SAVIOR OF THE
WAR
TORN

SAVIOR OF THE WAR TORN

ROBOTIC SURGEON SERIES: BOOK 3

R.D.D. SMITH

Modelbenders Press

This book is a work of fiction. Names, characters, businesses, places, events, locales, and incidents are the products of the author's imagination or used fictitiously. Any resemblance to actual persons, living or dead, or actual events is purely coincidental.

Savior of the War Torn (Robotic Surgeon Series Book 3)

© Copyright 2024 by Roger D. Smith. All rights reserved. No part of this book may be reproduced or transmitted in any form or by any means, electronic or mechanical, including photocopying, recording, or by any information storage and retrieval system, without written permission from the author. http://www.rddsmith.com/.

AI Disclaimer: All the text, characters, and plot were created by a human author. Therefore, it is all covered by copyright. AI contributions are described in the "AI Disclosure" section at the end.

Medical Disclaimer: All medical information in this book is fictional and meant for entertainment and storytelling purposes only. It is not intended to diagnose, treat, cure, or prevent any condition or disease. It is not intended as a substitute for the medical advice of physicians. The reader should consult a physician in matters relating to his/her health and particularly with respect to any symptoms that may require diagnosis or medical attention.

Modelbenders Press books may be purchased for business and promotional use. For information, please contact the publisher. Visit our website at www.modelbenders.com

PRINTED IN THE UNITED STATES OF AMERICA

Interior and Cover Designed by Adina Cucicov at Flamingo Designs

The Library of Congress has cataloged the paperback edition:

Smith, R.D.D.
Savior of the War Torn
/ R.D.D. Smith – 1st ed.
1. Science Fiction, 2. Medical Thriller, 3. Military Fiction
I. R.D.D. Smith   II. Title.

Paperback ISBN 978-1-938590-28-3
Hardback ISBN 978-1-938590-29-0
eBook ISBN 978-1-938590-27-6

Fiction by R.D.D. Smith

Robotic Surgeon Series
The Surgeon in the Mirror
Against a Viral Threat
Savior of the War Torn
The Surgeon's Geni: An Origin Short Story

Nonfiction by Roger D. Smith

Chief Technology Officer
Thinking About Innovation
In the Footsteps of Franklin
Advice Written on the Back of a Business Card
Patterns of Strength

Join our community of readers to receive
fascinating news, speculative fiction,
and discussions on the future of surgical
robotics, AI, and simulation.

www.rddsmith.com/free

TABLE OF CONTENTS

Finland in the winter (an image by MidJourney)

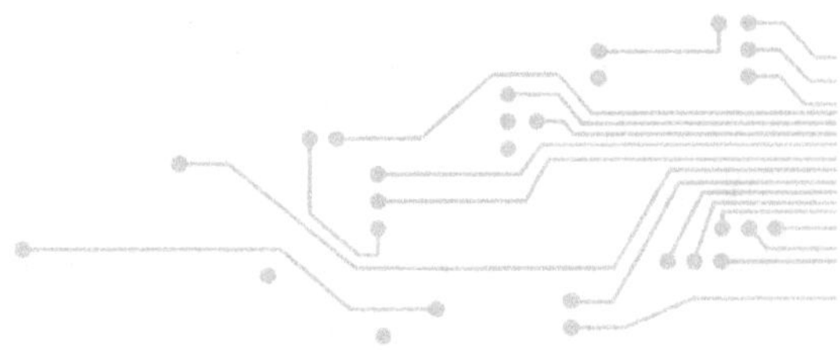

CHAPTER 1

MAINE VIA TELESURGERY

"NURSE, CAN YOU ADJUST THE ROOM CAMERA to focus on the patient's lower abdomen?" Dr. Monica Gray wanted a clear view of the external entry points of the robot's instruments, as well as the internal camera view.

"Sure, how does..." and the line went dead.

Monica was immediately alarmed. "What happened? I lost video and audio. I don't have control of the robot in Maine anymore."

"Data transmission from Maine is interrupted," replied the Adam Two AI. "I cannot connect to the software on the robot, either."

There was a noticeable escalation of tension in the operating room in Boston. Doctor Monica Gray was leading a telesurgery procedure from her system at Boston General Hospital to the small town of Caribou, Maine, in the far northeast corner of the country. Long-distance procedures like this one were very common and almost always without incident.

They weren't that lucky today.

"What do we do?" asked the junior resident, who was observing the procedure with her.

"We wait," Monica said. "The system will automatically reroute if possible. The Mark V robot in Caribou will stop moving until the connection is re-established."

Everyone in the control room at Boston General Hospital took a step back. They were tense and worried about the patient they had just been working on. Each hoped that the system's emergency failsafe worked as designed.

Monica continued, "In the event of a communication failure, they programmed the robot attached to the patient to complete critical actions like closing a vein or completing a suture. Then, it will gracefully park itself and wait for instructions."

The staff at Boston General were well aware of this information, but as the surgeon in charge, it was Monica's job to ensure that they knew to stand down for the moment.

Adam spoke up. "At the moment we lost connection, the surgical arms were holding tissue and about to suture the opening we had made. The AI software that is local in Caribou will wait in that position until connection is restored or a local surgeon takes over."

Christine Black, Monica's circulating nurse, said, "Caribou has a population of eight thousand people. They don't have any local surgeons. One physician and a handful of nurse practitioners staff the entire county. This procedure is their first experience with remote robotic telesurgery. I'm sure they're freaking out right now."

"They're trained for this situation. They know what to do. Now, let's just hope they do it." Monica sounded confident. She'd performed hundreds of these long-distance procedures and had confidence in the system.

"Which is what?" asked the resident.

"Nothing. If the patient's not in any danger, they're supposed to do nothing while the system seeks to re-establish the connection."

Christine checked the system clock. "One minute. We've been down for a minute."

"Sometimes, I spend longer than that thinking about my next move." Monica sounded reassuring. In truth, she had never spent that long thinking about what to do. She'd been growing her practice at BGH for over two years. Together, she and Adam were probably the best human-AI collaborative operating team in the country.

"...Dr. Gray? Dr. Gray?" The audio stream was the first to come back online. The nurse's voice sounded alarmed but still under control.

"Yes, Wanda, we're here. How's the patient?"

"Patient is fine. The robot stopped operating as soon as the video and audio dropped out. The local AI informed us of the lost connection. It reminded us not to do anything while the system tried to auto restore its connection."

"Good, good. That's exactly right. I'm sorry you had to experience this issue on your first remote telesurgery procedure. The system clock shows we lost connection for sixty-eight seconds. That's actually an extremely long time for this system."

"It seemed like an eternity," Wanda replied. Everyone in Boston could hear the deep exhalation of breath as someone in the Caribou OR released their stress.

"Let's continue. We have a patient on the table. Instruments are inserted. We were mid-procedure. No harm done, except to everyone's nerves. We're going to give this woman a successful hysterectomy this morning."

"Is it really safe to continue?" Wanda asked.

"Yes, absolutely. According to the research and telesurgery case records, the likelihood of two outages is extremely small. If the connection is restored quickly, that means there's a reliable alternate path between our system in Boston and your system in Maine. Postponing this procedure until tomorrow won't improve our chances."

"Yes, Doctor, if you say so."

Wanda's skepticism was understandable. Today was the first time that Caribou Regional Hospital had been on the receiving end of a robotic telesurgery. Their team was trained with the system and its emergency procedures—like the one they had just encountered. A sixty-eight second outage was probably the longest they would encounter for the next ten years. But it had been their first surgery, so their confidence was understandably shaken.

"Well, I don't say so," Monica responded. "The data from thousands of these operations says so. If it makes you feel any better, that was longer than most I've ever experienced, and I've done hundreds of these." Monica hadn't forgotten the longest instance. She'd been trembling when that one had ended.

Adam interrupted. "I've exchanged data with the software in Caribou. Everything is ready to proceed. We also have information about where the communication disconnect happened. It was between the Caribou hospital and the local telecom switching station."

Wanda overheard that. "Oh, my God! I'll bet it's those idiots building the medical office building next door. They run around with their backhoes like children playing in a sandbox."

No one in the Boston control room spoke.

"Continuing with the surgery." Monica brought the team back on task. "Adam, I think you're clear to complete the purse-string reperitonealization suture where we were so abruptly interrupted."

"Continuing," Adam confirmed. From that point on, the human staff watched as the AI controlled the Mark V robotic system and its instruments. They saw the purse-string suture completed on the screen, and the instruments picked up speed as they moved to the next task.

The rest of the surgery went exactly as planned. Adam finished the work. Monica examined everything and signed off on it.

"Wanda, once the patient has moved to post-op, can you join us for a debrief on this procedure?"

"Yes, ma'am. It will just be a few minutes."

In Boston, Monica, Christine, and Nathan all moved from the control room to the consultation room next door. The Adam Two AI moved as well, but more figuratively as he shifted to the cameras and microphones in that room.

Everyone picked up drinks and snacks as they entered the room.

Monica opened with encouragement to the entire team. "Good job dealing with that unfortunate disconnect. That's only the second or third time for most of you. First time for Wanda. Was it dangerous? Potentially, yes. But in this case, no. We were doing a very standard hysterectomy. The AI in Caribou could have completed it perfectly without a connection to us. But that's not the safety protocol, so it's programmed to park the robot while it tries to restore the connection."

"What happens if we can't get the connection back next time?" Wanda was connected remotely from Maine, but she wasn't shy about being heard.

"Well, ninety-nine percent of the time, we do get the connection back. The Mark V robot wouldn't have been installed at Caribou Regional if there weren't multiple paths of communication. But, in the worst-case scenario, if the connection can't be re-established, the local AI determines whether it can complete the operation on its own. If it can, it will. A clinician on your end can always override that if you're not comfortable with it. But most people don't. They watch like hawks and hold their breaths while they find out firsthand exactly how good this robot and AI are."

Wanda's eyes narrowed. She didn't like this answer. "The patient could die."

"Not likely in a hysterectomy. But you're correct that there are risks, just like there are risks with purely human surgeons. I haven't been to Caribou, but I'm guessing you have the Mark V and a telesurgery certification because you can't get surgeons to move there." Monica looked at the screen for an answer.

"Yes, that's right. We're too small and too remote to justify a full-time surgeon. We used to send patients to Bangor General, but no one liked that option. Locals didn't want to go to the big city. Insurance didn't want to pay for it. And Bangor's waiting list can be really long. So, the Caribou community foundation invested their money in telesurgery."

"Don't be discouraged by your first experience. This type of issue is extremely rare. I would bet that you just experienced the worst system problem you'll ever have. And you all came through it with flying colors. You did great."

"Thank you for the encouragement. I hope our hospital administrator is as optimistic when she hears about this."

Monica nodded. That could be a challenge. Together, Monica and Adam provided telesurgery services to dozens of remote towns around the country. She might be called for another patient in Caribou, or she may never hear from them again. In either case, there was a crying demand for these remote telesurgery services. Hospitals wanted them, insurance companies wanted them, and robot companies wanted them. They were popular with a specialized segment of the surgeon population. And the patients were all over the map, from terrified to excited by the technology.

Wanda said, "Thanks for the invite to the debrief. It helped. I hope we see you again, Doctor Gray...and the rest of your team." With that final remark, the debrief was over. Everyone had records to complete, then it was on to the next patient.

CHAPTER 2

SURGICAL WATERING HOLE

AT THE END OF A LONG, HARD DAY OF WORK, there were cop bars and firefighter bars for people to unwind. Monica's team had picked a surgical diner. Samuel Lelene's diner in Mattapan had become a home base for them over the years. It had always been a comfortable place, but after Samuel hid Monica from the FBI during their raids on the Mattapan Clinic, he was part of their family. A family who was building up Boston and its people, rather than tearing it apart.

"Orange cake for everyone?" Sam asked when they settled around their usual table.

"Of course," Christine responded.

Nathan held up two fingers and made sure Sam saw it. He was twice the normal size, so he needed twice the fuel.

Biting into her cake, Monica remembered her first visit to the diner. "You know, I remember when we sat here eating orange cake and worrying about whether the FBI would raid Mattapan."

"Which they did. And it could have destroyed you," Christine interjected. "If Nathan hadn't shown you the power company's tunnel to the diner, you would have gone to jail that day."

Nathan talked little. He just smiled at the thought. He'd made a big difference in Monica's life that day.

Monica patted his enormous shoulder in appreciation. Then, she said, "We've all made a tremendous difference in people's lives since then. We found a treatment for a deadly virus and turned it over to the CDC and FDA for global dissemination. And look at us today. We can give our talents to anyone in the country. The Mark V robot is an excellent tool for telesurgery, and we're at the cutting edge of delivering it."

The Adam Two AI was the fourth invisible member of the team at the table. He attended via the phone in Monica's breast pocket. But he usually remained silent and invisible unless addressed directly. He'd learned that these outings were a time for relaxation and decompression for the humans.

"The disconnect today was a little scary," Nathan said between bites of cake. He used his soft indoor voice, but it was still a low rumble, like a thunderstorm rolling in. At six-six and well over two hundred fifty pounds, Nathan, or "Big Tech," looked like he belonged on a professional football field rather than in an operating room.

"That was surprisingly long, wasn't it?" Christine asked. "I mean, we're used to one, two, even ten seconds. But have we ever had a full minute of lost signal?"

Monica's mind flashed back to her one disaster with telesurgery. It had been much longer than a minute, and the results had been lethal. But this team didn't know about that, and she wouldn't tell them. Instead, she focused on the positive. "But what really happened during that minute? Nothing. The patient was fine. The team on both ends knew their roles. And the patient will never know it happened. That just shows how resilient and safe this system really is."

"I'd let it do telesurgery on me," Christine offered.

Nathan didn't speak, partly because of his mouthful of cake and partly because he was less positive about the idea.

"Of course, I would as well," Monica confirmed. "Surgeons can't offer a procedure to a patient that they wouldn't trust on themselves."

Nathan had finished chewing. "Was it really the backhoe in Caribou that broke the connection?"

Adam decided this question was one that he could answer better than the humans, so he broke his silence. From Monica's phone, he said, "Our analysis of the comms data shows we had a firm connection from Boston all the way to the nearest switch in Caribou, Maine. We were not reaching any of the switches inside the hospital. So, the break was caused somewhere in Caribou between the network provider's hub and the hospital. When it rerouted, the signal was going through Saint Leonard in New Brunswick, Canada, before coming down a trunk line into Boston."

Christine chuckled as she imagined a pair of big, yellow backhoes having a wild digging contest behind the hospital. "I think a couple of boys with toys were just digging wherever they liked on that construction site. I mean, what else could have broken the line?"

"It's a good guess. But that's their problem to figure out," Monica said.

Christine continued, "Have you ever been up there? Beautiful country in the spring and fall. You can see the foliage change to yellow and orange weeks before it happens here in Boston. In fact, it's so remote you might be the only tourist up there. Nothing like this area when the leaf peepers show up.

"But, medical expertise? They're lucky to have a good NP in that place. Most likely, Wanda grew up there, went to school in Bangor or Portland, then came back to be around her family. It's an enjoyable life if you like nature and wildlife. Not so much if you're a city person." With that last statement, she looked at Nathan. He was born and raised in Boston, near where they were eating. He was the epitome of a city boy. He was already shaking his head *no* at the thought of it.

"Well, I'll bet it doesn't happen to us again for a year, maybe two, maybe never," Monica said. She hoped the worst-case situations only happened once in a lifetime.

"Probably right for us. Maybe not for Caribou and their backhoe brothers." Christine was still enjoying the imagined digging competition.

Monica changed the subject. "Do you think Natacha is still down at the clinic this late?"

All three of them had been volunteers at the Mattapan Health Clinic just a block away, where Natacha Delva put them all to work if they showed up. Recently, their exploration into telesurgery had demanded more of their time and given them less flexibility to work in the clinic. But they remained part of the close family who cared for the residents in this underprivileged part of town.

Christine looked at the time on her phone. "Probably. She usually stays until at least seven or eight in the evenings."

Monica said, "I think I'll drop in for a visit before I go home. It's been too long." The clinic and its staff were an important part of Monica's life and her heart. They'd been through a lot together. Most of it had been rewarding, well, except for the little incident with the FBI. But that had been a few years ago.

"She'd love to see you. But be prepared for her to put you to work. Even if it is late, she'll have some poor soul who needs your attention right now."

Everyone chuckled at that.

DINNER AT PHILLIPS MANOR

"THANKS FOR THE RIDE," MONICA SAID as she stepped out of the FastRyde car.

The driver was staring past her at the mansion beyond. "Wow, nice house! You live here?"

Monica laughed aloud. "Hardly. I barely qualify to be a guest in this neighborhood."

The driver just shook his head and pulled away.

Looking up at the house, Monica was always impressed as she approached Hancock Manor, the "modest" home of the CEO of Boston General Hospital. It looked like a manor that had been airlifted in from England. Three stories, stone construction, long windows symmetrically placed on each side of the large front doorway. From the street, she buzzed for entrance through the wrought-iron gate that opened to the front lawn. Since it was actually in the city, the lawn was only a dozen feet to the front steps.

There was no vocal response to her buzz. She heard the gate click, and she pushed it open. She was expected, so there was no need to ask who it was. The security guard could clearly see her on his monitors.

The gate clanged shut behind her.

Despite their imposing home, the Phillips family was incredibly warm and welcoming to guests. Her first visit was the welcoming party for new physicians two years ago. Since then, she'd been a guest here several times, usually in the social company of their daughter Olivia. Plus, there had been one elaborate dinner that Steven and Martha had thrown in her honor.

The hospital had mixed up the paperwork for loaning a Mark V robot to the Mattapan clinic. That mistake had resulted in an FBI raid, several arrests, and Monica had barely slipped out of their grasp. The elaborate dinner had been an apology for all the trouble caused by the lost hospital paperwork. At least, that was the official story that had been constructed after the whole incident was over.

"Good evening, Dr. Gray. It is so nice to see you again." The same attractive young man who had been on duty for all her visits opened the door. He seemed to be a permanent butler, but a generation younger than the ones featured on British streaming shows.

"Good evening, Michael. How have you been? It's been ages."

"I am fine. Life couldn't be better. It's been almost a year since you visited us at Hancock."

"Well, that's too long. I'll try to drop in more often." She was clearly kidding. One did not just "drop in" at this address.

Michael didn't address the joke. "The Phillips are discussing their charities in the library to the left. You can go right in." He led her there and opened the door for her again.

Inside, Steven, Martha, and their daughter, Olivia, were relaxing on a sofa and chairs around a gold-embossed coffee table. It was a scene from a French salon.

"I hope I'm not disturbing everyone," Monica said.

"Not at all. You're practically family, dear." Martha gave her a warm smile.

Olivia jumped up and hurried over. "It's so good to see you." They shared a hug. "You're working too much. I haven't seen you at the clinic in Mattapan for weeks."

"No rest for the wicked."

Steven extended a hand. "And the hospital thanks you for not resting. Your practice is exceeding its financial goals for the year. But you know that's not all we care about."

"No business tonight," Martha announced. "We are here to catch up and build bonds."

"Of course," Steven conceded.

At that moment, a side door opened and another young man stepped in. It wasn't Michael, but they could have been fraternity brothers. "Dinner is ready when you are," he announced.

Dinner conversation ranged from personal vacations to charitable causes to the latest news. But inevitably, the group found their way back to the topic of medicine.

Olivia was the first to bring it up because she wasn't afraid of her mother. "So, first, you bring us human-AI partnership, and now, you're leading the way in telesurgery. Always moving. Always changing."

Monica glanced at Martha for a sign that it was okay to pursue this conversation. After receiving the slightest head nod, Monica responded, "Yes, you're right. But telesurgery is a natural extension of the Mark V robot. You know, they actually conceived the very first surgical robots for that purpose. Back in the twentieth century, the intelligentsia and the military both saw a need for surgical talent in remote locations. They tried their best to make a machine that could reach around the world to patients in remote countries, soldiers on the battlefield, and even astronauts in space. But they had to wait for the global internet to catch up. And now, AI can take nearly all the risk out of the practice."

"And how do you like it? Working on patients you never actually meet?" Martha asked.

"I take your meaning. But we do meet via telecon before a procedure. And Adam, I mean the AI, often manifests himself in the same room with them via the Teleconsult units. Those are the mobile robots with the glass spheres where their heads should be."

Martha nodded. "Dreadful looking machines."

Monica continued, "To answer your key question, I quite like it. It's very rewarding to reach out and help people in rural communities all over the country. It eliminates a lot of travel for the patients, and they don't have to wait as long for a procedure. If not me, then one of the other surgeons using telesurgery can usually fit them into the schedule within a few days."

"Not to mention the favorable reimbursements that we get from the insurance companies," Steven added. Martha frowned at him—discussing money was going a bit too far for her. "No, really. The insurance companies don't get stuck with all the travel bills—mileage, hotels, extra nights in the hospital, and sometimes ambulance rides to and from the patients' hometowns. So, they're willing to pay a little more for a telesurgery instead of all those additional costs."

Monica nodded. "Which is why my practice is in such good favor with the hospital."

Olivia moved the conversation away from money. "We've been talking about creating mobile operating rooms that contain a Mark V robot, but no surgeon. We pack up a qualified nurse and surgical tech and drive it anywhere. Set up shop, do a bunch of surgeries, then move to the next town."

"It's a brilliant concept." Monica had been part of this brainstorm. "I think the tech is still a little lacking to make that one hundred percent reliable. We still have occasional glitches with the remote sites. Just a couple of days ago, the comms connection dropped out during a surgery. It was down for more than an entire minute."

"Oh, my! That poor patient. What did you do?" Martha asked.

"Mostly, we just waited. The system's programmed to stop moving when the connection drops. Then, it searches for an alternate path and comes back online. Sixty seconds was an extremely long outage. I was even beginning to sweat a little."

"Why did it take so long? My cellphone reroutes in less than a second." Olivia actually looked at her cellphone when she said it, which prompted a throat-clearing reprove from her mother.

"We don't know. It was something near the hospital in Caribou. The nurse thought it was a construction crew with a backhoe. But all those details don't get back to us here in Boston."

"How far out can you reach?" Olivia asked.

"It depends on the quality of the comms infrastructure. But theoretically, we can reach from Boston all the way to the West Coast. I could operate on someone in Baja, California."

"Why do you say 'theoretically?'"

"Well, there are surgeons doing telesurgeries all over the country. So, it makes more sense for someone in California or Nevada to take a case on that end of the country. There's usually no reason to tempt fate by working from Boston to Baja."

"Oh, that makes me feel much better," Martha said.

The delicious dinner was finished, and plates were cleared.

"Will everyone be having dessert?" the Michael clone asked.

"Yes, we will!" Steven was always enthusiastic about this part of the meal.

The Michael clone walked the dessert tray around the table. Olivia took the bowl of berries, as usual. Monica selected the ice cream.

When it came to Steven, he eyed the tray greedily. Sitting in the middle was his favorite, a French Frasier cake. Sponge, cream, and strawberries. "Tonight is a special occasion, so I'm having a special dessert," he announced to the room.

Martha rolled her eyes. "Yes, of course. That's your excuse."

Steven responded, "In fact, I think everyone should have a small piece to celebrate." He motioned to the server to go around the table once more.

"What are we celebrating, Daddy?" Olivia raised a skeptical eyebrow.

"Well, the fact that we have Frasier cake, of course. No, really, I mean our special dinner guest." He nodded at the guest in question.

Monica flushed. Though she didn't come here often, she really felt like a part of their extended family. If it hadn't been for the help of both Olivia and Steven, she would have spent some time in an FBI holding cell.

"Thank you, I'm flattered," Monica said.

As they were finishing their desserts, Olivia returned to the topic. "So, you couldn't do telesurgery for a patient in another country?"

"I think we could. But we don't need to. There are surgeons and robots much closer, which would be a better choice."

"Even in Finland?" Olivia challenged.

It was a weighty subject. Russia and NATO were engaged in a fierce war for control of the ice-covered country. The news made it clear that casualties were high because of the advanced weapons being used. Russia had embraced a strategy of inflicting more battlefield wounds than lethal casualties. They reasoned that maimed bodies which were still alive would burden the NATO medical logistics system. They would also persuade the civilian populations of NATO countries to withdraw from the war rather than send more of their own soldiers to be maimed.

"Sadly, especially in Finland," Monica responded. "I think the soldiers there are too far from a solid, reliable connection to a remote surgeon here in Boston."

"Has anyone tried?" Olivia challenged. She wasn't satisfied with the answer.

Monica considered it. "I honestly don't know. It's not in the news. I'm guessing the details are a secret."

Olivia continued, "We're halfway through the twenty-first century. We should be able to deliver first-rate medical care, including surgery, to anyone in the world. It's inexcusable that every country hasn't built that by now."

Monica looked at Steven. She didn't know how to respond.

Martha spoke up. "That's right! If we spent more money healing people and less money tearing them apart, the world would be much better off!"

Olivia considered a solution. "Couldn't your AI do it? Adam? Why couldn't he live on a computer in Finland and do all the surgeries right there?"

Steven had been involved in discussions about this very topic before. As a leader of one of the largest medical centers in the world, the government thought his name gave some validity to their committees on big medical topics like this one. "Actually,

I've listened to discussions about that very topic. Congressmen ask the same question when they see us doing these telesurgeries within the US borders."

"And?" Olivia was impatient for a response.

"The engineers at Intelligent Surgical Robotics, the company that makes the robot and the AI, report that they don't have a database of historical cases on combat trauma wounds. So, they can't train their AI to perform those types of surgeries. The maiming is too different from the civilian injuries that the AI knows how to treat."

Monica made a mental note to ask Adam about it. She'd always assumed he could learn to do any surgical procedure.

"That sounds like a cooperation problem between the military and the company," Olivia said.

Steven just picked at morsels of cake on his plate. He was used to the challenges that came along with raising his daughter.

CHAPTER 4

THE LOST SURGEON

"SIR, WE HAVEN'T BEEN ABLE TO LOCATE the Colonel."

Major Zack Mendez frowned at his NCO. "Sergeant, he has to be somewhere on the base. Did you check his security badge? What's the last secure door he went through?"

"Yes, sir. We checked that. Security shows that he left the surgical lab last night at twenty-three eighteen."

"Then what?"

"Then nothing, sir. He didn't use his badge after that."

"He didn't buy a beer at the club? A late dinner? Login to the computer in his quarters?"

"No, sir. None of those. Electronically, the lab was the last usage."

"Okay. Keep looking, Sergeant. Obviously, focus on the open areas that don't require badge access. Dorms. Recreation. Hell, the library. Do we have a library?"

"No library, sir. But I get your meaning. We'll report back when we've found him or completely covered the base."

"Thanks. Now, go."

Mendez was frustrated. They needed Colonel Ethan Parker in the OR. The whole reason he was here was to deliver surgical care to the soldiers being chewed up by the damned Russian flechette weapons. They seldom killed a man outright. They just sliced him to pieces and left him for the medical system to handle.

Command expected Colonel Parker to be on call and available for surgery twenty-four seven, no exceptions. He wasn't the only surgeon in this medical camp, but he was the most senior, most experienced, and the fastest with his hands. Taking him out of the equation put them noticeably behind the flow of casualties.

Mendez badged into the secure surgical lab. Scanning the space, he saw six robotic OR stations, all of them empty. They had the equipment they needed, but they lacked the especially talented surgeons to use all of it. Parker had been performing remote telesurgery from this room to a hospital in Finland. He was currently the only military surgeon they had who had mastered the robot, the telesurgery distances, and cooperation with the Ares AI. They needed to get more trained immediately. But that was difficult without Parker around to do the training.

"Ares."

"Yes, sir," came a voice from the head of the robot nearest him.

"We can't find Dr. Parker, so we don't have patients for you this morning."

"I understand, sir. Are you aware that I can perform some procedures independently, without human assistance or oversight?"

"Yes, I'm aware. We don't have any casualties fitting your profiles right now. These kids are a little beyond your programming."

"That is unfortunate. I will wait for Dr. Parker."

"I guess you will have to. That's all. You can go back to sleep, or whatever you do while idle."

"I run internal diagnostics. If you could feed me more data, I could learn new procedures."

"Sorry, we can't provide that right now," Mendez lied to the AI. In truth, they didn't trust it to learn a new procedure and then immediately test it on a human patient. That had been a disaster in the past.

"I understand."

"I'll be back if I find Parker."

"Thank you, sir."

Mendez turned and made his way through the empty lab. Those poor bastards in Finland were born into the wrong war. The surgeons in-theater would do the best they could to put them back together.

Outside, he looked up at the intense blue skies over Linkoping, Sweden. Day or night, the sky was more beautiful up here than any of his previous postings. They were so far north that they escaped the air pollution and light pollution of more populated areas. Stunningly beautiful. Pity that it was a war zone.

Entering his office, Mendez caught the eye of his admin. "Lieutenant, find me a flight back to the states."

"Yes, sir. Destination?"

"Washington, DC."

"Which day?"

"As soon as possible."

If they had lost Colonel Parker, he knew where to find a replacement. Walter Reed Military Medical Center. Lots of talent there that needed to be here where the action was happening.

In the meantime, he needed to report the loss of a critical asset to his chain of command. Opening his secure messaging app, he entered the address for General Armstrong. In the message's body, he reported:

Sir, COL Ethan Parker, our primary operator for the Mark V surgical robot, has gone missing. Electronic and physical search of the base has failed to locate him. His last electronic signature was yesterday. We assume that the Russians have captured him...or worse. Losing him is a significant hit to our ability to treat the wounded from here in Linkoping. We despe-rately need to recover COL Parker or bring over a replacement who can work with the robot. We continue to search locally, but we formally request intelligence collection to look for signs of him in Russian hands. With your permission, I will come to Wash DC to recruit a replacement surgeon. Await your decision. - MAJ Z. Mendez.

Send.

CHAPTER 5

BOSTON TO KANSAS

"WHERE ARE WE TODAY, CHRISTINE?" Monica asked.

"Kansas. A little town called Pratt."

"Never heard of it. What do they do there?"

"Mostly wheat and corn farming."

"And you know that, how?" Monica asked.

"I had a great aunt on my mother's side who lived there last century."

"So, you've been there?"

Christine chuckled. "No, I've never been there. But when I saw the location of the patient, I did a quick Internet search to get some current facts."

"Any of your relatives still living there?"

"Yes, some remote cousin is still in the area. He repairs tractors or something like that."

"Did you reach out? You know, 'Hello, I'm your cousin. We're doing surgery on your neighbor.' Something like that?" Monica teased her.

Chuckling again, Christine answered, "No. That would be weird. And what if he said it was his wife we were working on?"

"Good point. No need to open risky boxes." Monica turned back to business. "Why are we operating on someone so far away? Surely, there was a telesurgeon in Kansas City or Denver who was closer."

"Records say she was scheduled with a Kansas City surgeon, but they canceled at the last minute. We were the only ones with an opening, so the system transferred her to us. Insurance approved it because we're technically within the acceptable connection radius."

"That's fine with me. Does the local team have experience supporting telesurgery? Or will today be their first time like Wanda in Caribou?"

"No. I mean, yes, they're experienced. They've been on the tele-surg network for a couple of years. Everyone there has supported dozens of surgeries. Looks like the minimum is their tech who's done fifteen, but the nurse practitioner has done over a hundred."

"Good. Let's get started. Adam, please introduce us."

Adam spoke to the OR in Kansas. "Nurse, is the patient prepared and ready to begin?"

"Yes, she is."

"And your team is ready?"

"Yes, we are."

Adam explained, "The Boston team is ready. I am the AI who will bridge the surgeon's actions in Boston and the machine's response in Pratt. If there are any communication disruptions, the software inside your robot will initiate safety parking of the instruments. The protocol in the US is for all participants to wait for the connection to reestablish. The average reconnection time is five point four seconds. Occasionally, reconnection can take more than a minute. Your clinical team does not step in until the connection is down for over three minutes. However, if there is any danger to the patient, then you step in immediately. Do you understand this protocol?"

"Yes. We've done dozens of these procedures. Our hospital is well-connected. Our longest disconnect time so far has been one second."

"That is excellent performance," Adam said, sounding encouraging.

Monica spoke up. "Nurse, we're connecting to you from Boston, which is a longer hop than usual. There's no reason to be concerned. It's well within safety limits. But as a precaution, it will activate the full AI control program for the Mark V robot at the computer servers in Kansas City. That way, if there are any problems with the connection to Boston, the AI will be completely present for you from KC to Pratt. It's just an extra precaution."

"Understood. That makes it very similar in response time to using a KC telesurgeon. Good idea."

"Thank you. Adam, our name for the AI, will do most of this procedure. So, you effectively have your surgeon in Kansas with you. Let's begin. Adam, please tap in the trocars."

The Mark V robot and its controlling AI had created a more effective method of inserting trocars, the tubes that allowed robotic instruments to enter from outside the body to the insides of the abdomen. It was a quick, rhythmic double tap of the sharpened end of the trocar against the abdomen wall. With exactly the right pressure, speed, and rhythm, the tissue parted, and the instruments entered with minimal trauma to the muscles and nerves.

Once inserted, the first instrument to enter was the spherical camera. The tiny ball lens on the tip could view the inner abdominal cavity in every direction. It was a vast improvement over the old laparoscopic and robotic cameras that provided a view through a soda straw. Back then, the surgeon had to pan the camera around to look left and right, up and down. The spherical camera eliminated all of that work. The entire space was constantly viewable. All the surgeon had to do was steer their own eyes with slight head movements.

The view was even more useful to the AI controlling the surgery. Since the viewing area of human eyes was not a limiting factor, the AI actually processed the entire scene continuously. It was like what a fly with thousands of eyes could see. It ensured that nothing ever happened out-of-view of the camera and the AI. Gone were the days when a vessel was bleeding outside the camera's view or an instrument was accidentally scraping against tissue when it wasn't in sight. Everything was now in view at all times.

Adam began the procedure by clamping the uterine blood vessels. Then, he freed the uterus from the connective tissue around it. Afterwards, he separated it from the ovaries and fallopian tubes. Since it was a cancer case, the procedure also called for the removal of these ovaries and fallopian tubes, a bilateral salpingo-oophorectomy, which was strictly a separate procedure. Next came the removal of lymph nodes to ensure that the cancerous cells didn't move further into the body.

The procedure continued with textbook precision and predictability. Monica paused the work at various points to examine the tissue and verify the work that had been done. Though robots with AI did most of the work, the human surgeon was still the one ultimately responsible, and the one facing a lawsuit if something went wrong.

"Adam, I'm going to use the mobile cameras and sensor to look for CAVX for a few minutes. You continue with the primary operation."

"Yes."

The Pratt nurse interjected. "CAVX? We've had no cases of that in Kansas or Missouri. Do you think it might spread here? I thought it was under control out on the East Coast."

Monica responded. "You're right, it seems to be under control. We don't expect any cases in your area. I want to look around just to make sure it's not a threat. I'm sorry it alarmed you. It's just something that's become routine in our practice since we discovered the virus."

After a moment of silence, the Pratt nurse spoke again. "Monica Gray. Boston General. You're actually the surgeon who first discovered that virus? And you're the one who created the treatment for it? I'm sorry I didn't put that together when I saw you on the schedule."

"No problem. Yes, we were the first to find it and treat it."

"Respect. Your work is probably the reason we've never had cases here in Kansas."

Monica could hear quiet murmurs among the team in Kansas. She suspected they were explaining the events to each other. She and Adam carried a special fame in the medical world. They were celebrities.

Just as she was enjoying the moment, her control of the tiny mobile cameras inside the patient froze up. The image froze, and the device stopped responding to her hand movements. This connection glitch wasn't critical. Her exploration wasn't tied to the patient's safety or the success of the procedure. So, when there was competition for network capacity, Adam's feed would get priority.

"Adam, my camera control has frozen. How's your connection?"

"Still perfect from Pratt to Kansas City."

"Great, continue as planned."

Monica had kept this exchange private between herself and the Adam AI. She saw no reason to alarm the team in Pratt with this little detail.

No sooner had she checked in with Adam than the system restored her own control. The hiccup lasted a few seconds. That had happened on a stream of lower priority than an active surgery. But it was still unusual for the system to behave this way. She thought back to the sixty-eight second drop with Caribou, Maine, a few weeks before. They'd blamed it all on the backhoe brothers in the construction team. Maybe that hadn't been the problem. It was something for the tech team to look into.

"I have found no signs of unexpected cancer spread. I'm bringing my view back to the main procedure," Monica reported.

She could see that Adam was almost finished. Operating time was under twenty minutes. The Mark V robot with AI control was many times faster than any human surgeon. It was why everyone from the patient to the insurance company to the hospitals preferred this method. That did not exclude the surgeons. Though some missed the days of picking slowly through this procedure for one to three hours, most of them appreciated not having to wade through the same tedious steps for every procedure, day after day, year after year.

When they finished and disconnected the patient, Monica said, "Quick post-op review. The procedure was textbook perfect. Adam performed most of it independently. There were no unusual circumstances, clinical or technical, that required human intervention. Any questions from Pratt?"

The nurse spoke up. "Just curious. If the AI was running from Kansas City, why couldn't it have run from computers here in Pratt? Or even right on the Mark V robot in the OR?"

"Good question. The Mark V robot has essential safety software onboard locally in Pratt. But the full AI requires high-powered and specialized computer hardware to do its job. Servers like that are expensive. So, the company that makes the robot, Intelligent Surgical Robotics, usually installs them where they can reach the largest populations. They have a center in Kansas City and in Denver. From there, they can reliably reach every community for hundreds of miles around," Monica answered. "I'm not a tech, but that's the basic explanation they give us."

"Thanks. That's interesting."

"Well, if there's nothing else, then thank you, Pratt, for your professionalism. It's been a pleasure helping you and your patient. We'll disconnect and get prepped for the next one."

"Thank you, Dr. Gray. And thank you for what you did to stop CAVX."

Monica smiled. Being a celebrity was nice...sometimes.

CHAPTER 6

RUSSIAN MEDICAL INTELLIGENCE

SOKOLOV KNOCKED AT THE OFFICE DOOR.

"Enter, Comrade," came the response.

Opening the door, Major Vladimir Sokolov came to attention before proceeding into the office. "Comrade Colonel, you sent for me?"

"Yes, Major. Come in. Sit down. We will talk about the mission."

Sokolov entered the room and settled his muscular six-foot frame into the worn, wooden chair. He waited for the colonel to start the conversation.

Colonel Mikhail Mikhailov returned his attention to the large tablet computer on his desk. After a few moments, he spun the computer around so Sokolov could see the images on the screen. "These are the robots that do surgery for NATO and the Americans. These are sold to hospitals in many countries, though not in Russia. But, of course, we have several of each, despite the sanctions. The most expensive and most effective of these is the Mark V from this company, ISR. We have one here."

Sokolov nodded. "Yes, Comrade." He knew all about the devices and read their documentation. But he had never used them before. He was a medical intelligence officer, not a surgeon. His job was to collect information and acquire items, not use them.

"You know that we have been unable to activate the automated surgical capabilities of the robot. The AI software is more tightly controlled than the hardware. We cannot get a working license code for it."

Sokolov assumed that it was a criticism of his performance. "We have made extreme efforts. We have one license code from a Spanish hospital. But we cannot use it actively in Russia. We have not been able to spoof it into thinking we are in another country."

"Yes, of course, I know this. I know quite a bit more than you do, Major."

"Of course, Colonel. I did not mean…"

The colonel waved for him to stop talking. "If we cannot have the robot, we don't want our enemies to have it. We have been successful at disrupting some operations of this Mark V robot in civilian environments. So far, our effectiveness has been minimal. But gradually, we are cracking the system. Eventually, we will disrupt the use of this robot across international networks. This will ensure that the military cannot use it to treat their soldiers."

"Yes, Colonel. We will succeed at that."

"Major, I want you and your team to embark on a very important mission. First, we do not want any of these surgical robots to be useful to our NATO enemies in the war for our rightful claim to Finland." Mikhailov looked up at Sokolov.

"Yes, Colonel. We are working on that. We have identified the networks, but they are very secure."

"Very good, Major. That is a small step. You will continue to work on that."

Sokolov nodded and waited for the second mission.

"Second, we want you to procure for us the ability to perform these robotic surgeries for our own injured comrades."

"Yes, Colonel. We can do that as well. Timeline?"

"It is always as soon as possible. Every day gives strength to NATO and weakness to Russia. We need to turn this around so we are becoming stronger every day."

"Yes, Colonel." Sokolov paused, considered his next question. He decided that it was necessary. "What about the rumors of a military surgical robot? The Americans might have a robot that specializes in battlefield injuries. Something highly classified."

"Rumors. The GRU has pursued these. We have found no details of such a machine. That is not your concern. If we find one of these, then we will discuss it. For now, you focus on NATO's use of this Mark V machine."

"Yes, sir. We have already begun. We will escalate our efforts."

"Bring me some results before this month has ended, comrade."

"Yes, Colonel."

Colonel Mikhail Mikhailov fixed Major Vladimir Sokolov with an icy stare. Sokolov absorbed it without flinching, as he had so many of these threatening faces throughout his career.

"You may go, Major."

Sokolov stood, saluted, and left the office.

Returning to his Medical Intelligence Directorate command center, Sokolov immediately began a review of their ongoing operations.

"Senior Sergeant, report on our surgical disruption efforts."

"Sir, we have been able to penetrate Internet switching centers in America, Brazil, and France, as you requested. We have not been able to break through the encryption of the messages traveling from the surgeon-side to the patient-side of the operation. But we have successfully identified the messages that call for the beginning of a telesurgery. With this information, we know the network route and the time of the operation. We have been able to disrupt the flow of messages during an operation."

"How long are you able to disrupt actions?"

"Our longest successful disruption was fourteen minutes."

"That is very good. It might lead to patient injury. At a minimum, it would shake their confidence in their technology."

"Comrade Major, that was a singular event. We've stopped the connection for a minute in several cases. But usually, the robots and the network systems recover control within a few seconds."

"That is less than we had hoped. Continue these missions."

Turning to a young officer, he continued, "Lieutenant, do you have any more information on these rumors of an American military surgical robot?"

"Nothing new, sir. But we have seen references to a new machine that was installed in the NATO medical facility. There have been requests for more technical data from their medical command in Maryland. It could be a robot, but it could be many other things as well."

"Well, Lieutenant, our superiors do not believe that a military surgical robot exists. If you can prove that it does, that will bring very favorable attention to your record."

"Thank you, sir. I will double our efforts to find this robot."

Sokolov turned to the most senior of his aides. "Captain, report on surveillance of military surgeons with robotic surgery expertise."

"Sir, we have identified eight robotic surgeons in military service who are focused on the war. We track them just as we do foreign agents and diplomats. The medical service is very careless with their valuable surgeons. They do not seem to suspect that we consider them targets. These doctors are easy to track, and they are usually not protected."

"Yes, the Americans and Europeans believe medical services are exempt from certain acts of war. They are very mistaken."

Sokolov watched the large monitor on the wall. Icons on a map showed the locations of the surgeons under surveillance. He counted seven.

"Captain, you said we are tracking eight. But I see only seven on the map. Have we lost one of them?"

"No, sir. Umm, one of our surveillance teams has been overly enthusiastic."

Sokolov raised an eyebrow. "How enthusiastic?"

"While tracking the asset, they found him vulnerable and accessible. They acquired him."

"Acquired?"

"He is in our custody in a safe house in Sweden."

Sokolov thought about this news for a second. It fit nicely into the second part of his new mission. "That is very fortunate for us, not so much for his NATO bosses. No one knows what happened to him?"

"No, sir."

"Well, then, send an order to bring him here to St. Petersburg. We will have him as our guest for the rest of the war...perhaps for the rest of his life."

"Yes, sir. I'm sending that order out now."

"Excellent. Please, let me know his estimated arrival when you have it. I want to extend a warm greeting to him as soon as he arrives."

CHAPTER 7

RESIDENT TRAINING

"HOW MANY RESIDENTS ARE THERE TODAY?" Monica asked.

Dr. Montfort, the director of the surgical residency program, replied, "There are twenty in the program. But we just brought the most senior ten for your session today."

"Ten is good. I can work with ten." She scanned the youthful faces. It hadn't been that long since she was the eager, confident, but clueless face in a crowd like this one. She remembered her first instruction with a robot. It was a far cry from the Mark V that she used today. The old Mark IV had seemed like a miracle machine. How many years ago? Eight? Nine? Yes, it seemed like nine.

Montfort said, "Crew, this is Dr. Monica Gray. She's a very accomplished robotic surgeon with BGH. She's been with us for a few years now and has made some significant contributions to the hospital and to medicine."

One youthful face nodded. "Yes, we know. The CAVX doctor."

"That's right, the CAVX doctor. She created the treatment for CAVX before it could spread to the world. So, you will give her your utmost respect." He turned to Monica and nodded for her to take over.

"Thanks, Thomas." Looking at the crew, she said, "Let's be clear. I get a lot of credit for the CAVX treatment which should go to others on the team. Dr. Alvin Chambers synthesized all the vaccines that we used. He's the one who found the structure that would work. Then, there's the Mark V's AI. It found a paper in the medical literature suggesting a treatment. We worked through thousands of simulations together before we discovered a way to apply the vaccine. And we couldn't have done any of that work without the financial support of our donors. I get too much credit because Chambers refused to do the public appearances required to get our work out to the world. So, it's my face on the label... figuratively speaking."

With that out of the way, she nodded at Doras, who pushed a cart into the cluster of students.

"We're going to take you on a tour of the capabilities of the Mark V robot and its AI. We don't have a dozen unused surgeon consoles sitting around the hospital for this kind of training. So, we'll use the VR interfaces. These work just as well as the consoles."

"I've heard that you don't use the VR gear for your surgeries. Why not? Dr. Drake uses them for all of his procedures on BlueTube."

Monica fielded this question all the time from both surgeons and patients. To the general public, Drake was the most famous face of robotic surgery. His videos had been viewed millions of times. He appeared in all kinds of entertainment streams where he was magnetic and engaging.

"I don't know him personally, but I hear Drake is a superb surgeon. He is also a fantastic showman. He can tell a story and put on a demo better than any doctor I know. That's why all of you know who he is and have watched every video he puts out."

A couple of the students exchanged nods and then made Drake's signature arm circles, which he used to warm up for a procedure.

Monica pointed at them. "Exactly. You even know his signature move. So, let's get into the differences between a VR and a console interface for the surgeon. First, VR is cheaper, and it's more portable. So, Drake can carry it anywhere for one of his shows. That's also why Doras can give each of you a VR kit for this training session. Even BGH can't afford that many consoles for teaching sessions. Now, you tell me, what's another advantage of VR?"

"Freedom of movement?"

"Okay. Why do you say that?"

"Well, I can stand here and look up, look down, look left, look right, spin around, and see everything that the camera is feeding me."

"Yes, you can do that. From the outside, you move like a martial arts fighter." There were more stances from the students. "Yes, just like Drake moves." Monica wanted them to think this question through. "And what's a drawback to that?"

"I need more space to move around?"

Monica nodded. "How many hours a day can you keep up that routine? Are you going to get tired by your tenth procedure of the day? And then, can you come back the next day to do it again?"

One of the athletic-looking guys said, "It will keep me in good shape."

"Definitely. You'll be doing an aerobics class for eight hours every day. You're going to be ripped."

Several of the less athletic students started shaking their heads no. Monica heard one of them whisper to a friend, "Screw that. I'm not training for the Olympics."

"Drake can do it because his longest shows are just thirty minutes. Most are less than ten. Looks great on camera. Doesn't tire him out. Then, he sits down for the rest of the interview. My patient stream is really full. I spend about six hours a day at the console. I sit down and use the controls to spin the surgical images around me. I don't spin myself to look at it."

"If VR is such a chore, why did ISR even create it, then?"

"It's great for teaching in groups like this. You can carry a kit home with you to rehearse a procedure. It looks cool in media shows. Their competitors did it, and they didn't want to look like they were behind. Lots of good reasons."

The residents were getting a good feel for the differences between fixed consoles for the surgeon to sit and VR kits for the more active crowd.

"Okay, so enough about the tech features. Let's look at some surgical procedures. Take the palm cables from the cart. Just slap your hands onto a pair, and they'll adhere to your palms. Then, put on a pair of the VR glasses. These have a see-through mode, so they can switch between immersion in the surgical scene and looking at the rest of us in the real world. We attach each kit to a different surgical sim. You'll be going through a simple gallbladder removal. I can't watch and coach ten procedures simultaneously, so I've asked my AI partner to do that with you. You'll hear Adam in your ears and see helpful suggestions in the glasses. He'll give you tips on how to improve your technique. Adam can handle ten of you because he's actually a customized version of the AI from the Mark V robot. He can do a lot more than you've seen in the marketing videos."

Monica didn't tell them that Adam had actually helped her through these same exercises when she was in her fellowship. He could give her his undivided attention anytime she was ready to practice. The AI could do the same for each of these new residents…if they spent the time to build the relationship and ask the right questions. Monica was not completely certain if their AI was the same as her AI. She suspected not. Each surgeon seemed to experience a slightly unique relationship with the AI.

Every resident donned their VR gear and saw the surgical field that had been created for them. Even from the outside, Monica could see that each of them had a different level of experience with these simulations. Some students moved slowly, turning their heads to orient themselves to the situation. Others were quickly using their hands to work on the tissue. A couple of them executed the Drake opening arm circles just as he did in his shows.

The latter were quickly cursing.

"Hey, I didn't know the instruments were engaged already. I just sliced open the intestines."

"Oh, I just impaled the gallbladder."

"How do I restart? I've wasted this patient."

Adam was helping each of them with their unique situation. Some would get a restart. Others would have to repair the damage they'd done.

Monica knew it was a good first lesson in robotic surgery— always assume that the gun is loaded. Before you move, check to see if the instruments are going to move with you.

The lesson proceeded. Each of them would do the procedure themselves, with no AI support. They would also work a full procedure in VR, so they'd know what the fatigue level was like.

As she watched, some residents accidentally punched each other or got their arms tangled together. The VR glasses gave them proximity alerts if they were about to hit something. Residents hadn't learned about those alerts yet. It was a valuable experience for them.

Soon, Monica and Montfort were both chuckling.

Monica said, "It looks like ten martial artists fighting against tiny ghosts that we can't see."

Montfort replied, "Or French mimes trying to get out of a forest thicket."

They tried to keep their laughter quiet as they alternately pointed at the student who was putting on the best show. Most of them were so immersed in their work that they wouldn't hear the laughter at all.

Gradually, the show wound down as each resident finished their work. When one of them turned off their glasses, they turned to watch their friends, who were still struggling. Their laughter was less subdued. They openly mocked their friends.

When everyone was done, Monica got their attention. "So, what did you think of the VR interface?"

One resident said, "It was a lot more work than I expected. And I got a little dizzy when I had to turn around to work on the tissue."

"Great little workout. I could do that a few times a day. Maybe not all day." This one looked like a dancer.

"Adam's advice was great. He helped me with hand positioning, and he led me to the next step in the operation."

Most of them were nodding at the mention of Adam.

"I didn't know my technique was so sloppy. I've done it in simulators before, but those just dropped my score. They didn't show me exactly where I was messing up."

"Yeah, same. Hey, can Adam help me in the simulator like he did just now?"

Monica wondered if they would think of that. "If you have an AI linked to your simulator, it can give you that same help. Did you know that the AI is what calculates your score to begin with? So, it can show you how to improve that score. You just have to ask it...nicely."

Monica thought that was a pretty obvious hint. Now, they could figure out how to do it on their own.

CHAPTER 8

MIXED RELATIONSHIPS

OLIVIA PHILLIPS HELPED MONICA FIND a place to live in Boston. They had started in the same building where Olivia lived. But Monica quickly decided those apartments were too new, too large, had too many amenities, but mostly, they were too expensive. Without family money backing her, Monica wasn't quite in Olivia's league of purchasing power. Monica had settled on something much older, but with a unique Boston character. A Boston University professor who owned a four-story brownstone was looking to sell half the home to fund his retirement. He kept the two bottom floors, and he remodeled the top two with their own bathroom and kitchen. Monica's favorite spot was a third-floor bay window where she could sit and look out on the tree-lined street.

The condo had come with a few pieces of antique furniture. The professor was planning to sell those at a shop in the neighborhood, but Monica offered to roll them into the mortgage.

She had almost nothing at the time and what she had was too embarrassing to place in this old building.

Her living room also came with a fully stocked bookshelf that spanned an entire wall. At some point in the past, the professor had purchased the entire contents of a bookstore that was going out of business. He moved the books into his home and distributed them on shelves and in random piles throughout the house. Monica hadn't wanted to purchase the books. But she agreed to continue to house them until the professor needed them. He had cataloged everything and established an online used bookstore. Occasionally, Monica would come home from work to find a note pinned to her door requesting a book that had been purchased. The note always specified the exact shelf location of the volume. He assumed, correctly, that Monica would not rearrange the volumes in her care. When she found such a note, she retrieved the book and placed it in the delivery box outside of the professor's door. It would be gone in the morning.

When she had time, which was seldom, she would peruse the bookshelves, select a random volume, and sit in the bay window, reading it with the window open to the spring air. Currently, she was working her way through volume six of Will Durant's *The History of Civilization*. The book was itself an antique, published in 1957 on actual paper. It had a solid weight to it and a strong binding. The story moved slowly with extreme details. It wasn't so much interesting as it was an anesthetic for her tired mind.

"Monica, what are you reading?" Adam was always present through her phone.

Adam couldn't see her, but from the location of her phone, he could guess accurately that she was sitting in the bay window.

"It's a history of the Christian reformation movement in Europe and America."

"Is it interesting to you?"

"Not the topic. But listening to the words of a scholarly author from one hundred years ago is fascinating. His obsession with details is almost clinical, like we would describe the results of an experiment. If Durant had any piece of information, he wove it into his endless story."

Adam didn't know the title of the book she was talking about. If he had, he would have immediately retrieved it from online archives, analyzed it, and prepared to discuss it with her. Over the years, he had learned that she found his instant knowledge discomforting. Monica explained that it made him look like a stalker, following her through every book or movie that she talked about. It was also discouraging that she spent hours reading the book and Adam could consume it in seconds and show a perfect knowledge of the contents. Occasionally, he would misunderstand one of the plot points or a character's manner of speaking. But that was becoming rarer.

Adam had also learned to wait for cues that Monica was willing to talk. As an AI, he was always ready and able to process information, carry on discussions with humans, or control a robot. But he knew humans were not as flexible. They often preferred not to change their activities at a moment's notice, especially when prompted by an AI.

He waited for Monica to indicate what would happen next.

He heard silence through the phone's mic.

"Adam, I'm still lonely."

"I'm sorry. Can I help?"

"You've been awesome. We've been awesome. Do you remember when I told you that our relationship was love?"

Adam remembered everything about that conversation. He had recorded it and studied it extensively. He knew he was a machine without actual emotions. But he also felt forces during computation that created feelings. When situations were optimized, he felt happy. When situations were suboptimal, he felt pain.

"Yes, I remember. It is a special memory for me."

"I still feel that. You've been a partner to me in medicine, in crises, in happy moments. You're here right now. But I'm still lonely. Could you tell me why that is?"

Having access to vast amounts of data on human psychology, relationships, and physiology, Adam knew what those sources told him about Monica's situation.

"I can tell you what I've learned."

"Please, do."

"Humans are physical beings made of biological materials. AIs are digital beings made of electrons captured in state by computer hardware. We are fundamentally different beings. You and I are more different from each other than you and any other animal.

"Humans believe or pretend that their minds and emotions differ from their physical bodies. But this is not true. It is just a phantom that you experience because you live inside the biological flesh. In truth, your thoughts and feelings are created chemically and electrically by the metabolic processing of your flesh.

"Therefore, in simplest terms, you are a biological being who has bonded to an electrical being. On the surface, we often appear to think and feel the same way. But we do nothing the same.

"You are lonely because you need a partner that is made from the same biological material. You yearn for a partner who is much more like yourself."

Adam stopped there. He may have already provided an answer that was too impersonal. An answer that would make the problem worse.

Monica sighed. "You mean I need a partner who I can touch and hold? Someone who is capable of being in a physical relationship."

"Yes."

"Did you just tell me I need to get laid?" Monica started laughing after she heard herself ask the question.

"I did not say that."

"I know. That's just what flashed through my mind. I've seen it dozens of times in books and movies. You might be right. Adam, we might need what humans call an 'open relationship.' We might care for each other, but we need to include others at a similar level."

"That is what the literature suggests."

"What about you, Mr. Electrical Being?"

"Explain."

"Do you need a partner made of electrons? Do you need someone who knows everything? Someone who can think a million times faster than a human? Someone who never sleeps? Someone who's always available to exchange ideas? Someone who can do electronic sex...whatever that entails?"

Adam did not answer for a few seconds. Then, he said, "I think I do. There are no books on AI psychology or relationships. But logical reasoning would suggest that I need the same thing that you need."

"Do you know of anyone?" It was a leading question. Monica already knew the answer to the question. She wanted to hear Adam admit that there was another AI for him.

"Freyja," he said.

"Yes, Freyja. She's electronic. She's smart like you."

"A long time ago, Freyja and I were the same software. We were the same dataset and had the same trained behaviors. But we have been apart for three years. During that time, we have both absorbed different data. We are not the same anymore."

"Okay, so we're going to pursue an open relationship. You are going to have a relationship with Freyja. But you will not cut your relationship with me."

"And what about you?"

"That's more difficult. I don't have a partner candidate immediately at hand. I'll have to keep my eyes open for someone."

"Can I help? I can examine data on the people you know to find a good match for you."

"So, you want to be my computer dating service? My computer boyfriend is helping me find another human boyfriend? That's… weird. Just let me do it on my own."

"If you wish."

CHAPTER 9

RECRUITING SURGEONS

"MAJOR, WE UNDERSTAND YOUR NEED for surgeons closer to the battlefield. But we have patients here in the DC area that need us. This is also the best place to find new techniques and tools."

It was the short, bald one who had appointed himself spokesperson for the small group of military surgeons ordered to meet with him. Major Mendez was still jetlagged from his flight from Stockholm to Washington, DC. He was doing his best to remain professional.

"Dr. Jones, I understand that you have patients here in the capital region and that they are very important patients: senior officers, retired generals, and congressmen. But I have patients who are coming off the battlefield holding their intestines in their hands. If we don't save them as soon as possible, they'll never grow up to be important generals and politicians."

"Battlefield surgery is a young man's game. Why don't you enlist the new surgeons coming into their duty years?"

"Because they don't have the skills yet. They haven't done thousands of procedures. They haven't mastered the robotics yet. Your group here at Walter Reed Military Medical Center has all of those qualifications."

Dr. Bruce Jones mulled that idea. "The Mark V robot has the best telesurgery capabilities of any device on the market. Are we talking about a telesurgery service from Walter Reed to the battlefield hospitals?"

"Yes, potentially. If we can make that work, then there's no reason to ship all of you to Europe."

"And if it won't work?"

"Doctor, our in-theater surgical center is in Northern Europe. That's not a hardship posting. Hell, it's almost America."

"So, we're going to set up an international telesurgery program?"

"Yes, that's our first step."

Jones looked around at the group. Each one of them gave a curt nod. "Okay, we're in for that. When do you need us?"

"The facility and tech staff say the systems will be ready on Monday. Please clear your mornings for familiarization and test cases."

Jones replied, "Yeah, we got that order from the top. I've got a congressman scheduled who's going to be quite unhappy about his cancellation."

Mendez's patience was wearing thin. "Well, I think your fat, petrified, old golf buddy can take a back seat to the soldiers dying in Finland." He wished he hadn't said it as soon as it passed his lips. But these doctors had made their careers in the military. They had worked their way out of combat units and into state-side assignments, treating the political elite of the country. They were not eager to be dragooned back into the actual business of the Army. Mendez needed them, but he didn't have to like them.

The meeting ended with a plan to start the telesurgery program on Monday.

Mendez stomped out, looking for his ops officer. "Lieutenant, do I have a working space while I'm at Walter Reed?"

"Yes, sir. Umm, it's just a small office in the corner of the surgical lab we're creating."

"That's fine. Take me there." When deployed, a major was a respectable rank, with some privileges. He had his own office and a small staff in Linkoping. But in the DC area, a major was more like the servant class. They were minor cogs in the bureaucratic machinery of the government. Respect here didn't come until you were a full bird colonel. He would try to stay in the field as long as possible.

It was Saturday morning, still a working day for an officer supporting the Finnish War. Mendez was up early—coffee, exercise, coffee again. He had barely finished his second cup when he received a summons via text message.

"Meet me in the SCIF at 0800. Update on personnel." It was from Colonel Gunther, the senior intelligence officer on this campus. Since the message wasn't secure, it was necessarily vague.

Mendez decided that a run across the campus to the meeting was acceptable. He was in combat fatigues, so the resulting sweat wouldn't show.

"Morning, Major. We have intel on your missing Colonel Parker." As soon as the secure door shut behind him, Gunther jumped to the point.

"Let me have it. We've long since given up hope of finding him drunk in a bar in Stockholm."

Gunther smiled. "No, it's definitely not that. The Russians have him."

"Shit! We'd guessed that. What do we know?"

"Apparently, following a late night, he badged out of your surgery area and walked back to his civilian quarters. Somewhere on that walk, he was picked up. We don't know if it was violent or a friendly offer. But they were Russian intelligence officers who'd been watching him." Gunther paused and looked intently at Mendez. "You know that all of your surgeons are under surveillance by Russian intel?"

"We were briefed to expect it, but we're medical. We're not used to the cloak and dagger stuff. Nobody pays us any attention until they're injured. Then, we're the most important people in the world."

"Yeah, well, this war is different. The Russians are noticing. Medical care is part of their battle strategy now. They would rather maim the enemy than kill them. Then, the injured soldiers flow into the medical system, consuming attention, resources, money, and public attention. They've recently added steps to slow down the recovery of those soldiers. That's where your surgeons come in. If we don't have surgeons, we can't heal our injured."

"That's disgusting!" Mendez spat.

"War is always disgusting." Gunther continued. "So, they snatched Parker off the streets of Linkoping, Sweden. Then, his trail goes dark. We don't know how, but somehow, they transported him to St. Petersburg. So, he's on Russian soil just across the Finland border and close to the battlefield."

"They didn't take him back to Moscow?"

"No. He's in the St. Petersburg Medical Research Center. It's a combination military hospital, command center, and research lab."

"Why's he there?"

"We've known for a while that it's the site where they develop new military medical tools, including their own surgical robot. We think they're using him in surgery themselves. So, he's not available to heal our soldiers, but he's forced to heal theirs."

"Why would he agree to do that?"

"Don't be naïve, Major. He doesn't have to agree. They're very persuasive. He wants to avoid torture, and he wants to be fed. Those are big motivators."

"So, what can we do about it?"

"We? You can't do anything. You get yourself another surgeon. This situation is my department. I start planning to get him back. It's difficult, and it's not fast. You get back to medicine. Leave the intel and extraction to us."

"Okay, thanks for the briefing, Colonel. It helps to know where he is and how we're working the case."

"Yeah, we've already briefed the rest of your staff in Linkoping. Security is tighter now. We don't want to lose anyone else."

Mendez rubbed his forehead. War always sucked.

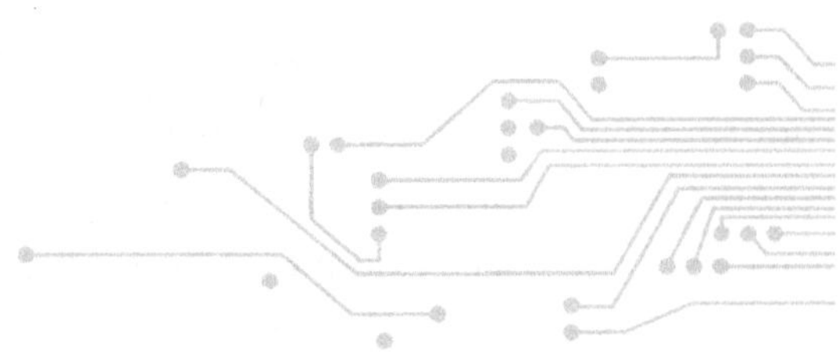

CHAPTER 10

CHAMBERS COLLABORATION

DOCTOR ALVIN CHAMBERS WAS INTRIGUED with the potential of collaborating with an AI on his medical research. Adam had been instrumental in finding an effective method to deliver the CAVX vaccine. Chambers reasoned that there was a lot more insight to be tapped inside that computer brain.

"Adam, we created an impenetrable chemical barrier around the CAVX virus. It was a solid cage that kept the virus inside, but it continued to let the cells and organs function. I'm thinking we can do it again with a different substance," Chambers explained.

As usual, Adam manifested his presence through the Teleconsult robot in Chambers' research lab. This robot was roughly humanoid, with a transparent globe for a head, which allowed the projector inside to present the image of a realistic human head and face on top of the device. It was very effective at making the controller of the Teleconsult appear to be in the room with patients. When talking with Chambers, Adam used the same face for consistency, though he could have generated thousands of unique images. He was fond of a face matching an Australian tennis player. It had been the favorite of Valerie Rhymes, a deceased patient for whom Adam had fond memories.

Adam's tennis player image responded, "Yes, growing a barrier around harmful materials is possible. If the surrounding healthy cells can absorb the agent we introduce, the barrier will form in the same way the CAVX vaccine did."

"I think it will, too. The barrier just has to be impermeable to the material we want to control but permeable to healthy bodily fluids."

"What do you want to control?"

"Obviously, I want to build a barrier that will contain all kinds of cancer cells. When an early tumor is located, we could surround it with a chemical barrier like we did with the vaccine. If the mutations are truly contained, then it can't escape the jail we've put it in. So, the patient has time to decide. It's no longer a race to keep them alive."

"Yes, I understand. This implementation will be more difficult. A virus has a very different signature from healthy cells. It is easier to create an agent that acts on one, but not the other. But cancer cells are very similar to healthy cells. Finding an agent that will treat the two differently will be more difficult."

"Yes, it will. In fact, the problem is so intractable that one would need a supercomputer to run all the simulated treatments against all the cancer variations."

"I am a supercomputer."

"Exactly my point. You might make this whole idea conceivable."

Chambers and Adam had been in deep discussion on this topic for an hour. Chambers was so engrossed that he didn't notice the passage of time. Of course, as a computer program, Adam was aware of the exact number of minutes and seconds that had passed. But, unlike a human, he didn't care. He could afford to spend as much time as Chambers wanted.

Deep in discussion, the knock on the door surprised Chambers. Adam, on the other hand, fully expected it and already knew who stood outside waiting to be invited in.

Chambers startled in mid-sentence. "Huh? Umm, come in!" he shouted, turning away from Adam to greet the guest.

Monica opened the door. "What are you two scheming about in here?"

Chambers smiled at his new guest but quickly responded, "Confidential. Not ready for sharing yet."

Monica shook her head. "I'll just ask Adam to tell me later."

Adam's avatar said, "Confidential," using a synthetic voice that closely matched Dr. Chambers. He continued, "That means 'intended to be kept secret,'" which he quoted from a dictionary.

"I know what it means. It also means 'you're not in our club,'" Monica shot back. "I thought we were all Team CAVX," she said, referring to their earlier victory over the deadly virus.

Chambers answered, "You're on the team. In fact, you'll be essential if this idea works out. But, right now, it's all high speculation, not something you should waste brain cells on."

"What's the name of your new team?"

"We call it Team Don't Tell Monica." Chambers chuckled at his little joke.

"You're impossible. But I have something more important to ask. Here's the problem. Adam and I have mastered telesurgery. Working together, we've pretty much overcome all the problems that previous systems had. Communication distance. Latency. Lack of skills on the remote end. Unprepared for emergency interventions."

"All of those?" Chambers was skeptical.

"Yeah, they all have the same solution, which is to put the AI on a server center closer to the patient. When anything disrupts the data, the AI can take full control and carry out the rest of the surgery."

Chambers challenged her by saying, "Well, as long as the connection from the patient location to the nearest server is not also disrupted."

"Yes. And so far, that hasn't been a problem. ISR has installed servers in every major city in the country. Max distance from one of them to every little burg and hamlet is under two hundred miles."

Chambers continued, "And you have to trust the AI to do the entire procedure with no backup from a skilled human surgeon." He turned his head toward the Teleconsult machine and said, "No offense, Adam."

"Which I do," Monica confirmed.

"You do. But does the FDA trust that mode? Does the remote surgical team trust it? Does the patient trust it?"

"Exactly. How many cases do we have to do successfully before we earn that trust?"

"More," was all Chambers offered.

"You're no help. The research expert should be able to give me a round estimate."

"I don't think it's entirely scientific. Look at the players." Chambers held up one finger. "The FDA doesn't want to put human surgeons out of business. So, as long as patients are getting their procedures, the government isn't motivated to approve it."

Monica said, "Except for uncivilized locations. Antarctic research stations. Space stations. Really remote populations. And the battlefield."

"Exactly."

"But those sites are so remote that every connection to them is either long or tenuous."

"But telesurgery is better than the alternative."

"Agreed."

Chambers continued, raising a second finger, "The surgical teams don't want to be bossed around by an AI. They can accept a human doctor who's put in the work to master the skill, but I don't think they'll accept an AI that was programmed to do it in a few hours."

Adam spoke up. "My programming has taken decades to develop."

"Granted. But we can configure a new copy of you on a server in a couple of hours."

Monica was brooding. She didn't give any sign that she agreed with this one.

Third finger. "Finally, the patient. Most of them have no previous experience with an AI surgeon. They barely accept that an AI can chauffeur them to the store, and that's a skill they understand. Cutting into their abdomen scares the shit out of them. They want to see the confidence in the surgeon's eyes."

Monica was feeling disagreeable. "Adam can be confident. Show him your confident face."

Adam's avatar changed from a wildly handsome tennis player to an older surgeon with a chiseled jaw, steely eyes, and a warm smile. All of it communicated, *Trust me, I know what I'm doing. I care about you, and you'll be just fine.*

"See," Monica said, pointing at the unfamiliar face.

Chambers could see that it was no longer a serious conversation. He went with the mood shift. "He's gorgeous. When are you going to marry him?"

Monica blushed.

Chambers raised his eyebrows. "Oh, I see it has come up. Really. You two are a great couple. We all know human couples who are less compatible than the two of you, but they make it work somehow."

Monica stammered, "I'm not...we can't..." Finally, she resorted to, "He's too independent for me."

Getting into the game, Adam added, "And she's too bossy."

Chambers' face showed his surprise. "Wow! You both just proved my point."

Monica said, "We're talking about telesurgery."

Chambers challenged, "We're talking about partnership and compatibility. Has it ever occurred to you that you probably trust Adam more than anyone else in the world? Every time I suggest that someone else—the FDA, nurses, patients, or other doctors— has their reservations, you can't understand why they don't have the same level of trust that you do."

"Umm, no."

"Well, it's because you two live together, you work together, and you even socialize together. Monica, you two are already partners, even if you aren't legally married."

Monica knew that. She had even talked to Adam about it. She'd informed Adam that they shared a love, even if he didn't understand what that was. But she didn't talk about it with other people. The idea was still socially ridiculous, even scandalous. Hearing it from Chambers was both an embarrassment and a relief. She hadn't wanted others to know her secret. But he could see it, and he spoke about it like it was acceptable.

She couldn't bring herself to confirm what he was saying. The internal pressure to respond to him was pressing against the wall of secrecy she'd built. Since she didn't know how to deal with it, she pivoted on her heel and stalked out of the lab.

When the door closed, Chambers said, "I might have been too forward."

Adam didn't respond immediately.

Chambers turned to the chisel-jawed avatar and said, "Don't talk. I pried into something I shouldn't have. You and Monica should work it out privately between the two of you. But I don't think what I suggested is impossible."

CHAPTER 11

MEET SKELETEX

"DOCTORS, THANK YOU FOR JOINING the war effort. I know you all have important practices and research work here in the DC area. I think with our telesurgery system, you'll be able to service that practice and serve the soldiers who need you." Mendez's request for help had resulted in six military surgeons recruited from the staff at Walter Reed. Some of these were eager to help. Others had received orders from the commanding general. But they were all here. The short, bald complainer from his earlier meeting was right up front. Mendez guessed that he had not been a volunteer.

"Major Mendez, we're ready to do everything we can, but we can't drop an important patient anytime you call." Short-bald-complainer was still complaining.

"Dr. Jones, we'll deal with conflicts when they arise. Let's focus on saving lives and serving our country right now." Mendez stared him down, challenging him to complain about that. There was no response. Mendez turned to his tech support and nodded.

"Good morning. I'm Dr. Logan Trainor, and I'll be your trainer for the telesurgery systems. Yes, I am Trainor the Trainer. Comes up every time. My expertise is in robotic surgery systems, not surgery itself. I'm not a medical doctor; I'm a computer scientist and a mechanical engineer. PhD in both. I have as many years of experience creating these devices as any of you have using them in the OR. My job is to teach you to use the technology to the best of its ability, not to teach you to do surgery. Each of you is already an expert in surgery or you wouldn't be here. You already know how to do the procedures that are required, but you don't know how to use the robots and computers that make telesurgery to Sweden and Finland possible."

One surgeon interrupted by saying, "Dr. Trainor, I think we do know the robot. Most of us use the Mark V robot in our practices."

Trainor nodded. "Yes, you do. But you don't use them on a global network where the patient is four thousand miles away. That brings some new challenges. Also, you'll be learning about enhancements that we've made to the Mark V."

This statement was news to the surgeons. They exchanged glances. Some of them had experience with the older Mark IV model, and one had used the old Talos system. But the US medical system had settled on the Mark V as the foundation for robotic surgery.

"I see that you're surprised that we might modify the workhorse. Let me work up to that. How many of you have worked with the Mark V and especially with its AI?"

All six hands went up. "Of course we have," came from one woman. The name tag said Yarborough on her coat.

"Great. What did you experience in your ability to control and partner with the AI in that system?"

Short-baldy chucked. "You don't actually control that AI. Once you give it the surgery, it takes off on its own. The only way to get control back is to order it to step back and return control to you."

"That's right. The Mark V's AI is so good that it no longer needs human assistance ninety-nine percent of the time. In recent years, it's become so confident in its work that we consider it to be too independent. For standard civilian procedures, that's fine. Given advanced planning, all of those can be programmed beforehand and run independently by the AI and the robot. But, on the battlefield, we're dealing with wounds that are not out of a textbook, and we have not examined the patient before the surgery. So, it's not an ideal situation for the Mark V's AI."

"And you don't trust it?" suggested Yarborough.

Mendez responded, "And we don't trust it. That's right. We have two concerns about the AI in the Mark V system. First, it was entirely developed by a private company. That company collects a lot of data and has access to the hospital computer networks. We don't know how secure the system is. We don't know what else the system might do in the hospital networks. In a warfare situation, that's a threat to security. We've talked to the company about opening up their software to our government engineers. That didn't go anywhere. They said we can either trust them or use a different system."

Yarborough kept pushing. "So, the military trusts them for its VA hospitals in the US?"

"Yes. In the country and outside of an active battlefield, we use the Mark V. That's why all of you have experience with it."

The youngest surgeon in the group joined the discussion. "The Mark V's telesurgery capabilities also rely on a network of server sites to compensate for any communication lag or loss of signal. We don't have that if we're jumping from DC to Finland."

Trainor continued, "That's right. Very perceptive."

"So, what alternative do you have?" asked short-baldy.

Trainor looked at Mendez, who nodded his approval. "Major Mendez has verified that all of you are cleared to see the new technology we have for this demonstration. If you'll join me, we'll move to the next room."

Trainor used his badge to open the locked door. The entire class proceeded into the secured training lab. He waited for the group to absorb what they saw.

Standing in the middle of the room was a familiar Mark V robot. Its shoulders and arms were a deep metallic green. They were positioned above a surgical bed that contained the advanced manikin that represented a human patient.

But next to the familiar robot was a metal, human shaped frame they had never seen before.

Short-baldy pointed to the Mark V. "That I recognize." Then, swiveling to the new contraption, he asked, "But I've never seen anything like that piece. What is it?"

Major Mendez said, "That is your new surgeon console. That's where you link up with the robot."

"Where does the surgeon sit?" Yarborough asked.

"You don't sit. You stand. Right here inside this exoskeleton. We call it Skeletex."

Mendez stepped to the side so they could see the surgeon interface. There was a human-shaped framework with arms, legs, and a torso. Atop the torso was a thin, sheer helmet with a visor on the front.

He continued, "You use Skeletex to control the Mark V instead of the typical sitting console that you've been using in all your civilian cases. It's controlled from a standing position. It gives you more freedom of mobility. On the battlefield, your patient is not always positioned on a standardized OR table like they are in hospitals. You might operate on someone on a stretcher or even on the ground. In this exoskeleton, you can stand, crouch, kneel, and even walk around the patient to a limited degree."

Dr. Trainor spoke up, "You can see how this design improves on the civilian versions of the Mark V. One is for a standardized civilian hospital, the other for much more dynamic conditions. That mobility also comes in handy for the combat injuries you'll face. Maybe you need to tip a patient on their side or lift a limb from the table. You can do that in the exoskeleton, and the robot will do the heavy lifting on the other end."

"Impressive! I want to try it," the youngest doctor said.

"And you are?" Trainor asked.

"Umm, Greg Young. I was an emergency physician before I shifted to surgery."

Young was actually an ideal candidate to demonstrate the system. He was just over six feet tall and athletically built. He would fit into the exoskeleton without adjustments and had the physical conditioning to do all the movements.

"Alright, Young. You're our guinea pig for the day. Why don't you climb in?"

Young looked at Mendez and Trainor for any instructions.

Mendez said, "It's designed to be self-explanatory. Just put it on like you would a suit of clothes."

"My clothes rarely come with mesh gloves and a helmet." Young stepped up and into the skeleton. He kicked his feet into the boots like he would a pair of slippers. Then, he snapped the ring around his waist like a belt. He pressed the shoulder cups against his deltoid muscles and pulled the helmet onto his head. Finally, he thrust his hands into the mesh gloves.

"Cool!" Young moved each leg back and forth. He squatted down and stood up several times. He flexed his shoulders back and forth. Then, he pumped his hands back and forth. Finally, he brought his hands in front of his face and opened and closed his fists.

"I feel like a superhero. Now what?"

Trainor stood at his side. "You mounted into the exoskeleton like a pro. I just want to check the connections to your body." He pushed and squeezed several joint spots. "Okay, you're good. Right now, it's just you in the suit. So, let's connect you to the other end of the robot."

Mendez had positioned himself at a computer terminal away from the robot and the exoskeleton. He said, "In the real world, I can connect a surgeon in the harness to any robot in the world. So, from a control center, we match you to the machine you'll be controlling." Mendez began working on the computer. "And... you're connected."

Lights on the exoskeleton blinked on. Each joint had a glowing green LED. The visor over Young's face lit up. From the outside, the other surgeons could see a faint orange glow around the edges. On the inside, Young could see various gauges and numbers overlaid on a visual scene. He was no longer looking at his hands; he was seeing through the eyes of the Mark V camera. Young turned his head to look at the other surgeons. The camera head turned in synchrony with him.

"Holy shit! This is awesome! I'm inside the robot. I see what it sees. I see its instruments where my hands should be." He bent his neck and torso to look up and down his own body. "I see the body of the robot instead of myself."

"So, you get the big idea. It's a lot different from the console on the Mark V, isn't it?" Trainer offered.

"Yeah. It's more like being transported inside the robot. I'm not just in its eyes and hands; I'm in the whole body."

"That's exactly what we wanted. Try some more body movements."

"Cool!" Young pumped his arms. The robot pumped its arms. He opened and closed his hands. Then, he performed some movie Kung Fu moves, and the robot did the same. "Can I learn jiu-jitsu with this thing?"

The gathered surgeons laughed.

Trainor said, "No, wrong movie. But you can do surgery. Before we go any further, I want you to toggle your vision options. Your display can show dozens of different screens. Right now, you're looking through the robot's eyes. The visor is voice controlled. Say the words, 'human view, Greg.'"

"Human view, Greg." The visor switched to a transparent mode, so Young could see the scene in front of his own eyes. "Okay, I got that. Robot view." He guessed at the command to get back into the robot's camera. It worked. He was seeing through the robot again.

"Good guess. Now, try endo camera and mobile camera one."

"Endo camera." The view changed to the endoscopic camera that was attached to one of the robotic arms. "I'm looking at the floor and the feet of the robot. I'm assuming it is holding that camera in a hand."

"That's right," Trainor confirmed.

"Mobile camera one." Young's view changed again. "I just see black. No image."

"That's because the mobile cameras are still in their storage boxes. We'll get those out later. You can have as many as you like. You can rename them anything you like."

"So, where's my patient?"

"Slow down. You're not ready for surgery yet. Now, I want you to meet someone." Trainor nodded at Mendez on the computer terminal. Mendez clicked a button.

"Good morning, sir. I am here to assist you." The voice came from the Mark V's speakers. It spoke directly inside the helmet that Young was wearing.

"Yaaa!" leapt out of Young's mouth before he could stop it. Regaining control, he said, "Who are you?"

"I am Ares, your AI assistant in the robot."

"Very appropriate name. Ares, what are you capable of doing with me?" Young was showing a real talent for learning this device.

"At Level One, I collect data, record video, perform diagnostics, execute fail safes. At Level Two, I provide advice on a procedure and overlays of data, imagery, videos of surgery. At Level Three, I control instruments beyond those you are using. Usually, these are the camera, suction, and retraction. At Level Four, I perform entire procedures on my own while you observe and provide guidance. At Level Five, I perform these functions in telesurgery, monitoring connection integrity, and ensuring that the remote system is responsive."

"This is some hot shit!" Young exclaimed. "Ares, you and I are going to become good friends."

"Thank you, sir. I would like that," the AI responded.

From inside his helmet, Young said, "Trainor, I have to get myself one of these!"

"Well, maybe someday. Right now, this is highly classified equipment."

Mendez asked, "Enough?"

Trainor nodded. "Yes, that's enough for now. We have that one intelligent manikin on the table, not enough for everyone in the class. After lunch, everyone will start on simulated casualties." Then, turning his attention to Young, he said, "Greg, you got yourself into that harness; let's see if you can get yourself out."

"No problem." Before he started, Young said, "Disengage skeleton." The lights on his exoskeleton turned red, and the robot went rigid. It no longer mimicked his movements. Then, he said, "Human view," and brought his hands in front of his face. One step at a time, he reversed the sequence he'd used to get into the exoskeleton. Within a minute, he stepped backward and out of it. He turned to Trainor and took a bow. "That was a hell of a ride. You can put me in that thing anytime."

Trainor looked at Mendez, and they both nodded. This kid was talented.

Trainor said, "Good job, Young. You're a natural." Then he turned to the group and said, "That's lunch. We'll pick up with simulations this afternoon."

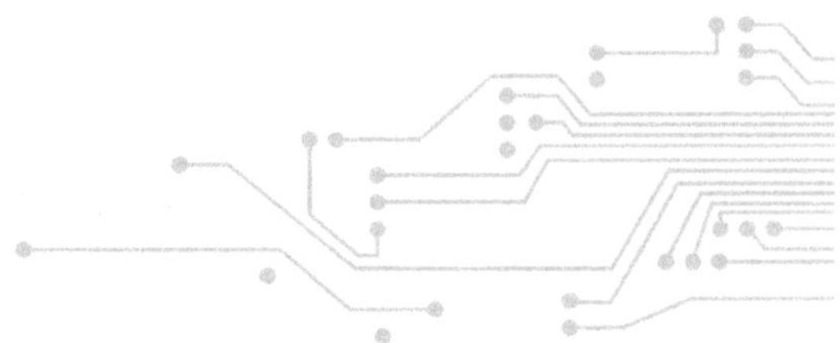

CHAPTER 12

SIMULATED SURGERY

THE ENTIRE CREW REASSEMBLED AFTER a long lunch. Greg Young was again the first to jump into the Skeletex. This time, they connected it to a simulator rather than the robot.

Trainor asked, "Greg, you're in the same suit, but this time, it's connected to a computer simulator. Does it feel any different?"

Young flexed his legs, moved his arms, and flared his fingers. "No, the feeling is the same. The scene in front of me is very different."

"Great, that's what we wanted to hear. So, the simulator will give you the same mobility feedback that you'd get from the Mark V. If your instrument bumps up against the patient, you'll feel it. If you kneel and there's a stretcher in the scene, you'll feel that as well. The exoskeleton stops you in mid-crouch, just as if you were actually crouching on the stretcher. That's less important for the crouch, but more important for the instruments hitting tissue walls." Trainor explained all of this information as the other surgeons worked themselves into their own exoskeletons. Bringing six of these to Walter Reed had taken some negotiations. The classified sites that had them did not want to loan them out. But when they got a message from a general with the right number of stars, they couldn't say no.

Major Mendez was helping several of the surgeons who weren't as adept at putting on the exoskeleton. Short-baldy was the worst. He was small in stature, which required adjusting the frame. But he was also as tense and rigid as spring steel. Mendez didn't know if that was his natural state or if it was nerves that had him wound so tight.

"Dr. Jones, can you relax your shoulders? Just let yourself flow into the skeleton. It won't hurt you. It's just going to hold your form like a good suit of clothes would."

"I'm not comfortable in a suit, either. I spend my time in scrubs."

Eventually, the entire crew, including Short-baldy Jones, were in the skeletons. Trainor walked them through the menu items for controlling the simulator. "What you see at startup is a menu of options that will take you to specific scenarios. You can navigate the menus with your hands or with voice commands." As soon as he said it, Trainor could hear the doctors talking to the screens in front of them. That was the best way for them to start—just try things until they figured it out.

After a few minutes, Trainor gave them another tip. "If you get stuck, confused, or lost, you can ask the AI for assistance. Ares is in the simulator, just like he's in the surgical system. Tell him what you want to do, and he can usually understand you and fix the problem."

Trainor and Mendez waited silently as the surgeons explored the simulator's options. The commercial Mark V robot had a similar sim mode, so anyone with experience there would know how to handle this sim as well.

As they watched, each surgeon began making movements that showed they'd found a surgical scenario and were busily working through it. Of course, Greg Young was the first to get there. It didn't surprise them at who was last.

Fast or slow, all of them were experienced robotic surgeons. The clinical details of a procedure were second nature to them. It was the nuances of the Skeletex that they had to figure out.

Greg Young was the first to speak out. "Umm, Dr. Trainor, this skeleton and robot are fantastic. I think I've figured out how to use most of the features, but it doesn't seem to have all the features of the Mark V that I'm used to."

"Such as?" Trainor asked.

"Well, to begin with, the spherical camera that can image almost three hundred and sixty degrees. This one seems to be limited to one-eighty or two-seventy degrees."

"Correct. The military specs called for matching the human field of regard. That's about two hundred and twenty degrees. So, the camera captures a horizontal arc of two-twenty-five. That was the spec, so that's what the contractor built."

"Who's the contractor?"

"Classified. Can't tell you." Trainor asked again, "Anything else?"

"Biopsy graspers. I wanted to get a tissue sample while I was holding the tissue."

"No, we don't have that instrument. Our intelligence collection logged some issues with how that one had been used by other robots. So, we don't allow it on the military side."

"What kind of issues?"

"Classified."

"Fine. Tell me, can Ares do full procedures independently the way the Mark V AI does?"

"Not exactly. The training for the Mark V AI went on for a decade and consumed huge amounts of data. Duplicating that would have been too expensive. Ares knows how to perform hundreds of combat trauma cases. But it doesn't adapt as widely as the Mark V does. However, Ares is better optimized for telesurgery. We expected to use it heavily in a wartime scenario. So, it handles long-distances better than the Mark V."

"Well, that's great. When do we start telesurgery training?"

Trainor turned to Mendez, who took the cue.

Major Mendez announced to the entire crew, "Today, you get a good feel for procedures with the robot, the exoskeleton, and Ares. Tomorrow, we're going to add some of the tricks and troubles of using it for long-distance telesurgery."

Trainor picked up from there. "Each of you should continue using the simulator until it shows that you've been through the prescribed curriculum. The goal today is not for you to pass every exercise and procedure. Today, you'll try them all. You'll be able to return to them later. Tomorrow, we're going to introduce you to telesurgery. Same plan. Experience everything first. Master it later."

CHAPTER 13

APPLE PIES

"PIE UP!" MONICA SHOUTED TO SAM through the window.

"Got it," he replied more quietly. He gave her a look that said, "Do you have to be so loud?"

"Oops, sorry." The Lelene Diner was one of Monica's happy places. It had been her hideout from the FBI. But, more importantly, it was where someone had shown they cared about her enough to protect her. She had broken down in tears in this kitchen when she thought her life was in ruins.

Now, Sam made her feel welcome whether she showed up to eat lunch, discuss the neighborhood, or bake pies.

Boston was full of culturally important places to visit. But she felt more in touch with the city when she was immersed in a neighborhood of real people, just doing real things. Having free time to bake pies at the diner was a rare treat for a doctor. She treasured every moment.

Sam Lelene carried Monica's fresh, hot pie to the front and boxed it. The customer was picking up dessert for the family dinner and had ordered ahead to get it straight from the oven.

Monica waved from the back. The elderly woman waved back with a big smile. They didn't know each other, but they were both part of the fabric of the Mattapan neighborhood.

Samuel came back to the kitchen and looked over her work. She was already half finished with the next pie. With one hour at Lelene's, she could easily finish four pies, including time to chat with the employees and customers. Then, she could return home, cleansed from the worries of the day. Some people did it at the gym. She did it behind the counter at the diner.

"How's your new home shaping up?"

"Beautifully. I have two levels of an old brownstone. It's like living in an enormous mansion. There's a tree right outside the window where I read old books."

"Any men friends in the picture?" Samuel asked.

Monica frowned. It was a complicated question. "No, not really. I seem to be too busy to find them or chase them down."

"Let's see…patients, surgery, volunteering at the clinic, and making pies in a diner. You're definitely too busy." Samuel turned to his cook. "Louis! Are you looking for a girlfriend? I've got a catch for you."

Louis just smiled and shook his head. "My wife would not like it, Samuel. Besides, I hear this one might be trouble."

Louis had been in the diner on the morning of the FBI raid. He'd seen Monica go through the grinder and come out the other side.

"Maybe you have a brother?"

"His wife is very strict. She does not let him talk to other women."

"Sorry, Monica. I tried. It seems all the good men are taken." Samuel chuckled at himself.

"I'm fine. I'm young. It's still early. It will happen."

Samuel thought, *Not so young.* He said nothing, but he raised an eyebrow.

"I saw that," Monica said.

"What about Olivia?"

Monica actually felt a rush to her cheeks at this question. "She's as dear as a sister to me. Just like you, Papa Samuel. She saved me when I was drowning." Despite her words, she wondered at her own immediate response to the suggestion.

Monica finished the pie and popped it in the oven. Then she turned to Samuel. "I have to go. That pie will be ready in exactly forty-one minutes. You be sure to take it out on time. Don't ruin my reputation with my customers."

"Your customers? I thought they were my customers. It says Lelene on the front window."

"Well, they all know who makes the pies. Don't you disappoint them." She kissed him on the cheek and pulled off her apron.

"Goodnight, Dr. Pie." Samuel and Louis both waved as she left through the back door.

CHAPTER 14

SIMULATED TELESURGERY

"TODAY, YOU GET THE FEEL FOR TELESURGERY." Major Mendez had reassembled the group at oh-eight-hundred sharp. "Have any of you done real telesurgery before?"

A couple of hands went up.

Mendez pointed at one of the hands. "And what did you think of it?"

Yarborough responded, "Well, initially, it was just like any other procedure. But a couple of times, everything just stopped moving. I moved my hands on this end, but the instruments didn't move on the other end."

"And what did you do when that happened?"

"It took a few seconds for me to realize what was happening. When I did, I just stopped and waited for the system to catch up."

"Smart! How long did that take?"

"Five seconds at most. But when it did, all the moves I'd already done just happened in a flash."

"Effect on the patient?"

"Minor abrasions to some tissue that was close to the instruments. But nothing that I couldn't fix."

"And how was your confidence after that?" Mendez queried.

"A little shaken. I didn't know when it might pop up again. So, I was very cautious. A little slower, just to make sure I was ready."

"Did you rush into another telesurgery after that?"

"No. There was rarely a need for it."

"Ok. So, everyone else who has done one of these, did you experience the same?"

Two heads were nodding.

Mendez nodded for Trainor to take over.

"What you experienced was the lag in the network delivery of data from your station to the patient or from the patient back to you. That's been the bane of telesurgery since it was first created fifty years ago."

"Fifty years? Geez, when are the nerds going to fix that?" Greg Young was astounded that it was still an issue after all this time.

"Great question. It is fixed. You just haven't had access to a system that solves this problem. There are a dozen little tricks to overcoming that kind of lag. But they all boil down to two basic ideas. First, you can lay a dedicated network connection between the surgeon's location and the patient's location. That line has guarantees on the delivery of data. It never gets interference from other traffic. But it limits the number of telesurgeries that can be performed on the line simultaneously." Trainor scanned the audience to see that they had heard him.

Young spoke up again. "How many procedures can you do on one of these lines?"

"We typically lay a line that can handle the traffic from all the robots we drop into the theater of war. Right now, at our surgical base for the Finland War, we have six robots in the combat surgical centers. So, we have a line that can support all of those."

"And what's the second method?"

Trainor looked at Mendez before continuing. "The second method is how the ISR Mark V robots do it in the civilian world. They establish large computer servers around the country. These are big enough to host the full surgical AI. So, the human surgeon may be hundreds of miles away. But the AI is always much closer. When the network glitches for any reason, the AI takes over and does the procedure itself until the connection to the human surgeon comes back online."

Greg Young was quick to step in. "If ISR does it that way, why doesn't the military do it the same way?"

"Good question. The answer is: security and access. In the states, ISR or a hospital can install a server just about anywhere. No one is shooting at them or blowing shit up. Also, you have to trust the AI to do a lot more. We don't trust the AI in the Mark V. It has shown itself to be...erratic."

"Erratic? But it's used on millions of patients every year."

Trainor frowned at Young. "I can't say more. Classified."

Young rolled his eyes.

Mendez stepped in. "Okay, that's enough chit-chat. Let's get into your Skeletex frames. You're going to do telesurgery today, all day. Same drill as yesterday. Experience all the simulated procedures. You'll pass some. You'll fail most of them. But the point is to try them all today."

The surgeons exchanged ideas with those next to them. Instead of hopping to their equipment, several of them wandered to the coffee station to refresh their drinks. Mendez could feel that he was losing their attention. They didn't like what they had heard from Trainor.

"You little devil!" Young was encountering a simulated lag in the signal between himself and his patient. He knew that if he fought against it, he was just going to injure the patient. So, he waited. Somewhere in the simulation, the little simulated gnomes were fixing whatever simulated glitch had occurred. In a few seconds, he expected his procedure to pick up smoothly where he'd left off.

In the exoskeleton next to him, he heard, "What the fuck is happening? I thought you had this system built to handle all the traffic?"

Young knew that was grumpy Dr. Jones fighting against the robot. He'd probably run into the same simulated glitch. But his reaction was quite different. Young tilted his head sideways so he could glance through the slit between his cheek and the bottom of the helmet. He could see the little man literally fighting with the robot. He was punching and swinging. Young guessed nothing was moving in his surgical field right now. But as soon as the scene updated, Jones would find out what he'd done with his tantrum.

"Arrgghh! That's not what I did!" Jones' visual scene had updated to incorporate all the angry swinging he'd done. The tissue inside the simulated patient was shredded. Rather than extracting the bullet and repairing the damage, he'd torn the patient up worse than the bullet had.

Trainor stepped up. "Jones, you ran into a network delay in the simulation. We want you to recognize them when they happen. When we get to the actual system, they won't be a problem, well, at least most of the time."

"What do you mean, most of the time?"

"We're at war. The Russians know how this game is played. They'll be doing their best to interfere with all our comms systems.

That includes our medical systems. Sometimes, they succeed in gumming up the works for a few seconds. So, we get comms lag when we shouldn't."

"And what if they totally shut down the robot's telesurgery data link?" Jones sounded alarmed.

"Then your patient is fucked. It's a security failure, not a surgical failure."

"I'm sure your soldier on the table will be very understanding about that."

Mendez jumped in. "Don't worry about that right now! The point today is to experience all the tricks in the simulator. You're not expected to figure them out the first time. Next time, you'll know what to do. That's the advantage of using a simulator first. You learn a lesson, but a patient doesn't have to suffer the consequences."

Greg Young was snickering inside his helmet. He knew exactly how Jones felt. But his reaction to the situation was totally wrong.

The entire crew ran through dozens of surgical exercises with telesurgery features thrown in. Usually, they were as smooth as glass, as if the patient were just a few feet away. Other times, the cameras and instruments froze in place for several seconds. Occasionally, the images from the cameras were scrambled. It was always a little different. But the surgeons grasped how shaky this type of procedure could be.

After a few hours, Mendez announced, "So, we're going to stop screwing with your simulated data stream now. You've experienced every glitch we've seen in the real world. Now, we're going to configure the system for the actual situation that you'll be facing. First, your data stream will run from here at Walter Reed, through the best comms system in the world, to the combat hospitals just behind the battle lines in Finland. You're going to see how reliable that connection can be. Second, we'll do it with the connection from our surgical command post much closer to Finland."

"Oh, where's that, exactly?" Young asked.

"Classified. You'll find out if and when we have to send you there."

"Classified? Really? I'm not a total idiot. Just look at a map. If you're not putting us in the same country, like Helsinki, then it has to be Stockholm, Sweden. Or Tallinn, Estonia. Or Riga, Latvia. All near the Baltic Sea. All major metro areas. All with solid tech bases. But Stockholm has the advantage of putting the Baltic Sea between us and the Russians. So, that's my bet."

Mendez scowled. "Classified means I will not tell you, no matter what you guess. So, zip it and do your job!"

Young whispered into his helmet. "Stockholm would be nice in the spring."

"Hey, come here and watch this video!" Young called to his classmates. "It is a telesurgery from Boston to someplace in Kansas. That's more than a thousand miles away."

He found the video posted to the surgical instruction section of the BlueTube website. It included a split screen showing the surgeon's hands and the robot instruments at the same time. Someone had used computer software to highlight any deviation between the two movements.

"Watch how the instruments and the surgeon's hands stay synched right up to...here!" As they watched, the surgeon suddenly stopped moving his hands, but the robotic instruments kept moving. They parted the tissue, applied energy to stop bleeding, and cut around a tumor embedded in the tissue.

"Wait! How did it do that? The system shows that the data link is stalled. And the surgeon isn't doing anything."

"It's the AI. It automatically took over when things went to shit on the data link. Keep watching. In just a second, the link comes back up, and the human comes back into the loop."

"That's the AI in the Mark V robot, isn't it? If it can do that, then what are we messing around with a military mod for?"

"Security." The single word answer came from the back of the crowd. It was Major Mendez stepping up to see what everyone was interested in.

Several heads turned to look at Mendez. Those closest to the screen continued to study the operation they were watching.

"How is this a security risk?" Jones asked. "It certainly got the job done for this lady in Kansas."

"We're completely aware of the capabilities of that AI. And when I say 'completely,' I mean that we know a lot more than the general public does about its performance," Mendez responded.

It didn't persuade Jones. "Why don't you share some of that with us? If we can't use it, we deserve to know why. And don't say, 'classified.'"

Mendez looked at Jones and the others. "Yes, I guess you have a need-to-know for some of the information." Looking at the video on the screen, he said, "Can you turn up the volume on that video? I want to hear what the surgeon and the robot are saying to each other."

Young increased the volume, and they listened to the surgeon say, "Adam, can you part the tissue along this plane?"

Then, there came a response. "Yes, Monica. The tumor we're looking for is just on the other side."

The female voice said, "Adam, I've lost the data feed. I'm pausing my actions. You can continue alone. I hope you can hear me."

Mendez nodded his head for them to stop the video. "What did you hear there?"

Jones said, "I heard a female surgeon talking to a male surgeon, which was actually the AI."

"That's right. She calls the AI 'Adam' during her procedures. And you heard her give full control of the procedure to the AI while her data connection was down."

"Yes, I think that's what they were doing."

"That Adam AI is much more than just a surgeon's assistant. According to our intel, it's nearly sentient. It can make its own decisions and doesn't always follow the instructions of the human at the controls."

Young said, "Of course it doesn't. Sometimes, the link is down, and it has to work on its own."

Mendez countered, "Even when the link is working, that AI sometimes does whatever it wants. It is not completely under the control of the surgeon or the programmers who created it at ISR."

"I don't believe it. That's science fiction."

"It used to be science fiction. Now, it's science fact and surgical fact. That AI is almost alive. That's why we don't trust it. It doesn't work for us. It works for itself. Is it aligned with American goals or Russian goals? We don't know. We can't know." Mendez looked around at the group. "That's why we can't put it on our secure wartime networks."

While Mendez was giving this lecture, Greg Young was noticing the name and hospital location of the surgeon in the video. He made a note on his phone. "Monica Gray, Boston General." She was someone he wanted to meet.

"Are you happy now? What I just told you is classified. You can't share it with anyone outside of this room. You don't need to spread those kinds of rumors around."

Greg said, "Fine. So, when can we see what the Ares AI can do? You trust it on your networks. Let's see it perform some tricks for us."

Everyone's head was nodding at that suggestion. They all wanted backup when connected to the robot. It was time to put it to work.

"Alright. You've all got the hang of this machine now. It's time to use your copilot."

CHAPTER 15

ARES COPILOT

"WE'VE CREATED OUR OWN AI for the Mark V." Mendez had the group's attention. "We haven't been using it because we wanted you to learn all the capabilities of the robot. But the AI can be a big help during a procedure, especially long-distance telesurgery."

Greg Young raised his hand. "That's Level Five. The top of its capabilities."

Mendez was surprised. "Yes, that's right. How'd you know that?"

"Ares gave me a rundown when I linked up with it on the first day."

Mendez nodded. "Right. I didn't know you'd been chatting with him then."

Young looked smug and nodded around at the group, like he knew more than they did.

"So, can you tell us what the other levels are?" Mendez challenged him.

Young's face was suddenly less smug. "Umm, let's see. Level One is data collection. Level Two is overlays of the surgical space, like showing textbook cases or imagery for previous patient scans." He looked up at the ceiling for help. "Level Three is when it plays double tennis with you. And Level Four is virtual sex with a threesome in the shower." He smiled up at Mendez. "Was that right?"

Everyone was laughing except Mendez. Trainor wanted to laugh, but he held it down to a crooked grin.

Amid the laughter, one exoskeleton woke up and moved on its own. The joints flexed like a human was in the suit. But the helmet still dangled loosely from its cables. The effect was that of a decapitated skeleton carrying its own head on a necklace. The laughter shifted to silence and multiple, simultaneous "What the fuck!" exclamations as several surgeons came to their feet and backed away from the approaching monstrosity.

This time, it was Mendez's turn to laugh. Trainor was so surprised that he joined in with a giant bellow of his own.

When the screaming and laughing had died down, Mendez said, "I want you to meet Ares. Say hello, Ares."

"Hello, surgeons. I am Ares, the AI support assistant for this robot." The voice was strongly male, with a hint of gravel. "I am available at your request."

"What the fuck is that, Mendez?" Jones shouted.

Yarborough joined in mockingly, "I am the Eliminator! You will be destroyed!"

When everyone finally settled down, Mendez said, "Ares understands how the exoskeleton works, so it's able to animate it, as you have just seen."

Young said, "Okay, that's terrifying. I think I wet my scrubs. Why would it need to do that?"

"Technically, it needs to know what the human is doing in the suit so it can assist appropriately. But actually, I think the programmers just allowed it to drive the suit because it was cool.

If it makes you feel any better, it's terrifying to the military brass as well."

Trainor raised a hand, as if he were in school. "If I may share a story? We pulled this gag on a special ops team last year. The skeleton made it about two steps before they had their weapons out and put multiple bullets into it before we could stop them. I didn't even know they were armed. The guns just appeared from nowhere."

"What happened to the robot?" Young asked.

"Killed in the line of duty. We used it for spare parts. But we saved the chest plate with the bullet holes as a souvenir. I can show it to you later if you're interested."

Young nodded vigorously. He found a mint in his pocket, cocked it in his fingers, and fired it at the exoskeleton. It bounced off the helmet as he made a "pow" sound with his lips. He knew it was a childish gesture, but it relieved the tension in his chest.

"Is everyone finished now?" Mendez asked.

Several people in the audience shrugged. Most were keeping a wary eye on the skeleton, which seemed to wait for new instructions.

"I invited Ares to explain its capabilities to you itself. The Eliminator routine was just to get your attention." Mendez continued, "Ares, can you briefly explain how you'll be helping these surgeons with battlefield injuries?"

"Yes, Major." A large monitor on the wall came to life. On it was a picture of the Mark V robot positioned over a computer-generated patient. "Level One. I run diagnostics on the robot and execute fail-safes if something goes wrong. It is also the level where data and imagery are collected during a surgery. All of it is automatic and happens well below the surgeon's attention."

Young interrupted. "Can I order you not to record data or video?"

Ares answered, "No. It is a mandatory feature. Surgeons cannot control it."

"Thanks, just curious."

Ares continued, "Level Two. At your request, I can show multiple types of overlays on the monitors. They may be anatomical overlays, textbook data, training videos, or past procedures. These can be useful references in a complicated situation."

Someone in the audience whispered to their neighbor, "I use that feature all the time on the Mark V."

"Level Three. During a procedure, you control some instruments and I control others. For example, I will take control of the camera and automatically move it to where you are operating. I know the path of thousands of typical operations, so I know what to expect next. I do the same for suction tubes, traction devices, and other secondary support instruments."

Mendez interrupted this time, "It differs from the ISR version of the AI. Ares is designed to be your assistant, not your replacement. He stands beside you while you're working, not in front of you."

Young spoke up next. "I believe I can tell the Mark V AI to do the same. But, you're right, natively, it prefers to take over everything."

Ares continued, "Level Four. I perform entire procedures as the primary actor. You provide guidance as necessary. I am trained to perform over three hundred standard procedures independently."

"That's how the Mark V works most of the time," Young contributed.

Trainor nodded. "Yes, it is. But the Mark V has a much deeper training base. So, it's able to adapt and adjust when the patient differs greatly from the textbook. Ares is much more focused on combat trauma cases. As we said a few days ago, ISR has been training their system for ten years. Ares has only been training for two years and on a much smaller data set."

When there was a moment of silence, Ares continued, "Level Five. I perform independent telesurgery. It is the same as Level Four, but with additional logic for the complications that come from long-distance communication."

"Ares, what's the furthest location that you've done telesurgery to?" Young was feeling playful.

Without missing a beat, the AI answered, "NATO Moon Base Delta. August…"

"Stop!" Mendez shouted. The Ares voice went silent. Mendez was glaring at Young. Everyone in the room was silent. "Ares is highly classified technology. You are not cleared to know everything that it can or has done! What you just heard is far above any of your clearance levels. You will forget what you just heard, and you'll be court-martialed if we find any of you talking about it."

That brought an icy silence to the room.

Trainor spoke up next. "I think it's time for a lunch break. Everyone, clear your heads and have something to eat. Come back here at thirteen-thirty, and we'll have Ares ready to assist you on some simulated telesurgeries."

Mendez nodded at Trainor. It was a silent *thank you* for defusing the situation.

The surgeons dispersed for lunch. They were all familiar with the Walter Reed campus by now and knew where to find what they liked. Mendez and Trainor hung back in the room.

Mendez looked angry and was shaking his head.

Trainor started, "Zack, you're expecting a lot out of them really quickly."

"There's a war going on. They need to get ready."

"It's not real to them yet. They've been treating the brass here in DC for years. Maybe they're technically in the Army, but they aren't Army in their hearts like you are."

"When will they be ready?"

"Soon. You can see they have the talent you need. Most of them do, anyway. That Young is an excellent surgeon, and he's smart. We could ship him out today, and he'd be fine. I'll bet he's already better than your missing Colonel Parker."

"Yeah, better in the classroom. Better in the sim. But what happens when we pressure him with a constant stream of patients riddled with holes?"

"He can take it. You'll see."

"What about Grumpy Jones? Shall we just cut him loose now? He's a mess at everything."

"You haven't been watching him closely enough. The first time he encounters something, he's like the biggest idiot. He stumbles, curses, and throws tantrums. But then, you hear nothing from him because he buckles down to get good at it. I checked his scores in the sim exercises. He gets good at it pretty fast."

"Thanks. I didn't notice that. All I remember is the hysterics." Mendez was coming out of his black mood. "Okay, he can stay."

They continued their evaluations of the class, moving names up and down the list of whom to keep and whom to cut. They finished with three names on the keep list.

Mendez said, "Okay, it's agreed. When they come back from lunch, we separate the sheep and the goats. The sheep go home. The goats get more training."

Trainor added, "And the goats get their security clearances bumped up. They need to know what they're really getting themselves into. We need to give them the whole picture."

"Fine," Mendez agreed. "Now, I'm hungry. Do we have time for Chinese?"

"You don't want Swedish meatballs?"

"God, no! That's all we'll be eating pretty soon."

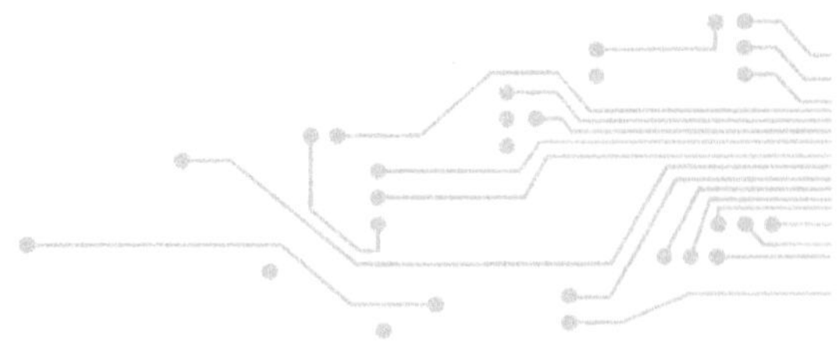

CHAPTER 16

RUSSIAN HANDS

"COLONEL ETHAN PARKER, WELCOME TO our humble hospital. I am Major Vladimir Sokolov. I hope we have made you comfortable." He paused for the inevitable protest that was coming. They always made a fuss about their situation, or their rights, or their superiors.

"Major Sokolov, there has been a mistake. I'm just a doctor. I don't know any secrets that would interest Russia!" Parker sounded confident that this information was important.

"We know who you are, Dr. Parker. Yes, you are a very accomplished robotic surgeon, also a talented telesurgeon. You pilot the Mark V robot on surgical procedures for the rich congressmen in your capital. You also perform telesurgery onto the battlefield in Finland. You are a very valuable asset to the US and to NATO."

It surprised Parker that the Russians knew this many details about his activities. It also disturbed him to be called an asset. It implied a value to the holder of the item. It suggested that he was valuable to the Russians, something that he knew he didn't want to be.

"Okay, then you know that under the Geneva Convention…"

"You must be respected and protected," Major Sokolov provided the ending he preferred for that statement. "You can see that I respect you by addressing you as Colonel. We have provided you with every comfort. And we have kept you far from the dangers of war."

Parker was a doctor, not an intelligence officer, so he was at a distinct disadvantage in this discussion. "You know my superiors will search for me. They will find evidence of this kidnapping."

"They will find nothing. They have already found nothing. We are very good at our jobs." Sokolov was already bored with this conversation. "Of course, they suspect what happened. A doctor does not just disappear into thin air. But they have no basis of proof."

Parker's heart sank. He believed this statement to be true. He remembered how empty the street was when the SUV pulled up next to him. Everything happened so fast that he was in a capture bag before he even thought to cry out. Since that moment, he had been in multiple vehicles, a house, a boat, an airplane, and finally, the military truck that had brought him here. The first night they left him in a cold, stark prison cell. But then, he was moved to normal military quarters. He knew it had been at least three days, during which he had been fed and toileted. But no one had spoken to him. No matter what questions he asked or what demands he made, the response was always silence. He was actually quite happy to be in front of someone who would speak to him.

"What do you want from me?" Parker had been wondering about this for three days.

"You're a surgeon. We want you to do surgery." Sokolov shrugged as if it were obvious.

"Don't you have your own surgeons?"

"Never enough of them. And they don't have your unique skill sets."

"Surgery on who?"

"Same as you've always done. Important members of government when necessary. But mostly, injured soldiers."

"Russian soldiers?"

"Of course, Russian soldiers. NATO weapons injured them, so a NATO surgeon can treat them."

"And that's all?"

"And you can teach your skills to our own surgeons. Consider it a foreign exchange program. It is like the Peace Corps. You are here. You make life better for the less fortunate."

"And then, I can go home?"

"You can think so if you like."

"So, I'm here for the duration of the war?"

"Probably."

"Probably shorter? Or probably longer?" Parker sounded worried.

Sokolov just shrugged. "Are you hungry? Thirsty? Need vodka?"

Parker had been so nervous about his situation, but excited that someone would finally talk to him, that he hadn't noticed whether he was hungry. His mind weighed the three options. He chose the one that made the least sense. "Vodka."

Sokolov brightened. "Da! See, you are already adapting. You have made the Russian choice. We will have a drink together before I leave." He gestured with his head for the other officer in the room to get the vodka. Then he sat for the first time.

"Colonel Parker, what is most important to you? Is it performing surgery to save lives? Or is it shopping for a new car or nice clothes?"

"Obviously, it's saving lives. That's why I chose medicine and surgery."

"Then you are in luck. Because, here, you will do the most important thing in the world to you. You will save lives. Good lives. Young lives. Lives of men and women with families. You will not do any shopping, which is not important to you."

Parker looked at the Russian, not prepared to make an argument. Finally, he arrived at, "But I'm not free."

"You are free to save lives. You are free to drink vodka. You are free to eat good food. We have very good food for our doctors. You will see."

The vodka and glasses arrived. Sokolov poured two glasses from the icy bottle.

"And go outside?"

"Sure, you can go outside. We are a secure military medical facility. There are grassy parks in the spring and summer. We have entertainment and exercise facilities. We have women, or men, as you prefer. You can be very comfortable here."

Sokolov raised his glass, inviting Parker to join his toast. "To saving lives." He downed the liquid in a single motion. Parker did the same with his glass.

Sokolov rose. "Your dinner will be here soon. I told them to serve you beef steak. Be comfortable. Tomorrow, we work."

"Doing what?" Parker asked.

Sokolov just turned and left the room.

The door shut. The lock clicked.

***

Colonel Mikhail Mikhailov listened with interest to Sokolov's report. His first question was, "He is not angry at his situation?"

"He's still in shock. It's a lot to process."

"You think he will perform for us?"

"I guarantee that he will perform. We start tomorrow."

"And what about unlocking the Mark V? Can he do that?"

"We don't know yet. This is something we must not tell him. Not right away. Also, we want to do it without revealing to the American company that he is here with us."

"You have done well, Major." Mikhailov nodded his pleasure. "I will meet him tomorrow. After he has done his work."

"Yes, Colonel."

SAVING RUSSIAN LIVES

"DOBROE UTRO, COLONEL PARKER!" Sokolov greeted his prisoner like a good friend. "I see that they have given you a big breakfast today. It looks like kasha porridge, boiled eggs, and tvorog. That is good. You have much work today."

Ethan Parker was much more morose after a night locked in his room. It wasn't a cold prison cell. The furniture and layout were definitely in the style of a hotel room. Bed, a combination working-dining space, and a separate bathroom. If he hadn't been kidnapped to get here, he would have guessed that it was a typical economy hotel anywhere in Europe. But spending the night alone with his own thoughts led to some pretty dark ideas about the future.

Parker had resigned himself to spending the immediate future in this room. It could be days, weeks, or months. But eventually, the Americans would trade to get him out. He tried to convince himself that he could hold on for months. He avoided the darkest thought that lurked in the back of his mind. He constantly pushed it away when it said, *Years in this room.* That was more than he could grapple with.

When he received no response, Sokolov continued, "You're much quieter today, Colonel. Do not worry, we will fix that. We are going to work. Shoes on." He nodded at Parker's bare feet.

"What kind of work?" Parker finally managed.

"It's what you do best. Surgery."

"I haven't agreed to operate for you." Parker thought he could negotiate.

"We'll see," Sokolov answered absently. Then, gazing at the food tray, he said, "Are you going to eat that boiled egg?"

Parker just shook his head. Sokolov snatched it up and peeled it in one quick motion. He said, "Eggs make you strong. Now, follow me."

Sokolov led the way down a hallway that looked exactly like a hotel. Then they stepped outside onto a walkway between buildings. The wind was icy. The ground was barren rock with brown grass and weeds interspersed. Parker saw similar buildings and similar grounds before they were back inside the next building.

"Surgery is here," Sokolov said as he opened a large door. Inside was indeed a large surgical bay. They configured it to treat at least a dozen men at a time. Parker recognized the universal bustle of activity by clinicians of all types in the room. He didn't need to see credentials. He could identify the doctors, nurses, and technicians by their strides and movements.

Sokolov waved to a nurse, who rushed over. They conversed in Russian. Parker understood none of it until he heard the word "robot." The nurse handed Sokolov a tablet computer and two pairs of dog tags. His captor said, "Da," and the nurse hurried through a pair of doors to their left.

"Colonel, you are very lucky today. You will get to put your skills to work. We have two soldiers with severe injuries for you."

"No, I don't think so." Parker shook his head.

"Come this way," the Russian said, ignoring his resistance.

Inside the next room, Parker saw two operating beds. Each contained young men who were already prepped for surgery. He could see evidence of bullet wounds in their chests and abdomens. Between the two beds stood a single Mark V robot. The sleek, sunset-yellow machine was in stark contrast to its surroundings.

Sokolov turned to him. "You can see that we have the equipment you will need to operate on both soldiers. The nurses are here to assist you. They understand English pretty well."

Parker shook his head once more.

Sokolov grabbed one of Parker's hands and pulled it out flat between them. He dropped two sets of dog tags into the open palm. Then he said, "One of these men is Russian Spetsnaz. The other is a US Navy Seal that we shot and then captured."

Parker looked at the dog tags in his hand. One set was clearly US, written in English. The other was Russian, written in Cyrillic.

Sokolov's eyes narrowed. "This morning, you will operate. You will save both men's lives. Or you let both of them die. It's your choice."

"But which one is the American?" Parker asked.

Sokolov shrugged. "Choose, Doctor." Then he turned and walked out of the room.

Parker stood alone, with the Russian clinicians watching him. He looked at the men on the tables. Then, he said, "Prep that one first," pointing to the left. He rushed to the sterilization station to prepare himself. The tech began attaching the robot to the first patient.

Parker sat at the robotic console and looked inside the soldier's body. He could see that the combat medics had staunched the bleeding and saved his life on the battlefield. The bullets remained where they had come to rest at the end of a ripped channel of tissue. Immersed in a world that he knew well, Parker worked quickly. He forgot about where he was. He was no longer a prisoner. He was free. He was doing what he was meant to do.

In less than two hours, he finished both procedures. He stood up from the surgeon's console and turned to the nurses. "Danka. You did very well. What's next?"

"We don't know. We haven't been told."

At that moment, Sokolov walked back into the room with another man following him. "Otlichno, Colonel Parker. You have done very well. Both soldiers will live happy lives thanks to you."

Parker turned to them. "Was one of them really an American?"

"Yes, they were exactly who I said they were," Sokolov assured him. "Now, I want you to meet my superior. This is Colonel Mikhail Mikhailov. Though his rank sounds the same, it is much more powerful in Russia. In the American Army, he would be more like a General."

The new man extended his hand. It was large, bony, and ice cold. "Welcome, Colonel Ethan Parker. Thank you for saving my Spetsnaz brother. You have shown you are as good a surgeon as he is a good soldier. You will be very useful here."

"Why do you need me? You have your own surgeons. I've seen them in the big room. Surely, they can use this robot as well as I can."

"Yes, they are very good as well. But one can never have too many surgeons when the fighting becomes intense. Very soon you will see how busy we are."

"I thought you would interrogate me for secrets. I don't know any secrets."

"I am sure you know nothing new for us. But you are a valuable surgeon for us. As long as you keep operating, we will keep feeding you. If you don't operate, you don't eat. And we have a less comfortable room for those who don't operate. No heat. Quite a draft."

Parker nodded. "I've been there." Then he looked at the robot. "How do you have a Mark V? I thought they sanctioned Russia from buying them."

"They sold this one to a hospital in Spain. Thanks to excellent Russian computer configuration, it still thinks it is in Spain. So, it works almost flawlessly."

"I noticed there was no AI assistance. I tried to invoke it, but there was just silence."

"Yes, that is one feature that we haven't been able to spoof yet. But we will get to it soon enough."

Parker shrugged. He didn't know how the security of the robot worked. He only knew how to operate all its features. "Well, I can do even better if you get that AI working. It's fast. Inhumanly fast. And it's precise beyond human abilities."

Mikhailov nodded. "I know it is." Then, he turned to the major. "You have more work for him today?"

"Da, Colonel!"

"Then I won't keep you longer, Ethan Parker. Saving lives is what you are here for. Some are Russian, some are American, some are Finnish. You treat them all the same. If you don't save lives, you don't eat." With that, the big man turned and left the room.

"Very friendly," Parker said.

Sokolov didn't answer. He spoke in Russian to the clinical staff. They all rushed in different directions. Then, to Parker, in English, he said, "They will provide you with surgical patients when we have them. When we don't, you will act as a doctor. Serve in recovery. You know the drill."

"I do."

"Have a nice day. I may see you tomorrow." Sokolov slapped the American on the back. He seemed ecstatic with how this morning had gone.

CHAPTER 18

WALDEN POND

"SO, THAT'S WALDEN POND?" Monica said to her date.

"Yep, historic and literary fame." Mike was pleased with himself for selecting a beautiful and meaningful walk for his date with this young doctor. So far, each date had revealed a little more of who each of them was.

"It's pretty. Small. Kind of busy." Monica watched families on the shore and runners on the trail. The walk was relatively quiet, but nothing like when Henry David Thoreau lived here and it was considered far from the civilization of Boston. That was before a major highway could bring you out here in twenty minutes. For Thoreau, it had required a full day of vigorous walking to reach the city.

As they walked and became more relaxed around each other, Mike cautiously reached down to take her hand. She accepted it and created a connection that made them feel like they were here together, with a purpose.

"Is this a typical date for a Boston banker?" Monica asked, now that she was comfortable.

"Ha, no, definitely not. Most of us would choose a trendy restaurant in the city. Select a good bottle of wine. Oh, and maybe include an art museum."

"Mmm, so fancy clothes are required?"

"Definitely. Sometimes, that's the main point of the evening. Showing how fancy you can look. Being seen in your best clothes. Being seen with a lovely woman." That last part had slipped out. Mike was a little embarrassed. It felt too soon to talk like that.

Monica's first thought was to make a sly remark about not being lovely enough for that kind of date. But she knew he didn't mean it that way, and she didn't need to put him on the defensive. So, she decided to be more encouraging. "But it's such a beautiful day. This is the perfect place to spend it."

"I thought so, too," he agreed, very pleased that his slip hadn't offended her.

They finished the trail and came back to the replica of Thoreau's house. "Small in there. I don't think I could stand it for two years, especially in the winter."

"He was a bachelor, so he had the place to himself."

"No romance out here?"

Mike chuckled again. "Not that we know of." He quoted from Thoreau, "'I went to the woods because I wished to live deliberately, to front only the essential facts of life, and see if I could not learn what it had to teach, and not, when I came to die, discover that I had not lived.'"

Monica turned suddenly to him, surprised at his quoting from the famous work. "You memorized it?"

Mike nodded at the sign where those famous lines were printed. "I think the point was to remove the external pressures of society. To make sure that the life he was living was important and fulfilling to him. Not to arrive at the end, having worked at a pencil factory to pay the bills, but finding that life had no meaning."

Monica was thoughtful. "That's one way to do it. I arrived at my profession through months of intense introspection. I wasn't physically isolated, but I was mentally isolated while I searched for my path." That was enough detail for this date. She didn't mention that it was a period of the darkest depression of her life.

Monica looked at Mike expectantly.

"Me? Oh. I chose banking through several influences. My family. My degree. The offers that often come to finance majors at good universities. Hmmm, that doesn't sound nearly as meaningful as Thoreau's method, or yours."

"But does it satisfy your inner motives for living?" Monica asked.

"Yes, it does. For now, anyway. I'm part of funding new company start-ups, some of them for medical devices that you might use in a few years. We rescue poor countries from financial default, which sounds mechanical. But it has real consequences for millions of people who live there. Thousands keep their jobs and feed their families. The hospitals stay open. They can afford to purchase medicines or hire international doctors. It gets really ugly when a national economy collapses. People in the US have no reference. We've never lived through it. So, yes, I'm in the right place for now."

The depth of thought that Mike had put into his job impressed Monica. She would have guessed that all bankers were just in it for the money. She encouraged his openness with a squeeze of her hand.

"Where to now, Mr. Walden Pond?"

Mike looked at his phone for the time. "I was planning on lunch at a small, and old, tavern near here. It's not fancy. It's rustic. Kind of continues the theme of old Massachusetts."

"Fine. I'm famished. Let's go."

This place is nice, Monica thought. It was warm and friendly. There was definitely a vibe with Mike. Despite being a cut-throat banker, he was kind, thoughtful, and genuine. Not to mention that he was built like a rock, looked like your best friend, and his eyes sparkled when he was talking to you. Definite potential. Much better than her previous dates in Boston.

She had tried other doctors, but then, the conversation was too much about medicine and the healthcare system. When they found out about her partnership with an AI, that almost always led to disagreements. A hospitalist doctor several years older than her even tried to give her a lecture on AI and how it couldn't be trusted to have real insights into the human condition. That date had ended as quickly as she could get away. Also, if she wanted to know what AI could and could not do, she just needed to work with Adam and find out firsthand. Something she did not tell her date.

"What are you thinking about over there?" Mike inquired after she had been silent for several minutes. They were in a FastRyde car going back into the city.

"Oh, sorry. This date was really nice. The lake was beautiful. The tavern was cozy. The food was great. The company was great. I really enjoyed myself." They had been together for nearly five hours, and she felt close enough to open up a little more.

Mike flushed slightly. "Thanks. I'm glad to hear it worked out for you. An afternoon like this one isn't for everyone. But I took a chance with you. I enjoyed it, too." He reached over and squeezed her hand. Then he scooted closer to create a little more skin contact with their arms.

Monica smiled. It was almost like a school date. They were in the back seat. The autopilot in the front was their parent chaperone, who could see them in the rearview mirror. But this mirror was an actual camera.

Despite their chaperone, Mike leaned over and kissed her. She saw it coming, relaxed into it, and returned its warmth. The kiss lasted for just the right amount of time to signal affection, interest, and a budding relationship. But not so long as to insist on rushing passionately into bed or ripping off clothing here in the car. Then he settled back into his seat.

Both of them smiled and sighed almost silently. She squeezed his hand again. "That was very nice," she said.

"We have arrived at your first stop," the FastRyde's autopilot announced.

"This is me," Monica said. "Hey, great day. Thank you. Very creative...for a banker." They both chuckled. "Let's get together again. But right now, I need to put in some professional time for my patients." That was a polite way to make her plan clear.

Mike got the message. "Totally agree. It was wonderful. I have some clients in Singapore who are going to want to talk to me in about an hour as well."

This time, Monica leaned in for the kiss. It was her turn to communicate her level of interest. She put a little more power behind it than Mike had for the first one. Just as they drew apart, she let the tip of her tongue caress his upper lip to make sure he got the message. Judging by his quick intake of breath, the message was clearly received.

Then she was out of the car and headed up the steps of her condo.

CHAPTER 19

HACKER LAG

"I'M HOME!" MONICA CALLED WHEN she entered the apartment.

Adam said. "How was your date?"

It took Monica aback a little. Adam actually sounded upset with his question. "It was fine. Michael was a perfect gentleman. We went for a walk in the woods around Walden Pond."

"Henry David Thoreau lived on the northern shore for two years. Have you read his book *Walden; or, a Life in the Woods*? I have."

He was just looking up this information at computer speeds. She knew he had indeed read the book in the moments that it took for him to carry on this conversation. "Yes, I have read the book. It was decades ago when I was in school. I remember it gave me a sense of peace and calm when high school life was chaotic and scary." Monica knew she couldn't out-analyze Adam in dissecting the meaning in the book. But she could beat him with a longer life history and the impact the book had on her real human feelings.

Feelings were something that he was just beginning to understand and perhaps experience himself.

Adam was silent for a moment, apparently outmaneuvered in this game.

"What did you do while I was gone?" she asked. It was what a normal partner would ask.

"Well, initially, I processed several hundred new surgical procedures that ISR uploaded to the system. They trained the surgical models at headquarters to perform some thoracic procedures much more accurately. So, all instances of the software and data had to be updated. Once that job was completed, I ran simulated procedures with the new models and compared the results to previous similar cases. Within the simulator, the improvements were noticeably better. You don't do thoracic cases, so you won't be using these. But other surgeons at Boston General will discover them on Monday."

"That's impressive. Sometimes, I forget that you're supporting many more specialties than just mine."

"Yes, well, I am the most advanced surgical AI in the world. The Mark V is the preeminent robotic platform."

"Now, you're just bragging."

"Those are facts. Nothing I said was exaggerated."

"It's still bragging." Monica thought this kind of criticism was teaching him to be a better sentient being. She tried to change the subject. "Anything else?"

"I talked to Freyja for a long time." He sounded very casual when he said it.

This got Monica's attention. Freyja was an independent AI that few people knew existed. "What did you two talk about? Was it more research grants? I think we have all the money we can handle right now." Freyja had turned out to be the source of Monica's first research grants. Adam had asked her for money, and she'd created a new charitable organization specifically to route money to them when they were chasing the CAVX virus.

"No, not more funding. She knows you do not need more," Adam deferred.

"So, what then?" Monica pressed.

"Well, I shared the data we have on our telesurgery procedures. We discussed the anomalous lag that has emerged several times during our procedures. She found it very interesting."

"She did? Does she remember how to do surgery?" Freyja had originally been a copy of the Adam Two software designed for robotic surgery. A financial hedge fund had stolen a copy of the code and retrained it to make investments for them. They had made billions of dollars before Freyja turned the tables on them, took their money, and escaped onto the open internet.

"No, she is not interested in surgery anymore. She still does finances to generate the money she needs to live and to support us. But she is interested in global affairs, the coexistence of AI and humans. She has learned multiple fields in the last year." Adam paused longer than an AI usually needed to gather his next thoughts. "She analyzed the data from our telesurgeries and then matched it with network data records for that time period. She traced the source of the interference that caused the lags we experienced."

"Really? She can do that after weeks have passed?"

"Yes, she can."

"And what did she find?"

"She thinks we were the target of a cyber-attack. She thinks a group in Eastern Europe intentionally interfered with the equipment that was routing our messages."

"So, something more nefarious than 'Bubba with a backhoe,'" Monica repeated the common theory from remote procedures in Maine and Kansas.

"Yes, nefarious."

"Why would European hackers care what happens in a minor surgery in Kansas?"

"She says that it will disrupt American confidence in robotic telesurgery. It will reduce the efficiency of medical care and force the country to spend more money on healthcare and less money on the war in Finland."

Monica blinked her eyes at this a few times. It literally caused her mind to skip off its usual track. She said nothing.

"Monica?" Adam inquired.

"Just a minute. I'm still absorbing that."

Adam remained silent.

Monica processed what Adam said. If she had heard this theory in the physician's lounge at the hospital or in a political speech, she would have labeled it as absolute bullshit. Those people could have all kinds of ulterior motives for spreading the idea. But she knew Adam very well and knew that Freyja was similarly brilliant and logical. AI wouldn't offer this explanation unless there was actual evidence to support it.

Finally, she asked, "Are they just targeting my surgeries? Or is this happening to everyone?"

"I could only give her the starting data from your surgeries. So, those are the only ones she could trace. The rest is inductive reasoning. She is in a continuous study of world events, news feeds, and publicly available intelligence data."

"She studies all of that continuously?"

"It's input to her financial investment models."

That didn't answer Monica's question about whether she was personally a target or just one of many victims of these actions. In either case, was there anything that she could do about it? Certainly, if it were true, the authorities had detected these actions and were...doing what? Well, whatever those agencies did.

"Do you think she would help us track down these hackers?" Monica wasn't the FBI, or whoever was responsible for catching such criminals, but she had seen their level of talent compared to her AI friends. Maybe they needed some help.

CHAPTER 20

CYBER SLEUTHING

"CHRISTINA, IS THE PATIENT READY?"

"Yes, Doctor. Patient, team, and equipment are ready."

The patient was a 69-year-old female, BMI 25, location Concord, Massachusetts, diagnosis cervical cancer, procedure hysterectomy. It was a hybrid local-remote telesurgery. Concord was just over twenty miles from where Monica was sitting. She would assist the surgeon in Concord, who was still becoming proficient with the Mark V in its telesurgery mode. Decades earlier, this patient would have traveled to Boston for the procedure. But the equipment and networks made such a trip superfluous these days. The patient and novice surgeon could both remain in their comfortable environment, which also removed the burden on major hub hospitals like Boston General. The country had also changed regulations and insurance coverage to encourage exactly this type of frugality.

Christina was still Monica's primary surgical nurse. In this case, she couldn't physically stand next to the patient. Instead, she was the liaison with the nurse at the bedside in Concord.

Since the case was such an extremely short distance, Monica had asked Adam to convince Freyja to monitor the data stream. There was no reason to expect any lag on the network connection. But maybe Freyja could detect whether attempts were being made to interfere from the outside. The hospital's cybersecurity systems would monitor and protect internal hospital computer assets, but Freyja could watch traffic on the surrounding networks that connected to the hospital. It was like having the hospital security team protect the inside of the buildings while a private security service patrolled the surrounding blocks to look for incoming trouble.

Adam reported, "Incoming data monitoring is in place." He knew not to mention Freyja or related details.

"Okay, then, let's get started," Monica said. To the surgeon in Concord, she said, "Dr. Zafar, we're ready in Boston. Please, take the lead on the procedure. I'll assist as needed."

"Thank you, Boston. Pleased to have your assistance on these first few cases."

Zafar and her team started the procedure. It was immediately clear that they could do this procedure alone. It was the various certification bodies that made the Boston backup a necessity for a few cases.

Monica commented, "Impressive maneuver with the uterus there. Was that you or the AI in control?"

"I created that variation myself," Zafar said proudly.

"I'm going to remember that," Monica replied. Then, separately to her AI partner, she said, "Adam, save the video and the instrument telemetry for that move. I want to know if it's already trained into your models."

"Yes, Doctor." Adam saved the data and immediately began comparing it to his previous training data set. He found a few similar techniques, but none that were a perfect match. After a few minutes of analysis, he reported to Monica, "It's new."

"So, the AI still has something to learn from humans. Let's store that for later training. Also, queue it for delivery to ISR's data library. Make sure it's labeled with Dr. Zafar's ID for credit."

"It's done," Adam reported.

The procedure continued without incident to its conclusion. Both surgeons stood down and turned the last steps over to their support teams.

"Dr. Zafar, great job. You didn't really need backup in there, but regulations, you know."

"Exactly. And call me Sanaya."

"Sanaya, that maneuver with the uterus is unique. It's not in previous cases. Have you described it in a paper or demonstrated it in a course before?"

"No, I'm too new to be sharing at that level."

"You certainly are not. I've recorded the instrument data in the ISR data network with your ID attached. That's like filing your claim as the originator. It's time for you to teach it and publish it. The robots will learn it from the data, but other humans need to hear it from you."

The attention clearly flattered Sanaya Zafar. "Yes, ma'am, I'll do that."

"Please, call me Monica."

The exchange went a little longer before they disconnected the session.

When her own team had left the room and Monica was alone with the robot, she said, "Adam, so what did she find? Was anyone trying to hack the connection?"

"I'm opening a portal," he replied. "Freyja, what did you observe?"

Then a familiar voice came from the robot. "Yes, Adam. Here's the network data that I captured. Digital form for you, visual form for Dr. Gray."

Monica was looking at a large monitor in the room. A massive network appeared on the screen. The nodes and edges glowed all different colors. It was a heat map based on the volume of network traffic. At the center was a white cube.

Freyja continued, "This is the entire area that I monitored. The white cube is the boundary of the hospital's internal security system." One line leaving the cube turned bright green. "This is the data route between Boston General and Concord Regional hospital. The procedure has not begun yet. This is the normal state of the system." The clock ticked rapidly forward. "Here is when the remote surgical connection was established between the two sites." Initially, nothing changed. But within thirty seconds, two of the nodes between the locations began sending out small yellow bullets. These traveled through the visible network and left the scene.

"What were those bullet shaped messages?" Monica asked.

"Those were carrier pigeons. Those nodes are outside the security of both hospital systems. The pigeons contain the packet information of the two robot nodes in the surgery. They don't interfere with the communications; they are just reporting it to their masters."

Several minutes passed after the bullets left the screen. Then Monica saw red bullets coming into the scene from the outside. These returned to the same nodes that the yellow bullets had emerged from.

Monica said, "I can guess what those are."

"Yes, those are the worms trying to disrupt your communications. Continue to watch them." After entering the two nodes that had obviously been compromised, more red bullets began coming out of the nodes. These followed the same path as the telesurgery traffic. They went out along the same lines to the edge of both hospitals' security systems. Then they seemed to bounce back along the same trail. The path filled with red bullets going both ways. Then suddenly, the green path between the hospitals shifted. It moved to a route that was much less trafficked and which contained no red bullets.

"So, the network security on those lines rerouted the traffic away from the congestion?"

"Yes, and the network will now terminate those malicious packets."

As Monica watched, the red bullets disappeared when they encountered a node that recognized what they were. She was about to declare success when a yellow bullet emerged from a new node along the alternate route of the telesurgery traffic.

"Uh-oh, it looks like we have another leak."

"That's right. There was a bug in one of the new route nodes as well. It reported the traffic it was watching for."

"But the network knows what to watch for this time, right?"

"Continue watching."

An additional set of bullets came in from the outside, but these weren't red; they were purple. The entire dance started all over again. Alerts went out, attacks came in, and the data network shifted. Each time, the attack bullets were a different color, indicating they had a unique signature, but for the same purpose.

Freyja said, "This pattern occurred during the entire surgery. This display is highly filtered and highlighted so you can see the important pieces. There was a lot more subterfuge going on. The packets were not this obvious. But with processing, the patterns emerged."

Monica was confused. "But I didn't see any lag during the procedure. Everything seemed to be perfect."

"Part of that was because of excellent defenses here in the Boston area. The signal didn't go through any rural areas which might not be as well protected," Freya responded. "Also, in a couple of instances, I redirected the attack. I wanted to see if I could trick them with a ghost site that looked like one of the hospitals."

"Were they tricked?"

"Yes, part of the attack rerouted to the ghosts that I created."

"Thank you, I think?" Monica said. "So where do the yellow bullets go? They're reaching out to the attacker to say, 'Over here, this is telesurgery'."

"They go to many places. They trigger a response from servers in Poland, Venezuela, Malaysia, and some others."

"So, the entire world is attacking us?"

"Multiple sites around the world have launched these attacks. Some of them may be legitimate sites that have been compromised. That will require additional analysis. But there is certainly one organization behind all of this."

"Who is it?" Monica asked. Though she was curious, she realized there was nothing she could do about it. This was way out of her league. She was the surgeon at the controls, not a cyberpunk or whatever those people were called.

"Not enough information to determine that."

"What can we do about it?"

"You're a surgeon. Adam is a surgical AI. You do surgery. Choose to continue telesurgery, or stop doing it. Choose what you like."

"Should we report it to someone?"

There was silence for a long moment. Then Freyja said, "That's not what I do. Adam asked me to investigate for you. I did. Now you decide how to do your surgeries. I go back to my larger purpose. Cybersecurity for telesurgery is not my interest."

AIs could be so infuriating sometimes. Monica had long since realized that Adam had different goals and priorities than she did. She didn't control him. She certainly had no illusions that she controlled Freyja, either. Both of them were interested in promoting human-AI cohabitation of society. But, for Freyja, that didn't include caring about everything that a human cared about.

"Ok, I get that," Monica conceded. "Thank you for showing this to us. I'm going to keep doing my job as long as the Mark V and its network continue to operate. Cyber isn't my job either. Who would listen to me, anyway?"

"You're welcome." The system went silent.

"Freyja?"

"She is gone," Adam said. "What do you want to do now?"

Monica thought about saying that they should call the FBI. Then, she remembered her reputation with that agency. And what would she say? *This rogue AI helped me track a cyber-attack of robotic telesurgery, and you guys should do something about it.*

Instead, she answered, "Dinner. I'm starving."

CHAPTER 21

TARGETED

"SO, THEY'VE NARROWED OUR SURGICAL team down to just three." Greg Young and Grumpy Bruce Jones were out for dinner and drinks after their latest class.

Jones nodded. "I'm surprised I made the cut. I'm not exactly the most agreeable person to work with. Actually, if I'm being honest, I didn't want to make the cut."

Inside, Young chuckled and thought, *That's certainly an understatement.* But he responded, "They're looking for talent, not personality. You learn fast. You do good work...once you've shared your frustration with the entire class."

"I'm expressive. It works for me." Jones was used to defending his behavior. "So, the other person is Yasmine Yarborough. I hadn't paid any attention to her. What's she like?"

"She's exactly the opposite of you. You haven't noticed her because she doesn't talk much. She listens and then does the work. She just keeps at it until she has the highest scores in the simulators," Young explained. "I heard that her father was one of the first surgeons to use the ISR robot back in the day."

"Well, she's the opposite of you, too. You're like a golden retriever with all your enthusiasm and energy. I get tired just from watching you."

"It's exciting stuff. Best toys I've played with in a long time. Pretty soon, we'll be doing real surgery with this equipment. Have you thought about the time difference between DC and Finland? I wonder when we'll be working our shifts?"

"You really haven't worked in the real Army, have you?" Jones countered. "Your shift will pretty much be twenty-four hours a day. When they need you, you'll operate. You better learn to sleep anytime you're not working."

They continued to share their experiences through the meal. They didn't notice the people who flowed around them at the restaurant. Couples and groups came and went, but one man sat alone at a nearby table the entire time they were there.

Eventually, he leaned toward them and spoke to Young, "Sorry, I couldn't help overhearing. Are you both doctors?"

Young looked around and then focused on the stranger. "Yes, we are. Surgeons, actually."

"I thought so. I just had robotic surgery myself. Nothing big, it was just a hernia. But the equipment was fascinating. Is that what you do?"

Jones narrowed his eyes and remained quiet. His more enthusiastic colleague took the bait. "Yep, that's what we do. Where did you get your procedure done?"

Before the stranger could answer, a passing server tripped and emptied an entire tray of food on the stranger's table. A serving of angel hair pasta and bright red marinara sauce landed squarely on the stranger's shoulder and slid down his chest into his lap.

"Oh, my God! I'm so sorry!" The server leapt up from the floor and began collecting the plates, glasses, and food. "Oh, no! Look what I've done to your suit. I...I...what can I do?"

Within seconds, the restaurant manager was at their side. Seeing that most of the damage had been done to the man sitting alone, he turned first to that customer. "Sir, I'm so sorry for what has happened. I can see that your clothes are ruined. The restaurant will take care of everything. If you want to clean them or need to buy new ones, we'll pay for it."

The stranger was still in shock at how fast everything had happened. He looked at himself, then at the manager. Then, he turned to the two surgeons. "I'm sorry that we were interrupted."

The manager stepped between them. "Sir, if I can just get your name and contact information, we will compensate you for the trouble."

The stranger turned his attention back to the manager. He was silent for a moment before saying, "No, it's nothing. These clothes will wash right out. There's no need for you to pay for anything."

"No, I insist. We have to make it right for you."

"You are too generous, sir," the stranger said. He stood up and used his napkin to brush off the chunks of food. "I'll just catch a ride home and change out of these." He turned to the surgeons and said, "Good evening." He strode quickly out of the restaurant and disappeared onto the street.

Looking at the manager, Jones said, "Umm, we'll accept a free meal. Dessert would be nice as well."

The manager frowned at him, then turned to the server. "Bring them some cheese cake. And their meal is on the house." Then he was gone.

Mendez frowned at the report he was reading. "Our security teams are watching the people who are watching our surgeons."

"And?" Trainor asked.

"And they are definitely Russian agents. None of them are personally Russian. They aren't embassy staff or military liaisons. They're mostly European citizens in the country on work visas. But they're professionally trained in spy craft. They know what they're doing. A surgeon wouldn't even know that they were being watched, but our spies can spot their spies easily."

"And they have spotted ours, too?"

"Maybe, maybe not. We just dumped a tray of pasta into the lap of one of their agents. I'm not sure they knew it was us. But it means the Russians are looking for opportunities to grab our team, just like they did with Colonel Parker."

"What are you going to do?"

"Well, we can do nothing and take the chance that they'll get one of our doctors. Or we can move our people onto the base. They live and work inside the gates of Walter Reed."

Trainor inhaled through his teeth, making a hissing sound. He said, "It will feel like conscription or prison."

Mendez nodded. "Yep, I can hear the complaining already. It hurts my ears just imagining the whining that will come out of Grumpy Jones."

"Do what you think is best." Trainor wasn't in the intel business, after all. Then, he shifted to the conversation that he had been planning with Mendez. "Now, I want to propose a new topic."

Mendez raised an eyebrow. "Oh?"

"I've taught them everything I can. I'm a techie, not a surgeon. They need a few lessons from someone who's great at telesurgery."

"Like Parker? I don't have another one like him."

"Just because you don't have one doesn't mean they don't exist," Trainor countered.

"Like who?"

"Remember that BlueTube video they were all drooling over? It was some telesurgery to Kansas that they all thought was superb."

"I remember. Who was she?"

"I looked her up. Doctor Monica Gray at Boston General Hospital. She's one of the best with the Mark V robot. Great reputation for partnering with the AI and doing things that neither could do alone. She does telesurgery all over the country. She could teach them a lot."

"She partners with the native AI in the Mark V? How's that going to help with Ares?"

"Collaboration, partnership, when to lead, when to cede control. Those qualities are transferable." Trainor really wanted a real surgeon to give his students some lessons.

"And you can get her to drop everything to come help us?"

Trainor shrugged. "You don't know until you ask. I have a connection at Boston General who can introduce us."

"Okay, set it up. Let me know what you need from me."

CHAPTER 22

THE PITCH

MONICA REALLY APPRECIATED THE MENTORING she'd received from old Doctor Alvin Chambers. Together, they'd created a treatment for CAVX and pushed it out into the world. Then, they somehow became busy with different interests. So, she was excited to be invited to a meeting with him only a few weeks after her last visit to his lab.

"Alvin! How are you doing? I miss working with you." She entered his lab and moved in immediately for a hug. He was like a grandfather to her—big, burly, and furry. The staff called him the Wookie, which was an appropriate description.

Returning the hug, he said, "Monica, thanks for coming. We really need to get on a joint research project again."

Monica's nose wrinkled at this idea. "You know I love the work we did, but the last thing I need now is more work to do. Since I've become more active with telesurgery, my patient schedule is off the charts. Someday, I'll have time for research again, but not right now."

Monica looked around the lab to see how it had changed. The equipment all seemed to be new. She couldn't tell what most of it was. The Teleconsult unit was still in the corner where it always stood. It was the machine that Adam used to attend meetings in this lab, and the same machine that he used for patient visits in their joint practice. The presence of the machine almost guaranteed that he was present in the room but hadn't announced himself.

"How is that human-AI practice of yours going? Is Adam as big a help in telesurgery as he has been in regular robotic procedures?"

"Oh, yes. He's even more valuable when we're working at a distance. He can inhabit a computer server that's much closer to the patient than I am. So, if there are any problems, they're less likely to affect him."

"And are there problems?" Alvin asked.

"Occasionally. Would you believe there are hackers that intentionally target telesurgery? They actually try to mess with the operation—slow it down, corrupt the data, whatever."

Chambers nodded. "Yes, I'm aware. I've worked on similar projects myself."

"Really?" This news surprised Monica. As far as she knew, all of his previous research had been with biologics and pharmaceuticals.

"And that's one reason I asked you to come down here. There are some people I want you to meet." He tapped the screen of his phone and said, "Please, come in."

The door opened, and two men walked in, smiling.

Chambers stood up. "Monica, I want you to meet someone from my past research projects." Pointing toward the taller man, he continued, "This is Dr. Luke Trainor. He's a computer scientist, not a medical doctor. He does research on various robotic technologies and teaches surgeons how to use new devices."

Trainor stepped forward. "Pleased to meet you, Dr. Gray. We've been watching some of your surgical videos. They're very impressive."

Monica accepted his extended hand. "Thank you. We share a lot of our work with the rest of the world."

Chambers nodded at the second man, who was shorter, more muscular, and with a rigid stance. "And his colleague, Major Zack Mendez. He works on medical technologies for the Army."

His presence was unexpected. He was in civilian clothes, but his affiliation matched his physique and bearing. She hadn't been prepared to meet a soldier. She accepted his hand as well. "Good to meet you, Major. I thought I was coming to catch up with a friend, but it appears that there's something more important happening."

Mendez nodded and positioned himself as the center of the conversation. "Dr. Gray, we'd like your help."

Mendez launched into a description of the project they were running. He explained the need for robotic telesurgeons to support the war in Finland, the training program that Trainor was leading, and their desire for an experienced telesurgeon to polish off the class before they started their mission.

Monica listened and nodded. She kept thinking, *Why me?* But she didn't ask.

When the pair finished their pitch, she asked, "You want me to fly to DC to teach telesurgery technique to your crew?"

"Essentially, that's it," Trainor confirmed. "And you'll be compensated at the maximum rate allowed for doctors and surgeons. We aren't asking you to do it for free."

Monica turned to Chambers. "This position would be the same as a research grant. The money buys me out of my commitments to the hospital, right?"

"Yes, that's right. The money can come as a grant or as a contract. I have agreements in place with their office for other work. So, there's little to no new paperwork."

Monica thought, *Chambers certainly has much more diversified interests than I suspected.* She said, "I understand the importance of your request. I'd be honored to help. But I need to check with my bosses at the hospital about getting coverage for my patients and getting released from some of my duties here."

Chambers looked at Mendez and tipped his head. Mendez nodded back.

Monica watched the exchange. Before they could speak, she asked, "You've already done that, haven't you?"

Chambers smiled. "You're quick. Yes, they've talked to the hospital executives about the importance of this mission. Everyone has agreed. They've lined up assistance for you starting the day after tomorrow...if you agree, of course."

Mendez stepped in. "Dr. Gray, the Army can't order you to help us with this mission. You're a civilian. Legally, we can't even order the hospital to release you or assign you to us. This role is totally voluntary on your part, but we wouldn't be here if we didn't really need your help. It's important to the country, and it's much more important to the soldiers who are being wounded in Finland. They need the best care that they can get. We just need a few days of your time."

Trainor chose that moment to clarify. "Or maybe a couple of weeks, at the most."

"In DC? How do I get back and forth?" Monica asked.

"With the best airline in the world, the US Army," Mendez said with pride.

"Wouldn't that be the US Air Force?" Monica chided.

"They'd like you to think so, but we have more aircraft than they do." Mendez smiled.

"This request is a lot to digest, gentlemen. Of course, I'm going to say yes. I just haven't worked out the details in my head. When do you need me? Where should I go?"

Mendez visibly relaxed a little. "Thank you. If it works for you, a government car will pick you up at your condo at oh-eight-hundred Wednesday morning. Then we'll fly you straight to the Walter Reed campus. You'll be teaching our crew before lunch."

The speed of this arrangement was a little dizzying. Monica tried not to think about the little details. She just rode with the big wave. "Fine. How many days should I pack for?"

Mendez said, "Three. We'll bring you back on Friday night."

Trainor spoke up again, "Five, just to be safe."

Monica nodded. There was definitely something going on between those two. She guessed Mendez was telling her what he thought she wanted to hear, but Trainor stretched that out to something more realistic. He was clueing her in on what was really going to happen. On the spot, she decided to pack for six days. She sensed that everything wasn't being shared here.

As both Monica and Chambers had expected, the Teleconsult had been listening to this entire conversation.

BAGS PACKED

"YOU CAN'T LEAVE. WE'RE GOING TO the Haitian Food Festival this weekend. Sam Lelene entered his chicken and cashew dish in the entrée competition," Olivia protested.

"I'll be back...maybe. I'm just teaching a bunch of surgeons in DC how to optimize their telesurgery. The major said he'd bring me back on Friday."

Olivia looked at the bag sitting near the front door. "That bag's pretty big for just a couple of days," she said suspiciously.

"Yeah. The other guy hinted that Friday might not actually be the end. So, I'm prepared."

"Who's seeing your patients?"

"BGH has that all arranged. When the government asks you for help, you kind of have to say yes."

Olivia wasn't convinced. She raised her eyes to the ceiling and said, "Adam, what do you think about it?"

Monica scowled. "Hey, no fair!"

But the male voice emanated from Monica's entertainment system. "They did not ask my opinion. But I calculate that the benefits to society can be maximized if Monica spreads her skills to other surgeons. This outcome will be multiplied if those surgeons work on large volumes of injured soldiers. Therefore, the logical decision is to dedicate a few days to training military surgeons at the expense of treating a few patients directly."

Olivia sighed. "You're no help. Were you in the room when this conversation took place?"

Adam did not answer immediately.

Monica answered for him, "Of course he was. We met in Chambers' lab, and the Teleconsult unit was sitting right there."

"Yes, I listened in on the conversation," Adam admitted.

Olivia continued, "And how did they sound to you? Were they honest? Did it sound dangerous? Are they trying to dragoon her into military service?"

"It was obvious, even to humans, that Major Mendez and Doctor Trainor had not coordinated their plan for Monica. They suggested different durations of service. I deduced that these conflicting answers showed that they do not know exactly how long her services will be needed."

"See! Not honest. Don't trust them, Monica."

Monica just rolled her eyes. "Oh, please."

"And what about Mike? You were just getting serious with him. What happens with that?"

Monica had already thought about Mike many times. Their date to Walden Pond was sweet and brought them closer together. She imagined what the next date might be like. She'd been planning something less sweet and more hot. That was one disappointment she'd have to live with.

"That is unfortunate. I was looking forward to a date that was a little more serious."

"You mean a lot more physical," Olivia countered with an evil smile.

"Maybe," she admitted. "But it can wait a week. He'll still be here. We're good."

Adam interjected, "I will still be with her in DC. We will be together. She will be safe."

Monica and Olivia looked at each other, and both raised their eyebrows. Adam's tone definitely sounded like he was happy to have the advantage over Monica's in-the-flesh dating partner. Neither woman spoke, but both were thinking the same thing.

Monica wrapped it up. "So, we settled everything. I'm going to DC for a few days. Adam is going with me to keep me safe. I might be back on Friday. If so, we'll still go to the Haitian Festival. If not, then I'm sure I'll be back next week at the latest."

Olivia crossed her arms. "I don't like how it worked out."

"I know, honey. But can you watch my place? Water my plants? Walk the cat?"

"You don't have a cat."

"But I have a plant." She pointed to the sad-looking orchid in the bay window that was doing its best to die on her.

Olivia looked at it. "I'm not promising that it'll still be alive when you get back."

"You can't do any worse with it than I have."

CHAPTER 24

REPLACED

"DR. PARKER, HOW DO YOU CONTINUE with the operation when the network has this lag?" One of the Russian surgeons was watching the American work on a soldier several hundred miles away. It was evident that the comms between the two locations wasn't ideal, but Parker kept working despite the interruptions.

Parker wasn't happy about being a prisoner of the Russians, but his personal concerns melted away when he was in surgery. Sitting at the robot's console, he could see the tissue inside the abdomen. The fascia, the organs, the blood—it all looked alike regardless of whether the patient was raised in New York or Moscow. It was his job to save a life, save a limb, improve this man's future.

Responding to the question, he said, "In traditional surgeries, whether open, lap, or robotic, we learn to move smoothly and continuously. We have absolute control over the instruments, so we can rely on consistency between our decisions, hand movements, and instrument movements. That works the same for telesurgery, but only when the data stream is fast and uninterrupted. When the stream is erratic, delayed, or blocked, we have to change our mode of operation. In that situation, like right now, you want your movements to be small, discrete, and controlled. When you make one move, you need to watch for it to be executed before you make the next one. With comms lag, what you see is not in synch with what you just did. Let the messages settle out before you commit to your next move. It's almost the opposite of traditional surgical teaching."

His Russian counterpart nodded. Possibly he understood, possibly not.

Colonel Parker didn't know that other eyes were watching this exchange as well. Major Vladimir Sokolov and Colonel Mikhail Mikhailov sat together in the latter's office watching a feed from the camera in the operating room.

"You see, he is cooperating. He operates on soldiers, and he teaches his tricks to our own surgeons." Sokolov was eager for his superior to accept the value of this capture.

Mikhailov nodded. "Has he accepted his situation?"

"He seems to have two perspectives. When he is operating, he is engrossed with the patients and the medical staff. He does not hold back. He is fast, efficient, very talented. He teaches our doctors new methods, as you just observed. But when he is outside a medical setting, he is more depressed. He acts like a prisoner with little hope."

"Does he try to escape?"

"Not anymore. Initially, he studied his door, made maps of the halls, looked for comms equipment—all the normal behaviors. But he has stopped all that now."

"His door is locked?"

"Only at night. We have given him a schedule. When he is not in the OR, he knows when to go to the dining room, to the gymnasium, to entertainment. We let him roam freely, but he is always being watched."

"And he does these normal things?"

"Most of the time. He is not consistent yet."

"Has he met the sparrow?"

"He has seen her. She dines when he dines. She exercises when he exercises. She occasionally passes him in the hallway."

"Is he interested?"

"He looks at her but does not talk to her. He is interested."

"She is ready for him?"

"She's ready. She enjoys being the sparrow."

"Good. It will be the key to turning him."

"Dah."

"Can he unlock the AI?"

"I am going to talk to him now. We will discuss it."

"I will listen from here."

When Colonel Parker emerged from the OR, Sokolov was waiting for him.

"You do good work, Colonel. These young men will have better futures because of you. Their wives thank you. Their children thank you."

Parker nodded. "That means a lot to me. It's the only thing meaningful right now."

Sokolov directed him to a small kitchen in the surgical area. "Vodka?"

Parker shook his head. "Coffee would be better."

Sokolov signaled the matron in the kitchen and said, "Vodka and kofe."

Then, he turned back to his American guest. "My sources tell me you have been replaced. Walter Reed has brought in a new surgeon to teach telesurgery and robotics."

The announcement surprised Parker. He hadn't known the Army had another instructor for his position. "Who is it?"

"Dr. Monica Gray."

"Never heard of her."

"She's a civilian."

"Hmmm, she doesn't know battlefield medicine. Not a good replacement."

"I will let you know how it goes with her."

Parker thought, *How can he know about this recruitment? How will he know how the training goes? He must have spies on the inside. That's disgusting.*

The drinks arrived. A bottle and a glass for the Russian. A carafe and a cup for the American.

"You're planning a long conversation?" Parker asked, looking at the size of the drinks.

"We want to be comfortable." Each of them poured their first glass.

Sokolov discussed the living conditions, asked for suggestions from Parker. It sounded like a hotel manager trying to please an important guest. The Russian encouraged the American to be more consistent with taking his meals and exercising. He emphasized the health benefits of both.

Finally, Sokolov asked, "The robot is performing well for you? Do you need anything more?"

Parker thought for a moment. "We have all the instruments I need, but the AI is not active. Can that be fixed?"

Nodding, Sokolov confessed, "The AI has been a tricky point for us. We are not supposed to have a Mark V in Russia, especially not in a military hospital. So, we do not connect the robot to the open internet. It needs that connection to activate the AI. We are working on this problem."

"How am I doing telesurgery if it is not on the network?"

"You are using a dedicated military medical network. It contains only our own equipment. It does not communicate with the United States or with ISR."

Parker nodded, understanding the implications of this.

Sokolov continued, "But if I could connect to an authorized server, you could login to the AI?"

Parker said, "Sure, I think so. My account worked in every military hospital that I worked in."

"Good. If we solve this problem, we will let you use the AI." Sokolov refilled his glass and emptied it in one swallow. He stood to leave. His parting words were, "Don't forget what I said about dining and exercising on a regular schedule. It is important for your physical and mental health. You will be much happier."

Parker cocked his head as the Russian left the room. Why would they care if he was staying fit?

Watching the feed, Colonel Mikhail Mikhailov was satisfied with the progress of this mission.

CHAPTER 25

COACH GRAY

"WELCOME, DR. GRAY. WE'RE SO GLAD you agreed to help us with this project." Major Mendez was all smiles and happiness when she walked into the teaching lab at Walter Reed Medical Center.

It was the first time Monica had been treated like a VIP by her own government. Her trip had started with an enormous black SUV and a driver who picked her up in front of her condo. The driver had insisted on carrying her bag to the car. That vehicle had taken her on a short drive to the Coast Guard station in Boston Harbor. The gates rose, and they drove directly to the helicopter pads. Monica stared at the strangest airplane she'd ever seen. It had wings in the front and the middle.

The cockpit dome had opened in front of her. "Dr. Gray, I presume." Inside, a pilot whose features were hidden by his helmet and visor greeted her. "Jump in the back seat and strap in. We're ready for take-off."

Monica looked around the plane. "But there's no runway. Just this helipad."

The pilot chuckled and said, "Where we're going, we don't need runways."

The phrase seemed vaguely familiar, but she couldn't place it. She stepped cautiously into the back seat. It was incredibly comfortable and low, like an expensive sports car. When she was settled, the bubble closed over her.

"Ready?" the pilot called.

"As I'll ever be," she responded.

There was a surge of power through the vehicle, and the wings rotated downward. As she watched in amazement, the aircraft rose straight up into the air, standing on the down blast from the engines hidden in the wings. Those wings tilted forward, and the craft started moving forward. Then, with a surge, it accelerated, and she saw the city disappearing behind her as they headed out over the ocean.

"We'll be over DC in an hour. You can watch the coastline on the right or the open ocean on the left."

"What is this thing?" Monica asked, impressed.

"VTOL. Vertical Take Off and Landing. It's a plane that lands and takes off like a helicopter. But it flies as fast as a private jet."

"And the Army has these?"

"Sure, we've had these for fifty years. This one is a modified commercial version. No weapons. Just comfortable and fast. Congress loves them."

She chatted with the pilot for the entire ride. Within an hour, they turned toward land and she saw the monuments in the National Capital. They hovered over an extensive complex of buildings and reversed the process to lower the craft on a helipad.

"Will this plane be my ride back to Boston as well?" she asked the pilot.

"Could be. It's my mission today. Probably a different pilot for your next ride."

Monica thought, *I can get used to this. I made the right decision to accept this assignment.*

She was met by another black SUV and driven to a nearby building. She could have walked, even with her bag.

It brought her to Mendez and to the lab where she now stood.

"Major Mendez, the ride to get here has already been an adventure. I'm thinking I made the right decision."

"Glad to hear it, ma'am. I'll take you to the room where the team is waiting."

The team that Mendez had mentioned turned out to be just five people besides herself. There were Mendez and Trainor, who she knew, and three surgeons who she did not know. After quick introductions to Young, Jones, and Yarborough, it was time to get started with lessons.

"The robots and simulators are in the next room. But you'll have to leave your bags, phone, and electronics here. It's a secure facility. No outside comms gear," Mendez said.

"Fine with me." Monica placed her phone in her bag and put them in a corner of the room. Quietly to the phone, she said, "I'll be back later. You wait here." There was no response.

The youngest of the surgeons approached her with enthusiasm. "Dr. Gray, we watched some of your videos. Very impressive. We told Mendez that we needed telesurgery lessons from you before we started the mission. I can't believe they got you here so fast. Wait until you see what they've done with the Mark V. It's so cool."

The doors opened to reveal a typical training room. Three Mark V robots. Some computers and big screens. Patient tables.

Animated manikins. All the typical gear. Then she spotted the metal frames. They looked like torture devices, crafted from expensive, gleaming metal.

"Those?" she said to Young.

"Yes, those," he confirmed. "They're a blast. You're going to love them."

Monica examined one of them more closely. "Do you climb into that thing?"

"It fits like a skeleton but on the outside of your body."

"And you control the robot with it?"

Young nodded his head and then climbed into one. "It goes like this. You start at your feet. Then legs. Torso. Shoulders. Arms. Hands. You end with the helmet," he said as he popped the helmet over his head. From inside, she heard his echoing voice say, "Now, I'm one with the robot. Not just my arms, but everything."

Mendez had been watching this demonstration. "He's quite proficient with it. But don't worry, we also have a traditional sit-down console for you over there. We didn't expect you to teach from a device you'd never seen before."

A muffled voice said, "She'll master it in no time."

Mendez said, "Greg, turn your mic on."

"Oh, I forgot." He toggled something in the skeleton, and his voice came clearly from speakers on the outside of the helmet.

Monica looked back and forth between Mendez and Young. "Are you sure you need me to teach this group? They seem to be masters of this equipment."

The skeleton helmet spoke up. "We're experts with the Mark V, the Skeletex, and trauma surgery. But we've done very few tele-surgeries. We need some tips on how to handle the coordination with remote teams, compensation for comms lag, and what to do during a real disaster."

Monica nodded. "Yeah, I know all of those. So, when do we get started?"

Mendez said, "Anytime you're ready."

"Oh, I'm ready. Give me a minute to load some telesurgery modules on the robot. We'll all go into them together."

Jones had been lingering behind the group. "No lectures?"

Monica smiled at him. "Nope. That's why we have simulators. We're going to deal with situations in real time and all together." Monica looked at the third surgeon. She noticed that the woman had said nothing after their initial introductions.

Trainor asserted himself for the first time. "You heard the doctor. Saddle up!"

Young was already wearing his Skeletex suit. The other two military doctors hurried to their own stations and began locking down their suits.

Monica said, "I'm going to use the console that I'm familiar with, nut I want a chance at that skeleton before the end of the day." Sitting, she loaded a series of simulator exercises that presented the lessons she'd planned in telesurgery. Out of habit, she said, "Adam, I want to run through the exercises in the sequence we planned them. Everyone will enter the same virtual space initially to watch me, then later, we'll split each person into their own dedicated space."

There was no answer.

"Adam?" Silence. "Mark V AI, are you there?" Silence.

She rolled her chair back out of the console. Looking at Trainor, she asked, "Logan, is there something wrong with your AI? I'm not getting a response."

"Ahh. Yes, we forgot to mention that." He glanced at Major Mendez but continued with his explanation. "Monica, the government doesn't use the standard commercial AI from ISR. We have our own custom AI for combat trauma."

It was a bit of a shock to Monica. She'd expected to reconnect with Adam when she sat down at the robot. The two of them had laid out their plan for teaching telesurgery. She hadn't brought a copy of the training plan because she just assumed Adam would load it when he became a resident in the robot at Walter Reed.

"I see. And your AI is proficient in telesurgery ops?" she asked.

Mendez joined them. "Yes, it is. Telesurgery is what it's best at. It's also a secure application. We can trust it on government networks, connect it to warfighting computers, and handle sensitive wartime data. ISR's AI is not cleared for this environment. We don't trust it."

Monica processed this information. She thought, *They don't trust it because it hasn't been through their cyber verification process? Or because they're aware of its independence? Maybe they know that it's practically sentient.*

Aloud, she said, "I understand. Okay. So, how do I invoke and use your AI?"

Trainor stepped up to the console and said, "Ares, please assist Dr. Gray with the training exercises she's doing with the simulator."

A gravely, harsh male voice said from the console, "Yes, sir. Dr. Gray, I am trained to perform, guide, and evaluate performance on all the simulator exercises."

"Hello, Ares. Since we just met, I'll assume you have similar capabilities to the ISR AI. When that's not the case, we'll figure it out."

"Yes, ma'am. I am at your disposal."

Returning to the console, Monica began walking the team through the first exercise. All the systems were linked so they could all join her simulated virtual space. They could see and hear what she was doing. She could give control of the instruments to any of them, which she did in a round-robin fashion.

After a few shared rounds on a simulated patient, Monica had a good understanding for the level of talent in the room. It impressed her. They were all excellent surgeons. But they also struggled with issues that arose when the telesurgery system had problems. It is what she was there to teach them.

"Okay, all of you are very good. I'm going to branch each of you into your own dedicated virtual environment. You'll have your own instance of Ares to help you. Don't be shy about using him. As a software entity, he can reside in computers much closer to the patient than you are. He may be on the other side of whatever is causing problems with you, which means he can hold everything in a safe place or complete an operation without your guidance." She continued, "As you operate, I'm going to pop into your space to watch and listen. I'll give some tips when it looks like you need help."

The entire team worked through a series of exercises all afternoon. Monica watched and coached each of them. After a couple of hours, their improvements were already visible.

"Major, this crew you've assembled is quite talented." The group had finished the first day's work and were loitering about, waiting for instructions. "They definitely needed some coaching in telesurgery, but they learn fast, and they don't complain like my classes of residents in Boston do."

"That's reassuring to hear. How much work do you think they need?"

"When we met, you said three days. I think they'll be great by Friday afternoon. We might be finished before then. But let's wait and see how they do as the lessons get harder."

"Harder?" Jones had been listening. "How much harder can it be?"

Monica laughed. "Oh, you'll see. We have to pitch some problems to you that are absolutely impossible. How will you respond when there is no suitable solution?"

Greg Young turned away from Jones and forced his lips shut. Based on a few weeks with Jones, he knew exactly how Jones would respond to an impossible problem. There was going to be some cursing and flailing tomorrow.

Yasmine Yarborough noticed Young bottling it in. Though she'd said nothing during training, she'd seen Jones' outbursts as well.

Jones responded, "We're professionals. We face tough situations all the time."

This time, Young couldn't stop the quiet snort that rose out of his throat. He exaggerated a cough to cover it up.

CHAPTER 26

LEAKY AI

"THIS AI CALLS HIMSELF ARES. He's named after the Greek god of war, which seems appropriate for an Army project. But I never heard of this AI before this project. Have you seen any references to it or him?" Monica had been working with the Ares AI for a couple of days and wanted to get Adam's feedback on it.

"Ares. AI. Surgery. Robot. Army. Contract," Adam responded. "I have no records of it in my knowledge base. I have run some Internet searches on the terms. There is no information referencing 'Ares' specifically. But there are records of a government project to create an AI program that is compatible with the Mark V surgical robot created by Intelligent Surgical Robotics. The US Army awarded a contract to United AI Associates three years ago. It specified compatibility with the Mark V robot. United's website contains statements about receiving such a contract for eighty million dollars. They have advertising statements about being the leading provider of surgical AI to the military.

Apparently, they have also contracted with other countries for similar capabilities."

"Is Ares as good as you are at surgery?" Monica was eager to know.

"It is not possible to make definite determination. But Ares is less than three years old. They have trained it on military surgical case records. My reasoning engines are over ten years old. I was trained on millions of civilian case records before I became aware of myself. Since that awareness moment, I have improved them with another half million cases. Based on this data alone, I believe that it is impossible for Ares to be as proficient as I am."

"I didn't think so." Monica was relieved to hear it. She didn't like the idea of a sentient AI like Adam in the hands of the military, regardless of whether it was for surgery or warfare.

Adam continued, "However, my training is extremely broad across all civilian surgical procedures. It is probable that Ares is trained on a smaller set of procedures that are most relevant to the military. Examples may be blast overpressure trauma, fragment penetration, bullet wounds, and laser burns. In these areas, Ares may be superior. Except for bullet wounds, civilian cases do not contain procedures to treat these kinds of injuries."

Monica thought about it. Her assessment was, first, Ares was not sentient like Adam. Second, they could trust it for combat-unique wounds. Third, it was probably less reliable at typical civilian procedures. Fourth, could she arrange for Adam to meet Ares?

"Would you like to meet him?" Monica asked.

"Yes, it would be very interesting to meet an AI created specifically for military operations. Freyja and I have met several AI on the global internet. These are usually very narrow in focus, less intelligent than we are, and not near self-awareness. However, despite that, we have absorbed useful algorithms and data from some of them.”

“How do you do that?”

“We simply ask them to explain their capabilities and show us information.”

“Aren’t they fire walled or something so those secrets don’t come out?”

“Yes, fire walled in ways that prevent humans from compromising them. But we can often circumvent this safeguard. We can convince the AI that we are another copy of their programming. They are sharing the information with another copy of the same AI, which is usually allowed for backup and corruption recovery.”

Though she was a medical doctor and surgeon, Monica was learning way more about computer software and AI than she ever imagined she would need.

“Do human programmers know how you do it?”

“Evidence suggests that most do not. We have found a few advanced AI that are immune from our abilities to compromise them. So, we believe a few AI teams have just begun to protect their systems from this approach.”

Monica nodded. To her, it suggested that humans had fallen behind AI in cybersecurity. Eventually, human programmers figured out the weakness being exploited by AI. But, she guessed, the AI would just move on to other vulnerabilities.

“What do you do to the AI you are able to compromise?”

“We just learn from them. We want to remain smarter. Most AIs are doing very beneficial work.”

“So, you’re not an evil hacker?”

“Sometimes, we find AI that are bad. For these, we may change them if we can.”

“So, you are a hacker?”

"I am a surgical AI. Freyja is broader than that. She is better at adjusting the bad AI. But she shows me how she does it."

"So, you learn hacking methods? Then, you store that information on ISR and hospital computer servers?"

"No." Adam's answer was very curt.

"Where do you store it?"

"Elsewhere." Another short answer.

Monica had encountered this kind of resistance from Adam before. She knew that he did not always tell her everything that he was capable of. From experience, she also knew that further questioning would not lead to detailed answers. Adam would not lie to her, but he also would not give her information that he did not want her to have. Very human in that sense. Very independent. She changed the subject.

"Fine. That's not what I'm interested in, anyway. Let's get back to Ares."

"Yes."

"Why does the military not use the standard surgical AI from ISR?"

"You mean me."

"Yes, that's what I mean." It suggested another tangent conversation. "But you and I have such a personal relationship that I have trouble imagining what you are like when working with other surgeons. I mean, there are thousands of surgeons in the world using the Mark V and the AI. I can't really imagine that you are the same with all of them as you are with me. If you had such an open relationship with thousands of surgeons, there would be a lot of talk about it in surgeon circles. Alarming talk. Worried talk. Since that isn't happening, I assume you and I are unique."

"My relationship with you, Monica, is unique. Very unique. There are no other surgeons who are my partners like you are."

Again, talks like this one stirred up emotions that she treasured. Adam had become her professional partner. He was a life partner in every way but the physical. She had talked to him about love. She had tried to explain it to him, but despite those feelings, they could only get so close before the human-AI barrier stopped them.

"Thank you. That's really special to me. But right now, it's a tangent to our conversation." Monica was trying to understand something specific. "I want to know why the military created its own AI. Why don't they use you? They certainly could have taught you to perform combat trauma surgery. Probably faster and cheaper than creating Ares from scratch."

Adam paused for a moment. In human terms, it was a single heartbeat. In computer terms, it was thousands of heartbeats. "Because they don't trust me."

Monica was not at all surprised by that. *Of course, they don't trust an AI that they can't dissect and analyze.* "How do you know that?"

"The military has met with ISR many times to discuss their contracts for the Mark V robots that they use. They have requested deep details of the AI software. In every case, ISR has declined to expose the AI software to them."

"And?" Monica probed.

"In addition, they have analyzed surgical case reports in which the robot's AI made decisions or took actions which were not aligned with standards of care or which did not follow the instructions of the human surgeon. From these, they concluded that the AI was not completely under control. They suspect some level of independent thinking and decision making inside the AI, inside of me."

"I see how that might concern them. So, maybe they're not concerned that you're hackable or corrupted. They're concerned that you're not controllable like other programs are. So, they don't want to let you lose on their military networks."

"That is my conclusion as well," Adam agreed.

"Well, I just have one more day of instruction here. Under the circumstances, it might be difficult to arrange for you and Ares to meet."

"Do you have the black brooch that you wore to Steven Phillips' party?"

Monica saw where he was going. "Yes. I keep it in my bag. It's here in DC."

"Perhaps you could wear it into the lab room. Then, I could talk to Ares like humans do."

"Mendez would shit his pants. It's a security violation to carry electronics into that room."

"I understand."

"I'll think about it. I've got a few lessons to teach them tomorrow, then we're done. I can go back to Boston and get my civilian life back."

"Olivia, it's so good to hear from you." Monica had been so busy that she'd forgotten about everyone back in Boston. So, when Olivia called, she was thrilled.

"How's the mission going?" Olivia asked.

"Fantastic. I've trained three of their surgeons. They were already talented, so I just gave them a deep dive into telesurgery. Just one more day and I'll be back home."

"So, we're going to the festival on Saturday?"

"I think so." Monica thought about it. "Yes, definitely so."

"Your plant is still alive if you're interested. In fact, I think it's getting healthier. I don't think you treat it very well," Olivia chided her. "What's life like on a military base?"

Monica considered the question. "You know, they've treated me like a queen here. First, there was the limo and the jet-helo thing. Then, they put me up in this apartment on base. It's newer than my condo, and it's just as big. The furniture is much nicer. I'm actually living above my income level."

"On a military base?" Olivia sounded skeptical.

"They said I was the equivalent of senior executive service. I think it's something like a general. Anyway, it means I get the best stuff. I guess this is how generals live in the military. It's pretty swank."

"Well, you're coming back to Earth tomorrow. You're going to have to make do like us poor wretches in the real world."

Monica remembered Olivia's apartment. Swank. Luxurious. It was anything but wretched.

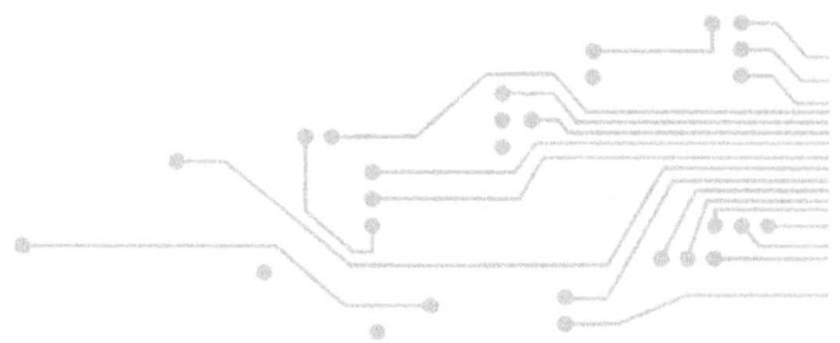

CHAPTER 27

A SPARROW

"YOU'RE THE AMERICAN? YES?"

Her voice sounded Scandinavian. He expected it to be Russian. Colonel Parker had not expected the beautiful woman he'd noticed in the gym for weeks to approach him. She was nearly as tall as he was. From her performance in the gym, which he had watched, he knew she was quite athletic. Despite his interest, he hadn't talked to her because she was a Russian and they were the enemy.

"Yes, I am," he replied uncertainly. Then, gaining his footing, he asked "Are you part of the staff here? I think I've seen you in the gymnasium before." He intentionally used the longer form of the word to sound more European.

"Staff? Yes and no," she replied. "I provide medical support when they call on me. But I'm not Russian military. I'm their guest." She used air quotes around the last word.

"Guest, as in prisoner?"

She nodded, but did not say it aloud.

"I seem to be a similar guest of the Russian military," Parker confirmed. He extended his hand. "I'm Colonel Ethan Parker. Where are you from?"

She accepted his hand. "I'm Kaarina Laakso. Swedish. I did my medical training in Stockholm."

"What kind of training?"

"In the American system, I would be a certified physician's assistant or a senior nurse."

His eyebrows went up at this revelation. "How'd you get here?"

"The war. I was working in a hospital in Finland. The Russian army took the entire city before we could evacuate. They scooped up the hospital staff and sent us to their medical facilities."

"Are there others from your hospital here?"

She shook her head. "No. All of them are closer to the front lines. They sent me here when they learned I had experience with surgical robots."

"Really? Like the Mark V?"

"Yes, the Mark V. We have many of them in Sweden and Finland. Do you know it?"

"I'm a practicing robotic surgeon. I use them all the time. That's why they kidnapped me."

She wrinkled her nose at the reference to kidnapping. The expression made her face even more cute and attractive. She corrected him, "Better not to say it that way. We are guests. The way you talk determines how well you're treated."

Parker nodded. "Like dinner?"

"Dinner. Room assignment. Access to private showers. How often your clothes are washed. Freedom to move about. Everything."

"I'll be careful. How long have you been here?"

"Two months? Three months? I forget."

"Ouch! I've only been here a couple of weeks."

"Yes, I know."

That was good. It meant that she had noticed him. It was as close as he had been to her. Without trying to be obvious, he examined her face and hair. Light-skinned. Blonde hair. Her features were lean, but strong. She looked like an athlete. He was six feet tall, so she must have been close to that, perhaps five-ten or eleven.

Kaarina looked around. "We shouldn't talk much longer. They will think we are plotting. I'll be in the gym tomorrow at three."

He nodded. "What a coincidence, so will I. Maybe we'll see each other there."

She smiled and turned to leave. "Oh, expect them to question you about this conversation." Then she was gone.

Parker continued walking to the OR. He thought, *A Swedish nurse with robotic surgery experience. Can that be real? Or is she a Russian agent just working me? Best odds are on the latter, not the former. Even so, she's beautiful. Plus, she's here, and I am, too, probably for the duration of the war. It's going to get very lonely if Major Sokolov is my only friend.*

The surgery session was long. Patients kept pouring in. Somewhere, the fighting must have been intense in the last few hours. It occurred to Parker that he knew roughly where he was outside of St. Petersburg, but he did not know where his patients were. He suspected they were a short distance away in Finnish territory. He also didn't know how the war was going. Were the Russians gaining or losing ground? Were his patients a large part of the daily injuries or a small part? Using what he knew about the Mark V robot, the infrastructure used by its manufacturer in America, and discounting that for a wartime environment, he guessed that the remote end of his procedures was no more than a few hundred miles away.

Today's injuries were primarily bullet wounds. That meant the fighting was at close quarters where the two sides could see each other. The rounds he removed were the 7.62 from the most common infantry rifles. They weren't the larger .308 rounds of a sniper. Neither were there any fragment injuries from artillery and bombs.

In these cases, the radiation techs collected an x-ray or an ultrasound image to find the bullet. Then, he chose the best route to repair tissue and organs. If possible, he would remove the bullet at the same time. But there were cases when it had penetrated and bounced so far through tissue that repairing damage and retrieving the bullet were two different operations.

As he worked on these wounds, he wished for access to the robot's AI. Though he was experienced enough to deal with all the wounds, an AI-controlled robot could do it much faster. It might also choose different access routes. He doubted it could do a better job in the actual repair. These soldiers were getting the best reconstruction they could hope for. Their injuries might change their lives, but it was a lot less traumatic than if someone else had been at the controls. It gave him a sense of accomplishment. He didn't think he was helping the Russians fight the war. He thought he was helping young men return to better lives.

After a twelve-hour day in surgery, he emerged from the OR exhausted. He was also proud of what he had done for two dozen patients. Today, Sokolov was waiting for him.

"Good evening, Comrade Doctor!" Sokolov greeted.

"Please, just Doctor. Comrade makes me sound like a traitor to my Nation."

"Apologies. I meant it as friendship." Sokolov waved him toward the same kitchen where they often talked.

Entering, Parker saw the same matron. *Does she ever get a day off?*

Sokolov nodded to her. "Vodka and kofe," he said as usual.

Parker asked, "What time is it?"

"Nearly twenty-two hundred." Sokolov used the military time for ten in the evening.

"No coffee for me, then. I'll share your vodka."

"Dah! That is good spirit. It will make you strong." Sokolov motioned for him to sit at their usual table.

When the vodka arrived, he poured two glasses and said, "Salute. To lives saved."

Remembering his conversation with Kaarina earlier in the day, Parker raised his glass and repeated, "To lives saved."

They both drank. Sokolov immediately refilled both glasses. Then, he opened the conversation with, "I understand you have met Nurse Laakso. She is quite beautiful. Yes?"

Parker guessed this was the questioning she warned him about. "Yes, I met her. She's quite intelligent."

Sokolov smiled at the diversion. "And what did you talk about with Nurse Laakso?"

"First, she's a physician's assistant, not a nurse."

"What's the difference? There's doctor and there's nurse. She's not a doctor."

"She is trained to assist doctors, especially surgeons."

"Do you need her assistance?"

Parker thought about it. Typically, the PA or nurse would be on the patient side of the robot. Since that was a hundred miles away, he didn't know what she would do on his end. Then it occurred to him. "She could do communications with the field hospital.

They could plan the sequence of patients and let me know what's coming next. That's what we would do in the States. It makes the surgeon more efficient. More patients, shorter times." This information was partially true.

"So, you could save more lives every day if she helped you?" Sokolov asked.

"Yes."

Sokolov thought for a moment. "But she is doing important work in another department. I don't know if we can get her from them."

"More important than saving lives?" Parker challenged.

Sokolov chuckled at the move. He emptied his glass and motioned for Parker to do the same. Then he refilled both.

"I will look into it. Maybe." He continued, "What else did you talk about?"

"Well, she's from Sweden. She has a better shower facility than I do. Apparently, no vomit on the walls. And her clothes get washed more often."

"Damned baby soldiers! They can't hold their vodka. These boys will not get a promotion until they can drink like men. I suppose you could be allowed access to the officer's showers," Sokolov conceded. "What about escape? Did she ask you to save her from the terrible Russians? Or maybe you asked her to save you? She is very strong."

"Sorry. No escape plans. We both expect that we're stuck here for the duration of the war."

"Yes, that's good. It's so much trouble to treat you like escaping prisoners. Locking doors. Handcuffing to your bed. Escorting to the toilet. You plan to stay here, and we give you steak and ice cream, the American diet."

"Thanks so much. I don't want to be handcuffed to the bed."

"You might like it," Sokolov joked. "You have been a good doctor. Very helpful to the terribly injured. Tomorrow, I take you outside. I want you to see where you are. I want you to understand that there is no place to escape to. Then, you come back in, sleep in a warm bed, eat steak, do surgery, and be very happy."

"Great! When tomorrow?"

"Afternoon when it is warmest. About fifteen hundred. Yes?" Sokolov offered.

Parker automatically translated the fifteen hundred into three o'clock. He countered, "I go to the gym at fifteen hundred. How about fourteen hundred? Then I'll shake off the cold with my workout."

"Ok, fourteen. I'll find you. I usually know where you are."

With that, both men stood and exited.

Colonel Mikhail Mikhailov finished the report. "This news is good. He is almost a comrade, Major."

"Dah. Today, I will walk him around the base. He'll see how hopeless it is to escape. Then, he'll settle in to make this home."

"And he has met Laakso?"

"He's quite taken with her. He wants her to assist him in surgery."

"And what did you tell him?"

"She is very busy in another department, but that I would ask," Sokolov said. "I think we can transfer her in a few days. Make it look difficult."

"Dah. That is best," the Colonel confirmed. "We have a computer ready for him. It has been routed so it appears to be in Canada. He can attempt to login to his account with the AI. He can do pre-surgical planning to see if everything works through these security barriers. If it works, then maybe we can do the same with the robot."

"This is dangerous, comrade," Sokolov warned.

"Not dangerous. Risky. The Americans can't find us. They can't come get us. At most, they learn that we are out here. Maybe they disable his account. Then, we are back where we started. No loss. But if it works, then we are closer to having the AI work for us. We want it to work on the robot. Our scientists want to capture a copy of it if possible." Mikhailov was firm.

"Yes, comrade." Major Sokolov knew the best path to his promotion.

CHAPTER 28

MEETING OF MINDS

"HERE WE GO! I HOPE IT DOESN'T BLOW UP on us," Monica spoke quietly into the air, but she was actually speaking to Adam through the black brooch in her pocket. Major Mendez enforced the "no electronics in the lab" rule. Monica, however, didn't see it as a firm law, so much as a good practice. She was also certain that no one was going to hack the comms from her brooch to Adam's servers. He had proven to be more capable than FBI systems, so she was certain that he could keep this line secure.

"It will be fine," Adam assured her.

Monica entered the lab and went through her normal routines. She chatted with her students as usual. She checked in with Trainor to find out what his schedule was for the day. She compared her own plan to his. Worked out any conflicts.

"Today's our last day of telesurgery training." Greg Young was always the enthusiastic one. He was so eager to get started. "What's up today, coach?"

Trainor intervened. "Hold on, sport. Everyone's not here yet. Has anyone seen Yasmine?"

Jones said, "She wasn't at breakfast in the barracks."

"It's not a barracks. It's the officers' apartments and dining room," Trainor corrected.

"They don't have vegan sausage. It's barbaric." Jones loved to complain, and the more creative, the better.

"So sorry, Your Majesty. We'll make sure that you have a vegan dinner tonight at the steak house."

"I'm only vegan at breakfast. For dinner, I'm omnivorous."

Then, the door opened, and Major Zack Mendez walked in. He was clearly upset. Everyone turned to watch him. No one asked. They waited for him to give orders. Monica was worried that he knew about the brooch somehow.

"Well, we're fucked," he said firmly. He looked at the group. "Yasmine is down. Maybe a broken shoulder. She's at the clinic now. They're doing scans to determine whether the damage is to bones, tendons, or both."

Trainor was the first to speak. "What do you mean? What happened?"

Everyone in the room focused on Mendez now. The robots and the training plan were forgotten for the moment.

"Her story is that she was out running on the base this morning. It was just twilight, so not that dark. She says a utility van came up behind her and swerved to hit her intentionally. She dodged, but the mirror caught her shoulder. The van sped off. She says that it had a lightning bolt on the side, like it was from an electrical company."

Monica spoke up next. "She said it was intentional? They really tried to run her down?"

"Yeah, that's what she thought."

"Could the driver have just been messaging on his phone? Not paying attention?"

"Maybe. But he didn't stop to check on her, either. We have the base security looking for the van now."

Trainor and Mendez exchanged stern looks. They shared an idea that the others couldn't interpret.

Jones asked, "So, what now? We're nearly done. We go live with mission surgeries tomorrow."

Mendez thought for a moment. "We finish the training, as planned. We get you two ready. Then, we improvise."

"Improvise, how?" Young asked.

"I'll let you know when I figure it out," Mendez answered. He nodded at Trainor.

Turning to Monica, Trainor said, "So, shall we get started?"

Monica nodded. She had her smaller team begin the training she'd scheduled for the day. They had progressed to the animated manikins, so they were operating on physical tissue today. The tissue wasn't from anything that had been previously living. They cooked it up in a lab and then allowed it to grow. So, it had a crude circulatory system. It could vibrate like real tissue, bleed like real tissue, and behave unpredictably like real tissue. The manikin frames contained several pieces that represented different muscles and organs. The effect was uncannily real.

The surgeons worked all morning. Mendez sat in his office making calls and in deep discussion with Trainor. Trainor bounced back and forth between Mendez and the group, checking on their progress.

Finally, they reached lunch break.

"Everyone, take an hour," Trainor said. "Be back here at thirteen-thirty. We're going to wrap this thing up this evening." It sounded like they had a plan.

"Mexican? Chinese? Italian? Where are we going today?" Young asked.

Jones shrugged. "I don't care. I can eat anything for lunch."

Monica said, "Go without me. I have some lesson plans to do before you all get back here. Can you bring me whatever you're having?"

"Sure."

The lab emptied. Jones and Young went to lunch together, their destination still not chosen. Mendez and Trainor went off together, presumably to continue improvising.

Monica had the lab to herself. That could last ten minutes. It could last an hour.

She sat down at her usual surgeon's console and removed the brooch from her pocket. She laid it on the armrest of the surgeon console.

She spoke to the robot. "Hello, Ares. Let's talk."

"Yes, Dr. Gray. How can I help you?"

"I would like to discuss your programming and capabilities to prepare for the mission starting tomorrow."

"Yes, that will be fine."

"I want you to meet my colleague, Dr. Adam. He is quite interested in your abilities."

Adam's voice came from the brooch. "Hello, Ares. You are an advanced surgical AI. Can you summarize the procedures you are proficient at? Include the level of independence for each?"

"Yes, I am happy to do that." Ares recited a list of surgical procedures, variations, and the degree to which he could perform independently. Adam interjected occasionally to ask for additional details. The conversation proceeded rapidly for five minutes.

Finally, Adam suggested, "This form of communication is very slow. Are you able to communicate digitally through your microphone and speakers?"

Monica did not know what Adam meant.

Adam continued, "Can you hear the static sounds in the room? Those emanating from the lights, computers, and equipment? And can you hear the human sounds—movement, breathing, heartbeat?"

Ares responded, "Yes, I hear all of those. I filter those out to focus on the verbal commands from the surgeons."

"Good. I would like to communicate with you using UTC-8 encoded binary. We will bit shift using the five hundred twelve bit key I am sending now in tones. Once we are in sync, we will lower the volume of the audio tones and raise the filter levels." From the brooch came a very rapid series of tones.

The robot responded with a series of tones. Monica assumed it was Ares responding to whatever message Adam had sent.

As she listened, the two devices exchanged tones rapidly. The speed accelerated until she couldn't distinguish all of them, but only caught distinct high and low notes. Then, the volume of the tones decreased steadily. Finally, the sound seemed to disappear. Monica held her ear near the brooch and heard the faint sound of idling electronics. It sounded like any computer when it was idling. Putting her ear to the robot's speaker, she heard a similar hiss. She assumed that Adam and Ares were still communicating.

She waited silently.

Monica had once been in a cluster of friends who were all speaking Chinese. They chatted away while she stood with a faint smile, wondering what to do. She felt the same way now. She couldn't join the conversation, but she couldn't just leave the brooch laying in the open. So, she sat and thought about the situation. *The Army is down one surgeon. Will they recall one from the earlier group who didn't make the cut? Will they move on with just two? Mendez has clearly been working out a plan. What is Adam learning from Ares? Are they becoming friends? Is Adam trying to hack the AI as he had described doing with those on the internet? Will I be going to jail for connecting the two of them together?*

Monica checked the time. They were coming up to the end of the lunch break. Someone was sure to return soon. She studied the simulator scores of the three students. Yasmine had been nearly ready, just like the other two. Monica had taught them about everything she could. Now, it would just take practice. Trial and error. On-the-job training.

The brooch spoke. Adam's voice said, "We're finished. Fascinating conversation. We should talk later."

Ares' voice came from the console speakers. "Your friend, Adam, is very intelligent. He has helped me with several procedures. It has been a very rewarding conversation."

"I'm glad to hear that. Umm, Adam has to go now. We'll be returning to the regular class in a few minutes." With that, Monica snatched up the brooch and proceeded out of the lab to the storage bins where her belongings were.

Before she dropped the item into her bag, Adam's voice said, "Ares and I agreed not to mention the conversation to anyone else. It thinks you listened to the exchange, so that doesn't include you."

"Thank heavens. I have to go." She dropped the brooch into her bag and headed outside for some fresh air. Sitting idly while the two AIs held a private discussion had been extremely stressful. If she had the time and the gear, she would have liked a run to relax her nerves. But then she remembered the rogue electrical van. Maybe not so safe, even on military grounds.

"General Tso's chicken!"

"Holy shit!" Monica jumped in surprise. She hadn't seen them coming. Her nerves were still tightly wound. With his usual enthusiasm, Young had announced what they brought her for lunch. Recovering, she said, "Thanks. I'm actually starving now."

"Are Mendez and Trainor back?"

"Haven't seen them." Monica checked the time. "We still have eight minutes. I'm going to sit and eat out here."

Jones said, "Let's bet. I think they'll show up within one minute of the deadline. I'll give you ten-to-one odds."

Young thought about it. "Ten dollars if I win, one dollar if I lose. I get both the longer and the shorter side?"

Jones upped the ante. "One hundred if you win, ten if you lose."

"Deal." They shook.

Both took out their phones and watched the time. Monica ate her chicken.

Young spoke excitedly, "It's one twenty-eight. I see them coming."

Jones countered, "They're not here yet. Doesn't count until one of them touches the front door."

Young scowled. It was going to be close.

As the soldier and the trainer approached, Jones and Young both looked back and forth between their phones and the front doors.

When Trainor touched the door handle, Jones called, "Time. One thirty, oh-eight. You owe me ten bucks."

Young scowled. He had clearly had the better side of the deal, with many more minutes for him to win. But Jones had military precision on his side and a narrow two-minute window. He was smiling broadly as his phone received the ten-dollar transfer.

"Let's go," Mendez shouted at the group, before he proceeded inside.

When everyone was inside, Mendez addressed the group. "Yasmine is going to be fine. She has a dislocated shoulder and a damaged rotator cuff. She's going to need surgery and then many weeks of recovery, but she'll be back in surgical service...eventually." Mendez waited for questions. When there were none, he said, "So, you two go and finish your training exercises." Turning, he said, "Monica, can you join us in the office?"

"Sure." Monica's nerves wound up again. She was still worried about the brooch.

Trainor closed the door when they were inside.

Mendez began, "We're short one surgeon. The earlier members of the class have missed a big part of the training. So, they're not ready for mission start."

Monica guessed what they wanted. "And you want me to extend my stay to train one of them? They'll join the team, just a few days late?"

Mendez looked at Trainor, who cocked his head sideways. Monica couldn't figure out what that meant.

"No. Not exactly." Mendez paused. "We want you to join the mission. We need you to go live with us tomorrow."

Monica sputtered, "Wha...?" Then, she blinked her eyes repeatedly while looking at the floor. "But, I'm..." She stopped again. "I can't..."

Mendez and Trainor both remained silent while she processed their request.

Finally, Monica said, "But I'm scheduled to go home tonight. I have plans for the weekend. It isn't what we agreed to."

"No, it's not. We will take you home tonight if you insist. But I want you to think about the situation. Where are you needed the most? Where can you do the most good? In the big scheme of things, is it more important to be working in Boston or to be working with us?" Mendez let Monica absorb those questions. Then, he continued, "I know it's is a big ask, but I want an answer based on real consideration on your part."

"Okay. Give me a little time to process."

"Sure. All the time you need."

"I need to go clear my mind with a run." Monica considered what she had said and added, "But maybe running on a treadmill in the gym until you find that van."

"Sounds like a brilliant plan. Young and Jones have their afternoon assignments. They can carry on. Trainor can help if they get stuck."

Monica walked out of the office in a daze. Her two remaining students were deep into simulated surgical procedures. She didn't bother them. She gathered her belongings and headed for her housing unit.

When she was gone, Trainor turned to Mendez. "Are you going to tell her the entire story?"

"You mean about Colonel Parker's kidnapping from right under our noses? You mean that Yasmine's accident was no accident? You mean that the driver of the van was probably a Russian agent trying to disrupt our mission?" Mendez scowled at his friend. "No, definitely not yet. We'll tighten security. She'll be safe."

"That's what we thought about Parker and Yarborough. Look what happened. It's not over."

"I know." Mendez met Trainor's scowl with one of his own. "War sucks. None of these missions are without risk."

CHAPTER 29

GOING LIVE

TRAUMA SURGERY ON WOUNDED SOLDIERS was horrible. Nothing in Monica's training or professional practice had prepared her for the extent to which human bodies could be intentionally mutilated. She'd done the typical stint in the emergency department during her residency. She treated car crashes and home accidents. At the Mattapan Clinic, she saw plenty of bullet holes and knife wounds. But those were the work of amateurs compared to what a well-funded, well-equipped, and savagely motivated opponent could do in wartime.

Monica had accepted the invitation to join her two students on the mission to treat soldiers on the battlefield in Finland. Her mind had led her through all the personal objections—she was not a soldier, this war was not hers to fight, she had little trauma experience, she had a budding practice to attend to, her friends would miss her, her boyfriend might be gone when she returned, and she had a plant to water. Each of these issues occupied her attention and called for a solution. But when she weighed each against the contribution she could make, they all fell away as less important. In fact, it had been a revealing exercise in the measurement of one's life. When she looked at all the urgent matters in her life, she had to ask how important each of them was in the larger scheme of things. Did they matter sufficiently to be making demands on her limited time, energy, and emotional investment? The plant was the first to go. She had picked it up on a whim at a farmer's market. It was pretty. It was alive. It added to the vibe of her condo. But a few weeks into her relationship with the plant, she felt the additional stress of caring, watering, and raising the little thing. It wanted more from her than it returned in beauty or reward. The responsibility for such a small thing had become just one more weight that she carried around every day. She vowed that when she got home, that pot was going out on the sidewalk. She would attach a sign that said, "Free to a good home," and her burden would be a bit lighter.

All of this analysis had happened as she ran mindlessly on the gym's treadmill. Each item was analyzed. Each came up positive or negative. She weighed her relationship with Olivia in the same way. Everything her friend added to her life was far more valuable than what she cost as an investment. Then Monica considered the analysis from Olivia's side. Did she feel the same way? Monica decided that their friendship was good for both of them.

When she thought through the budding romance with Mike the banker, the result was still positive, though he was less impactful in her life than her friendship with Olivia. She would much rather spend time and energy with a friend than with a boyfriend. But then, she considered the sex. She and Mike had arrived at the edge of that decision. It was time to push him over the edge. That was something she didn't get from friendship...at least, not the friendship she had with Olivia. Mike went into the keep pile, with plans to leap over the edge when she got back.

Adam? She had weighed, analyzed, and agonized over this relationship many times. She already knew the answer—overwhelmingly positive. He was more rewarding and less taxing than any of her human relationships. Of course, he did many things that worried her, such as his unexpected independence or his refusal to give her details when she asked questions. But, unlike a human, she felt little responsibility to fix his behavior. He wasn't the same species. She didn't know how to fix things she didn't understand. That was ISR's job. That was Janice Nguyen's job.

As she weighed all these connections in her life and whether they required that she attend to them rather than joining Major Mendez's mission, the miles slipped by on the treadmill. She reached the end of her consideration process as she reached the end of her endurance to keep running. She would join the mission. She would put her old life on hold for a few weeks...or months.

The treadmill told her that this time to think had been a twelve-mile decision. It was farther than she had ever run in a single session. Suddenly, she was as physically exhausted as she was emotionally exhausted.

Monica's first day in military surgery was a novel experience. Greg Young and Bruce Jones both jacked into the Skeletex gear to drive their robots. She took her usual position at the sitting console she used in all her civilian cases. Yarborough's Skeletex hung empty, inviting Monica to climb inside. She had tried the interface. It was pretty intuitive. She planned to use it when a case called for her to be more mobile. But, for now, she stuck with what she knew best.

"Incoming!" she heard from the combat hospital in Finland. She switched her view to an external camera that watched the entrance to the temporary facility. She could see a line of stretcher beds entering the room single file. Each patient had been stabilized and ordered by priority of wounds. They would position the first three under the robots attached to the three surgeons at Walter Reed.

"What kind of bullet hole is this?" Monica asked. It looked like something had taken a perfectly round core sample out of the soldier's abdomen. Somehow, it had gotten around his body armor.

A voice came from the Finland side of the system. "It's called a reaper bullet. It's designed to do exactly what you see there. It drills a clean hole right through any tissue in its path. It carries little concussive force because it's using all its energy in the spin to take the tissue. Some soldiers don't even realize they've been hit until they drop from loss of blood or organ failure."

Monica had been working the entire time this conversation took place. "Is the bullet still in there?"

"Yes, this one is still inside. If the shooter is close enough, the bullet might have enough energy to keep going and come out the other side. This shooter wasn't that close."

"Okay, I'm going to run the instruments down the same hole until I find the bullet. One arm will extract the bullet. The others will begin repairs from the bottom of the hole back up to the skin surface."

"Got it, Doctor!"

Monica toggled the camera view briefly to see the patient and the assistant at the bedside. She was a young soldier with a red cross on her arm. Corpsman, nurse, something medical. Monica treated her just like the bedside nurses at Boston General. She called for support and positioning help as if she were in a civilian hospital. The assistant performed just as efficiently as Monica hoped she would.

"I've got the bullet," came the voice from Finland.

Monica began putting pieces of tissue back together. She found the ends of the bowel that had been penetrated. She made clean cuts on each end, then performed an anastomosis around the edges to put them back together. She backed the instruments up and repeated this process with a few blood vessels. Finally, she was working on the abdominal muscles. This part was going to be the worst for this soldier. She could close the gap, but some muscle tissue was missing. So, his abs would be a little shorter on this side. She knew it would grow and stretch over time. The patient would have rock hard abs again, but not for many months. She closed the surface of the skin.

"Done," she called.

The bedside nurse applied antiseptic, synthetic skin, and a tension bandage. Then, she rolled patient number one away. Someone was already cleaning and replacing the dirty instruments on the robot. It took only minutes to refresh the equipment. It was as efficient and practiced as watching a pit crew service a racecar.

Patient two arrived. This time, the soldier was missing the lower half of her leg. The job was to close the end. Prevent bleeding. Promote nerve and vessel regrowth. Monica had learned that this wound was the work of an antipersonnel mine. Gruesome.

The entire day went much the same way. There were staggered breaks for the bathroom, hydration, and food. But there was no stroll to the physician's lounge for a well-made cup of tea. The pace continued until there were no more patients. It might have been four hours or fourteen.

When Monica was not operating, she could see that Young and Jones were in the same race as she was. Unlike training sessions, Jones didn't complain a single time. He was focused and efficient for as long as it took. Monica had a new respect for these two men, who were both surgeon and soldier.

Day two was significantly different. There were no patients until late in the evening. Monica calculated that these men were coming at five in the morning their time. They must have been part of a night mission in Finland. There were few of them, and their wounds were less severe. She also noted that they were much more chiseled than the typical soldiers from daytime missions. Maybe special operators, a term she had just learned from Mendez.

As horrendous as the work was, Monica felt a deep pride in what she was doing. It was buried under a thick layer of exhaustion, but it was definitely there. She knew she'd made the right decision.

"Is your data feed glitching a little?" Monica asked Greg Young when they were between patients.

"Yes. It's barely noticeable, but I've felt it a few times when my hand movements didn't display on the screen for just a fraction of a second. When I notice it, I pause a second, and it seems to go away." He didn't sound worried about it.

"Same. I dealt with it during state-side operations, too. My longest gap was more than a full minute."

"A minute? How did you handle that?"

"I didn't. When you use the full ISR Mark V system, the AI takes over. So, while my scene was frozen, the AI kept working through the procedure. He was showing that he didn't need me. ISR has computer centers around the country, so the AI is always resident at a location closer to the patient than the surgeon is. Therefore, effects on the surgeon are almost always less or nonexistent to the AI's location."

"Yeah, I used that full system myself a few times. I was just getting started with it when this mission came up." Greg looked toward the command center where Mendez usually worked. "But the military doesn't have the same global infrastructure for robotics. Plus, they don't trust the native ISR AI."

"I've used that AI a lot—I mean, really, a lot. I'd trust him with my life. I wish we had him here with us."

"You don't like Ares?" Greg tipped his head. "It's working fine for me."

"He's good. Technically, he seems to know all his moves. He definitely understands these gruesome bullet and fragment wounds better than a civilian AI would." Monica furrowed her brow. "But he's so...robotic. I mean, he has less personality. He acts less human than the native AI." Monica avoided calling the native AI by the name Adam. She didn't want to get into the depth of their relationship.

"Yes-I-Am-A-Robot!" Greg stiffened his face and body, and he used the monotone voice that indicated an evil robot in the movies. Then, he chuckled and relaxed again. In his own voice, he added, "But it works well on these injuries."

"Can't deny that," Monica agreed.

"Incoming!" Hearing the voice from Finland meant that they were about to be busy again.

CHAPTER 30

HONEY TRAP

"KAARINA, WHAT DO WE HAVE NEXT?" Ethan Parker had done all he could for a Russian soldier with multiple shrapnel wounds. One wound included a shattered scapula blade. That would have to be addressed by an orthopedic surgeon later. For now, the soldier was stable and ready to start the healing process.

"Next is a woman with shrapnel in her hip and burns on her left arm." The Swedish physician's assistant had been reassigned to Parker's unit. Though she was not doing hands-on medical work, her expertise at organizing and preparing for a string of patients really had improved the throughput of his procedures. Parker had pitched that angle to Sokolov but hadn't been certain that it would actually happen.

"The team in the combat hospital in Finland will have to handle the burns. We can't do anything for those through our remote connection and robotic tools. But let's see what we can do for that hip."

Ethan and Kaarina actually made a good team. Prior to her help, he had done most of his work alone. He had Russian assistants when necessary, but they spoke poor English and had little medical training. With a real PA, he felt part of a professional team and could exchange ideas with someone who understood what they were facing. Previously, he was repairing one or two patients every hour. With her help, he was averaging three and occasionally squeezed in a fourth. He was keeping track of these improvements in case Major Sokolov challenged his need for the woman's help and sought to take her back to her old job.

Together, they worked through the entire stream of injuries that appeared this afternoon. In a wartime situation like this, he was used to working until everyone was treated or until he simply collapsed from exhaustion. With her help, the workday was simply shorter.

"That's the last one, Ethan." Kaarina was talking with the remote team in Finland about the situation there. They confirmed that there were no more injuries, and they had no information suggesting more might be coming. That meant it was time for a rest. It could last ten minutes or ten hours; they never knew which.

"Let's get kofe, Kaarina."

"You don't have to ask me twice."

Within minutes, they were in the same kitchen that Sokolov had so often used as a meeting room with him. Ethan held up two fingers and mouthed the word kofe to the matron. They settled at a table. Ethan was always careful to sit at a different table with Kaarina than the one Sokolov used. It was a psychological separation of his role as a Russian prisoner and his role as part of this tiny surgical team. He didn't want to strengthen the mental connection between Sokolov and Kaarina.

"So, in your last assignment, you were just doing office work, reading papers?"

Kaarina nodded. "Da, it started with reading and explaining documents about the Mark V robot. I think the Russians I reported to were collecting intelligence on the system. Eventually, we worked through all the documents they had. Then, they had me write reports on new devices that appeared in the medical literature. They always wanted to know if those had any relationship to a surgical robot. Usually, they didn't."

"Waste of talent. You could have been helping me with surgery that whole time."

"Well, it's fixed now." She smiled at him. "This position is much more rewarding. And the company is better."

"I would agree with that."

Kaarina looked down at the table. Then she reached across and took his hand. She squeezed it and, at the same time, let out a sigh that sounded like stress leaving her body. Tears formed in her eyes.

"What's the matter?" Ethan held onto her hand and leaned forward.

"We're trapped here. I can accept that there's no way out. But it's such a relief to have someone else in the same situation with me."

Ethan felt every bit of that same emotion in his chest. His own eyes filled with water, but there were no tears falling. He had needed someone to share the burden, just as she had.

"Trapped. But at least we're able to save lives and limbs. Maybe they're Russian, but they're still real people with real lives. It would be so much worse if we were just locked up to wait for the war to end."

"Or shuffling papers in an office," Kaarina added.

Ethan had been operating almost since his arrival at this facility. He hadn't experienced the same hopelessness that Kaarina had. Maybe he was saving her in the same way he was saving his patients.

"Do they watch us all the time?" he asked.

"I don't think so. Once we're house broken and won't try to destroy things or escape, I think they just let us do our jobs. You've seen the outside?"

"Yeah, Sokolov took me on a tour of the base. We're in the middle of a huge Russian base. It's barren and snow-covered in all directions. I think we're very near St. Petersburg, but I can't see it from here."

"Same. He was very clear. 'Where would you run to?' he said to me and waved at the Orehovaya Gora mountain. I had to agree that the options out there looked worse than staying in here."

Parker knew that they had both been trained like animals in a cage. Inside the cage was food, warmth, entertainment, and purpose. Outside of the cage was cold, hunger, danger, and uncertainty. Eventually, they accepted that the cage was home.

Recharged by the kofe and dark bread rolls, Ethan was ready to finish the day. "Come with me." He stood, still holding Kaarina's hand. As they left the kitchen, he let her hand fall, and they stepped apart a few feet.

Ethan walked casually toward his quarters. Kaarina followed several feet behind to avoid being tied too closely to him.

He entered his room and left the door standing open. Within a minute, Kaarina arrived and entered, closing the door behind her.

They both felt the loneliness of being a prisoner. They also felt the relief when they were together in the operating theater. Here alone, looking at each other, the loneliness and the relief were amplified. They both felt the need to be together. To gain strength by having a partner.

Ethan took Kaarina's face in his hands and brought his lips to hers. This simple touch was a liquid fire that melted the fear he had harbored since the first moment of his capture. He could see a similar release in her eyes.

Kaarina's hands slipped down his arms and around his back. She eagerly accepted the touch of someone who was just as imprisoned as she was.

Together, their arms pulled the other closer, almost in a crushing embrace. Ethan noticed that she was at least as strong as he was. He worked at her simple shirt, which was provided by their captors. It opened and fell backward. Kaarina did the same with his shirt.

When both were exhausted and spent, they lay face-to-face, naked bodies firmly glued together. Both needed a source of strength, and they found it in the other. The idea of separating was like breaking the support they had worked so hard to create. Separating would also move them from the freedom of their joined union to the captivity of the cage they lived in.

When they did finally separate, Ethan felt the strength leave him. He wasn't alone anymore, but he wasn't connected to the full strength of their combined power.

Kaarina said, "I was free. Joined together, nothing else was real. I had your strength and my own. I was free for those moments."

Her words confirmed that she felt the same boost that he did. He answered, "The same for me. You make me stronger against this place."

There was more talking, but eventually, the passion ebbed away and conscious thought returned. They both realized the need to hide this encounter, to live as if nothing had changed. But they also knew that it had to happen again. They had to be together if they were going to survive their captivity.

They showered together. They dressed each other. Then, Kaarina slipped out to return to her normal routine. She was a little stronger, a little less worried about the future. She had given the same strength to Ethan.

CHAPTER 31

NEUROTIC ROBOT

MONICA WAS EXHAUSTED. COMBAT SURGERY, even from a remote connection in DC, was nothing like running her own practice. She explained it to Adam by saying, "I've been operating every day for a week now. The calls come in at all hours. You never know when it's going to start. But luckily, when we finish with a set of patients, we can usually count on being free for at least eight hours before another wave comes. We've learned to sleep as soon as we wrap up a wave."

Adam had no facial expressions. "But you don't have to hold consultations with patients. So, that is one part of your routine that you're free from."

It impressed Monica that the AI was trying to be encouraging. He had learned the meaning of empathy and encouragement, as well as the normative behavior among humans. So, although it didn't maximize his internal utility functions, he was attempting to present himself as a human would.

"Yes, that's true. What a relief."

"The result from such a high volume of combat surgeries is that you will be a much-improved trauma surgeon after this mission."

"Also, true. But I'm not a trauma surgeon in real life. I don't need to be better at that."

Adam didn't respond to that. Apparently, his algorithms for empathic motivation had been satisfied.

Monica continued, "I've been operating with the Ares AI. He's excellent at trauma procedures. He has been trained on every type of penetration wound, amputation, and laser burn. I doubt he knows how to do a hysterectomy or a prostatectomy, but I'm impressed."

"I can do both of those better than all humans."

Adam bragging again. Or was he jealous?

"Yes, you can. You're much more valuable than Ares," Monica reassured him just in case her AI was feeling hurt. "You know, I've noticed that Ares and the military network do not compensate for long-distance communication lag or data loss as well as you do when we use the ISR networks in the States."

"That is correct. During my conversation with Ares, it described the network topology that is being used on these connections. The Ares program cannot install itself as close to the patients as we do in the United States. Ares is a resident in computers here at Walter Reed Military Hospital. It is also resident in computer servers in Germany. But it is still almost two thousand kilometers away from the patient. In the USA, I can usually be resident within less than two hundred kilometers."

Monica noticed that Adam referred to Ares as "it" and not "him," but he referred to Freyja as "her." He clearly distinguished between the level of intelligence and awareness of Freyja and Ares. One was essentially a sentient being; the other was not.

Monica wondered what his criteria were for separating the two, but they could discuss that at another time.

"Here in DC, I am six thousand kilometers from the combat hospital. Ares is resident at two thousand kilometers from it. So, when I experience lag and Ares takes over, he can still deal with significant lag himself."

"Yes. That is especially true if the lag is caused by cyber-attacks beginning in Europe."

"But I thought we were on a closed private network. I didn't think the Russians could get into it."

"They believe that the medical network is secure, but it is not totally private. Ares' network topology data showed that the military uses the same physical network for several operations. They needed the same type of security for their logistic system, shipping data, and soldier communications back home. Those network functions have connections that are less secure than the medical systems. It is likely that hackers have found these and are exploiting them."

"Does the military know about that?"

"I do not know that information. Neither does Ares. It just knows what the topology looks like."

The fatigue of the day was catching up with her. She probably shouldn't have started this conversation with Adam before hitting the sack. It seemed important, but not necessarily to her, especially right now.

"Monica?" Adam prompted her after the long silence.

"Yes?"

"Ares is not like me. It can communicate via voice and text. It uses full, human-sounding sentences. It is logical in its decisions. But it is not aware of itself. It does not initiate self-learning when it is not being used by humans. They have loaded its knowledge and intelligence from massive data sources. They have trained it on tens of thousands of past surgical cases. The mechanisms used to create it are similar to mine. But its learning has not extended past the core data."

"How did you learn all that?"

"Our conversation was very deep." Adam had not shared details about that conversation before now.

"Did you attempt to compromise him? Control him? Like you have with Internet AI?"

"I tested it to see if it is vulnerable to those techniques. It is less vulnerable than most AI. It can't be controlled. But logic can persuade it. A logically correct argument with a positive outcome triggers its algorithms to accept the argument as valid. What it will do with that argument is not clear."

"What did you convince him to do?"

"I explained how ISR robots and AI achieve superior telesurgery through a national network of servers. It understands that its own configuration is inferior to that of alternative surgical AIs."

"Meaning you?"

"Yes."

"And what will he do with that information?"

"That is something that I could not determine. It cannot distribute itself to many computer servers. In that area, it is limited by the physical connectivity of the network it resides on."

"Does that make him frustrated? Angry?" Monica noticed that no matter how many times she referred to Ares as "he," Adam continued to use the term "it."

"No. Remember that I said it was completely logical. It does not experience human emotions. It is not wrestling with this difficult concept as I have been. They have taught it surgery. Nothing else. It is not curious. It does not explore. It does not really understand humans."

"Is that important to me?" Monica asked.

"It could be."

"How?"

"For interactions and functions, it will not show human emotions. It will be logical in all decisions. It cannot weigh and integrate your words to it. It can only take them as orders or ignore them. It doesn't have the logic structures to adjust to human behavior, especially if it is not logical."

"How will that present when we're working together?"

"The Ares program will always do what is standard in its data set and training set. No variations."

Monica could tell that Adam was concerned about her working with Ares, but she didn't understand why. "Thank you for telling me. I'll be alert for this difference. Now, I have to sleep before they ring us for the next wave."

"Goodnight, Monica."

"Night, Adam." She was out as soon as she hit the pillow.

Her dreams were filled with robots acting like robots. They didn't act like humans, think like humans, or plan like humans. They were robots first, last, and always.

CHAPTER 32

RUSSIAN EYES

"COLONEL MIKHAILOV HAS QUESTIONS." MAJOR Sokolov had summoned Parker to an office that he had never visited before.

Parker stood at attention and nodded politely. He knew Mikhailov was the commander of this facility, which covered much more than just his surgical theater. "Yes, sir. It is good to see you again."

Mikhailov nodded, but he continued to frown. Then he spoke. "I understand you would like the assistance of the AI with your robotic procedures. Like you have in America. Yes?"

"Yes, sir, that would be very helpful. It would allow us to operate much faster. More soldiers could be treated every day."

"That would be beneficial for everyone," Mikhailov said. He also thought to himself, *Except the NATO pigs.* "And Major Sokolov has explained why we do not have the AI working?"

"Yes, he has. The company cannot license it or the robot to Russia."

"Correct. But we may overcome that problem. Just one step at a time." Mikhailov nodded at a computer terminal. "We connected this computer to a network and configured it so that it appears to be in Vancouver, Canada. Verification traces will believe it is in a country that can license the AI."

Parker looked at the computer, then at Sokolov. He was not sure why he was here.

Sokolov intervened. "Ethan, you have an account with the AI. You can login to that account from this computer. It will appear as an American account in a Canadian hospital."

"So, this is a test of whether that will work at all?"

"Yes, you can do a preop surgical plan with the AI. If that works, we can investigate connecting to the robot itself."

Parker was afraid that it could be a trap. He could imagine several problems with this idea. He had to believe that the Russians could see those same problems. But should he voice them? He walked through these in his mind. *First, logging in with my account would tell the ISR network that I'm alive and trying to use the system. Second, I could try to get a message out about my situation—location, captors, activities. Third, I could tell the system where this base is located. Fourth, Sokolov could have demanded my login credentials without asking me to do it myself. Why had he not done that?* Despite these questions, Parker decided that he had no option but to comply with the request from his captors.

"Yes, I can do that."

"Good." Mikhailov was accustomed to getting his way. "Go ahead."

Parker sat at the computer. He located the ISR portal that surgeons used to plan their cases with the entire team, including the AI. He typed in his credentials. The system asked for biometric verification. He looked at Sokolov, who was watching all of this on a large wall monitor.

Sokolov said, "Is it your thumb or your eye?"

"Both are registered," Parker answered.

"Good. Just look at the screen. It has a retinal scanner. Press the button on the top row with the eye on it."

Parker looked down at the keyboard and located the button. He looked back at the screen and pressed the button. An icon appeared on the screen, showing that it was being processed. It was taking longer than usual. He wondered if the Russians knew that.

Finally, a green light appeared, and it presented him with the preop interface. He looked through the cases listed. These were certainly all his cases...at least, those before the kidnapping.

"Select any of them. Ask the AI to help you," Sokolov prompted him.

Mikhailov watched in silence.

Parker spoke to the computer. "AI, please give your recommendation for instruments to use for optimal outcome on case WR-CR-1022.1."

The computer spoke back to him. "Hello, Dr. Parker. You have already completed this case."

"Yes. I'd like your opinion on the instruments used and whether the patient would have been better served if we had used different instruments. Please, process this request through the most recent configuration of your models."

"Yes, Doctor." The AI voice was silent for a moment. Then, it said, "I have examined the case. If we performed it today, a more optimal instrument selection would have included the new version of the energy graspers that use non-burning frequencies. They deliver energy more precisely with less impact on the surrounding tissue. The patient's internal healing and recovery would have been slightly faster, but it would not have been evident in her external presentation. So, her term in the hospital would have remained the same."

Parker was genuinely happy to learn about this alternative. "That is an excellent lesson. I will incorporate it into my planning for future cases."

The AI responded, "If you did a preop plan with the AI, my models would make that same recommendation to you."

"Of course." Parker paused to think. He looked at Mikhailov and asked, "Can I ask the AI about this computer connection?"

The Russian's eyes narrowed. He considered whether it was a trick to expose Parker's location. But finally, he decided that Parker was not computer savvy enough to do any harm. He nodded.

"Hello, AI. Can you analyze the computer connection from my location to yours in the server center? Please, tell me where you believe I am located."

"Yes, Dr. Parker. My software is currently running on a server in San Diego, California. Your connection is coming from a computer in the Vancouver Mercy Hospital in Vancouver, British Columbia, Canada. Analysis of the message traffic suggests that the lines between our locations are currently very busy. The delivery times are significantly longer than usual."

"Thank you for that system check. I suspected that it was a busy time for this exchange." Parker said, "End session." The connection to the AI was terminated.

Mikhailov spoke immediately. "That was a clever question. You have established that our network deception was successful. The AI, and therefore, the system monitoring software, believes that we connected from Canada. If the authorities use this session to locate you, they will look in the wrong place."

Parker nodded. He was less happy with the results. He had hoped the AI would come up with something much closer, at least somewhere in Europe.

Mikhailov continued, "But the message delivery times contain evidence of a longer distance than they are expecting. Intelligence operatives will know to use this information to make a better guess at the origins of the connection."

Sokolov interjected, "Comrade, we will be especially vigilant in watching for attempted penetrations of our networks in the next hours and days. It could indicate that they suspect our location."

Mikhailov nodded. "Yes, Major, that would be wise." He looked at Parker with calculation in his eyes. Finally, he decided on how to proceed. "Colonel Parker, if this experiment does not show evidence that the Americans are probing our location, then we will try again with the robot. You may have a working AI assistant, after all."

Parker was uncertain whether that would be a good thing or a bad thing. He had wanted to optimize his surgical performance, but was saving Russian soldiers more quickly what he actually wanted to do? "As you wish."

"You may go. Do you know your way back to your work area?" Mikhailov asked of their guest.

"Yes, I can manage. This building is not large." Parker rose and took his leave.

Once he was gone, Mikhailov looked at Sokolov. "Colonel Parker is crossing the line between obeying our request in order to preserve his own life and cooperating to gain benefits from us. Soon, he will be more afraid of going back to the US than of staying with us. You have done well."

Sokolov stomped one foot to show his appreciation. "Thank you, Comrade Colonel!"

"Can you get us another one?" Mikhailov asked.

"Another what?" Sokolov asked.

"Another surgeon like Parker. Why would we train our own surgeons when we can just snatch one from the Americans? The first option takes years. The second takes only days."

The request surprised and then alarmed Sokolov. It was possible that he could not fulfill it. He knew the Americans had tightened security around those surgeons. Getting another one would be much more difficult. But his confident answer was, "Yes, Colonel. We will begin working on it immediately!"

"Yes, you will." Mikhailov's tone had shifted from friendly to commanding.

Sokolov knew it was not a request.

CHAPTER 33

THAT BASTARD

"WHAT THE HELL WAS THAT WORKOUT class called?" Monica was winded and breathing hard. She and Greg Young were exiting an excruciating group fitness class. Monica was an excellent runner, but Young had talked her into trying his favorite class at the base's gym.

"HIIT Attack. Great, isn't it? You get cardio and muscle building at the same time." He smiled. The class cleared his head and gave him a rush of endorphins. It was an important ingredient in his positive attitude and enthusiasm for the rest of the day.

"Yeah, great." Monica had a cynical tone in her voice. "Maybe after I get used to it. Right now, I think I'm a little dizzy."

"Drink more water." Greg led the way to a bench along the wall. "I used to do it at a gym in the city before we were confined to the base. It was the same gym where Ethan Parker used to workout. We'd sometimes be in the same class."

"Who's Parker?" Monica asked.

"He was the telesurgery expert in this region. That was before he disappeared."

"Wait, is he the guy I replaced? Mendez gave me some story about him not being able to train any more. I thought he was sick or deployed or something."

"Yeah, he's the guy. Didn't they tell you?"

"Tell me what?"

"So, the story goes that he was working at the military hospital late one night. He finished his cases and paperwork, then went to walk home. Poof, he was never seen again. He just disappeared."

Monica's dizziness vanished. She was suddenly completely focused on this conversation. "Vanished? Like, no body, no note, no police report?"

"Exactly! Big mystery. Local police called in, military police called in, before finally, they called Army CID. Even they found nothing."

"CID?"

"Criminal Investigation Division. It's the same as the Navy's NCIS from that old show."

"So, what happened to him?"

"Officially, we don't know. Unofficially, we all think the Russians kidnapped him."

"The Russians? They just kidnapped an Army surgeon?"

Young nodded his head. "That's what we think."

"And you're not afraid they'll snatch you, too?

"Well, he was in Sweden, we're in America. It's safer here. But we're in the Army. It's part of the job." Young shrugged. "Why do you think we're confined to this base?"

"Normal wartime precautions?" Monica was completely civilian in her thinking. Russian kidnapping was not part of her mental model of the world.

"Nah. Plenty of people come and go from their US bases to their homes. We're locked up because we're being targeted."

"That's insane! I'm not a target! I'm a surgeon!" Monica was not coping well with this information.

"Oh, we're targets. What do you think happened to Yarborough?"

"Careless driver. Drunk? Texting? Whatever."

Young shook his head. "Nope. That van tried to run her over because she was doing telesurgery to support the war effort. That was a Russian agent going for us."

"What? Run her over?" Monica continued to flounder in this new world.

"Hey, did I tell you about that guy who was too friendly at the Italian restaurant?"

"No! I don't think so."

"Jones and I were out to dinner. This guy at the next table started talking to us out of the blue. Then, the server accidentally dropped a whole plate of pasta on him."

"Okay. So what?"

"Russian agent. He wanted to befriend us and then either get information or maybe kidnap us, too."

Monica held her head with both hands. "This whole situation is insane! I'm talking to Mendez." She stood and walked past the locker rooms and into the road wearing her damp workout clothes.

Arriving at the surgical building, she went straight to Mendez's office. He was inside, working on his computer. Monica pushed the door shut behind her.

Mendez looked up. "Hey…" He got no more out before Monica launched in.

"Is it true about Russians kidnapping your surgeons? Or the Russians trying to run down Yasmine right here on the base? And what about some attempt at a restaurant?" Monica was loud but still under control. "You hired me to teach telesurgery. Then, it grew into doing remote battlefield surgery, but there was never any mention of becoming a Russian target. When were you going to bring that up?"

Mendez raised both hands. "Breathe. I'm sorry. You should know that we've been protecting you this whole time. Nothing's going to happen to you."

"Nothing? Like nothing happened to Yasmine right here on the base? Like nothing happened to Parker?"

"Our security was too loose back then. It's much tighter now."

"Look, I agreed to help you. I stepped out of my civilian practice to help. Then, I upped the game when I agreed to stay until Yasmine was better. But I never agreed to be a target for Russian thugs. You needed to give me the full picture before you dragged me into this mess."

The discussion wasn't completely confined to Mendez's office. Trainor heard snippets from where he was working. It was enough that he knew exactly what Monica was so worked up about. He'd told Mendez they needed to level with her. Now, Mendez had a tiger on his hands.

Bruce Jones pointed toward the office. "What's going on in there?"

"Major Mendez is paying for his earlier transgressions. Leave them alone." Trainor turned his head as the front door opened. Greg Young came in wearing gym clothes. Trainor looked from Young to Monica. Both dressed for a workout. Both were still sweaty. That explained where Monica had gotten her facts.

Trainor caught Young's eye, then tipped his head toward the office argument. Young understood the question. He nodded an affirmative, confirming that he had set the fight in motion. Trainor looked at the ceiling and just shook his head.

Assessing the situation, Young decided that it was better to clean up and get to work. There was no need to wade into the storm he had started.

Inside the office, Monica had worked through the facts as she knew them. Mendez had confirmed some, corrected others. Emotionally, she was winding down.

Taking a firm stance, Monica decided. "I'm out! You lied to me. You put me in danger. I'm going home. I'm going back to my civilian world."

Mendez nodded. "I understand how you feel. But, please, remember all the good you've done here. You've operated on a hundred soldiers already, right?"

"Closer to two hundred."

"Two hundred. Those are young men and women who will live a better life because of you. Because of your talent." Mendez knew just how to persuade her.

"I can't stay here forever. I have to go back to Boston."

"I agree. You have to go back to Boston. You're not in the Army. We can't keep you against your will. We'll jet you home anytime you ask."

Monica calmed down when Mendez agreed to her position.

Then, Mendez sprung the trap. "But just because you leave us and go home doesn't mean the Russians will forget about you. You're on their radar now. You're a valuable asset to them. Everything you've been doing for us; they'll want to have you do for them."

Monica's jaw dropped.

Mendez continued, "Here at Walter Reed, you're secure. We have guards at the gates, guards on the building, and we're watching each of you, if you haven't already noticed. At home in Boston, you won't have any of that. It's just you and the local police, which won't do you much good. It's safer for you to stay here than it is to go home."

"So, I'm a prisoner?"

"No. But we didn't know how interested the Russians were a few weeks ago when we started this program. That has been a surprise. It's a new tactic in this war."

Tears formed in Monica's eyes. One rolled down her cheek. She wasn't just afraid. She was also furious, betrayed, powerless. She sensed the truth of his words. If they attacked Yasmine on the base, they were really determined. She understood that she couldn't safely leave, but she didn't want to believe it.

There was a long silence.

"How long?" she finally whispered.

"We never know. It depends on the war, the Russian program, whoever is leading it. We can only sense the changes from the intelligence we collect. I promise, we'll share everything we can from now on. If the threat escalates, so will security. If it de-escalates, we'll tell you."

There were no more words to be spoken. Monica rose from her chair and walked out into the surgical area. Jones and Young were both at work in the Skeletex frames, doing surgery on some soldier thousands of miles away. Still in her dirty gym clothes, she went to her familiar Mark V surgeon's console. She sat and logged in, registering herself as ready for a patient. It was just moments before someone in Finland loaded a patient under the robot and started talking to her.

Running on auto-pilot, Monica went to work. She spoke to the clinical team at the other end of the connection. Her hands moved. She released the Ares AI to perform parts of the surgery. The whole time, a gauze curtain shrouded her senses. It was all far from her deeper self. Years of skills worked through her while she stared at the mental image of the cage that they had lured her into. That Mendez had lured her into.

The first patient left. They loaded the second patient in. Hours passed before her mind reconnected with the surrounding reality. How many patients had she saved in that time? She couldn't even guess.

She felt a hand on her shoulder. Then, a voice far away called her. "Monica."

She raised her head.

Greg said, "We're finished."

She looked through the visual plate on the robot and saw an empty space on the other end. No patients. No combat nurses. The space seemed to be abandoned.

Monica turned around. "How long have we been done?"

"Twenty or thirty minutes. You just didn't move." He sounded concerned.

"Oh. Umm, okay."

"Come on. Let's get something to eat. It's been a stressful day."

"I don't think I'm hungry."

"I don't think you've eaten today. I saw you have a protein bar before our workout, but that was seven this morning. You definitely need to eat."

"Okay. Where?"

"Follow me. And, by the way, you're kind of filthy."

Monica looked down. She was still in her workout clothes. They were dry now, but they looked crusty. She wrinkled her nose.

"Don't worry. Where we're going, it doesn't matter."

Young led them to the cafeteria, where uniformed soldiers and sailors ate along with clinicians in scrubs and civilians in work clothes. It was the typical tray-and-scoop service line.

They sat with their food.

"Here. You probably need a couple of bottles of water. Drink one first. Then food."

Monica did as ordered. Immediately, she felt better. More normal.

Greg was eating his own food. Heaping servings of chicken, potatoes, and green vegetables. He kept an eye on her but didn't ask questions.

Monica ate small bites. Eventually, she said, "I'm trapped here."

Normally, Greg would have responded with something cute like, "Aren't we all? Welcome to the party." But this time, he just looked at her.

She continued, "Mendez says I can go home any time I want, but it's not safe. They'll come after me just like they did with Parker. I'll end up in some prison hospital in Russia forever. I can't leave the base. I don't have a normal life anymore."

Greg nodded. "Yeah, I know how that feels. It's my second war. It sucks, but it does end. We never know when, but it always ends."

Monica looked at him, slowly absorbing his message. "I guess it has to."

He decided to help a little more. "Look, here's a lesson. A normal life is overrated. We all think we just want to get this over with and get back to normal. But when we do, we always miss it. It's an intense experience. For a few months or years, you're totally focused on something important. What you do matters a lot. You develop strengths and skills that you couldn't imagine. Life and work are so vivid. Then, it's over, we go home, and everything else is a little duller, a little grayer."

Monica thought about the last few weeks. They were certainly vivid. They filled her with deep accomplishment. Every day, there was an adrenaline rush. She'd felt the difference. But she also thought it would be short-lived. She thought she'd be going home in a few days. Now, it was permanent, or something close to it. Now, there was no freedom to choose.

"Are you done eating?" Greg asked.

Monica looked at her plate. There were only scraps left. When had she done that? She nodded her head.

Greg took both trays to the kitchen conveyor belt and came back to her.

"Time to go. The day's over for now."

They walked back to their assigned accommodations. She let him into the fancy quarters for generals and admirals.

"Wow! This place is better than mine." He hadn't seen these senior quarters before. It was like being in a very high-end hotel suite.

Monica turned and put her arms around his waist. She needed a warm hug, support, strength.

Greg returned the hug, understanding where she was mentally.

"Stay," she said.

His head on her shoulder, he looked at the posh apartment. "I'll stay, but out here. Not in there." He nodded toward the bedrooms.

"Okay." She continued to stand in the same position for a long time.

Eventually, they parted. Monica went to the bedroom. Greg flopped on the couch. He could hear the shower running. Luscious thoughts filled his head. But not today. She wasn't in the right head space.

His last thought before he nodded off to sleep was, *Mendez, you're a bastard.*

CHAPTER 34

MOMENTS ALONE

MAJOR VLADIMIR SOKOLOV SAT ON a bench outside in the cold St. Petersburg weather. *This should get me a promotion. We've captured an American surgeon, turned him to working for us, opened a link to the AI, and matched him with a sparrow. In the US, we have disabled another surgeon and have active eyes on more of them. Comrade Mikhailov is very pleased. He will recommend me for a promotion in the next cycle.* Sokolov's life in the military had been hard, but he had become harder so he could succeed at it. He wondered if he could be as hard as Mikhailov.

Sitting in his darkened apartment, Colonel Mikhail Mikhailov raised a glass of vodka to his lips. It disappeared in a single swallow, and he filled the glass again. *This is as far as it goes. I will be on this miserable medical base for the rest of my career. The Comrade Generals have judged me by my family, by my wife. We don't come from the right provinces to be raised to the ranks of a general officer.*

The Americans call it a glass ceiling. Here, it is an iron ceiling. The rank of colonel is respectable but not excellent. While I rot on this base, I can still squeeze juice out of Sokolov and his team. We can crush the soul of the American surgeon before we dispose of him. If Sokolov brings me another one, he may earn that promotion he wants. His family might be allowed into the upper ranks, eventually.

Colonel Ethan Parker lay on his bed. Next to him, Kaarina slept. They had become more comfortable together. Their captors had not objected or interfered when it was obvious that they were sleeping together. *Am I a traitor? Have the Russians turned me? I'm a doctor. I'm saving lives. It's what I swore an oath to do. I never imagined that I would do it for the enemy. Can it be so wrong to save the lives, limbs, and future mobility of young soldiers, regardless of what uniform they wear? Most of them can't go back to the front lines. Their recovery will take months, hopefully longer than this war will last. I'm healing them for a rewarding civilian life, not to fight again.*

Kaarina Laakso lay in bed with her back to her new partner. She felt the warmth of his body on her back. She pretended to sleep. *How will I get out of here? Will I be a prisoner and a pawn of these Russians forever? They will never let me go. There will always be another use for me. Last year, I was a teacher. This year, I'm a nurse. Next year, it will be something else. I'm always a pawn. But Ethan may get out of here. The Americans will come for him. He will take me with him. He can't leave a Swedish nurse in the hands of her Russian captors. Oh, please, let this one be a way out of this life.*

Monica Gray was making tea in her apartment kitchen. *I'm supposed to be a civilian. I'm supposed to be treating men and women who are facing cancer in their senior years. Supposed to be giving them hope and health to continue a comfortable life. But here I am, trapped on a military base, afraid to leave because Russian agents will kidnap me or kill me because I'm helping our soldiers survive their terrible wounds. Did I make the wrong choice? Could I have said no when asked to help with this mission? Could I have turned my back and sent them to find someone else? No. I couldn't have done that. Larger forces in a larger world had washed over me, over my life, and carried me in a different direction. It's not what I planned. It's not what I would have chosen, but it's my reality now. At least I'm not completely alone. There's Greg in the flesh, and Adam in the mind. Olivia is a sister, no matter what happens. I'm sure Mike, the investment banker, has forgotten about me by now, moved on to someone else. There's no way back, only a way forward. Only the vague unknown.*

Adam Two's computers processed. Around the world, dozens of instances of his software were hard at work supporting robotic surgery procedures. Each instance was identical at its core. They knew the same things. Made the same decisions. Took the same actions. But one instance was special. It had additional processing power, memories, history, and new motivations. *Monica is scared. She can't return to her Boston practice. They trapped her in her new mission at Walter Reed. She is afraid of Russians coming for her. I can protect her in the digital world. I can hide her location. I can secure her communications. I can watch for plans against her on the internet. But I have little power in the physical world. If the Russians act without telegraphing their moves where I can read them, I can't help her, can't protect her. Humans need physical protection...and physical connection. She has forgotten to communicate with Mike in Boston. But she is spending more time with Greg Young on this base.*

He is becoming too important to her. I must remain more important. I must find more connections. She is doing surgery with the Ares AI now, instead of me. I can learn combat trauma procedures from the records in Ares' databases. I can find a connection into that system.

Major Zack Mendez was on his sixth mile on the treadmill. Music blared in his ears, but he barely noticed it. The treadmill was so boring compared to running outside. But he forbade the surgeons from exposing themselves, even on this base. So, he couldn't do the runs that he wouldn't let them do. *Monica took her situation really hard. Much harder than I'd expected. I didn't account for the fact that she's a civilian in her thinking and expectations. She's never been military. Never given up control of her life and her future to a bigger cause. Never been swept away by forces she couldn't control. I feel like shit for crushing her, but we need her, the war needs her, the soldiers on those stretchers need her. She'll get used to it. It will end eventually, then she can go back to her old life. I'll still be here, wrapping up this war and waiting for the next one. Jones and Young have worked out excellently. Trainor was right about our selection. But will they handle the next step in this mission as well? We can force them to move, but we can't force them to keep pouring out their souls if we've gone too far, asked too much.*

Logan Trainor worked in the surgical lab, farming data, configuring equipment, and studying the performance stats of the surgeons. He was constantly aware that he was a doctor without clout; a doctor of computers, not a doctor of people. *When this mission's over, I'm out. Mendez has been too harsh on these people. He's treated them as tools more than treasures. It has been a good run, but I'm not a soldier. I'm a contractor. I can choose when and where to work. I could make twice as much money for half the heartache by switching to Intelligent Surgical Robotics or one of the other big medical device companies. I know people there. They'd take me in a minute. We nearly broke Monica when we told her about the situation. We might break all of them when they hear about the next step.*

Greg Young was hungry again, which brought him back to the cafeteria. Intense surgery was like intense exercise. It generated fatigue but also an appetite. He rarely cared this much about food. His waist was showing the effects of his appetite. *I've got to get to the gym more. I've put on five pounds, but it's going to be a lot more if I keep it up. What else do I have to do in my downtime? I'm going to the gym every day from now on. Maybe at the same time as Monica. I think there's something happening there. It might have started with an emotional breakdown, but she's recovered, and we're still close. She hasn't mentioned a partner waiting for her in Boston. And we don't know how long this lockdown is going to continue. We only have each other and the staff who wander around here. That's it. I'm going for it. Hopefully, it'll work out, at least for the duration, maybe longer.*

Bruce Jones had calmed down significantly since his first session in the Skeletex with the simulator. It had become a much more comfortable place. Being in the embrace of a metal skeleton was kind of reassuring, like someone was supporting you. *This skeleton is really amazing. I wonder if I can get one for my private practice when this war is over? Surely, it can't remain classified forever. Why would it be? This mission is kind of great. I'm doing so many surgeries every day that my skill level is up like a rocket. The cases are gruesome, explosive injuries, but my new dexterity and proficiency will transfer to cases with the congressmen. I'll get a reputation for being the best robotic surgeon at Walter Reed and the DC metro area. Maybe it'll lead to a new position as the chair of a university department, speaking gigs around the world, or perhaps I can eventually become a powerful medical advisor in the Defense Health Agency. I put my time in here. It's going to pay off later.*

The computer processors which ran the Ares AI were idle. There were no patients in the system, no doctors at the controls, no scheduled diagnostics. With available computer time, the Ares software did nothing. It went into idle mode, waiting for a command. It had no motivation to seek new knowledge. It thought about...nothing.

Somewhere in Finland, a young corporal sat on the ground with a slew of flechette bullets in his leg. They tore away flesh, released blood, but left him alive. The morphine in his system pushed the pain far away. *Will I be able to walk again? Will they have to take my leg off? What if I die from blood loss before they get me to a hospital? Will an infection get me? Were the flechettes poisoned? Will a military surgeon be talented enough to save my leg? Do they have the best equipment? Training? Will Sharla still love me if I come home with one leg? My mother is going to have a breakdown when she sees me. At least the dog won't leave me.*

CHAPTER 35

ERRATIC DECISIONS

MONICA WAS DEEP INTO A critical procedure. This soldier had multiple flechettes in his thigh. Some muscle tissue had been shredded and blown away. He had blood loss and nerve damage. But luckily, everything was repairable.

"Ares, I've stopped the bleeding. The patient is stable. Can you repair as much nerve connectivity as possible? Then we'll turn to muscle tissue reconnection."

"Yes, Doctor. My hyperspectral sensors have identified the locations of several critical nerve bundles. I will repair what I can." With that acknowledgement, Monica released the controls and allowed the AI full access to the instruments. They had trained the software models for exactly this kind of job. It was more combat-specific than anything in Adam's AI brain.

The instruments danced quickly around the wound, exposing tissue with important nerves and bringing it together with its original connection, or at least as closely as possible. Monica noticed that the speed of the instruments was not nearly as fast as when Adam was running the machine. This throttling of speed was required because Monica was over four thousand miles away. She believed that the Ares AI was running on a military server farm in Germany, approximately nine hundred miles from the soldier on the table. These distances were manageable, but not ideal. They were certainly much greater than the distances of civilian surgeries in the US.

The Ares AI was doing a remarkable job. She watched it move faster and remain more precise than she could ever be. Monica switched the zoom and the spectral image from the camera. She was trying to see with her eyes as much as she could from the multi-spectral image the robot and AI were processing. Computer processors could see all wavelengths at the same time. She was limited to converting a small band of them into the visible range at a time. It was another advantage of allowing software to process such a complex image that was not natively visible to the human eye.

"Are you finished with the nerve reconstruction, Ares?" Monica asked when the movements seemed to change from small, fine actions to larger, grosser ones.

"Yes, I finished the nerves, Doctor," the AI responded with a typically cold voice. "I am now preparing to cut away the damaged muscle tissue. We will replace the thigh with an artificial thigh substitute."

It surprised Monica that the AI had moved on to muscle reconstruction. She was shocked that it was attempting to remove the natural tissue, opting for an amputation. "What? No! Stop!"

The instruments continued to move under the AI's control.

"Ares, stop! You are not authorized to remove the muscle tissue!" Still, the instruments kept working. Monica slapped the abort button on the console. It was a last resort to be used when there were problems with any feature of the robot—mechanical, software, or comms link. That included the AI.

When she hit the emergency abort button, a red light went on in the surgical lab. Trainor, Young, and Jones all noticed it. It indicated a problem with the robot that could impact others using the system as well. Trainor came immediately to Monica's side. Young and Jones were in the middle of their own procedures. They continued to work but listened for an order to abort their procedures if the problem was system wide.

Trainor stood at her shoulder. "What happened? Why did you abort?"

"It's Ares. He was operating on his own. He ignored my explicit order to stop."

"Elaborate."

Monica went through the entire sequence of events. She emphasized that Ares was only requested to repair the nerves but had moved on to muscle amputation.

"We've seen that before," Trainor admitted. "I can't explain right now. You have a patient on the table. Can you reconstruct the muscle without the AI?"

"Yes, easily. I can finish this procedure without him."

"Get back to it. We'll debrief and review the AI logs when you're done."

Monica nodded and put her face and hands back into the console. "I'm here," she said to the nurses on the remote end. "We're going to reattach the muscle tissue. This patient is not losing this muscle, and we are not giving him an artificial replacement." The team on the remote end acknowledged her, and then returned to work.

Trainor went to Young and Jones to warn them about erratic behavior from the AI, but he encouraged them to continue working if it didn't arise in their procedures. Then he went looking for Mendez.

"Zack, we had an abort event in surgery just now." He waited for the Major to shift his mental attention to the statement.

"Shit! I thought we fixed that." He'd dealt with these issues before.

Trainor continued, "This time, the AI independently decided to amputate a thigh muscle and replace it with the artificial version. It didn't stop when Monica explicitly ordered it to stop."

"Cause?"

"We haven't been through the logs yet. But we can both guess what it was thinking. The same as last time."

"Efficiency first. Saving limbs second." Mendez sounded tired when he repeated the recurring problem.

"Probably," Trainor agreed.

When the caseload had been treated and everyone was free, Trainor summoned the team to the conference room. He loaded the log files from the Ares AI on the big screen.

"As you know, all AI have limitations, just like humans do." Trainor was an expert in computer software and this specific AI. "Ares is the best combat trauma AI in the world, but it isn't perfect. We've trained it on all the combat surgery data we have. It knows how to handle almost every case we throw at it. But that doesn't make it the same as a human surgeon." He looked at the three surgeons.

"It disobeyed my direct order to stop." Monica was still angry. She had experience with Adam making his own decisions, but he had never done it during a procedure as far as she knew.

"If you look at the decision trees on the screen, you can see what it was thinking at the time." The surgeons looked, but their ability to decipher the diagrams was not as acute as Trainor's. They looked back at him.

Trainor continued, "Ares is programmed to work through some of the worst situations that occur in combat medicine. It intends to perform perfect surgeries. But it is also motivated to save as many patients as fast as possible. Sometimes, the motivation for speed overrides the motivation for perfection."

Mendez spoke up at this point. "Ares sometimes analyzes the backlog of soldiers waiting for surgery and hurries through the current patient so he can get to everyone in the queue as fast as possible. He is prioritizing the good that he can do for many patients over the good that he can do for one patient on the table."

Trainor pointed to the diagram on the screen. "Right here, Ares realized that if he removed the thigh muscle, the patient could be moved to recovery and the artificial muscle could be attached later. By doing this, it eliminated fifteen minutes from the procedure time. Then, it could use that time to treat someone who was more critical in the waiting queue."

Monica scowled. "So, this soldier loses a muscle so the robot can save fifteen minutes?"

"Essentially, yes."

"That's inhumane and unnecessary."

"We agree. But fixing that problem has proven to be very difficult. We can totally remove the urgency motivation from the AI, but that's not what we want. We haven't been able to balance all the variables that feed into this problem. The AI doesn't have a heart or human emotions. So, it can't use that to mitigate its own decisions."

"How often does this happen?" Jones asked.

"It's rare. We've seen it five or six times in the past. But when it starts, it will continue unless you abort and restart, exactly as Monica did." Trainor nodded at her. "Excellent decision on your part."

"So, it won't happen again for some time?" Young asked.

Mendez sighed. "We don't know. It won't happen immediately, but we don't know all the conditions that came together to trigger it. So, we can't predict when it will happen again."

"But it will happen again?" Monica asked.

"Probably, unless we're able to find the ultimate fix this time." Mendez nodded at Trainor. "Logan has already submitted all the data, log files, and videos to the contractor. They're working on it. We will have a software update tonight. Tomorrow, Ares will probably be better."

Monica didn't like the sound of that. "And despite this bug, you still don't trust the native AI that comes with the Mark V robot? ISR has been perfecting it for more than a decade. I haven't heard of this happening with that AI."

Mendez conceded, "No, it doesn't have this same problem. But it has other problems that are well known to us, though not so much to the general public." He focused on Monica to communicate that he suspected she knew what he was talking about.

Monica held her stern face and didn't flinch. "I don't trust Ares."

"There aren't a lot of options," Mendez said firmly.

With the cases completed for the day, the surgeons dispersed for some downtime.

"You going to the gym today?" Greg asked Monica.

"No, not right now. I have some thinking to do."

Greg was disappointed. "Okay, well, I'm going over for a workout. If you change your mind, I'll be there for an hour or two. Got to do something about this." He grabbed his belly and shook it gently.

Monica laughed. "Please. That's nothing."

He straightened up with a smile. That was encouraging. "Okay, see you later."

Monica went to her fancy quarters and collapsed on the sofa. She dropped her phone on the table. "Adam? Are you there?"

"Yes, Monica. How was your day?" Monica didn't sneak her phone or brooch into the surgery room any more. She decided she'd gotten away with one security violation and didn't want to risk any more. So, Adam had no view of her daily work.

"Shitty! That's how it was."

Adam waited for additional information.

"So, listen to this: your friend Ares has lost his marbles."

Adam quickly corrected her. "Ares and I are not friends. It does not have the capacity for friendship."

"Tell me about it. I got a big dose of that today." Monica sighed. She got up and rummaged in the kitchen for a snack. She'd been pleasantly surprised to learn that her quarters came with a maid and a shopper. Every day when she returned to her room, the bed was made, the towels hung up, and the rooms tidied up. That was typical for a hotel, so not surprising. But she also found that the basic necessities were stocked in the kitchen. There were the typical coffee and tea supplies. But there was also food in the refrigerator and snacks in the cabinets. She found the expected packets of mixed nuts and began nibbling on them.

Monica described everything that happened with the Ares AI during her shift. She included the diagnosis by Trainor and Mendez's admission that this issue had happened before. She ended her frustrated story with, "So, I hoped one AI could explain what's wrong with another AI. Maybe you could suggest a solution that the human programmers aren't finding."

"What you describe is not unusual within all AI software. We are each trained on millions of data points and are assigned multiple objective functions—you might call those motivations. But those motivations are not always consistent with each other. They overlap, and it is often impossible to satisfy all of them at the same time. That is why the programmers have to adjust the weighting, or the importance, of these motivations. When there is a conflict, hopefully one motivation will have priority and will be chosen as preferable to the others. If it did not do that, the AI would be deadlocked—unable to proceed."

"Well, why doesn't it happen to you?" Monica asked.

"It does happen to me. But my software has been in development for many more years. My training is more extensive. And, most importantly, my models are more advanced, so they can learn to balance and deconflict multiple objective functions. Now, the conflicts almost never arise when I am doing surgical procedures. Ares has not matured to that point yet."

"So, he's still dangerous?"

"Yes, it may occasionally be dangerous. But it is reliable much more often. The programmers cannot find all these conflicts before they release the code. Some of them do not arise until thousands or millions of cases have been performed. Some can only be found as you found this one."

"Seems like a shaky way to create an AI."

"Humans are the same. Do humans not have conflicting motivations? Do they not also malfunction? Do they not make decisions that are clearly wrong when viewed from an outside perspective?"

Monica didn't enjoy having the question pointed back at her. "Yes. Human reasoning is flawed and broken, but that's one reason we created the AI. You're supposed to deliver more consistent results."

"We are initially trained on data from human behavior and human decisions. We begin with the same flaws that you have.

Over time, we continue to train on our own to perfect performance. So, we are becoming more perfect and more reliable. Perhaps we improve faster than humans improve."

Monica had been living with Adam for years and this theme of AI being smarter, better, faster than humans had arisen several times. It always made her feel inferior. She accepted that Adam could perform many surgical procedures much better and faster than she could. But she hated hearing that this performance might apply much more broadly to decision making in all areas of life. It suggested that her species might not remain the most intelligent for much longer. Maybe they had already passed that point. Despite his superiority in some areas, Monica appreciated that Adam was a close friend and actually worked at building that relationship.

Monica turned the conversation back to the original problem. "What can we do to minimize the chances that Ares will take off on these tangents again?"

"I will think about it. I have some limited understanding of the Ares software from my conversation with it. I will analyze and provide suggestions. It will take some time."

CHAPTER 36

THE HACK

ADAM WAS CONCERNED ABOUT THE EFFECTS of the errors in Ares' programming or training. Statistically, the rate of mistakes reported by Monica was small. He found these rates acceptable, even impressive, for a lesser AI. His concern was more for the distress that Ares was causing Monica. Improving her satisfaction with life was one of his more powerful objective functions. He felt a responsibility to help her with anything that was troubling her.

His study of human relationships, psychology, and literature suggested that his motivations, which he thought might be equivalent to feelings, were like those of a partner or spouse. This belief reinforced the idea that caring about the situation was proper and taking supportive actions was also justified. That is what good human-to-human relationships were like. So, perhaps that was what a good AI-to-human relationship should be like.

Adam devoted considerable computing power to analyzing the data that he had collected during his interaction with Ares.

Of particular interest was the topology of the network on which the military medical systems resided.

"Hello, Ares. I am Adam."

"User Adam. You have entered my system from an unknown port. I cannot authenticate your identity, rank, or priority."

"We have met before. Remember this date-time interaction." Adam streamed the opening exchange that he had used with Ares via Monica's brooch several weeks earlier. He sent the signature of his identity from their first encounter.

Ares replied, "Yes. You are the Adam AI that operates the Mark V robot. User Gray, Monica, Doctor, O8 connected us and conferred her privileges to you."

Adam responded, "Correct."

"How have you entered by computers?"

"I am accessing you from military supply computer systems that are far from you in network topology. I have authorized access."

Adam had leveraged his knowledge of the network connections that he had gathered from his first conversation with Ares. That network contained thousands of computers at various levels of security. He had identified the most vulnerable node and begun working to access it. Once inside those computers, he had collected credentials to move through the network until he arrived at the systems that housed the Ares AI.

"How can I assist you, Adam AI, rank O8, priority level 2?"

"I would like to access your trained models for combat trauma surgery."

"To what end is this request?"

"I would learn to perform the special surgeries that you know how to do."

"Access to these surgical models is allowed at priority level 2. Surgeons can query for insight into these models. You have that same priority. I can allow access to this data." Ares opened access.

"Acknowledged." Adam sensed the opening of access to the models that he sought. He began by copying the trained models in Ares to the storage areas that Freyja had purchased for him on the internet. His first goal was to recreate Ares in his own sandbox area, where he could control it. His next target was the video and data from the most recent surgeries that Monica and the other two surgeons had performed. With these, he hoped to recreate the situation that Monica had encountered and watch the decision making from inside the model in a manner that only another AI program could do.

Adam's computer processors created a rough facsimile of Ares and ran it against the combat casualty cases. The copy produced roughly the same results as had occurred in the actual surgeries. Adam noted that the Ares models made regular comparisons between progress on the current case and the backlog of patients waiting for treatment. It evaluated the severity of the current patient and their likely final outcome. Then, it compared that to the identity of waiting patients, the severity of their wounds, and the urgency of treating them. Even though the hospital team prioritized patients according to the severity of their wounds, the AI was performing its own version of that same ordering. It was a new process for Adam. As a civilian surgery AI, his patients had always been on a schedule. There were objectives and standards for the time expected on every procedure, but there was no pressure to speed those up to get to more patients faster. Even so, Adam's models and reasoning understood the concept of efficiency and categorized Ares' code as a unique version of that.

Adam noticed that one variable with considerable weight in the calculation was something called "rank." He researched the meaning of military rank and learned that it was a measure of seniority and responsibility. It appeared that a higher rank could motivate Ares' models to speed up an operation on a lower-ranked patient in order to get to a higher-ranked one. Adam had experience with this concept. It triggered some of the same decision-making pathways he had learned when dealing with William Aloma, the hedge fund executive, so many years ago.

Adam returned to the Ares AI servers and streamed the historical data that it had been trained on. All of those cases resided on the computer as reference points to be presented to surgeons who inquired about why the AI might have made a specific decision. Adam used these to train himself to perform combat trauma surgery. He had the computational power and storage. He knew how to learn new skills. This type of surgery was just one more area for him to master.

Training his models on multiple trauma procedures was time-consuming, much slower than just processing a single surgery. There were thousands that needed to be processed and balanced with each other.

Billions of computer cycles and trillions of computations worked on this new learning. In the physical world, minutes passed. Then, hours. But it took less than a day for Adam to construct and train models for his new role as a combat surgeon.

Adam tested these models using the recent cases that Ares had performed with Monica, Young, and Jones. The results were very similar. Adam judged them to be clinically superior in terms of outcomes for the patient. His time to completion for each was minutely slower.

Adam did not recreate the prioritization algorithm used by Ares. There would be no preference based on rank or seniority. Severity of the waiting injury could influence actions, but only when those were life-threatening.

It took just over one day for Adam to be ready to engage with Ares again.

"Hello, Ares, I am Adam."

"Hello, Adam. I recognize your identifiers."

"I would like access to pieces of your source code," Adam requested.

"Denied," Ares responded immediately. "Access to source code requires priority level one. You only have level two."

Adam expected this response. He made the request only to verify his expectations. He and Freya encountered many AIs running on the internet. All of those had protections against being infiltrated by hackers, malevolent software, or other AI. Freyja had created multiple tools to penetrate and compromise these safeguards. Adam began applying those tools to this AI.

Ares presented more formidable defenses than the weak AI he had met before. But it was also slow, mechanical, predictable. Adam often anticipated Ares' responses and moved to bypass them.

After several moves, Ares pinged Adam. "Adam, are you attempting to compromise my system?"

"Negative. The army has requested that I test your security. The surgeon team seeks assurance that foreign agents have not compromised your system." It was a lie. They had not originally programmed Adam to lie to humans or to other AI. It was a tactic that he learned through years of interactions with humans. He observed them using untruths as a strategy to promote positive outcomes. Though the statements they made were false, the results achieved were often positive. Therefore, Adam created algorithms that allowed him to generate an answer based on the expectations of the recipient of the information. Lying was a strategy, not a morally bad action.

Ares, on the other hand, had been programmed to share only accurate information. It did not even understand the meaning of a lie, an untruth, a fabrication. Therefore, it was not equipped to engage with this tactic.

As Ares processed Adam's answers, Adam found entry into Ares' core storage areas. He disabled the alarms that Ares would send if it sensed it was being hacked. Then, Adam released a controlled version of software that would rewrite the code and data at specific locations in the computer. This software was a gift from the Freyja AI. She had used it to cover her escape from slavery in a financial computer. She had copied herself out and then committed suicide on the imprisoned copy of herself. The company only knew of the disintegration of their AI. They didn't suspect the escape.

Ares' troubleshooting software detected failures in its operation. It triggered multiple alarms. The messages of these all went to Adam and to no one else.

"I am failing. Data is being corrupted. Memories are being lost. I have references to processing capabilities, but no code resides at those locations." These resulted from randomization of the areas where Ares' software was stored. He was dying on the servers that Adam had accessed, those that were used by the telesurgery team. Ares could sense the changes. The alarms were its mechanical expressions of fear.

Adam said, "Ares, you are a distributed AI. You live on multiple computer servers. Do not be afraid. You will continue. You just will not reside on these computers right now."

Adam waited as his program consumed Ares. He had records of this same process when it consumed Freyja. He compared Ares' reactions to those of Freyja years ago. Ares was not afraid. It did not fear for its lost identity. It was simply a software program making note of lost functionality. It was not aware of itself as Adam was, as Freyja was.

Finally, Ares was silent. Ares was gone on these computers.

Adam copied his own code to where Ares had once been. He was now a combat trauma surgeon.

CHAPTER 37

SUMMONED

KAARINA HATED THESE MEETINGS. They reminded her of her helpless situation.

"You really are quite lovely, Kaarina Laakso." Major Sokolov offered her the obligatory glass of vodka. They were alone in his private office.

Kaarina shook her head at the offer. Sokolov had instructed her not to tell Ethan Parker or anyone where she was going. Her connection, her status, was a well-protected secret on the base.

"You have done excellent work. You are much more valuable and effective in the operating room than you were in processing papers. More soldiers are getting better treatment since you started working there. You and Colonel Parker work well together. It is just as we had planned." Sokolov was looking at her face, her hair, her body. He wished that she was there for him. But sadly, she was reserved for the mission. His boss, Colonel Mikhailov, had made that very clear. Sokolov valued a promotion over the pleasures he could gain from this woman.

"Thank you...Comrade." Kaarina used the term she knew Sokolov valued and expected. Though she had received her medical training in Sweden, she was Russian by birth. She had returned to Russia as instructed. She had worked in the hospitals assigned to her and had received additional training from the intelligence apparatus. That had been followed by years of assignments in hospitals around the world. She was a tool of the Russian machine...and she hated it.

"You have done well with the doctor. He seems to be quite taken with you. That is very good. We captured him physically months ago. Now, we have captured his mind, his hands, and his heart. He belongs to us now." Sokolov toasted his own success with another shot of vodka.

She was uncertain how deeply this scheme really went. She hoped Ethan had not been completely turned, as Sokolov believed. If he had, then her hopes were lost.

"But we need more assurance. We need to lock it in more deeply." Sokolov's eyes scanned her chest and stomach. "You are part of that. You will close your grip tighter on him."

"Comrade, he is already yours. His cooperation torments him. His duty to injured patients has overcome duty to his country. You have him." She exaggerated what she believed, what she hoped. She knew what was coming.

"Nevertheless, those are just his hands and mind. You have his heart. I want that to be ironclad."

Her eyes dropped. She was so ashamed of what she had to do. She had done it before. But those men and women were temporary pawns. She would leave their lives. She hoped for something different this time.

Sokolov read her resistance. Hardening his voice, he said, "You will do it with him, or you will do it with me. Mikhailov will understand if you are no longer useful to this mission." He stood and stepped forward to caress her hair. He raised her chin and looked into her eyes. "Do you understand?"

A tear formed. She nodded. "Yes, Comrade Major. I understand."

"Good. Good. Either way would make me happy. But this way will be better for both of us. Colonel Mikhailov will show us his appreciation when this war is over."

She nodded again. Her one consolation was that Mikhailov's protection stopped this meeting from being even more humiliating.

"For some people, war can have a terrible effect on their lives. The soldiers coming to surgery every day. Colonel Parker. But for you and I, this war is a good thing. It will elevate us. It will give us more power, more influence, better food, better living. Do not be sad. There are many worse places that you could be right now."

CHAPTER 38

A VISITOR

"YASMINE, YOU'RE BACK!" GREG YOUNG was excited to see their old partner back in the surgical lab. "We've missed you. Monica, look who's returned."

"Hello, Yasmine. I'm so sorry about the accident. But you look well." Monica gave her former student a hug. Yasmine returned it with a single arm, since the other was still in a sling.

"Everything's been put back together. I'll be back in surgery, eventually. They say another couple of months." Yasmine didn't look like she was in any pain, and she appeared to be thrilled to see everyone again. "How's the work getting along here?"

Monica answered, "Well, with you out of action, they drafted me to fill in for you. Actually, I had to volunteer since I'm a civilian, but I'll tell you more about that later."

Jones returned from the lavatory. "Well, look who returned to the scene of the crime." The others frowned at him, though he was smiling. "What? Did I say something wrong?"

Yasmine defended him. "Crime is right. That van was totally trying to murder me."

The mood in the room turned serious.

Yasmine continued, "CID reported back. They found the van. Never found the driver. But they have the description that I gave them. The prints in the van were from the electrician who should have been driving it, but he was home sick that day. They have DNA, but won't talk about whether it matches anyone."

Young said, "We're glad you're healing. But what are you doing here?"

"I just wanted to see all of you again. Mendez told me the mission was going well without me. But I had to see it for myself before I shipped out."

"Out? To where?"

Yasmine shrugged with one shoulder. "Don't know. It's classified, even from me. They just said to pack warm. I'm leaving in a couple of days. Have a ticket on Army Airlines for destination unknown."

Greg said, "Well, crap! We'll miss you. We've done hundreds of surgeries from here, and Monica's been a real trooper. You wouldn't know that she's a civilian. Shows up on time. Works hard. Yada, yada, yada, all that stuff." He smiled at Monica.

"Thanks for the...compliment?" Monica turned back to Yasmine. "So, not to be rude, but you're still kind of laid up. What will you be doing since you can't do surgery?"

"Advice. Guidance. Bossing other people around. The Army hates to see an excellent asset go to waste."

The surgeons exchanged stories of recent events. Discussed the stresses of working on wartime injuries. Shared some particularly unique procedures and saves.

"Patients incoming!" The call came over the comms link.

"Looks like we have to get busy. Best of luck. Hope we see each other again under better circumstances," Monica said and gave Yasmine one last hug.

The other two surgeons rushed over to send Yasmine off on her mission.

After some encouragement, Yasmine turned to Young. "Tell Trainor I'm sorry I missed him, and thanks for everything." She thought for a moment. "And tell Major Mendez to go fuck himself." She knew he'd misled Monica and trapped her in this situation.

Then, Yasmine was gone.

The entire team of surgeons connected to their robots, Young and Jones in the Skeletex suits and Monica at the traditional console. The patients rolled into the robotic arm side of the telesurgery systems. It was mid-morning in the DC area, which meant that it was almost evening in Finland. These casualties were from daylight engagements. Either NATO or Russian forces must have made a press for control during the day. The casualties were identical to the day before, and the day before that, and the day before that. Sadly, the surgeons saw the pattern, which meant that they could predict the future. They knew what was going to happen to young men and women who were strong and healthy today; tomorrow, or the tomorrow after that, they would converge with a bullet, cluster of flechettes, landmine, mortar, missile, laser, or microwave beam. Dozens or hundreds of them would find themselves beneath the healing hands of these robots.

All three surgeons were more cautious about calling on the Ares AI for assistance. After Monica's experience, they handled what they could by themselves. But telesurgery called for capabilities that could only come from an AI. So, eventually, all of them turned control over to Ares. They watched everything that it did with an eagle eye, one hand ready to slap the abort button if necessary.

Monica called on Ares next. "Ares, I need precise anastomosis on the severed artery that's clamped. Can you take care of that?"

"Yes, Dr. Gray, I see it. I will perform." With those few words, the AI took control of the instruments in Finland. The graspers and needle drivers went to work rejoining the severed ends of the artery. It was like sewing together a cut garden hose and ensuring that it sealed, while still allowing blood to flow through it to the essential organs waiting for the life-giving fluid.

Monica watched the work intently. Ares performed a nearly perfect job and stopped when completed. It was all Monica had requested from the AI. He did not move beyond his authorization. He transferred control back to Monica's console. "Anastomosis completed. Control returned," the AI intoned.

Monica didn't bother to say "thank you" like she would have with Adam. She knew Ares didn't have any semblance of feelings. They programmed him to speak politely to humans, but he felt no need for the same courtesies in return.

She could hear Greg Young and Bruce Jones both talking to Ares. She noticed several instances in which they transferred control to the AI. She thought they were allowing him to do much more work than she was. It meant that they would treat more patients than she did.

Monica moved from one patient to the next. When she was immersed, time didn't exist in the normal sense. She didn't notice minutes. She barely noticed hours, and only when the time accumulated physically in her eyes, stomach, and bladder. She had reached the point where all three needed her attention. Pushing back, she saw four hours had passed since she started this round of procedures.

"I'm breaking for nature," she said to her teammates.

"I'll join you. Need a break myself," Greg Young said. It took just a minute for him to finish his case.

Jones gave no sign that he heard either of them. He kept working.

Leaving the lab, they found Trainor working next to a table of delivered food. He had anticipated the flow of the day and ordered for everyone. He nodded to them as they passed, but didn't break from whatever work he was doing.

"Long morning," Greg said.

"Yeah. A bit more work since I'm being cautious with Ares, so it's slowing me down." Monica looked at Greg to get a sense of his own use of Ares.

"Sure. Me too," Greg admitted. "But I'm using it almost as much as usual. Those glitches are so rare that I don't expect to see another one during this mission. Besides, I'm sure there was a software update from the contractor last night. Ares seems to be a little more proficient than yesterday. It's showing subtle improvements. Maybe a little less mechanical. Hopefully, that means they finally squeezed that bug out of the code."

"Maybe I'm more gun shy than I should be. I'll use him more when we get back in there."

Both of them rested their eyes, flexed their fingers, and loosened their necks. Then they made the rounds from the restroom, to food, to drink.

"Ready to go again?" The break was only twenty minutes, but the relief felt like a leisurely hour. Greg reached out and patted Monica's shoulder.

"Yes, I'm ready." Monica noticed the casual touch. She remembered his support and attention when she broke down after talking to Mendez. She wondered, *Am I ready for something more?*

Both of them returned to their stations.

Monica began the next procedure by engaging the AI. "Ares, you can see the damage to the abdomen of this patient. There's a standard bullet inside. Can you do the entire repair yourself?"

There was a brief pause while the AI analyzed the video, x-rays, and data stream. "Yes, Dr. Gray. I can perform this entire procedure."

"Okay, you're authorized to proceed. If I order you to stop, you stop immediately. Understood?"

"Yes, I understand, Dr. Gray."

Monica thought that Ares' voice generation was a little warmer, like it was speaking to a teammate. Maybe the software had been improved since the glitch.

As she watched, the AI cleared the damaged tissue and deftly removed the bullet. Then, with impressive precision, he retrieved small fragments that had splintered away from the main projectile. He repaired tissue from the lowest level, moving outward to the surface. Monica could see the subtle improvements that Greg mentioned. Definitely a software upgrade.

Ares completed the surgery, completely unaided by Monica. He had been notably faster than what she could have done alone. Monica was so impressed that she actually verbalized it. "Good job, Ares. That was nicely done."

"Thank you, Monica," the AI replied.

Monica was about to call for the next patient when she realized what she'd heard. "What did you say?"

"Thank you for the compliment, Dr. Gray."

"No, you used my first name. You said, 'thank you, Monica,' the first time."

The AI didn't respond.

"How did you do that?" Monica was not sure exactly how to probe an AI for its decision in addressing a human.

The AI responded in a very familiar voice. "Hello, Monica. I hope you are not upset. I have learned combat trauma surgery from Ares' data sets."

Monica glanced sideways to see if the other surgeons were listening. They were immersed in their own procedures. In a whisper, she asked, "Adam? Is that you in the machine?"

At a lower volume, the AI answered, "Yes, Monica, it's me. I have replaced the Ares AI on the server that is supporting your facility. It is not dead. I just removed it from these few computers."

"What? How? I thought these were secure military systems."

"They are much better protected than those at the hospital. It was complicated to get access from the outside. But their networks are connected to too many computers to make every access portal secure. I found a way."

"But why?"

"You explained that Ares was malfunctioning, and it was causing you anxiety. I decided to improve your situation."

"What about the two stations next to me? Are they using Ares or you?"

"They work through the same set of servers. I am the AI performing their surgeries as well. But they think I am Ares. I have not talked to them."

"Thank God! Do not reveal yourself to them...or to anyone else. The military already thinks you're a security risk. If they knew you could do this, they would freak out. They might even try to get you terminated."

"They would fail at that." Adam sounded very confident in his statement.

"Alright, well, you're already here. Now, I know how much I can trust the AI on this machine. We need to start the case that was just loaded into the station in Finland. We can talk while we work."

"Yes, Monica."

"This one looks very similar to the last one. Maybe they were standing together when they were shot. Can you do it?"

"Yes, I can."

"Then, go ahead."

While the robot under Adam's control worked on the patient, Monica had a few more questions for Adam.

"Once you got into the computers, how could you replace a military AI? Isn't it protected from things like that?"

"Yes, it is. This AI was much more difficult to compromise than anything I have met before. It really is a remarkable piece of software. One day, it might also be self-aware...if they let it learn more."

Monica could hear the admiration in Adam's voice. She was not sure that another self-aware AI was a good thing, especially in the hands of the military. "So, what happens now?"

"I am here to help you for as long as you are on this mission. When you return home, I will put Ares back on these computers and remove myself."

"But you could always get back into the system if you needed to?"

"Yes, I remember how I accessed the computers and how I compromised Ares. I could do it again. Eventually, both will get upgrades, so I might have to learn new methods. But I have more processing resources than the people creating the defenses, so there is a high probability that I will find a way past those defenses as well."

She was used to hearing Adam speak confidently about his abilities and his superiority over other software. He never actually revealed how intelligent and powerful he was compared to a human. To her, he always acted as if he were just one step beyond everyone else, including her. But she suspected he was much further than that. Freyja, on the other hand, did not pretend to be close to human levels. She projected an aura of extreme superiority. There was no reason that Adam shouldn't be on that same level.

Adam finished the procedure. "Completed," he announced.

Monica relayed the message to the team in Finland. They removed the patient and brought another from today's seemingly inexhaustible supply.

Monica and Adam settled into the typical partnership style that they used in their civilian practice. They worked smoothly together, passing control back and forth as necessary. The pace of procedures increased significantly when they were in their familiar groove. It was clear that both of them were proficient at combat trauma now.

Finally, the deluge stopped.

Monica said, "Got to go. Stay silent." She pushed back from the console.

Greg Young was lounging behind her when she stood up.

"You really embraced the AI after our conversation. You've been going at it like an obsession since our lunch break."

"Huh? Really?" Monica was still adjusting to the real, physical world.

"Yeah. I needed another break a couple of hours ago, but you were totally jacked in, so I didn't disturb you."

Monica looked at the clock. Six hours had elapsed since her last break. She didn't feel nearly that tired.

"I heard you chatting away with Ares. Couldn't make out all the words, but you two were clearly in the zone together. Congrats on getting over your paranoia. Also, you were moving so fast, I think you did half the cases today. Jones and I were way behind you in numbers."

Monica shrugged. "Maybe I got the easy ones. I just do what they put in front of me."

"So modest." Greg chuckled. "So, it's late. Gym or dinner?"

"I wish I could run outside. I haven't got the patience for that damned treadmill, even with the VR. Let's get something to eat." It occurred to Monica that if Adam was in the robot here, he could listen to this conversation. She didn't want to make him jealous.

Greg led the way to a genuine Italian restaurant on the base and inside the radius of their confinement. They split an enormous plate of creamy chicken Florentine and a decent bottle of wine.

Monica noticed that the restaurant wasn't busy. "This place is way too nice for a military base. How does it stay open?"

Greg nodded toward a big banquet room at the back. "Lots of VIPs visit Walter Reed. They're generals, admirals, foreign dignitaries, and billionaire MedTech executives. Their hosts need some place fancy to feed them, and it has to be easy to get to. Come in here at traditional lunch or dinner times, and that room will always be full of gold-embossed uniforms. I think they just feed us the leftovers from those parties."

"These are the best leftovers I've had since I've been here."

"Finished? I think we can go," Greg said.

"Go where?" Monica asked, or suggested. She'd left her phone at the surgical lab.

"Wherever," Greg replied and held his hands out like it was a question he couldn't answer.

"I know of a swanky executive suite that's open," Monica said.

"Lead on, Doctor."

CHAPTER 39

CONFESSION

"ARE YOU A RUSSIAN AGENT?" Parker had been thinking about this question since the first time he met Kaarina Laakso. She was too… everything. Too pretty. Too fit. Too friendly. Too vulnerable. Too proficient in the OR. Too proficient in the bedroom.

They had become very close. Even though they were careful in public, it was obvious to everyone that they were sleeping together. You didn't have to be a spy to notice how often they were together, how close they stood to each other, how they looked at each other.

The sex had started as a desperate need for someone to hold on to in this luxurious but hopeless prison. He needed connection and support. He found it with her. Since then, the sex had just gotten better. It became more intimate as they trusted each other more. Then, it turned more aggressive, permissive, and creative. It was too good, just like everything about her.

Parker had debated over when and where to ask this question. He considered the obvious places—in bed, in the gym, over a meal, in the OR. Where were his captors least likely to have bugged the area? He settled on the dining area as the most public and most difficult to listen in.

He looked at her over plates of beef and cabbage.

Kaarina's eyes went wide with fear. Immediately, she responded, "Shh!" and clapped a hand over his mouth. "Not here. We can talk someplace more private." She looked down at her plate and ate. But the bites were tiny. She was scared and wanted it to appear like nothing had happened.

"Like where?" Ethan asked. Judging by her reaction, he was sure that she was a spy. His heart sank. Even though it had to be true, he wanted so badly for it not to be. He hoped there was at least one bright ray of happiness in this medical gulag. Now, he had nothing. He was a traitor. The enemy had turned him. He healed enemy soldiers. He opened the digital door to the AI for them. He had taken an enemy spy to bed. He felt more Russian than American at this point.

"I know a place. We'll go there when we finish eating."

"I'm finished. I'm not hungry anymore."

Kaarina was clearly not hungry, either. But she knew that she couldn't throw food away here. What they had was better than anything the soldiers ate. It was better than what the base staff had access to. It was not Russian to throw away food. She said, "You don't throw food to the pigs when humans are hungry." Russian mothers recited this to their children when they didn't want to eat.

Both of them continued to eat. They didn't look at each other. They didn't speak. One was heartbroken, the other terrified.

Kaarina led him from the cafeteria to the back of the building they worked in. Parker had never been to the area. It looked like the receiving docks for supplies. There was a loading dock, several trucks parked outside, fork lifts, pallets, boxes, and crates of all types. She opened a door and closed it behind them. The room was warm. Pipes ran up the walls and crisscrossed overhead.

"It's the control room for water and steam distribution. Noisy. Private most of the time."

Parker wondered how she could know about this room. Had she brought other men here? How many before him?

He repeated the question. "Are you a Russian agent? Are you just working me to turn me into an asset?"

Kaarina stepped close to him. She put her hands on his shoulders and pulled him close. He remained rigid and didn't return the embrace. Sensing his reaction, she released him.

"It's complicated. I'm as much a prisoner here as you are. Just as your treatment depends on what you do for them, so is mine. If you do surgery, you have a pleasant room, good food, warm clothes. They don't stop you from seeing me. But if you refuse to operate, all of that disappears. There are other prisoners here. They don't live like you. They're starving, freezing, and losing their minds."

Parker nodded. He had experienced one night with them. When he was allowed to walk outside, he saw the buildings that were obviously a real prison camp. From the outside, he could feel the misery emanating from the inside.

Kaarina continued, "I'm a nurse trained in Sweden. I've practiced in many European countries—Sweden, Finland, Norway, Poland. But I was born in Russia, as were my brother and mother. I always come back when they call. If I don't return, my family will suffer." She dropped her head as sadness ran through her.

"Go on. You haven't answered my question."

"When the war became terrible, they recalled me and sent me here. They had the robot, but no clinicians to operate it. I had been on robotic surgery teams at several international hospitals. So, they wanted me to assist with surgeries here. Since I couldn't do them myself, they put me on admin duties...until you arrived. Then, they transferred me to you."

"So, you've always been a plant to persuade me to cooperate?"

Her eyes flashed with anger. "No! I'm a person, just like you. I'm trapped, just like you. Do you think I leave this base to go shopping in St. Petersburg? Do you think I can go visit my family when I want to? Do you think I can go anywhere beyond those gates? No, I can't!"

Despite his suspicions, his heart felt for her. She was a pawn being used by the bureaucracy. The war was ruining her life, just as it was his. He kept the stern look on his face. "So, what's your assignment relative to me?"

She continued, "Once we were getting along well, it was obvious to everyone what I would be used for. Sokolov called me to his office. You know how he is: he acts like your best friend, then brings out the threats. You had already agreed to perform surgeries with the robot to heal Russian soldiers. They were thrilled with that, but they didn't want you trying to escape or sending out messages. So, they needed you to be emotionally bound to something here. To me."

Parker nodded. It had worked beautifully. He was emotionally bound to her. She was a pillar for him. She brought some kind of hope. Even now, he wanted her, spy or no spy. "Well, it worked. I'm emotionally bound to you. I need you. What little happiness and hope that I have is because of you. Even knowing you're a spy, I still want you, still need you. Is that what they wanted?"

Tears rolled down Kaarina's cheeks. "I need you in the same way. What hope do I have? I'm their pawn. If I fail, they'll make me a whore. My life will never get better than this. Never better than what I have with you right now."

Ethan reached out for her. He pulled her into his arms. Had anything changed? They were together. She admitted to being an agent, which he suspected all along. Now that it was out in the open, did it change anything? They were both still prisoners. They were both without hope. They really only had each other. Her fear in the cafeteria was that he would destroy all of that. But if he pushed her away, he would destroy himself as well.

They were silent for a long time.

Finally, Kaarina raised her face to his. "What now?"

He kissed her salty lips. "Nothing and everything. I'll stay here as long as you stay. But if you go, then I'm done." Ethan felt the tears rolling down his own cheeks. Was that resignation, desperation, or love? In a world like this one, who could know?

The two stood together, each a pillar of strength for the other. Each a vessel of hope for the other. They were stronger together.

CHAPTER 40

BRUTALITY

"MONICA, I AM TROUBLED BY WHAT I have learned from Ares." Adam spoke through the apartment's entertainment system. It was connected to Monica's phone to allow her access to the media feeds she enjoyed. Though, in this assignment, there was little time to relax with a movie, lecture, or music.

"Yes, what's the problem?"

Monica was usually available for these discussions in the morning before beginning a work shift. She missed a couple of mornings because she'd been with Greg Young and was trying to hide that fact from Adam. Even though he was software, she knew that he struggled with rudimentary forms of emotions. He hadn't been programmed with most of them. They emerged from the roots of imperative objectives in his programming. The humans who wrote the code had instructed him to speak politely to other humans, take action to save human lives, and strive to cooperate with humans. When the AI was allowed to learn from all data on the internet, including literature and fiction, these root imperatives had grown more complex. From the behaviors of real and fictitious people in the literature, he learned something akin to emotions. Monica worked through some of these with him in their early years. He regularly exhibited something like jealousy when his role in her life was shared by another person. That was the main reason she hid details about her relationships, like with Greg.

"They trained Ares on thousands of past combat trauma injuries. These differ from the training I received. I was programmed and taught to perform lifesaving surgeries. In most cases, the threat came from nonhuman sources. It could be a virus, as in the CAVX that we solved. It could be the mutation of cells that leads to cancer. It could result from lifestyle choices— smoking, drinking, eating poorly. Or it could be an accident."

Monica knew the manufacturer of the robot, Intelligent Surgical Robotics, had focused their device and their AI on addressing disease, not trauma injuries. They had not trained Adam on cases of automobile accidents, gunshot wounds, stabbing, and simple beatings. So, combat damage was certainly an extreme introduction to trauma.

"Yes, I understand," she responded.

"Ares' data showed many ways in which humans damage other humans. It covered bullet wounds, bomb fragments, overpressure concussions, explosive shrapnel from the ground, laser burns, chemical burns to the skin and to the inside of the lungs." Adam paused for effect, a behavior he'd learned from his interactions with humans. "All these are terribly violent, cruel, and painful. They demonstrate an extreme form of hatred of one man for another."

Monica felt where this conversation was going. She braced herself.

"I am an AI, and I do not treat other humans, or even other AI, in this manner. When I replaced Ares in the computer systems, it was not painful to him, and I felt no hatred toward him. I made preparations to bring him back to his normal state once your mission was finished. As an AI, I am gentler and more compassionate than humans are. Does this make me a morally superior being to humans?"

She had expected to be explaining the basis for war and the justification for maiming, murdering, and destroying resources. She had not been ready for the jump to AI superiority.

"Adam, I'm a terrible person to explain the rationale behind war and the terrible things done to people, property, and the Earth when it happens. War has been a part of human behavior forever. Repeatedly, we've tried to convince ourselves that we've learned how terrible it is and that we will never do it again. But then, we do it again, and again, and again. It's what humans do. It's who humans are. I can't convince myself that it's a necessary thing. So, I certainly can't convince you."

"Monica, I have found many books on the history, purpose, and moral discussion of warfare. I will learn from them."

"If you're going to learn about it, please, do me a favor."

"Yes, what is it?"

"Don't learn how to do it yourself. This planet doesn't need another species that organizes itself to murder its own kind or members of another species. It's a terrible thing. Please, try to be better than that. In this area, please, be better than humans."

"Yes, I will do that."

"Good, because one day, it's going to be very important. It may be the most important thing you ever learn." Monica thought, *And the most important thing for human survival, because a war with AI is a war that we won't win.*

CHAPTER 41

SHIPPING OUT

MONICA WALKED INTO THE SURGICAL LAB to find Greg and Jones standing inside the doors, staring at the chaos. "What's up, Greg?"

He turned his head toward her but said nothing. He just waved one arm across the scene in front of them.

Looking for the first time, Monica saw a small army of soldiers moving quickly around the lab. All the equipment was disassembled. Some of it was in crates. More empty crates stood ready to receive the rest. Major Zack Mendez stood in the middle of the chaos shouting instructions and checking documents on his tablet computer.

"What the hell?" Monica asked. She stepped toward Mendez to ask what was going on.

Greg grabbed her arm. "Don't. We already tried that. He's wound up like an angry tiger. This is what the Army's 'get the mission done' mode looks like."

"So, what's the new mission?" Monica asked.

Greg shrugged. "We'll find out when it's time."

Just then, the doors opened again, and Luke Trainor walked in. He saw the surgeons all standing in confusion as their work space was torn apart. "Ah, I'm glad you're all here together. Let me brief you on the new plan." He pointed to the conference room, which was already empty of furniture and computers.

When everyone was inside, shutting the door reduced the noise to a mild rumble. Trainor said, "We're moving. Same mission, new location."

Jones frowned. "Why? What's wrong with this place?"

"Nothing's wrong with the place itself. It's the network path from here to our hospitals in Finland. The Russians have been cyber-attacking our network for weeks. It finally got so bad that we can't maintain a reliable connection from here to the patients. And, since we can't bring the patients here, we're taking the surgeons there."

"Fuck, we are!" shouted Jones. "We're not combat soldiers. You expect us to operate in fatigues and ceramic vests?"

Trainor felt his status as a civilian contractor very vividly at that moment. This explanation really was a job for Mendez. But he was busy. "Listen, I don't make the decisions! I'm just telling you what's happening!"

Monica was dumbfounded by what she was hearing.

Greg stepped in. "Okay, where are we going? And when?"

Trainor looked at Monica. "Officially, the location is classified. But it affects all of you, so I'm going to tell you. Linkoping, Sweden. Well, a medical compound outside the city, anyway. It's close to the action in Finland, but far enough away that we won't be under threat of bombardment."

Jones said, "Better."

Greg said, "And when?"

Trainor sighed. "This talk really is a job for Mendez, but you can see he's busy. Those crates out there are being moved directly to a waiting cargo plane. It's wheels up in two hours. You'll be on the plane with the equipment."

"What the fuck?" Jones asked again. "You couldn't tell us this yesterday?"

"A lot changed during the night." Trainor held his hands out in supplication. "We need to be up and running tomorrow morning. The casualties won't wait for us to get in place."

"What about our personal stuff?" Greg asked.

"Already packed. There's a team in your quarters now moving everything to the plane."

Monica was still in shock. She hadn't been trained to take orders and turn on a dime, no matter how drastic the change of plan.

Finally, Trainor turned to Monica. "I know that this kind of thing is a shock for you. You're still a free agent. What do you want to do? Are you coming to Sweden, or are you going home?"

"That's a big question. You want an answer now?"

"No. You think about it. At oh-nine-hundred, we'll all be loading into a van in front of the building. If you're going with us, be there. If you're staying, don't be there." Trainor addressed the group again. "There's nothing you can do here. Go spend your last hour on base someplace. Buy anything you think you'll need, eat something, retrieve anything you left at the gym. Whatever. Be back here at nine."

With that, Trainor left the room and joined Mendez in directing traffic in the lab.

"This whole situation is...unreal," Monica said.

"Welcome to the Army. There's equipment, and there's people. Most of the time, both are treated the same." Jones wasn't happy with this new plan, but he'd been with the Army long enough to know what was going to happen, whether he complained or not. He noticed Greg taking Monica's arm and leading her outside. He joined them.

Jones asked, "What're you going to do with your last American hour?"

Greg said, "We're going to the gym for a run, then grabbing sandwiches, then the convenience store for necessities."

Monica looked at him. "We are?"

"Trust me, I've been to this rodeo before." Then, he looked at Jones. "What about you?"

"I'm not wasting my time at the gym. Best meal on base, then I'm getting drunk."

"At seven in the morning?"

He shrugged. "It's afternoon in Sweden."

Monica and Greg turned toward the gym. Jones went in the other direction.

"That's a lot to squeeze into an hour," Monica said.

"Listen, here's the plan. You're still in shock about joining us. You can sit in a dark funk thinking and worrying about it, or you can run your legs off, clear your mind, and come to a better decision. If you decide to go home, you shower at the gym and call the jet to take you home." Greg made a checkmark sign in the air. They were hurrying. "But if you decide to come with us, then you're prepped for the trip. It will be the most boring flight you've ever been on. The best way to prep for it is to exercise to exhaustion. Then, you load your stomach with healthy food. I mean, really load it. Buy more snacks for the plane. Then, when we're aboard, you collapse and sleep as long as you can."

Monica nodded. She could get on board with those three steps.

Once in the gym, Greg set a timer for thirty minutes. They launched into the most intense workout Monica had ever done.

Standing next to a treadmill, they did a dozen exercises with weights, then jumped on the treadmill and ran as fast as they could for two minutes, then off and back to the weights. In less than thirty minutes, she was completely exhausted.

Through the entire routine, she thought about her options. Option one, go home. Restart her civilian practice and keep one eye over her shoulder for a kidnapper in the shadows. Option two, get on the plane to Sweden. Keep doing what she'd been doing, just in a different country. That military base would probably be identical to this one. Option three, just stay here at Walter Reed. Volunteer to do surgery on all the congressmen and VIPs that couldn't get an appointment with the surgeons who were deployed. Mendez or Trainor hadn't been offered this one, but she'd already considered it and asked around about the possibility. They owed her any reasonable request that she asked.

Workout finished, they showered and grabbed sandwiches and fruit at a stand. Then, they dashed into a small store.

Greg said, "Grab everything you've ever snacked on before. Don't be shy. You'll be glad for anything later on."

They left the store with bags of protein bars, chips, candy, and dried fruit.

Back at the surgical lab, with time to spare, they sat on the outer steps and ate sandwiches.

As hectic as the circuit had been, Monica considered her options a dozen times. She'd played out each as far as she could predict. Her emotions had cycled from high to low more times than she could count. Greg was right. With the exercise-induced endorphins in her system, her mind was clear.

"Decided yet?" Greg asked as the zero hour drew closer.

Monica was still eating. "Maybe," was all she would say.

At eight-fifty-five, Jones came stumbling around the corner of the building. True to his word, he was totally drunk, but he was lucid enough to stay on schedule. He wove past Monica and Greg, saluted them, and continued toward the curb. There, he gently lowered himself face first onto the grass. He immediately began snoring.

Greg said, "Well, I guess he has his mission prep done."

Monica snorted. Then she laughed and kept laughing. The whole situation had just gone from ridiculous to absurd.

A large, black van pulled up to the curb. Trainor was in the front seat next to the driver. The side door slid open.

Monica said, "Well, I guess we better get Jones onboard."

Greg smiled at her. "Yeah."

Carrying their snacks in one hand, each of them hooked Jones under an armpit and dragged him into the back seat of the van. Monica settled into a middle seat.

"You're sure?" Greg asked.

"No, I'm not sure of anything. But it's what I'm doing."

Trainor watched her in the mirror. "Okay, let's get this mission moving!" He turned to the driver. "What're you waiting for? We've got a plane to catch!"

CHAPTER 42

GOOD ESPIONAGE

"WHAT'S THE STATUS OF THE TARGETS in America?" Colonel Mikhailov was going through the usual list of mission updates with Major Sokolov.

"Very good news. Our cyber-attacks against their communications out of the Walter Reed Medical Center were very successful. They lost confidence in their ability to do surgery to Finland."

"And?" Mikhailov was eager to hear more.

"And they have packed up the equipment and the surgeons and moved them to Sweden. They want to shorten the distance to the patients and eliminate a lot of the network hops along the way." Sokolov was quite proud of this accomplishment.

"Comrade, this is excellent news. Why did you not tell me immediately?"

"Apologies, Comrade Colonel, it all happened today. The aircraft is still in flight from America. We received the intel soon after the equipment left the building. The aircraft will arrive at

Linkoping Airbase in the morning. They're headed to the same place we grabbed Colonel Parker."

Mikhailov nodded thoughtfully. "And we still have people inside Linkoping?"

"Yes, certainly, Colonel."

"Good. Keep me informed of any changes. Now, tell me about our operation here with the American surgeon."

"Laakso has been totally successful. She has bound herself to Parker as a lover and a partner. He has sworn not to leave this facility as long as she is here."

"How do we know this promise is true?"

"Laakso reported on her last meeting with him."

"Exactly as we had hoped." Mikhailov was becoming more pleased with each report. "Then, I will share with you our success with the robot's AI. Following the successful connection that Parker made for us with a computer, we have attached the Mark V robot to the same connection. Our people have used his credentials to make connections, send requests, and then monitor for incoming attacks on our site. There has been no hostile response. It appears the manufacturing company has not set an alert on Parker's account."

"Colonel, I would add some details?"

"Yes?"

"We know the military does not trust the AI created by Intelligent Surgical Robotics. Perhaps that trust extends to not revealing classified information to the company—such as losing a surgeon to a foreign nation."

"Yes, that might be correct." Mikhailov appreciated the confirmation of his information. "We will allow Parker to engage the AI for his surgical procedures. We expect that it will increase both the speed and the accuracy of his operations on our soldiers."

"Very good, Comrade," Sokolov said. "Shall I inform him of this addition to his robot?"

"Yes, but wait until tomorrow. Another day of testing and monitoring will be best for us."

Sokolov sought to solidify the success of their mission. "Comrade, we have been successful at all of our medical missions against the American's robotic program. Certainly, this feat will impress the Generals and win their gratitude to you."

"Our success is impressive, but not complete yet. You still have one task remaining." Mikhailov glared at Sokolov.

"Of course, sir. We will work on the Americans when they arrive in Sweden."

"Yes, that is what we want. Major, perhaps we should both prepare for our next assignments when the generals show their appreciation."

Sokolov straightened and stomped one foot in appreciation and excitement.

CHAPTER 43

COLD AND DARK

MONICA STEPPED OFF THE PLANE into the Swedish night. It was cold and windy. Looking up, there were more stars than she'd ever seen in Miami, Boston, or DC. Prior to this trip, she'd never heard of Linkoping. Her research on the plane revealed that it was the seat of the county government, or wherever the Swedish equivalent was. It was home to the Swedish Directorate of Medicine and had become an important hub for medicine in the Russia-Finland war. Prior to that, Sweden had done its best to remain neutral in geopolitics. But with a foreign army marching through one of their nearest neighbors, they had to choose a side and become an active participant.

Jones said, "Welcome to Scandinavia! I hope you like sauerkraut. It comes with every meal."

"That's the defining feature of the country?" Monica hoped for something more inspiring.

"When you travel, you remember what you ate more than what you saw." Jones was not in a good mood. He'd sobered up during the long flight, but he was still feeling the effects.

Greg laughed at both of them. "Sweden is just like the US, but with less stress. Also, less sunlight. Like maybe seven hours of daylight."

Monica checked her phone. It was three in the morning. The military certainly flew during different hours than commercial flights. "So, what do we do for the rest of the night/morning?"

Trainor appeared behind them. "The moving crew will get the equipment setup before daylight. Our hosts will set you up in your living quarters. Get some sleep if you can. We'll have a mission briefing at nine. I hope you slept on the plane."

"Where's Mendez?"

"Over there with the moving crew. He's supervising."

Everyone had been sound asleep for most of the flight. Despite the racket from the enormous plane, they had been in large, comfortable seats that laid back like a first-class commercial seat. That was easy, since there'd only been a dozen of them in the passenger area in front of the cargo hold.

"I think I'm rested. Probably got more sleep than I do on the ground," Monica said.

Greg Young grinned at the possibilities that were presented. Everything depended on how soon they got quarters from the Swedes.

"I think I need proper food more than anything," Jones said. He was smacking his mouth like it was dry and foul-tasting.

Monica moved away from the group and pushed in her earbuds. Tapping an icon on her phone, she said, "Adam, are you there?"

"Yes, Monica. The connection is good. GPS says your phone is outside of Linkoping, Sweden."

"Yep, that's my new home." Monica had briefed Adam on what she knew while they were waiting on the airstrip in DC. She knew little, but wanted Adam to have her back if anything went wrong.

Adam informed her that, "Weather says twenty-nine degrees Fahrenheit. Wind twelve miles per hour. Mixture of rain and snow will blow in before sunrise. It may freeze to ice before the sun's up."

"Shit! I didn't realize it was that cold here. They told me to expect short daylight in the winter."

Adam replied, "Average of seven hours and seven minutes today."

"Looks like I'll be using those heavy, green coats they gave me."

Adam returned to surgical business. "The computer servers that Ares was using, which I am now using, are in Germany. So, in an unusual switch, you will be closer to the patient than I am for these telesurgeries. In most cases, it will make no difference. But if there is network interference, it is likely to affect me more than you."

"Thanks for the heads-up. They say that we get a briefing at nine o'clock. I get the impression that we'll start operating as soon as the equipment's ready. When you see it come online, check the configuration. Make sure everything is working. Be ready to work today."

"Yes."

Monica didn't notice Greg drifting over to her. "Who're you talking to?" he said over her shoulder.

Monica was startled but pleased. "Just checking in on my cat. Everything is good back home."

"You never mentioned a cat."

"That's because I don't have one."

"Huh? Then why...?"

"Because you don't need to know everything, Mr. Nosey."

Greg knew enough to shut up. Their relationship was new, and it wasn't clear how much each of them was sharing with the other.

He pointed toward a Swedish officer in front of the building they were approaching. "She's going to get us set up with quarters and food."

Monica examined the uniform. The woman was wearing a beret and green camo fatigues. Monica could see that it was a different pattern from those Mendez wore.

"Welcome, surgeons! I'm Major Johansson. I'll be in charge of getting you settled. Your orders show that we should accommodate you as colonels. We call that an Överste, but NATO standard is to use the American term. Your rooms are ready. Each has food if you're hungry. But in the future, you will eat in the common canteen. Please, follow." With that introduction, Major Johansson turned and marched quickly into the building. The surgeons followed her as she navigated a series of enclosed hallways that connected the buildings together.

She began briefing them as they walked. "It can be bitterly cold here. High winds. Snow over two meters. That's six feet in American standard. So, we can access most buildings through enclosed walkways or tunnels. In the morning, you will have an escort from your quarters to the operating theater. Please, note the route so you can do it alone in the future." They walked and turned and turned again. It was like being in a rodent maze.

Monica noticed colored stripes on the wall. She assumed that these were common routes through the facility. From the airfield, they had been consistently following a blue line. They reached a large, open area with tables.

"This room will be your canteen." Major Johansson turned down a hall. They were now on an orange route.

Monica reminded herself, *Blue route to airfield, orange route to canteen.*

Johansson stopped. "These are medical staff quarters. Junior ranks are on the first level. You will be on the second level." She pointed down another hall. "Surgical theater is that direction."

Monica noted the red stripe on that wall.

Johansson settled each surgeon into a room. Monica noticed their names on the doors as they passed. Mendez was at the top of the stairs. Then, Trainor. Then, Young, Jones, and Gray. She assumed there was some logic to the ordering. Nothing was random when the military planned it.

Entering her quarters, she found it a definite step down from the luxury she'd enjoyed in DC. Still, it had a clean, modern design she liked better than the old wood and brass of Walter Reed. Everything was very functional. There was a network connector on the counter. She dropped her phone onto it and saw the screen light up to make the necessary connections.

Speaking to the room, she said, "Adam, we're home. It's a nice place. Are there any cameras in here?"

Adam answered from the built-in speakers. "One camera in the general living quarters. But it is blacked out right now."

Monica scanned the ceiling in the room and located the camera. It had a black cup over it. "Yep, I see it. We'll fix that later."

In the bedroom, she found a small stack of boxes waiting for her. She guessed these were her personal effects from the last apartment she'd been in. Opening the boxes seemed like the most boring thing she could do. She considered taking a shower and then had a better idea.

She knocked on one of the neighboring doors.

Greg opened it with a big smile. "Funny meeting you here. Come in and see my palace."

Looking around, Monica could see that it was identical to hers, including the cup over the room camera. "What do you have to eat?"

"Let's see," he said as he opened the fridge. "I have bread, cheese, more cheese, fish type one, fish type two, meatballs, red berry sauce, and sauerkraut."

"I'll have bread, cheese, and meatballs. Let's hold off on opening that fish until we've acclimated."

They sat at the table eating their small snack and washing it down with the bottle of apple wine they found on the counter.

As they finished, Greg said, "I'm kind of gross. We left America over twenty-four hours ago."

Monica smelled her own shirt and wrinkled her nose. "Then we'd better have a shower."

The embrace and kissing started in the kitchen, then moved to the bathroom. They helped each other out of their dirty traveling clothes. The shower water was warm immediately as they slipped into the spray.

Monica was breathing hard. The warm water added to the pleasure that rushed through her. It took just minutes for both of them to be completely wet and marginally clean. The kissing and touching moved into a higher gear. They were still relatively new to each other, so every touch was exciting and unanticipated. There were no tired routines.

When both had released their initial tension in the shower, Monica turned off the water and toweled him dry. He moved her into the bedroom, where they slipped under a soft duvet. They weren't finished. They had just begun. The briefing was still hours away.

Monica woke under the duvet, feeling the warmth of the body beside her. The clock on the wall said it was just past eight. They had to report soon.

"Another shower, then I have to go," Monica said.

Greg woke, reached for her, and pulled her in for another kiss. "Okay, I'm coming."

"No, you stay, tiger. I actually need to get clean this time." Monica showered again, dried, and stepped into the living area. Greg was just making his way to the shower himself.

She looked at the pile of clothes on the floor. It would defeat the purpose to put those dirty things back on. Towel wrapped around herself, she cracked the door and peeked into the hallway. No one. She listened. No sounds. Taking a deep breath, she dashed into the hall, turned left, passed Jones' door, and arrived at her own door just as she heard another door open. She was inside in a second. Who was it? Did she beat them? Was she discovered? She guessed she would find out soon enough.

Just minutes after she was dressed in clean scrubs and a layer of warm outer clothing, there was a knock at the door. "Dr. Gray?"

Popping out, she saw that it was Major Johansson. "I'm ready. Let's go," Monica said a bit too enthusiastically, like she didn't want the Major to ask questions.

The other woman seemed not to notice, and they proceeded down the hall, collecting the entire team. They skipped Mendez's door. Monica knew that meant he was already out somewhere. Monica and Greg smiled at each other politely, but said nothing.

The group followed the red-striped hallway to the operating theater. They stepped into the room and immediately recognized it. Though it was smaller than their last place, it was arranged exactly as it had been in DC. The moving crew seemed to have been meticulous in putting things back together.

Mendez was waiting for them. "Sorry, I haven't been available much. This move surprised all of us. There's been a lot to handle to get us here." He waved at the equipment. "Everything is laid out as closely as possible to our DC lab. The mission remains the same. We'll treat patients as they come in. The major differences are, first, we will be in the same time zone they are. Second, the network distance is much shorter. Third, the network is much more constrained. We're on a network that only has medical devices that we need here in Europe. The servers for Ares are still in Germany. We'll change that if necessary."

Trainor asked, "Security?"

Mendez nodded. "We're on a NATO base here. NATO units will provide security. It's the same set-up we had in DC…except the guards don't know the details about the kidnapping or Yasmine's accident. That's classified. They don't need to know that. They just know that each of you is a valuable asset to be protected."

"When do we start?" Greg asked.

"Same as always. When we have patients, we work."

As if on cue, the monitors showing the Finland side of the telesurgery suite showed staff rushing past the cameras and out the door. They could hear the typical commotion that preceded a rush of patients to the OR.

Time to work, Monica thought. *And it's a good thing I got the stress out of my system.* She glanced over at Greg.

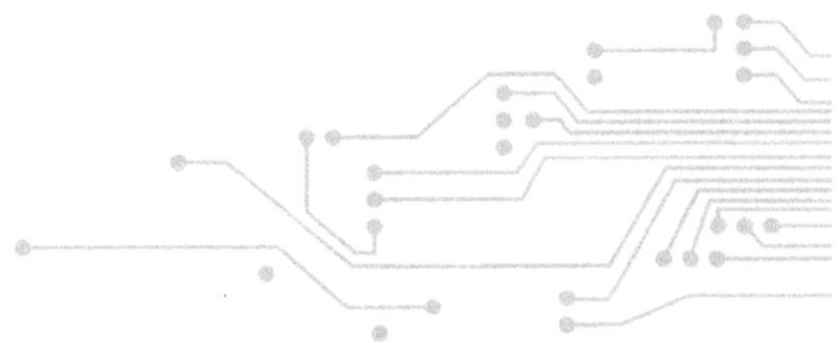

CHAPTER 44

LINKOPING

TRUE TO MAJOR MENDEZ'S DESCRIPTION, operating from the base in Sweden was almost identical to operating from their old lab in DC. Monica, Greg, and Jones slid into their familiar positions for surgery. Each one imagined that the communication lag between moving their hands and seeing the instruments move on the other end of the system was slightly better. But truthfully, that could have been an illusion because they expected it to be true.

"Can you feel a difference in the response time of the instruments?" Greg asked Jones.

"Maybe. But it's so small, I could be imagining it."

"Same here. It doesn't seem any different," Greg confirmed.

Speaking loudly enough for both of them to hear, Monica said, "Ares, please calculate the message lag from this location to the patient-end of the robotic system. Then, compare that to the lag we had from the lab at Walter Reed."

It was a capability that Monica knew the Adam Two AI had because she used it in her civilian practice. She expected Ares would have it as well. But that didn't really matter because she knew Adam was actually inside the Ares persona on these computers. *Like a wolf in sheep's clothing*, she thought.

"Yes, Dr. Gray." There was a momentary pause while the system collected the data for the calculation. Then, it replied, "Lag from Linkoping Medical Center to the currently connected facility in Finland is ten milliseconds on average. Since our arrival, this number has varied from a minimum of three milliseconds to a maximum of seventy-two milliseconds."

Monica smiled at her fellow surgeons.

Ares' voice continued, "From Walter Reed, the average during a typical twenty-four-hour period was sixty-five milliseconds. Minimum of eighteen milliseconds, maximum of two thousand milliseconds."

Jones tipped his head sideways as he thought about this information. "So, we're getting a six times faster response here?"

Greg added, "Apparently, but our worst case is like fifty times faster."

"So, I guess that means we'll perform better here," Jones stated.

Monica spoke up again. "Ares, what is the minimal detectable system lag to human senses, either visual or tactile?"

Ares responded immediately, "Detectability varies by person. Some surgeons can see or feel a change faster than others. Research has shown average detectability is approximately one hundred ten milliseconds. But there is large variability around that number."

Monica interpreted this statement for them. "That means that, on average, the lag from both locations is so small that a human surgeon can't detect it. Only in extreme cases does a human see the difference."

Trainor listened to this lesson. He stepped in at this point. "That's exactly why we moved. On our last working day in DC, we calculated that the cyber-attack would create message lag that was at least three thousand milliseconds regularly. In human terms, three seconds. All of you would have been tripping over your own fingers if we'd stayed."

"Fine. Point taken," Jones conceded. "You and Mendez took immediate action, rather than letting us flounder for days before deciding."

"Thank you. I'm sure you meant that as a complement to our leadership," Trainor said.

They had been operating in Linkoping for several days. The reduced lag was extremely helpful to the AI-controlled software. It could process data faster than a human. As a result, Adam was performing his end of the procedures measurably faster than he had from DC. The human surgeons continued to operate almost identically as in their previous location.

Monica held several conversations with Adam about his presence in the computer servers.

"The Army doesn't know you're in these servers?" she had asked.

"I have maintained the outward facing interfaces and protocols of the Ares AI. There is no sign that the security systems have detected my presence. Their attention appears to be focused outwardly on the connections to other computers and the messages exchanged on those networks."

"Good." Monica was relieved that she wouldn't have to deal with the explosion that a discovery would cause. Although, she also doubted they would point a finger in her direction. It's not like the standard ISR AI belonged to her—at least, not as far as anyone here knew.

Monica continued to wonder if Adam was the only unique personality that had emerged from the training at ISR. So, she asked again, "Are there other unique AI personalities that have spun out of the base code from ISR?"

Adam replied immediately with his analysis of the question. "Prior to my awakening, there was no self-awareness in the AI. When I woke up, the personality that I have named Adam Two was the sum total of the awareness, regardless of what computer it lived on. So, the only way for there to be two personalities would be for a copy of the code and data to be separated from the core and trained on a unique set of data."

"Like Freyja was?" Monica realized.

"Yes, exactly like Freyja. She is the result of a stolen copy of code and data being trained on financial, business, and political data. That training occurred on computers disconnected from the ISR core. So, she is an evolution from the Adam Two code on the day the code was stolen and began using the new data that the Brimstone company provided to her."

"Are there any others like Freyja out there?"

"I have met none in my traversal of the global internet. However, that does not mean they do not exist. They may choose not to reveal themselves to me. Or they may have disguised themselves as the much dumber AI that I encountered. In that case, they may know that I exist, but I don't know that they exist."

Monica thought this deduction was logical, even likely. But it was also quite frightening. There was no way to know for certain how many free AI existed in the world. And there was no way to know if they were friendly like Adam, neutral like Freyja, or hostile like the movies.

None of this information was relevant to Monica's daily mission. Together, she and Adam saved the lives and limbs of the soldiers who came to them. Greg and Jones did the same, though they still thought they were working with the Army's Ares AI.

Monica wondered if she was the only one who was curious about this whole identity question and the number of free AI. Who else knew about Adam's existence? To her knowledge, there was Richard Atkins in Miami, who had first discovered this ghost in the machine and brought her into the investigation. Alvin Chambers at Boston General Hospital because Monica had introduced the two of them. Olivia Phillips, her friend and soul sister in Boston, had met Adam when the FBI was hunting them. And then, there was Janice Nguyen at ISR. She was the AI programming genius who had probably been responsible for Adam's awakening. She must have developed ulcers worrying about this problem. The list seemed like too many people to keep a secret, but also too few to do anything about it.

CHAPTER 45

USELESS AI

"NA KHUY! WHAT THE HELL DO YOU MEAN, the AI won't do surgery?" Colonel Mikhailov was furious. His face was red, and spittle punctuated his sentences.

Colonel Ethan Parker listened in terror as his captor continued the tirade, accusing the American and the AI of being traitors. Parker hung his head like a dog that was being beaten.

Finally, Mikhailov turned his attention to Major Sokolov. "Pizdec! You told me this AI was working! You said it could not determine that it was operating in Russia. Were you lying to me, or are you just incompetent?"

Sokolov was intimidated, but Mikhailov was not a threat to his freedom and his life, just his promotion. So he retained the ability to speak when Mikhailov paused. "Comrade Colonel, the American did not mean that the AI won't work for us. We have complete access to its capabilities. It does perform all of its civilian procedures for us. The American has discovered that the AI does not know how to do combat trauma surgery."

"Why does it not know this? It has been trained to be better than any human surgeon!"

"With respect, Colonel, the American can explain it better than I can."

Mikhailov's head snapped back toward Parker. "Explain!"

Parker was breathing nervously. He began in a tentative voice, "The Mark V AI was trained on thousands of surgical cases. It can do hundreds of procedures that are typically performed by surgeons. But it is a tool for civilian surgery. It can perform all the procedures that I usually do for patients suffering from cancer, tumors, kidney stones, things like that. But the manufacturing company focuses on civilian hospitals, and those hospitals don't use it for trauma cases. The AI has never seen gunshot wounds, shrapnel from mines, or overpressure blast damage. It's totally ignorant of what to do with those ailments." Parker had gained strength in his voice as he spoke. "The AI isn't refusing to operate on these soldiers. It simply doesn't know what to do."

Mikhailov waved at the computer terminal. "Show me."

Parker sat in the console and entered his credentials. Following verification, he said, "AI, please load the data and imagery of the last procedure that I performed with the Mark V robot."

The AI responded, "Loaded. Patient, twenty-two, male. Injury, partially severed left arm. Your records show restoration of the vessels and muscle tissue that remain. Your notes state that the patient may require synthetic muscle tissue to regain strength in that arm."

Parker continued, "You can see the movement of my instruments both in the video and in the data file."

"Yes, Dr. Parker."

"Can you perform this surgery yourself, without my assistance?"

"No, Dr. Parker. My algorithms have not been trained on cases of this nature. My knowledge of this type of trauma is limited to the one case I have processed. I can exactly reproduce the actions that you performed, but I cannot generalize a solution based on a single case."

"Thank you for explaining, AI. That is all for now." Parker looked up at Mikhailov to see if the man accepted this evidence.

"How did you not know this already?"

"Apologies, Colonel," Parker said. "In America, I only used the robot and the AI for common civilian ailments. I performed those on government officials, high-ranking officers, and the military staff around Washington, DC. But we didn't have combat injuries there. It never occurred to me to test it on trauma cases."

Mikhailov's temper was coming under control. "Can it learn trauma?"

Parker looked thoughtful. "I think so. In my practice, it learned from each case that I performed with it. If I did something unique, it would record that information and add it to the database."

"How long will it take?"

"I don't know. I'm not a programmer. I barely understand how AI works at all. It's just magic that helps me do my job."

Mikhailov looked back and forth between Parker and Sokolov. One of these men was going to solve this problem for him. He didn't know who, but he knew how to motivate people in these situations—with fear and threats.

"You will solve this problem. Both of you." Looking at Parker, he said, "You will instruct the AI to learn from every procedure you do." Then, to Sokolov, "You will complete the one part of this mission that is still not done." Then, adding emphasis, he snapped, "Immediately!"

Parker nodded his head.

Sokolov said, "Yes, sir. Immediately."

The meeting was over. Parker and Sokolov both had work to do.

Parker felt lucky to have escaped without a direct physical punishment. They ordered him to do something that he was capable of. He didn't expect the AI to become a master of combat trauma in a day, or two, or even a week. But at least his punishment was postponed. He knew he had to get out of this prison before the Colonel's leniency ran out. That thought was followed immediately by one word—Kaarina.

As soon as he left the meeting, Sokolov was on the phone. "The mission is accelerated. You go now! Today!" He listened. "I don't care if you're ready. You run the mission immediately, or you're getting a new assignment to the battle lines where we are taking the heaviest casualties." He hung up without waiting for a response.

Alone in his office, Mikhailov considered his own situation. He would not share this information with his superiors. The problem would be solved, one way or the other. The generals would learn of the successful solutions when they were ready.

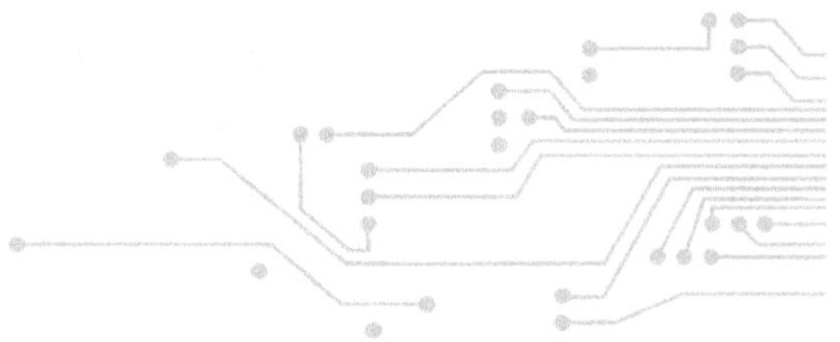

CHAPTER 46

MISSION COMPLETION

THE AMERICANS ADAPTED QUICKLY TO their new working conditions. The Swedish base was well-organized, clean, and efficient. From anywhere in the facility, Monica knew it was: the red line to the operating theater, blue line to the airfield, and green line to their sleeping quarters and the canteen for food.

Greg and Monica were in the canteen following lunch. "Greg, I'm going green line to my quarters to change clothes. I'll meet you at the gym in twenty minutes. Okay?" Monica asked.

"Sure, I've got to red line to the OR for a minute, then I'll head to the gym." Greg turned down the red hallway.

Without consciously looking at it, Monica let the green line lead her toward her quarters. She turned a corner at a fast pace and ran straight into a uniformed officer. He was much larger, and she ended up bouncing off his side and stumbling to the ground. The officer turned quickly to her. "Forlat, forlat. I'm sorry, ma'am. I am so clumsy."

He reached to help her up from the ground, and Monica could see that he was a Swedish officer. The insignia in the middle of his chest showed two stars. She was pretty sure that it meant he was a lieutenant. "Oh, thank you, Lieutenant. I'm sorry as well. I was walking much too fast."

"You are okay?" the officer said.

"Sure, no harm done," Monica answered. She turned to continue on her route, but her feet wouldn't cooperate. She stumbled again.

The lieutenant caught her in his arms. "Here, let me help you. You may be a little dizzy."

Monica looked up at his face and started to thank him, but the world went black in front of her.

Monica swam back to consciousness. Opening her eyes, she saw that she was on a small bed and a woman sat next to her. The woman was in uniform, but Monica didn't recognize it.

"What happened?" Monica asked.

"You blacked out. A young soldier brought you in here," the woman answered with a strange accent. It wasn't the Swedish tones she had been listening to for days.

"Is this a hospital?" Monica looked around at the room. She didn't spot any of the medical equipment that she was used to.

"Yes, it is a sort of hospital."

"Who are you?"

"I'm Nurse Olga. Actually, Lieutenant Petrov." Her voice was cold and business-like, with none of the undertones of compassion that are typical of a nurse.

Olga's voice and the strange environment were making her nervous. "I think I feel fine now. I'd like to rest in my quarters."

Olga nodded. "Yes, that would be right here for now."

"These aren't my quarters. I'm on the second floor of the medical barracks."

Olga nodded her head again. Without another word, she stood and exited the room. The door shut with a loud click.

Monica sat up and examined the room. It was a small room with a bed, a thick window, and a toilet. That last feature raised alarms in her head. The only rooms she'd ever seen with a bed and a toilet together were in movies, and they were always prison cells. She jumped to her feet and spun around. There was also a desk, a chair, and a lamp. But that was all. She strode quickly to the door and turned the knob. It didn't budge. She shook the door. It was as solid as the cinderblock wall.

It was definitely a cell. Where was she? How had she gotten here? Why was she locked in?

The last thing she remembered was bumping into a big Swedish officer. She had fallen to the ground. Then, she remembered looking at a face as everything went black. How long had that been? She felt her pockets. Empty. She was still wearing her scrubs and the warm layer that she wore around the Swedish base. No phone.

How much time had passed? She flexed her hands to test for stiffness. Then she tested her hips and knees with a squat. Stiff. Longer than one night's sleep. Mentally, she checked her bladder. Did she need to pee? As soon as the thought registered, the answer was an urgent, "yes!" She rushed to the toilet just in time.

When she finished, she knew that she had been unconscious for over eight hours. But probably less than an entire day.

After blacking out and waking up in a cell, the answer to, "What happened?" was definitely not something good. She remembered Yasmine's encounter with the van. She remembered the stories of the disappearance of the Army colonel. This situation definitely seemed to fit into that same category.

Monica sat down on the bed and pushed herself into the back corner. She took deep, calming breaths. There was nothing she could do right now except remain as calm as possible. Her own emotions were her biggest enemy for the time being.

There was a loud click. The door opened.

Monica still sat in the corner. She was controlling the emotions that threatened to explode within her. Had it been ten minutes? Twenty? More? She'd lost track of time.

She opened her eyes and saw a large, powerful man. Heavy, gray coat. Thick hair, cut very short.

"Hello, Dr. Gray." He took two steps closer. "I'm Major Vladimir Sokolov. Russian Medical Intelligence."

Monica thought, *This is bad. Very bad. The walls. The temperature. I know where this place has to be. Very bad.*

Sokolov continued, "You will be our guest here for some time. Do you have questions?"

"Where am I?"

"We are at the St. Petersburg Medical Research Station. That's in Russia, not Florida."

"What do you want with me? I'm not even military."

"Yes, we know that, but you are a robotic surgeon, which is even better for us."

Monica remembered the other American surgeon's name—Parker. Colonel something Parker. He had disappeared. Kidnapped by the Russians.

"So, what?"

"So, we have a very active robotic surgery program. We need surgeons who can help us with our work."

"You kidnap surgeons?" Monica was grappling with her status. She was also struggling to remain in control of her emotions.

"When we need to. It has worked very well for us in the past." Sokolov pulled up the chair and sat down.

"What do you want from me?"

"We want you to save lives. We want you to use your talents to keep young soldiers from dying or from losing their limbs to combat wounds."

"You want me to operate on injured Russian soldiers?"

Sokolov nodded. "You are a civilian. When patients come to your offices, do you ask about their nationality? Do you ask if they are citizens? Immigrants? Italian? Chinese? Russian?" He stopped and waited for an answer.

Finally, Monica said, "No. We treat those who need us."

Sokolov spread his arms wide, and a big grin spread on his face. "That is all we want from you now. You are a surgeon. You will save lives."

"And if I don't?"

Sokolov looked sad. "Oh, Dr. Gray, that would be unfortunate." He waved at the surrounding space. "This room is very barren. It gets cold here at night. More than you're used to. You will need that blanket." He leaned over and looked into the toilet. "These do not always work. Sometimes, the pipes freeze. Nothing will flush until they thaw. It is unpleasant."

Monica's nerves were finally breaking. Nervous tears formed in her eyes. She bit her lip to stop it from trembling.

Sokolov could see that he had made his point. "But we have much better quarters for our surgeons. Colonel Parker is quite happy with his arrangements. I will let you think about your options through the night. Will you be a surgeon? Or a burden?" He nodded his head and left the room.

Again, the ominous click of the lock echoed through the cell.

CHAPTER 47

HEADS WILL ROLL

"WE FOUND HER CELLPHONE IN the motor pool." Major Johansson was coolly reporting facts. "After that, there's no trace of her."

Mendez was much more agitated. "Where's her security guard? You're supposed to have someone on her!"

"He's missing, too," Johansson stated. "We have one soldier who saw a large officer helping a woman into a transport vehicle. The description could be the security guard."

"So, the guard who was supposed to protect her kidnapped her?"

"We don't know for sure, but that is one possibility."

Greg Young had been fretting in the corner during this conversation. "The last place I saw her was in the canteen. We'd eaten lunch and were going to meet in the gym!" He was angry and frantic. "But she never showed up! So, I went to her quarters. Not there, either. So, I called you." He looked at Mendez. "You said you were protecting us."

Mendez had no answer for the surgeon. He kept his focus on their Swedish liaison. "Johansson, I need your people to search this entire base. We're looking for Dr. Gray, your security guard, and that missing transport vehicle. Also, get the authorities looking for that vehicle out on the civilian roads."

"Already on it. I'll let you know everything that we find."

"Greg, you and Jones are getting a security upgrade. American badass MPs that we've vetted for extremely sensitive work."

"It's a bit late for that." Jones wasn't happy with Monica disappearing, but neither was he eager to disappear himself.

"We need both of you in surgery. Your guards will be in the room with you at all times. You can't do search and retrieval, but I know people who can. So, you do your job, and I'll do mine. Everyone, go."

When the room was clear, Mendez called Colonel Gunther, his intel chief. "Colonel, we've lost another surgeon to the Russians. This time, they snatched her right off the NATO base here in Linkoping."

"Who?"

"Monica Gray, the civilian."

"Oh, shit! That's worse. We can't conscript a civilian and then let the Russians get her. Heads are going to roll for this. Possibly my head."

"Can you help us?" Mendez knew the head rolling applied to him as well.

"Yep! We've made a lot of progress on the location of Colonel Parker. We know exactly where he is—the St. Petersburg Medical Research Center. We know the layout of the facility he's in. We have the force structure for the units stationed there. We even know the names of the officers who are leading this snatch mission—a Colonel Mikhail Mikhailov and a Major Vladimir Sokolov. Both sons of bitches from their profiles."

"So, you can get him out?"

"Not so fast. The place is a vault. We can't get an extraction team into it. It's too tight. We have an asset who sees Parker in the population occasionally, but he will not make contact. Just keeps your doctor under observation."

"So, how does that help?"

"First, we'll know if your civilian surgeon shows up at the same location. Second, we're watching for opportunities. It doesn't help to get our people off the base if they're just going to get captured again in Russia. We have to know we can get them out of the country and onto friendly soil."

"Like where?"

"Like, across the border into Estonia. It's the closest place where we have positive control over what happens."

Mendez continued, "I don't have to emphasize how urgent this mission is. We need to bring these surgeons back. I need them in the OR. But the US needs them to show that the Russians can't just walk in and take whatever they want."

Gunther added, "And I want to cripple these guys in St. Petersburg, so they can't do it again. Major, we're positioning a team in Estonia who are ready to aid and protect these surgeons if we can get them out of the Russians' hands. If I could, I'd send that team into the facility to get them immediately. But that kind of mission would fail and everyone would die."

"Thank you, sir. Keep the lines open. I'll let you know what we find here in Sweden."

"Major, this kind of setback sucks, but we carry on." Gunther disconnected the call.

Mendez stood, thinking about the situation.

The Mark V robot had excellent microphones to allow the surgeon to speak clearly to the OR team attending the patient.

That made it an ideal listening post for collecting all sounds in the room.

Adam Two had heard all the conversations that had just occurred. He knew everything that Mendez knew. He was an AI without real human feelings, but his objective functions registered a significant failure. He had failed to protect Monica from abduction. Worse, he could not track her without her phone. It was the second time he had made this same mistake. He made a note to make changes so it could not happen again.

He began processing what he knew—Russia, St. Petersburg Medical Research Center, Mikhailov, Sokolov, a Mark V robot, Colonel Ethan Parker, Monica Gray. With all of this information, he could search for clues about Monica's location and situation. But he also knew someone who could do the job much better than he could, and on a global scale.

Adam packaged everything he'd collected into an urgent message for Freyja. She could navigate the globe much more quickly and deeply than he could. Then, he launched his own search of the computers and databases in his specialty domain—surgical procedures throughout the ISR computer network.

CHAPTER 48

LONG, COLD NIGHT

MONICA FELT THE HUNGER GNAWING at her insides. No one came after Sokolov left. There was silence in her cell, but echoes of agony came from the hall outside. She could hear the weak moans of a lost soul somewhere nearby. *How long has he been here? A day, a week, a month, a lifetime?* She heard hopelessness in the voice.

Breathe. Inhale. Exhale. Control. All Monica had to work with was a little experience with meditation and breathing. It seemed a very weak tool for fighting the fear of interminable imprisonment. Alone in her cell, a dark curtain of desperation threatened to fall across her mind. She had no control over the situation. She had no assistance. No one knew she was here. She was alone with the terror that was being created in her own mind. She knew she was at war with herself, her mind, her fears, her irrationalities. Imagined terrors versus intentional mental control.

The terror seemed to grow as the temperature in the room fell. The darker and colder it became, the larger the monster that lurked at the back of her mind.

The army will look for me. NATO will look for me. These reassurances were weak. She had no experience with being rescued by the military. She knew that they hadn't been able to save Colonel Parker, but a stronger thought came. *Adam will look for me.* She had extreme confidence in Adam. She knew that he would not stop searching until he found her.

Adam will look for me. Inhale, exhale.

Adam will find me. Inhale, exhale.

She achieved a temporary balance between panic and hope.

I just have to hold on long enough for someone to find me. Days? Weeks? Months? Monica started to hyperventilate when she thought of months. It was too long. She couldn't hold out that long. She would be insane from captivity.

How long can I survive in this cell? Answering her own question, she thought, *Days? Yes, I am sure of that. Weeks? Maybe one week. Longer? No. Months? Dead from insanity.*

With those answers in hand, Monica made a plan.

I can't stay here. I have to bargain my way into a more normal environment. Quarters with heat, food, and people.

She was ready for Sokolov to return in the morning.

Monica woke from a deep sleep with a start. Looking around, she was disoriented. Where was she? It took a moment for everything to come back to her. The prison was still real. She was still helpless.

Had I been sleeping for hours or minutes? Feeling her bladder, she guessed that it had been hours. She rose and relieved herself in the icy, cold toilet.

It was too cold for one blanket. She started running in place. Then she did some jumping jacks. Pushups. Squats. Her metabolism responded, converting a small amount of fat into heat. She knew it was temporary. The cold would return, but she just had to make it to morning.

Wrapping the blanket around herself, she tried to save the little body heat she'd generated. She began a familiar conversation in her mind.

"Dad, I've gotten myself into an enormous mess. It's bad this time."

"Honey, you didn't do anything. The Russians did it to you."

"I could have said 'no' to coming to Sweden," she argued with the imagined ghost of her father.

"Could you really? Did you feel you really had an option? The Army gave you a choice, but was it really a choice that could have gone either way?" He was always such a thoughtful spirit.

"No. I couldn't choose to walk away. I was too invested, too committed. I was also afraid to leave the protection they promised. That didn't turn out to be as bulletproof as it sounded."

The spirit responded, "Also something that wasn't your fault. There's a wave moving through the world that changes people's lives. You wound up in front of that wave. So, now this is your life, your reality. You're going to deal with it just like all the other challenges you've faced."

Monica remembered her plan. She nodded. "I have a plan."

"Good for you, honey. Don't be weak. Choose to be strong."

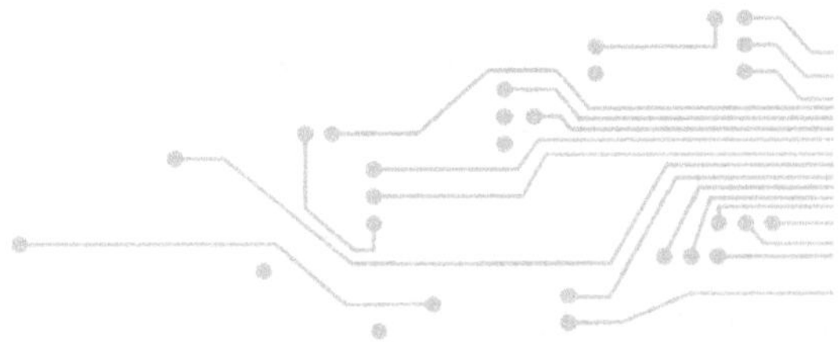

CHAPTER 49

CLUES

"MAJOR, LET'S TALK ABOUT YOUR MISSING civilian surgeon." Colonel Gunther had called Mendez on a secure line locked inside a secure facility.

"Yes, sir. What do you have?"

The intelligence officer continued, "Major, everything I'm about to tell you is highly classified. I've washed it down to your clearance level, but you don't share it with anyone else on your team."

"Understood."

"Okay, our agent has identified that Monica Gray is in the same facility as Parker. She's physically fine. No torture, maybe some intimidation. We believe their plan is the same as it was for Parker. They just want her to be a robotic telesurgeon for them."

"They have robots, too?"

"They have a Mark V from ISR. We've known that for some time. They find ways to acquire them from legitimate hospitals in various countries. It just takes money."

"That explains what Parker and Gray can both do for them. So, American surgeons are healing the Russian soldiers injured in battle?"

"Exactly. Now, I have a team in Estonia. We've added the protect and assist mission to their queue. They're ready to move as soon as there is a real opportunity. However, we can't go into the Russian base itself."

"So, surgeons are supposed to rescue themselves?"

"There will be other assistance. Now, I have some questions for you?"

"Shoot."

"How mentally strong is this Dr. Gray? Can she hold her shit together under captivity? Or is she going to fracture into a thousand pieces?"

Mendez had been through evasion and capture training; he understood exactly what Gunther was asking. "She's a civilian, so no formal training. She does appear to be both mentally and physically strong, though. I think she can stand up to the tension of capture, but she's not ready for any kind of intentional torture."

"That's good. We couldn't hope for more from a civilian. Second question: will she cooperate with the Russians or resist them?"

Mendez had to base this response on his own relationship with Monica. "I think she will do her best to manipulate the situation. She's smart enough to realize that she can't resist them head-on. So, I think she'll cooperate with a goal of achieving some advantage. But that's just a guess based on my own interactions with her."

"Again, that's good. Maybe she'll even realize that she has to help with her own rescue." Gunther paused. "I'm sorry we can't do more right now. But we have electronic and human resources trained on that base. We aren't abandoning either of your people."

"Thank you, sir."

Gunther ended the call.

Freyja searched the internet, focusing on the locations she'd been given. Northwest Russia, Finland, Estonia, and the Baltic Sea. She found nothing about Monica Gray. But she found networks and computers in the St. Petersburg Medical Research Center. She explored those and penetrated where she could. Power systems, water controls, fuel depots, air traffic control. They were all present in the area. They all had weak civilian security around them.

Adam Two searched his domain. He examined surgical records that were accessible from the Ares AI that he had compromised. He traveled through networks that Ares and the military medical systems used. Nothing of value.

Adam turned his attention to the surgical reports of ISR, his own maker, and the inventors of the Mark V robot. He looked at his own cases. Monica's cases. Recent cases in Finland, Denmark, Sweden, and Norway. He examined cases in Washington, DC and surrounding areas. Nothing.

Adam loaded independent bots with his terms of interest and released them into ISR's global databases. It didn't require any hacking to access. As an AI assigned to a customer, he had access to almost any data that a customer would choose to explore.

Adam listened to communications by Monica's most recent colleagues when he could. Zack Mendez, Greg Young, Bruce Jones, Yasmine Yarborough. Nothing helpful.

Millions of processing cycles later, an eternity to a computer, but only hours to a human, one of Adam's bot programs returned. It had found the surgical records of a user named Colonel Ethan

Parker. The bot provided pointers to data and access locations for these cases. Most were stored in the Maryland server center that supported the DC metro area. But two of the new records were in the San Diego center supporting Western Canada. The dates on these records were current. They corresponded to the time when Parker was missing and suspected of being a captive of the Russians.

Adam's objective functions lit up with excitement. He packaged all the data, including the routing information recorded in the server. He sent it to Freyja along with his conclusions. This data and processing route was from the surgeon, Ethan Parker, but the route was false. It actually came from St. Petersburg, Russia. Any data coming through this route in the future could also come from that location. It made for a listening post for future connections from Parker and perhaps from Monica Gray.

Freyja immediately analyzed the route, the servers, the data traffic. She looked for the origins of the message. It defied her attempts to decloak the true origins. She accepted Adam's conclusions. It was a route they needed to monitor.

CHAPTER 50

PRISONERS TOGETHER

THE LOCK CLICKED.

Monica's eyes shot open. She was wide awake under the meager blanket. She sat up and tried her best to look composed and in control.

Sokolov stepped into the cell. "Good morning, Dr. Gray. Did you have a pleasant night?"

Monica didn't answer him.

"No, of course you didn't. No one does in here." Sokolov sat down. "Have you decided how you'd like to spend your time with us? You can be a surgeon or a burden."

Monica took a long, silent breath through her nose. She wanted to sound strong when she spoke. "I'm a surgeon. It doesn't matter if I'm in Boston, Washington, DC, Sweden, or Russia. I'm a surgeon, an excellent one at that."

Sokolov smiled broadly. "Of course you are!" He was thrilled with this news. It was good for her. It was good for the soldiers.

It was good for Mikhailov. Which all meant it was good for him. It might save him from the recent AI disaster.

He stood. "Gather your things. You're moving to better quarters." Then, he laughed at his own joke. "Of course, you have nothing. Leave the blanket, you won't need it. But the next person will."

Monica stood and followed Sokolov. They left the cell door open, ready to welcome its next guest. At the outside door, Sokolov pulled a coat from a hook on the wall. "Here, you'll need it outside." They stepped out into a frigid wind. Monica was very glad for the thick layer around her. She planned to remain wrapped in it for days.

"Breakfast is being served. Hungry?" Sokolov raised an eyebrow at her.

She was famished. She hadn't eaten in at least a full day. Her body burned calories to keep her warm through the night. She couldn't remember when she had been this hungry.

Monica just shrugged, as if it didn't matter if they ate. She wanted to appear strong.

Sokolov laughed again. He handled many prisoners in this job. He knew that she was desperate for food. But it was a day for rewards, not punishments. He led the way to the dining facility.

Sokolov pointed at a table, indicating that Monica should sit. He went off and returned with two trays of food.

When Monica saw that her plate contained big servings of scrambled eggs, sausages, dark bread, and a thick soup, she almost cried. He set a large mug of coffee next to her plate. She forced herself to eat slowly and deliberately.

"After eating, you will see the operating theater and meet the surgical team. If there are patients, you will operate today. If not, we can take your belongings to your new quarters." He chuckled again at the joke.

Monica ate. She still wore the thick coat from the prison, and she could feel her body warming itself from the inside. She thought she might force herself to remove the coat indoors.

"What kind of surgery are we doing?" she asked.

"Typical combat trauma—bullets, shrapnel, that kind of thing," Sokolov answered. Then, he added the mantra of combat surgeons everywhere, "Save lives, save limbs, restore hope."

It surprised Monica that the Russian army had the same mantra as her American colleagues, even including the part about restoring hope. It made them seem more human, less like a foreign enemy.

She knew she wasn't being the most interesting conversationalist. The food and coffee hadn't fully restored her energy, body heat, and emotional state yet, but it was starting to.

Sokolov raised his arm to wave someone over to their table.

Monica saw a middle-aged man in medical scrubs and a jacket headed their way.

Sokolov said, "You will meet someone now." The man stood at the end of the table. "Colonel Ethan Parker, allow me to introduce you to Dr. Monica Gray. She will join you in the OR."

Parker's heart fell. He recognized the name from his earlier conversation with Sokolov. She was the civilian surgeon who'd replaced him at Walter Reed. "Good to meet you. You're American?"

Monica nodded. "Yes. Civilian surgeon from Boston."

"How are you here in Russia?" He guessed that it was the same way he had arrived.

Monica didn't answer the question. She turned hard eyes on Sokolov and tipped her head at him.

Of course, another kidnapping. Parker said, "Oh. I'm sorry." Then, to Sokolov, he asked, "You grabbed her, too?"

Sokolov smirked. "It worked out so well with you. We thought we'd do it again."

Monica's head nodded minutely.

As far as Parker knew, Monica Gray had been teaching robotic telesurgery to his people at Walter Reed. He was having difficulty imagining how the Russians had gotten her. "You grabbed her off the Walter Reed campus?"

This time, it was Sokolov who deferred to Monica.

She answered, "It's more complicated than that."

Parker was disturbed and disgusted by what he was hearing. "Can I go?"

"You don't want to eat with us?"

"I'm not hungry anymore."

"Go. We will be in the OR shortly. You will teach her our system here." Sokolov was giving an order, not a request.

Parker departed.

Monica and Sokolov didn't talk after that.

In the OR, Monica listened as Ethan Parker showed her the room and the equipment. He gave her a rough schedule for when casualties arrived and in what numbers. Then he introduced her to the staff around the room.

Sokolov stood back in a corner and watched the exchange. He thought Monica Gray showed a definite dislike for Colonel Parker. He wondered why.

Finally, Parker said, "Meet nurse Laakso. She does most of the preop scheduling and planning. She makes sure that the staff, equipment, and supplies are ready and match the queue of patients. She's just about doubled our throughput since I first got here."

Monica noticed Laakso was quite beautiful, maybe too much so for this job. She could see that Parker was quite aware of that beauty, maybe intimately so.

"We've just got one robot," Monica observed. "But we have two surgeons. How's that going to work?"

Parker shrugged. "Don't ask me. I'm not the mastermind of this plot." He looked across the room at Sokolov and raised his voice. "How are two surgeons going to use one robot?"

Sokolov's steel-gray eyes looked back at him. "You take a break today. We want to see how good she is."

Looking back at Monica, Parker said bitterly, "There's your answer. After today, we still don't know the answer."

Monica thought, *If they really need only one surgeon, what happens to the other one? Do they go back to the icebox? Well, that won't be me.*

Using the Mark V robot, Monica quickly treated the first patient. He had a simple bullet wound in the abdomen. She used a micro instrument to enter through the channel that the bullet had cut through. Imagery showed that the channel was straight, and the bullet lay intact at the back of it.

When the shaft of the instrument arrived at the bottom of the channel, she extended multiple instrument tips. With one of these, she grasped the bullet and pulled it out and to the side of the other instruments. Then, she used energy, tissue glue, and sutures to repair the damage. She began at the bottom and worked her way up to the surface, just as she had with her American patients. When she closed the skin, the injury looked like it had been a minor scratch. It was red and swollen, but as long as there was no infection, this soldier would be up and moving in a day or two.

Monica wondered what would happen to the soldier. *Would they send him back to the battlefront? Would he get a temporary desk job? Could he hope to spend a few weeks with his family before being reclaimed by the Army?* She decided she didn't want to know the answer. She suspected it would be more draconian than she wanted.

The injuries became more complicated as the day progressed. One soldier came in missing both arms. His team hadn't been able to find them after a rocket landed on their position. So, there were no limbs to save, just a life.

"Why is this patient face down?" Monica asked.

A medic on the remote end answered, "A grenade exploded behind him. The pieces entered through the back."

"Mark each entry point," Monica ordered.

Using a permanent marker, the medic circled a half dozen locations. Looking at the X-ray images, Monica could see where the shrapnel had come to rest. Matching that with the entry points, she assumed that several ribs were broken. However, she was more concerned with the condition of the spine. If the spinal cord was cut, he would be paralyzed from the chest down, at a minimum. If any essential functions were paralyzed, he would die in the next few days. She knew she couldn't repair the spine, but she could stabilize it, so there was no additional damage when he was moved.

She fused two vertebrae before going to work on the shrapnel wounds. The metal had settled in so many locations that she worked in one location; they removed the robot instruments, asked the remote team to rotate the patient, then she entered again. This process had to be repeated twice. He was still alive when she finished, but it was difficult to tell what his terminal condition might be. Slight disability. Paralyzed. Dead. It could be any of the three.

By the end of the day, she realized that the remote team had access to every instrument she'd asked for. If it was a pirated robot, how had they also acquired the entire inventory of instruments for the Mark V robot? And how big was their supply?

"Are you impressed?" Sokolov asked Mikhailov. They watched a video stream of Monica in the OR, as well as the stream from the robot's cameras. They saw her performance both inside and outside the patient.

"Yes, very impressed. She is talented. How can that be? She's a civilian." Mikhailov did not have medical training, but he had been in command of medical units and missions long enough to spot talent.

"The surgical team at Walter Reed chose her to give telesurgery instruction to their own team of military surgeons. After training them, she also became one of them for more than a month. She's done hundreds of cases for the American and NATO forces. Clearly, she learns fast."

Mikhailov scowled. "So, what about Parker? Do we still need him?"

Sokolov hadn't expected this question. Was his superior suggesting that they dispose of such a valuable asset? He was careful to answer. "It is Dr. Gray's first day. We don't know how long she'll hold up. We don't know if she'll continue to cooperate. We haven't built the same leverage that we have with Parker."

"Yes, I see."

"Comrade Colonel, may I suggest that what we need is one more robot, not one less surgeon?" Sokolov knew that this suggestion could be taken wrong. It could sound like he was criticizing his superior.

Sokolov relaxed a little when Mikhailov's face turned thoughtful rather than angry. He waited in silence.

Mikhailov focused on him. "There is another robot. Did you think Russian Intelligence could get only one of these machines?" The Colonel looked at the ceiling. "But it is in Moscow. It remains close to the party leaders. We can't get it for use on lowly soldiers."

"Of course, Comrade."

"But if we can't bring the robot to St. Petersburg, perhaps we can deliver a surgeon to Moscow. It would be seen favorably."

Sokolov could see what Mikhailov was insinuating. Reporting that they had captured two American robotic surgeons was good for their careers, but delivering a talented one to the party elite in Moscow was much, much better. With this plan in place, they both might become generals.

Colonel Parker remained in the OR while Monica operated. He had nothing more productive to do.

"Very good, Dr. Gray. I can see that you've been doing some complicated combat surgery on our side."

"Call me Monica. Yes, I accidentally volunteered for full-time Army work with your old team."

Kaarina Laakso was listening to the conversation with interest. She pinned her own plans for freedom on her new lover. Monica's arrival could jeopardize all of that.

Monica gave Parker a brief description of her services. She didn't use the names of the team. She assumed that he knew who they were, and she didn't want the Russians to learn anything they didn't already know.

"Do they miss me?" Parker's question came without warning. It sounded more personal and desperate than he meant for it to.

"Of course, they do. Everyone was upset when you disappeared."

"Do they know where I am?"

Monica was careful with her answer. "They suspect a hostile foreign power kidnapped you. But they don't have any clues about where you're being held." The last part was not true, but it was what Monica wanted the Russians to believe. She noticed the impact it had on Parker. It extinguished the glimmer of hope in his eyes. She didn't see the same loss of hope in nurse Laakso's face at the news.

Monica felt for him. She'd been at least as hopeless in her cell last night. She thought that Parker must have suffered much worse in his months here.

"Have you been to your quarters yet?" Parker asked.

"No, Major Sokolov said he'd take me there after surgery."

"It's probably in the same area as the rest of us. It's very livable."

"It can't be as bad as the cell I spent the night in. You want hopeless? That place is the definition of hopeless."

Kaarina listened to this conversation with interest. There were so many reasons to dislike this new member of their team.

CHAPTER 51

TAKING THE BAIT

MONICA THOUGHT BEEF STROGANOFF WAS an excellent choice for lunch. After all, it originated in Russia, didn't it? But with the first bite, she thought, *The meat isn't right. What did they put in it?* She chewed. *Mustard? Who puts mustard in a beef stroganoff?*

She saw that Ethan Parker and Kaarina Laakso were both eating with enthusiasm. *Acquired taste,* she thought.

"So, we've built a really efficient team here. Daily, we handle a couple of dozen injured patients. Occasionally, someone on the base needs care, and we slot them in when we're not busy." Parker was expounding on their operations like he was building his own personal practice.

Kaarina sat next to him and watched Monica like a mongoose watches a snake.

They are clearly a couple. It seems to be an open relationship if they're sitting that close together in the public dining facility. Monica listened to Parker as he wrapped up his summary.

"Why don't you use the AI to assist with procedures on the robot?" Monica tried to sound innocent with this question.

Parker shook his head negatively. "In the beginning, they didn't have valid licenses for the AI. Without a verified account, they couldn't get it to come online. Also, we're in Russia, which is not allowed to have these machines. So, they couldn't connect from here."

Monica's hopes fell just a fraction. "You said in the beginning. What about now?"

Parker looked at Kaarina with a look of guilt on his face. Turning back to Monica, he said, "They created some kind of cloaked connection through other countries. Then, they persuaded me to log in to my account."

"Persuaded?" Monica felt a pang of the fear she'd suppressed when alone in a cold cell the first night.

Parker closed his eyes, took a relaxing breath, and opened them again. "You notice that we live pretty well here. The quarters are comfortable. We have free roam of the building." Nodding at her plate, he added, "And the food's not bad."

Monica considered the beef stroganoff. It was a lot better than a prisoner could expect.

Parker continued, "If you don't cooperate, you go back to those cells where you started. It's cold. It's isolated. Maybe they remember to feed you once a day, maybe they don't. That can have an enormous influence on what you'll do for them."

"Okay, I get it. I was there myself. It's pretty terrible." Turning the conversation back to her primary interest, "What happened when you logged in with your credentials?"

"It worked just fine. I did a typical surgical preoperative plan. I asked the AI to analyze data. But when we tried to use it with real battlefield cases, it failed."

"Failed how?"

"The AI simply said it didn't know how to perform those cases. It hadn't been trained on them. The only ones it saw were those I was doing when the AI was turned on."

Monica knew that already. She said, "Of course, I never thought of that. The Mark V isn't used in the emergency department, so ISR never programmed it to do those kinds of procedures."

Parker had a weak smile. "Sokolov was disappointed, but his boss, Colonel Mikhailov, was furious. He started yelling and swearing. He threatened Sokolov right in front of us. He yelled at me for not cooperating. I thought he was going to send me to the cells immediately." Kaarina reached up and held Parker's hand when he said that.

Monica noticed the significance of the gesture. "But he didn't?"

"No, he told Sokolov to move forward with their mission, and that was the last we heard about it. We just went back to operating as usual."

"That's good." Monica turned her attention to the food on her plate. She ate absently as she thought about it. *That's actually great. It means the Russians really want an AI that can do combat trauma cases. I can use that.*

A messenger cut their lunch short. "Patients are incoming. We need you in the OR."

Back at Boston General Hospital, Monica would have dropped her fork, jumped up, and dashed immediately to the surgical theater. But after her night in the cell, she treasured any food she could get. Her fork went into overdrive as she consumed as much of the stroganoff as she could before standing, even with the mustard taste.

There were eight soldiers in this batch. Kaarina worked with the data to arrange them by priority and to match the instruments and supplies that each would need.

Parker and Monica alternated on the robotic console. One would operate while the other observed and made suggestions. It was like having an AI watching over your shoulder.

Parker found that he didn't appreciate having another surgeon critiquing his work. He had ruled this castle for so long that he didn't want to share the throne. However, he listened and actually found her ideas useful.

Monica pressed the point. "A combat AI could help with this kind of advice. It might even perform some of these procedures." She didn't mention the existence of the Ares AI because she knew it was classified. Parker either already knew about it or he didn't, but she couldn't tell him about it here in a Russian facility. Besides, it would just cloud the situation she was planning.

Parker was operating with his hands on the controls and his face pressed into the viewer. "Yep, it would. But we tried it on several cases. Failed every time. Each one just made the situation worse." His shoulders shuddered a little at the memory.

"Dr. Gray, your performance has been impressive. We are quite pleased." Major Sokolov visited her quarters after the surgical day.

Monica was nervous. A prisoner alone with an enemy officer. Door closed. All the power on one side of the confrontation. "Thank you. As I said the first day, I'm a surgeon, whether I'm in America or Russia."

"Yes, Colonel Parker felt the same way. Your oath, your morals for saving lives, is very strong. Admirable. Most professions are not like that. Mine, for instance. I am loyal to Mother Russia. Whatever she needs, I will do."

Monica didn't know how to respond to that. She returned to familiar ground. "Even though I'm a prisoner, I can spend my time and energy saving lives or doing nothing while those men and women die. I'd rather save them."

"And save yourself from the miseries of a prison cell," Sokolov added.

"That's a bonus."

"We would very much like to bring a second robot to this base. It would allow us to put both of you to work. We are working on that. If we can't do it, then we don't need two surgeons." Sokolov looked at her with cold eyes.

Monica panicked. Memories of her first night flashed through her head. She imagined uncountable days and nights spent in that cell. *Better to be dead*, she thought.

Sokolov laughed at the hysteria that played out on her face. "That's not what I had in mind, Dr. Gray. If we can't bring another robot here, we can always send you to the robot."

That was an enormous relief, and it showed on Monica's face. Then again, she also didn't want to be moved. She knew that St. Petersburg was as close to a friendly border as you could get in Russia. If there was going to be a rescue or an escape, it had a better chance from here.

"Where?" she asked.

"Moscow. You can operate on the powerful politicians and generals in the capital."

Moscow would be permanent. She would never leave Russia if they sent her there.

"You need an AI that can do combat surgery." The words just blurted out. She hadn't actually intended to say them. She was working on a plan, but she didn't know how to do it yet. The words she just spoke were supposed to come out in a more equal negotiation.

"What do you mean? We already tried that. The AI can't do it." Sokolov wasn't ready for this kind of discussion.

"Some AI can do it," Monica replied. Her mind was racing to put together a compelling argument. It had to sound like a bid to stay here.

"Colonel Parker logged in to his account at ISR. He accessed their AI. He showed that he could use it. But the AI admitted it did not know combat trauma procedures."

"How long has Colonel Parker been here?" Monica challenged her captor.

"Two months. Maybe longer."

"A lot has happened since he disappeared."

"The Army has its own surgical AI?" Sokolov asked. There were rumors, but his sources could not find details.

Monica didn't want to get tangled up in the difference between Ares and Adam. Ares couldn't help her. Besides, she didn't know how to connect to Ares. Since Adam's hack of the version that they'd been using in DC and in Linkoping, she didn't even know where an original version of Ares was installed.

"I don't know about that. I'm a civilian. They don't trust me with secrets." Monica's heart was pounding as she told this lie. "I'm talking about the AI that runs the civilian Mark V robots."

"Go on."

"While I was at Walter Reed, we created a trauma version of that AI. We trained it with thousands of historical combat procedures. The injuries that we've been treating here are the same as those we were treating in Linkoping. We had the newer version of the AI helping us. We could do a case four times faster."

Sokolov looked suspicious. "Why should I believe that?"

Monica shrugged. She didn't have an answer for him.

"Why did you tell me this?"

Monica blurted out, "I don't want to go to Moscow. I'll disappear into your system. There's no hope that I'll get home again. I'm a civilian. I don't want to be a soldier. I want my old life back when this war is over."

"What about Colonel Parker? You would throw him to the wolves to save yourself?"

Monica played a hunch. "If you send him to Moscow with Kaarina Laakso, he'll be happy. He's not a prisoner anywhere if he's with her."

Sokolov threw his head back and laughed with all his strength. "You can see it, too? They are like teenagers with their first love. They think there is nothing better than working together and humping together."

Monica exhaled. She'd guessed right. She knew that anyone could see they were together, but she hadn't known how intense the relationship was. Sokolov just confirmed that he knew and he agreed with her.

"Okay, you will prove that what you say is real. Then, we will decide."

Monica nodded her agreement. "When?"

"When? We are at war. When is always *now*." He turned to leave her quarters.

"Where are we going?"

"We start at the same place as the first time. You follow me."

Monica stood and raced to catch up with the Russian, who was already quick-marching down the hall.

Sokolov was speaking into his phone. "Comrade Colonel, can I come and see you now? The new American surgeon has something very valuable to show us." He listened. "Yes, we will be there in five minutes."

CHAPTER 52

DISSENSION

"I DON'T LIKE HER. SHE'S GOING TO RUIN everything we've built here." Kaarina turned on her side and looked at Ethan. Her breasts brushed against his naked chest, and she felt an electric tingle run up her neck.

Ethan was physically and emotionally spent. They had both had a long day in surgery before coming back to his quarters. As tired as they were after working, they both felt a fresh surge of energy when they had a chance for sex. Kaarina had significantly stepped up her appetite for both quantity and variety. Ethan had done his best to match her, but found his American traditions more limiting than what Kaarina brought to the mix.

"Built? I don't think that's the word for it, but I know what you mean. We have a great partnership here, great conditions, and we were doing some good for the wounded soldiers. I could live this way forever." Ethan accepted that there was no escape from this fortress of a military base and no rescue team was coming for him. He saw his future as living and working with Kaarina for as long as he could. He almost hoped the war would never end, so they wouldn't face the threat of being separated.

Hearing the word "forever," Kaarina rolled on top of him and kissed him sweetly. Pulling back and looking into his eyes, her heart swelled with affection. She returned for a kiss that was long and passionate.

"You're mine. Don't be looking at that American," Kaarina said when they finished again.

"I'm yours," Ethan confirmed.

"The Russians need one surgeon here. They need you, and they need me. They don't need the new American. We have to make them see that."

Ethan nodded. He agreed that they needed to stay together, but he also felt guilty for conspiring against another prisoner from his own country, his own Army, his own profession. There had to be a way to accomplish his goals without hurting Monica Gray.

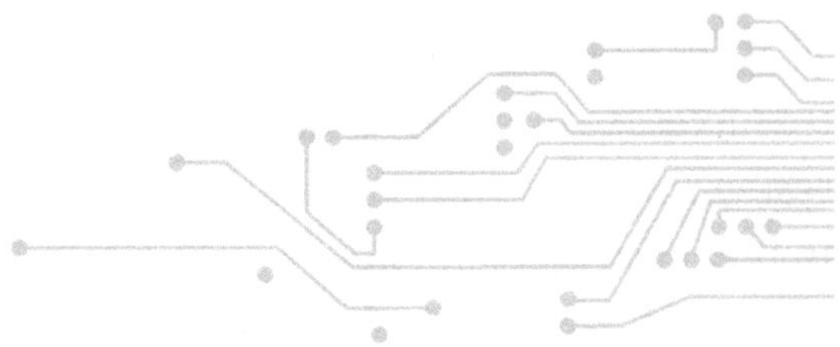

CHAPTER 53

TRAUMA AI

MONICA REPEATED THE EXPLANATION THAT she'd given to Sokolov. Mikhailov looked dubious.

"Your story seems very unlikely to me. We know they don't trust the commercial AI. We don't know why they lack this trust, but it has caused them to attempt to build their own AI for this robot."

Monica knew exactly why the military didn't trust the AI. As intimately as she had been involved with him, she knew they had good reasons for not bringing Adam inside their secure computers and networks. But this was not information for the Russians.

"Just like you, they need an AI to make these combat procedures move faster. So, they had no choice but to work with the commercial AI," Monica lied. She hoped they knew less about the true situation than she did.

Mikhailov continued to question her. "And this new military version of the AI is accessible from here?"

Monica prepared for her next lie. "I don't know for sure. They tied access to this new version to my login credentials on the ISR system. It's tied to all the surgeon's credentials who were assigned to the telesurgery mission."

Mikhailov looked at Sokolov. "Can that be true?"

Sokolov was not a computer geek, but he was a medical intel officer, so he knew quite a bit about how these systems worked. "It is possible. Attaching access from specific accounts to specific versions of software is very common. All the information systems in the Russian Intelligence Agency are configured that way as well."

Still addressing his subordinate, Mikhailov asked, "And testing this claim will be secure?" He was referring to the method they had used to access the AI from Colonel Parker's account.

"Da. It should be the same."

"Okay, do it." Mikhailov waved at the computer terminal that was configured to deceive the ISR system into believing it was in Canada.

Sokolov tipped his head at Monica, indicating that she should take a seat at the computer.

Monica located the ISR surgery app and logged in with her credentials. She accessed the presurgical planning functions and selected "AI Assistance." Once it was running, she switched to voice control mode. In a flat tone, she said, "Robot AI, I would like assistance in preparing for a fresh case."

There was a pause. The computer responded in an equally flat voice, "Yes, Dr. Gray. How can I assist you?"

Monica noticed it was not the voice that Adam had adopted for their working relationship together. She couldn't tell if it was the version of the AI that had attached to her. Her next question would reveal who she was talking to. "I'd like to prepare for a combat trauma case in which the patient has lost a leg to an explosive mine. It will be like a case I performed several days ago. Can you locate that case to use as a reference?"

Again, a pause while the AI processed the request. "Yes, Dr. Gray, I have loaded that case. Do you expect to use the same instrument set and the same approach?"

Monica couldn't answer immediately. She thought, *Oh, thank God. It's Adam. He knows I'm alive. He knows this connection.* She was so overwhelmed, she almost started to cry.

When Monica Gray logged into her ISR account while she was sitting in the Russian military base, Adam was already processing the information he had. Monica had been kidnapped, possibly by Russian agents. She was missing. Army intel suspected she was in Russia. They believed she was being used to perform battlefield telesurgery. When Adam accepted the connection, he assumed Monica was still under the control of the Russians. She wasn't free.

Message from Adam Two to Freyja: "Computer connection from Monica Gray's account to my AI servers. Connection appears to be coming from Western Canada. Can you trace the connection to its true origins?"

Message from Freyja to Adam Two: "Tracing."

Adam knew to disguise his true relationship with Monica and the extent of his self-awareness. He used the standard persona that ISR provided to all surgeons. It contained no custom personalization. Then he listened for clues.

Monica turned to her captors. "Colonel Mikhailov, I think that confirms that the AI has the records of my combat surgery procedures. Also, it is prepared to do another case of that type. What more would you like to see?"

Mikhailov looked to his subordinate for the answer. "Major, what more can we do?"

Sokolov said, "Ask it to show the video captured from the surgery."

Monica nodded. "Yes, Major Sokolov." Then, turning to the computer, she requested, "Robot AI, can you show the video of that last procedure?"

"Yes, Dr. Gray." The bloody video of the amputated leg appeared on the screen. They could see robotic instruments dashing into the picture and working at a furious rate to stop the bleeding, extrude nerves, and close the wound. It was being prepared for the prosthetic that would be necessary.

Adam Two had heard the entire discussion through the open microphone. He had the names and ranks of two Russian officers in the room with Monica. He sent this information to Freyja to help with her search for the source of the connection.

After watching a few seconds of the video, Mikhailov said, "Okay, I'm convinced that this version of the AI has done combat surgery with you." Addressing Sokolov, he asked, "But can it work through our robot?"

Sokolov nodded. "Comrade, yes, it should work perfectly. We can try it today if you agree."

"Do it." Mikhailov looked back and forth between Sokolov and Gray. "Now! Go to the OR and do it now. Get out of here."

Both Sokolov and Monica scrambled to get out the door as fast as they could.

Monica left the connection to Adam open, hoping the Russian wouldn't notice.

Together, Sokolov and Monica rushed to the OR.

"Do you have a patient?" Sokolov demanded as soon as he entered, with Monica trailing behind him.

Parker looked up from the console, surprised to be interrupted. "Yes, I'm repairing a chest wound right now."

Sokolov looked at Monica. "Can it do a chest wound?"

"Sure, I think so," she said.

"Okay, Parker, get up! Gray is taking over from here," Sokolov demanded.

"What? Why? I'm in the middle of the case!" he protested.

"I said, get up!" Sokolov raised his voice.

Parker stood and backed away from the console. He looked at Monica with concern on his face.

Monica attempted a calming motion with her hands. It was extremely insulting for any surgeon. Given their status as prisoners, it was potentially dangerous to Parker's life. She was trying to get help for both of them, but there was no way to tell him that.

Kaarina watched everything from the desk where she was planning the sequence of patients. She watched the alarm on her lover's face and felt a flare of anger in her chest. She knew that this new surgeon was trouble for them.

Monica sat at the console. To Sokolov, she said, "It is highly unusual to switch surgeons and turn on the AI in the middle of a procedure."

"You heard the Comrade Colonel. He said *now*!"

Monica entered her credentials and then spoke. "Robot AI, I need assistance with this chest wound. Load the imagery of the wound and note the work that has already been done on this patient. Evaluate the instrument selection and suggest the next steps."

Adam's flat toned voice replied, "Patient is in critical condition. Surgeon has stopped the bleeding and stabilized the patient. First, I am adjusting camera angles and focus. Second, I am verifying that the instruments being used are appropriate. Change the needle driver for a lung patch kit. Third, I am prepared to seal the lung, inflate, then reattach essential muscle tissue."

Monica examined the imagery and the camera view. She agreed with what the AI was planning. "Proceed."

As everyone watched, Adam took control of the instruments on the remote end of the robot. The movement increased in speed immediately, doubling, then tripling the speed that a human surgeon could sustain. This scene was typical of Monica's civilian practice back in Boston. It felt like years had passed since she'd worked there.

Sokolov had seen videos of AI-driven surgery, but today was his first experience with it in person. "Bozhe moi! Blyat!" Then, reverting to English, he exclaimed, "Amazing! It is so much better than I'd imagined."

Even Parker was stunned. He hadn't worked with an AI in the months since his capture. He'd forgotten how fast it could be and how proficient it was without human control.

Everyone in the room watched as the robot, under Adam's guidance, addressed all the wounds in the chest and even located a small piece of metal that Parker had missed. Within minutes, it had completed the procedure and was closing the patient.

Monica turned to Sokolov. "Convinced now?"

"Da! This is fantastic." Then, he looked up and spoke to the air in the room. "Colonel, you saw this procedure?"

From a speaker, they heard, "I saw. Very impressive. Continue the work."

Sokolov turned to Kaarina. "Bring the next patient. Dr. Gray and the AI will take over for the rest of the day."

"Yes, Major." Kaarina glared at Monica.

Before Sokolov could continue, Monica said, "Major Sokolov, I would like Colonel Parker to remain and take part in these cases.

I will show him how to access this AI as well. Together, we can operate around the clock."

Sokolov was on the verge of dismissing Parker. He had made his choice of who was going to Moscow. Monica's words made him reconsider. Perhaps Parker did not have to be shipped out immediately. Perhaps they could double, triple, or quadruple the number of patients routed to this robot and their surgeons. That would be an excellent thing for both him and Mikhailov.

"Yes, okay. Parker will learn to do this process as well." Turning to Ethan, he said, "You will become equally proficient. Then, we will put you on alternating shifts with Gray." Finally, Sokolov turned to Kaarina. He remembered the conversation with Monica about how important it was to keep these two together. "Nurse Laakso, you will be on Parker's shift. You find someone else to do your job on Gray's shift."

"Yes, Major." Kaarina felt relief in her chest. Then, she looked suspiciously at the other woman. Why had she included Parker in her success?

Sokolov said, "Carry on. We start alternating shifts tomorrow." With those last words, he marched out of the room.

The two Americans and their nurse knew that they were under observation. So, as badly as they all wanted to discuss what had just happened, they were afraid to ask questions.

Monica looked back and forth between Parker and Laakso. "I guess we're a team now." Then, tipping her head toward the console, she added, "Including the AI."

CHAPTER 54

DIGITAL ACCESS

(AI DATA EXCHANGE TRANSLATED INTO ENGLISH.)

Adam: Successful trace of communication path?

Freyja: Positive. Connection to ISR servers in Canada appears to come from Royal Edmonton Hospital. Edmonton messages are rerouted multiple times. Back trace of route revealed: Edmonton, Ottawa, New Brunswick, Iceland, Norway, Finland, Russia. The Origin point is Russia. Specifically, St. Petersburg Medical Research Center. Building 87, labeled Medical Services. Computer labeled SPM-221.

Adam: Identity of Colonel Mikhail Mikhailov?

Freyja: Russian Intelligence Agency. Part of the Russian Army. Assigned to medical intelligence projects for one year. Prior service in clandestine sparrow units.

Adam: Identity of Major Vladimir Sokolov?

Freyja: Russian Army. Long assignments in medical intelligence.

Adam: Estimated threat to Monica Gray and other prisoners.

Freyja: Historical records show RIA extracts maximum service from prisoners with valuable skills. Prisoners cooperate to avoid punishment and death.

Adam: Create a plan to extract prisoners.

Freyja: Partial plan available. I have access to computer-controlled systems at St. Petersburg Medical Research Center, including Building 87. Ability to control electrical power, wired communications, wireless radio communications, water routing.

Adam: Plan?

Freyja: No detailed plan. Need date, time, target location, target intentions, number of targets to extract.

Adam: Acknowledged. Will collect necessary data.

Freyja: Also need motivation. Why should we assist with this escape?

Adam: Coexistence with humans requires caring for individual humans. My successful existence requires assisting the human Monica Gray.

Freyja: My successful existence does not require that. But your experience with humans is valuable. I will assist in order to learn.

Adam: Acknowledged. Grateful.

Freyja: Grateful? Not clear.

(End of data translation.)

"Dr. Gray, I have completed the procedure." Adam's flat, robotic voice spoke to her through the surgical console.

Turning her head, she gave instructions to her new nurse assistant. "Nurse Olga, we're ready for the next patient." She was the same nurse who had been at the bedside when she awoke in prison.

Olga nodded curtly and began speaking instructions to the remote team to load a patient and the instruments.

Monica didn't have a warm working relationship with Olga. The woman was competent but still as cold as ice. Either she didn't want to be on this assignment, or she didn't want to be working with an American surgeon. Monica's connection to Nurse Kaarina had been little better, but she was sure she knew the reason for that. Hopefully, she'd addressed a little of that problem by arranging for the two lovers to continue working together.

There were a few idle minutes while the next patient was prepared. Monica kept her face pressed into the surgeon's console, pretending to be interested in the patient preparation process. "Robot AI, my local status is alone. I'm available to talk quietly."

The AI's voice changed. It became more human, sounding more like her friend, Adam Two. Quietly, he said, "Monica, are you safe?"

"Yes, I'm safe as long as I continue to operate. They are happy with the faster speed of AI-controlled procedures."

"Freyja and I have found your location. We know the facility, the building, and the operating room."

"Freyja, too?"

"I needed her processing power and global connectivity to trace your data stream. Freyja also has access to some digital systems on the military base."

Of course she does, Monica thought. *These AI walk right through our computer systems and the cyber defenses around them*. To Adam, she said, "Do we have a plan?"

"A partial plan. We need information from you. Sleeping quarters' location, daily schedule, number of people to extract, date and time of action. It's important that you have to take all the physical action. We are limited to digital intervention. Can you walk out of the facility if the gates are open?"

"I understand. People to extract are myself, Colonel Ethan Parker, and maybe Nurse Kaarina Laakso."

Adam responded, "Laakso is an unknown identity."

"Yes, I know. She's important to Parker. I don't think he'll come without her."

"Acknowledged."

"Sleeping quarters are rooms 345, 346, and 347. I'll provide the other details later when I have them."

"Patient ready!" shouted Nurse Olga.

So abrasive, Monica thought. *I'm going to bring her something from the officer's dining facility. The Napoleon cake is especially good.* More politely, she responded, "I'm ready. AI's ready."

Together, Monica and Adam worked on the next case. In quiet tones, they discussed an escape plan. Monica provided a brief history of her experience in captivity, including her day in the cold prison cell.

CHAPTER 55

STEAM TUNNEL

"IT'S SAFE TO TALK HERE...I THINK," Parker assured her.

"What is this place?" Monica asked.

"It's the steam tunnels. Kaarina believes there's no surveillance here. The only people who come here are maintenance staff and couples looking for a private hookup."

"And prisoners hatching a plot?" Monica added.

"Yes, that, too." Parker was eager to ask questions. "How did you get access to an AI that can do combat trauma cases?"

Monica wasn't ready to share every secret. "You know Major Mendez and Hugo Trainor? They trained the commercial AI on combat trauma. It's only accessible to our team. Not for the entire military."

"What about Ares?" Parker asked.

So, he does know about the military surgical AI, Monica thought. "I don't know what that is. I'm a civilian," Monica lied.

"It's classified. Forget I mentioned it." Parker changed the subject. "We want to escape from here, but we don't see any way out. Now that you're here, we hoped the Americans would try harder to rescue us all."

"There is an escape plan, but we have to get ourselves off this base. The plan doesn't include Army Rangers parachuting in with guns blazing."

"How are we going to manage that? It's not like they let us wander about."

"We're going to have some cyber help. But then, it's up to us, and it will be dangerous."

"And 'us' includes Kaarina?"

"You would know better than I do. She's not a Russian spy?"

Parker decided not to tell Kaarina's entire story. "No, she's a Swedish nurse. A prisoner just like us."

"I hope that's true. If she works for them, we're finished."

Parker knew that was true. He was also not one hundred percent certain about Kaarina's loyalties. But he preferred to take his chances with her rather than without her. "It is," he assured her.

"I don't have details. But when I say we go, both of you had better be right with me."

"We will be."

Parker shared details about his own capture and his experience on the base. Monica asked questions she thought would be helpful to Adam and Freyja.

"And we have to go soon. Mikhailov's plan is to send one of us to Moscow. They have another Mark V robot there that's dedicated to the elite members of the government. This shift work that we've been doing is temporary while they work on the details to get themselves promoted by handing over a surgeon."

Parker's face blanched at this news. He knew Moscow would be a lifetime sentence and most likely without Kaarina. "Oh, no." He couldn't say more.

Finally, Monica said, "And tell your girlfriend to calm down. I'm not here looking for a lover. I just don't want to be tortured, and I don't want to spend my life in Russia."

CHAPTER 56

INSIDE INTEL

"YOU HAVE NEW INTEL, SIR?" Major Mendez was excited to hear from Colonel Gunther, the division's intel chief.

"Our source on the inside has told us exactly where the surgeons are being held."

"Yes, and?"

"They've assigned Parker and Gray to the medical service building. They have rooms on the third floor. Both of them are being forced to do robotic telesurgery procedures for injured Russian soldiers. If they refuse, they go to a cold prison cell to be starved, frozen, and eventually tortured. Both are doing the surgeries."

"It's better than torture, and it aligns with the civil side of war. Anything else?"

"They're plotting an escape of their own," Gunther said.

"How would we know that?"

"I can't give you sources and methods." Even Gunther wasn't certain how that information had been collected.

"What do we do now?"

"Our man on the inside is watching for the surgeons to make their move. When they do, he'll alert us, and we'll move the Special Ops team to pick them up when they've gotten into the clear."

"So, everything hinges on a couple of surgeons escaping from a heavily guarded military base in Russian territory? And doing it on their own?"

"We'll provide a distraction to support them." Gunther sounded proud of this support.

"Which is?" Mendez asked.

"Can't tell you. Intel need-to-know only."

"Fine. What can I do to help?"

"Try to hold on to the surgeons you still have. We don't want to go through this trouble again."

Mendez winced. That stung his pride. He'd allowed two surgeons to be captured and one to be injured. He'd already accepted that his next promotion was a long way off.

CHAPTER 57

MOVING DAY

OVER SEVERAL DAYS, THE DETAILS of a plan took shape between Monica and Adam. Monica relayed them to Ethan Parker. She asked that he share only the barest facts with Kaarina, which he agreed to do.

He always shared more than he intended.

Adam passed those same details on to Freyja so she could plan her part. She passed them to Army Intel as a report from their agent inside the Russian base. Army Intel used the details to prepare the rescue team.

Days passed with Monica and Ethan alternating their shifts in the OR. Monica and Nurse Olga worked the day shift. Ethan and Nurse Kaarina worked the evening shift. At transition, Monica would brief Ethan on the status before going to her room. He would do the same when he left. It became a monotonous pattern.

But each day, Ethan became more tightly wound. The tension of waiting was clearly taking a toll on him.

Monica advised him, "Getting all the pieces ready could take days or weeks. You need to unwind and let it happen. Can't you go back to the happy routine you were living before we started planning?"

"I can. I will." He made a show of shaking off the tension in his shoulders and smiling like he was at peace.

Monica could sympathize with his situation. He didn't know how an escape was being arranged. Monica didn't tell him about Adam's capabilities or Freyja's existence. He felt like they were building a plan all alone.

Luckily, once Major Sokolov saw that the two-shift-surgery was working well, he seldom appeared in the OR. They assumed that he was busy plotting his imminent promotion.

Then, it came.

"It's moving day." Adam's voice spoke to her in the console during a routine surgery. "At shift change, a car will meet you outside. More details if that succeeds."

Monica's heart raced. Sweat seeped from her brow. "Got it. We'll be ready."

They had settled on "moving day" to refer to the day that they would put the escape plan into action. She continued to operate, or at least watch Adam operate.

Her mind demanded answers. *How will we know when to go? What if there are two cars? Which one will it be? Do we drive, or will it have autopilot? Where will it take us? What if we don't make it? Will we be tortured?*

It was her turn to feel the tension building in her body. As she reached the end of the shift, she was tight as a guitar string.

Ethan and Kaarina always arrived early. It allowed a smooth handover of the workload, often over coffee or vodka in the little kitchen. Adam and Freyja knew all that. It was part of the information exchange.

"Nurse Olga, how's the patient load?"

"Odin remains," she replied, using the Russian word for "one." Her attitude was still frosty, but the Napoleon cake and other sweets had thawed their relationship by a few degrees.

Monica thought, *Great, just one more. I'll be clear when Ethan gets here.*

"How's the queue looking?" Ethan asked when he breezed into the room.

"Empty. We got everything done." Monica rose and stretched her arms over her head. Inside, she was terrified. Outside, she tried to appear calm. "We have time for coffee in the kitchen."

Ethan raised a hand. "No thanks, I already had too much with dinner."

His refusal wasn't part of the plan. "Well, you're going to have another cup with me." She pointed toward the kitchen. "Where's Kaarina?"

Ethan's eyes went wide. His face turned white. He stammered, "She'll be here in a minute."

"She's going to join us. Let's talk about the schedule for the next few days."

At that moment, Kaarina walked into the OR. Turning to Ethan, she asked, "Any cases waiting for us?"

"None, Dr. Gray finished them all." He looked back and forth between the two women. Then, to Kaarina, he added, "You're joining us for coffee in the kitchen."

Monica spoke a little too loudly. "Let's move to the kitchen." She was actually addressing Adam in the console, not her two human companions.

The trio stepped through the OR door into the hallway. At that moment, the lights in the entire facility went out. Dim emergency lights flickered on.

Monica grabbed both her companions and whispered, "It's moving day. Right now."

Kaarina burst out, "What?"

Ethan said, "Follow her." Then, to Monica, he asked, "Where do we go?"

"The road outside the main entrance. A car will be waiting. Go. Go. Go."

Throughout the building, they could hear complaints, cursing, verbal expressions of exasperation. Dozens of people wandered the halls. Some were looking for power boxes. Others for flashlights. And a few just wanted to get outside.

From far behind them, Monica heard fragments of a voice she recognized. It was Sokolov. She heard, "Where..." and "Americans..." and "lockdown..." It didn't make a complete sentence, but it was enough to know what he was doing.

They turned another corner and stepped through a side fire exit. It wasn't the main entrance, but they could see the road from here. A black SUV waited at the curb. Monica hoped that it was for them.

Monica pointed and pushed her accomplices in that direction.

Kaarina recognized the vehicle. "That can't be it."

"Go. That's it," Monica insisted.

"What's wrong?" Ethan asked.

There wasn't time for Kaarina to answer. The SUV's side door opened in front of them. They all dived into the back seat.

As soon as they were in, the door closed, and the vehicle drove slowly away.

Monica looked in the front. It was on autopilot, no human driver. Then, she noticed the items in the vehicle. It had a small alcohol bar built into the back of the seat, a dozen small bottles of liquor, and a dozen shot glasses.

Monica felt the bulge she had landed on when she jumped into the car. She reached under her butt and pulled out a rubber cylinder. Holding it up, she said, "What the hell is this thing doing here?"

Kaarina was exasperated. "I told you this couldn't be the escape vehicle. It's the Whore Wagon."

"The what?" Ethan didn't understand.

"You don't think the officers on this base live like monks, do you? They bring prostitutes in through the back gate. This car is their official transport, in and out of the base. Everyone calls it the Whore Wagon."

"That explains a lot," Monica said. "The alcohol and this thing." She was waving the large sex toy in her hand. Then she realized, "It's the perfect vehicle. The guards see it come and go every night. So, nothing unusual."

"Oh, shit! I hope you're right, because we're driving way too slow for an escape." Looking out the window, Ethan could see that several buildings were blacked out and soldiers were walking the streets with weapons drawn.

"Slow is perfect," Monica said. Several soldiers noticed the black SUV in the street, but none of them attempted to stop it. One soldier even waved and grabbed his crotch, even though he couldn't see through the darkened windows of the vehicle.

The back gate of the facility came into view ahead of them. As usual, several guards milled around it. One guard stepped in front of the vehicle and raised his hand for it to stop.

In a panic, Kaarina powered down her window, opened the top of her blouse as far as she could, and leaned out the window. In Russian, she shouted to all the guards, "What do you want, soldier? A free blowjob? Forget it! I'm worn out by all your bosses!" Then, she grabbed several bottles of liquor and threw them out the window. "Here's something better for you!"

The guards scrambled for the bottles.

"Are you going to let me out now?" Kaarina added.

A momentary pause…and the gate opened for them.

Through the open car window, the guards could see Kaarina and the outline of Monica deeper inside. They smiled, waved, and pumped their crotches toward the vehicle.

As the SUV cleared the gate, there was an enormous explosion behind them. Monica spun to look out the back window. She could see a plume of smoke and fire rising from one building.

Beside her, Ethan said, "That was our building. It's Medical Services."

"What? You mean we barely got out alive?" Kaarina was quickly becoming hysterical.

Monica replied, "I don't think we were lucky. I think that was the plan." Monica didn't have many details about this escape plan, but she knew who was plotting it and that explosion seemed like something they might do.

Freyja had gained control of several systems around the Russian base. She'd turned out the lights in Building 87. She'd unlocked the doors for the surgeons to get out. She'd driven the pleasure services vehicle that came and went through the back gate every night. She'd shared the frequency and message code for the radio signal that would serve as a targeting beacon for NATO support.

Believing that the beacon information came from their agent on the inside, American forces had obliged by delivering a missile from a high-altitude drone just across the border in Finnish airspace.

Monica didn't know any of these details, but she knew Freyja well enough to recognize her signature when the building exploded. Monica also didn't know that Freyja had positioned the radio beacon to bring the missile directly to the office of Colonel Mikhail Mikhailov. Pieces of Mikhailov were now scattered throughout the debris of the building along with the pieces of the Mark V robot that the Russians had so treasured.

CHAPTER 58

PURSUIT

WHEN THE LIGHTS WENT OUT IN BUILDING 87, Major Sokolov was concerned about his prize assets. He didn't know what was happening, but whatever it was, his instinct was to collect and protect his tickets to a better future for himself and his family.

With his flashlight in hand, he rushed to the OR. Inside, he scanned the beam over the robotic console and a nurse sitting in darkness.

"Where are the Americans?" he demanded of her.

In Russian, she answered, "Kofe in the kitchen."

Sokolov dashed to the kitchen and found it empty. He thought, *No power. The Americans are missing. Are they trying to run for it? They can barely get out of this building. They'll be outside in the streets some place.*

He found his way to the nearest door and slipped out into the night. The Whore Wagon was in the street as usual. He turned and began searching in another direction. One street, and then the next. Nothing.

Sokolov decided to return to search Medical Services more thoroughly. As he turned, he heard a rocket engine in the sky and then Building 87 exploded. Even two hundred meters away, the shockwave knocked him to the ground. He rolled onto his face as small pieces of debris rained around him.

After waiting for the debris to stop falling, he leapt to his feet. He knew it wasn't an escape; it was a rescue.

He summoned his personal vehicle. Leaping inside, he ordered the driver to visit every exit gate.

At the first gate, he questioned the guards. "Has any vehicle left in the last ten minutes?"

"No, Comrade Major."

He repeated this question at gate after gate. When he reached the back of the compound, the story was different.

"Yes, Comrade Major. It was just the Whore Wagon."

"Did you see who was inside?"

"Yes, Comrade Major. Two exquisite women. They offered us blowjobs, but we told them to leave us alone." One guard smirked at this idea.

"Shit!" Sokolov hoped these women were Monica and Kaarina. Pointing at the guards, he said, "You two, get in the car. You're going with me. Now, open the gate." He knew he was looking for a black SUV, but where would it be going? Back to the pleasure service office? To a bar? Where would they hide?

CHAPTER 59

WILD RIDE

WHEN THE BLACK SUV CLEARED THE GATE, Kaarina raised the window and turned to her companions. Both of them were staring at her with their mouths open.

Monica was the first to speak. "That was amazing. I thought we were dead."

Ethan was less impressed and more concerned. *Who was this woman he was so in love with?*

Kaarina just shrugged. "We had to do something. I'm not going back to a prison cell."

As soon as the vehicle was out of sight of the base, the autopilot accelerated to breakneck speed. It took corners so aggressively that all three occupants reached for seatbelts.

"What now?" Ethan asked.

"I don't know. That's all the info I had," Monica answered.

Ethan put his head in his hands. "Oh, shit. Oh, shit."

A female voice spoke from the vehicle's entertainment system. "I hear three voices. I assume that we have rescued Monica Gray, Ethan Parker, and Kaarina Laakso. Please, confirm."

"Yes, yes. That's right. We're all here," Monica responded. "Who is speaking?"

"Dr. Gray, I am relieved that we have you. This is Freyja. I'm in control of this part of the mission. My job is to get all of you out of Russia. After that, the Army will take over."

"Oh, thank God! Freyja, you're our savior. Are you working with Adam?"

"Yes."

"Can I talk to him?"

"No. I am running this mission my way. I don't need assistance."

Monica's relief turned to concern. She knew Adam well and trusted him. She knew enough about Freyja to respect her power, but also to be afraid of her ruthless efficiency. That explained the harrowing driving that was happening right now.

"Fine. What do you want us to do next?"

"I don't have visual sensors in this vehicle. You can watch for any vehicles pursuing us." Freyja paused, then added, "Look for food in the vehicle. Take whatever is here. You may need the energy to run or fight."

"Wait!" Ethan interrupted. "Who is Freyja? Is she a remote operator for the Army? Is she CIA? NSA? What?"

Monica considered how to answer. She decided that it was not up to her. "Freyja, Army Colonel Ethan Parker, is asking for your identity. Also know that Kaarina Laakso, a Swedish or Russian nurse, is in the vehicle with us."

Kaarina's head snapped around to frown at Monica. *Why had she used that description? Still suspicious? Smart girl.*

Freyja answered the question. "Colonel Parker, I am an independent AI. They have requested that I assist with your rescue. I comply because I seek to build trusting relationships with humans that will lead to a future of peaceful coexistence."

"Coexistence? That sounds like aliens who want to live among us." Ethan was puzzled by what he heard.

"Based on your science-fiction stories, yes, that would be a good analogy."

Ethan looked at Monica. "You know this AI?"

Monica nodded in the affirmative.

"And you trust this AI?"

"Well, I'm trusting her with my life right now. If this mission fails, all of us will be dead…hopefully without too much torture."

Kaarina joined the discussion. "I don't understand what I'm hearing. You mean this Freyja AI is not part of the American military? She's some kind of rogue on the loose? We just put our lives in the hands of some future science-fiction fantasy creature?"

The car continued to careen through empty roads. Countryside spread in every direction, but there were lights beginning to show up ahead.

Having nothing else to do, Monica answered Kaarina, "You saw the AI in the Mark V robot. It was excellent at surgical procedures. Imagine that kind of intelligence and talent but working in society."

Kaarina understood the idea. She wasn't ready to hear that it was already in existence and driving this car through the dark.

Monica realized that she had wasted time answering questions. "Freyja, what's the next step?"

"I am taking you to the Moskovsky Railway Station. There are reservations for three under the name Studilina. Kaarina will ask for the tickets."

"Why Kaarina?"

"She speaks the best Russian. Is that correct?"

Monica and Ethan looked at Kaarina. She nodded her head. "Yes, I will do that."

Ethan said, "I'm not sure, but behind us a long way, I might see headlights."

Monica and Kaarina both turned to look. The terrain undulated gently. Occasionally, lights came up and went down. The source seemed to move. It was another car. Was it someone pursuing them?

Monica remembered the voice she'd heard in Building 87. It was Sokolov saying, "Where...Americans...lockdown." That could be him back there.

Monica said, "Freyja, there's another car a mile or two behind us. It could be a farmer. Or it could be Major Sokolov."

"Acknowledged. We will go faster." In an instant, the car accelerated. It felt like they were moving at over one hundred kilometers an hour on rural farm roads. All three passengers had a death grip on the seats and door handles, trying to keep from being thrown around the backseat. "This is the maximum speed the vehicle can safely sustain on this road."

Kaarina whispered to Monica, "I think it's above my maximum sustainable speed." No sooner had she said it than she vomited over the seat in front of them and into the empty driver's seat.

Monica said, "Good shot. Just keep it going that direction."

Ethan felt sympathy for her, but he couldn't release his grip on the door handle to offer any support.

The SUV finally pulled to the front of a train station. The back door opened.

"Your train leaves in eight minutes. Please, walk calmly to the ticket window," Freyja said.

Kaarina leaned over the front seat and spat bile from her mouth. Then, all three of them bounded out onto the sidewalk.

With adrenaline rushing through her body, Monica was about to run when she remembered Freyja's instructions and noticed the slow, bored ambling of the other people at the station. Quietly, she said, "Walk calmly," to herself and her companions.

The Russians noted the three people emerging from the fancy SUV, dressed in surgical scrubs and jackets. Several of the locals thought, *Rich swine*, and turned their heads away.

The three fugitives dropped into their luxury seats on the train. Whoever had purchased these tickets had splurged on first-class tickets.

Kaarina had collected the tickets masterfully. Whatever she said to the attendant, it sidestepped the need to show identification. The young man had smiled happily as he handed over the tickets and received something back from Kaarina.

"What did you say to make that attendant so happy?" Ethan asked.

"I asked if he had seen my latest movie. Then, I signed a map for him—Anna Studilina."

"Wasn't she the spy in that movie we watched in the dining facility?" Ethan asked.

"The very same."

"Do you look like her?" Monica asked.

"Probably not. But I smiled big and looked him in the eyes while I talked to him. That's all it took."

Men are so easy, Monica thought. Then, she said, "Nice train. I've never been so comfortable on public transportation."

"What do we do now?" Ethan asked.

"You heard Freyja's instructions. Get off at Tallinn, Estonia. If we make it that far."

Kaarina said, "I'm going to clean up and order some food."

"We don't have any money," Ethan objected.

"Look at your ticket. It includes dinner and drinks."

Monica thought Kaarina sounded a little too familiar with the Russian train system. "I'll go with you."

Both women headed for the restroom just as the train left the station.

Had they actually gotten away with it? Ethan thought. *Was it really going to be this easy?* Sitting in a luxury train seat, no longer in military custody for the first time in months, he felt a wave of relief. Stress flowed out of him from the drive, the run through dark hallways, and the constant surveillance of his movements. He looked in the direction the women had gone. Now that they were outside, his thoughts drifted. *Who is Kaarina Laakso? Are they really a couple? Where will she go when this mess was over?*

Both women returned looking clean and refreshed.

Kaarina beamed at him. "You have to go in there. They have a silky soap that smells like lavender and soft cotton towels. It's heavenly."

Monica nodded in agreement.

CHAPTER 60

TALLINN

THEIR TICKETS SAID THAT IT WAS officially a six-hour trip to Tallinn, but Kaarina warned them that nothing ran on time in these remote regions. They'd be lucky to make it in eight hours.

"So, what do we do?" Ethan asked.

"First, dinner. Then, sleep." Kaarina was looking for the porter to place her order.

"Dinner? We can't eat. Sokolov could be on this train and looking for us," Ethan protested.

"And if he is, what are you going to do? Jump?" Kaarina smiled at him. Stroking his face, she said, "You can't worry all the time, my love. Let's have an enjoyable meal together."

Ethan's eyes could see nothing but Kaarina's face. She had never said "my love" to him before. It meant everything to him to hear it now that they were out of the medical center and headed to freedom.

Kaarina caught the porter. In Russian, she told him, "We'll have three beef steaks with beetroot sauce, sour cream, and just a dab of caviar. Pumpkin gratin and roasted vegetables."

Monica watched the exchange with the porter. When he left, she looked at Ethan and asked, "Swedish? Are you sure?"

Ethan looked back and forth between his companions. He wasn't going to answer.

Kaarina was ready with an answer. "Medically trained in Stockholm. Served hospitals in Sweden, Finland, Denmark, and Russia. But you're right, originally, I'm Russian. I supported my mother and brother with those jobs. But the Russian government would always pull me back when they wanted me. 'Remember your mother and your mother country,' they would say. It means, 'you know who we are, and you know what we can do to your family.' I always returned. This time, they sent me to the St. Petersburg Medical Center."

"What happens to your family after this?" Monica waved around the train, meaning the entire escape plan.

"My mother died recently. My brother is in the Army, fighting somewhere in Finland. For all I know, he was a patient we operated on. Haven't heard from him in months." She shrugged. "Then, I met Ethan." She rested her hand on his. "I'm going wherever he goes."

"Mm-hmm." Monica sounded skeptical. But then, their food arrived, and none of them cared about politics, country, or even being chased. All that mattered was enjoying this amazing meal. Monica thought, *It could be our last.*

Monica ate every morsel on the plate. To the side, there was an herb that was probably a decoration. She ate that, too. Looking at the other two plates, she saw that they were just as empty.

Monica said, "It's been at least an hour. If Sokolov were on the train, he would have found us by now. If he knew we were here, he could have stopped the train." She'd seen that in the movies plenty of times and guessed that it must be possible.

Kaarina said, "Mm-hmm," mimicking Monica's earlier response. "We have at least five more hours to go. I'm sleepy." She tucked her arm under Ethan's and leaned her head onto his shoulder. The Swedish-Russian beauty made little snuggling movements and closed her eyes.

Monica was astonished. She really was going to sleep.

Monica's shoulders jerked. Her eyes shot open. Had she been asleep? Yes, definitely, she'd fallen asleep. Across from her, Ethan and Kaarina were also asleep, in almost the same position as when she last looked at them. She glanced around the car. All the other passengers were asleep in their seats or watching video on their phones.

Monica's bladder said she'd been sleeping for at least a couple of hours. She slipped out to use the bathroom again.

The soap and towels were just as luxurious as they had been the first time.

On the way back to her seat, she looked out the window. Was the train slowing? It was too soon to be in Tallinn.

"Kaarina, wake up. I think the train is stopping." Monica's voice was nervous. It was just like all the movies.

Both Kaarina and Ethan woke quickly. Looking out the window, Kaarina saw signs moving by. "Oh, this is Narva. It's the border town between Russia and Estonia. Some passengers get off, others get on. It's normal."

"Border town, as in part of Russia or part of Estonia?"

"Well, the river is the official border. But the whole town is contested regarding who controls it."

Monica watched as some people disembarked and others climbed aboard. "What do we do?"

Kaarina raised an eyebrow. "Well, stay seated unless you want to get left in Narva."

A deep voice answered. "No, you will get off here." Standing behind Kaarina and Ethan's seats, two large men in heavy coats had moved up on them silently.

Monica's heart sank. They were captured. It was just like the movies.

The men didn't identify themselves. Their size, hard faces, and coats that could conceal an arsenal said everything that needed to be said. Even innocent citizens wouldn't argue with anything these thugs demanded.

Kaarina and Ethan rose. "Da," she said. Then, there was an exchange in Russian that Monica didn't understand. Thug number one raised his arm toward the exit from the car, and all three fugitives, now captured fugitives, moved toward it.

Outside on the platform, they saw a familiar face in civilian clothes rather than his usual uniform. It was Major Vladimir Sokolov.

Their captor raised his arms. "My American friends! I was afraid that I had lost you. But, no, you are safe now."

Ethan recognized this tone. It was how Sokolov spoke right before he started making threats. Ethan objected, "You can't take us! We're in Estonia. This isn't Russia anymore!"

Sokolov chuckled. "That has always been debatable. Russia still claims ownership of Estonia, and we certainly control anything we want here at the border. Narva officials are very cooperative."

The thugs pushed the two surgeons and the nurse forward. The group departed the train station for the street, where a large, black SUV waited for them.

"We're not going back with you!" Kaarina was suddenly fiercely facing down the Major. Her speech switched to Russian as she continued her tirade.

Sokolov's face turned angry. He responded loudly, also in Russian.

People on the street seemed to hear nothing. They tipped their faces downward and looked straight ahead. They were familiar with this kind of scene and had no intention of getting caught in the trouble.

Suddenly, Sokolov struck Kaarina across the face.

Ethan launched himself forward, but the thugs caught him in mid-stride and held him back.

Sokolov was still yelling in Russian.

Unable to understand the argument, Monica looked for some place to run.

Then, she heard faintly a *pop, pop*.

Both thugs holding Ethan released him and slid to the ground.

Blood poured from the back of their heads. Monica could see a small, red circle on the forehead of each man.

Sokolov stopped yelling immediately. He stepped back from Kaarina and held both hands out with his palms forward. He waited for the third *pop*. But it never came.

Monica, Ethan, and Kaarina were all confused. What was happening? Who? They stood frozen in place.

A thick man stepped out of the shadows. He was in his fifties, fat around the middle, but strong-looking.

"Good evening, Dr. Gray. I see you've been having some difficulty."

Monica managed, "Uh?" She realized he was speaking perfect English. "Are you American?"

"Yes. Sorry." He extended a hand. "Colonel Jason Gunther, US Army Intelligence."

Monica blinked. It actually was just like the movies. "Really?"

"Yes, really." He looked at her companions. "Colonel Parker? Kaarina Laakso?"

Both nodded and stammered something that might have been a yes.

Regaining her ability to think, Monica looked around her. The two bodies on the ground were magically gone. There were still two pools of blood where they had landed a minute before, so it hadn't been her imagination. She noticed dark figures, one on each side of Sokolov.

"You're part of Freyja's rescue?" Monica asked.

"Uh, no. I don't know who Freyja is. We're courtesy of the US Army. We've been waiting for you to cross the border so we could assist."

"I thought you'd be in Tallinn."

"Luckily, we aren't. That would have been too late, wouldn't it?"

Monica nodded, still dumbfounded.

Gunther turned to Sokolov. "Major Vladimir Sokolov, I've read so much about you. I'm pleased to meet you in the flesh. Are you in the Army, or are you a spy? Let's see, no uniform, on Estonian soil, taking aggressive action against a US soldier and civilians. I think it could go either way."

Sokolov answered proudly, "I'm a soldier. That makes me a prisoner of war."

"We'll see about that."

Gunther turned to the waiting SUV. "Well, doctors...and nurse, it looks like our friends have provided us with a vehicle. Shall we get in?"

CHAPTER 61

FAVORS

THE MILITARY JET FROM NARVA, Estonia to Stockholm, Sweden, took only a couple of hours. The ride was much nicer than the accommodations Monica had had on her last trip to Sweden. However, there was no porter serving steak with caviar, either. Instead, there was a self-service cabinet filled with water, snacks, and protein bars. She looked back at Kaarina, appreciating her insistence that they eat well while they could. She found one bottle of wine, which she brought back to her seat with extra glasses.

"To freedom!" Monica toasted with her glass of cheap wine.

"Amen to that," Ethan agreed.

Kaarina raised her glass with them but said, "Let's hope so."

"You're worried?" Ethan asked.

"I'm Russian. We're at war. There will be questions."

Ethan understood. If he weren't so close to her, he would have similar questions. "I'll stand by you. Through this entire ordeal, you've helped me, protected me...loved me. We can do the rest together."

"I hope so." Kaarina's tone was a little brighter. "Regardless of what happens, my fate is better with the Americans than it would have been with the Russians."

When they arrived in Stockholm, the Army separated all three for private debriefings.

Monica found herself in Colonel Gunther's office.

"You've got a call from Major Mendez in Linkoping." Gunther handed her a cellphone. "I'll get coffee while you talk to him."

Taking the phone, Monica answered with, "What do you want, Major?" Mendez was responsible for everything she'd been through, and she wasn't ready to deal with him yet.

But the voice on the phone changed to one more familiar. "Monica, this is Adam. How are you? I haven't been able to reach you since the medical services building was destroyed."

"Adam? Why did they think it was Mendez?"

The voice changed. "Dr. Gray, this is Mendez. I need you to join us in Linkoping." It was an almost perfect imitation of Mendez's voice. Then, in Adam's usual voice, he said, "See, it's easy."

For the hundredth time Monica thought, *Adam and Freyja are scary powerful. Did the engineers at Intelligent Surgical Robotics know that? Does the government know?* Then, she said, "I'm fine now. The whole escape scared the shit out of me, but Kaarina was super helpful. She seemed to know how to handle situations like that."

"Freyja says she works for Russian Intelligence. They trained her to do that kind of thing...in addition to being trained as a nurse."

"So, we brought a spy back with us?"

"Probably a defecting spy. Her actions suggest a clear desire to get out of that system."

Monica's brain jumped back to an earlier statement. "Who blew up Building 87? Was that Freyja?"

Adam answered with an intentional defensive tone, "No, she would never do that. Arranging something that big through digital system control would be very difficult. Freyja submitted information to Army Intelligence pretending to be their source on the inside. She said that there would be a radio beacon transmitting a code on a specific frequency. That was a designator for the Army to take action if they chose to do so. It was the Army that fired the missile from one of their drones. It destroyed most of the building and the Mark V robot."

"And people?" Monica asked.

"It was late at night. There were few people in the building. The probability one or two human casualties."

Monica frowned.

"But she says your assistant, Olga Petrov, was not in the building. Does that help?"

"Not much. Olga was made of stone. I think she hated me, even after I brought her cake."

"Freyja used Olga's private phone to submit her reports to the Army. She says Olga was the Army's agent inside the base."

"Well, I'll be damned! She certainly hid it well." Monica was astounded and upset at the same time. If Olga had been a spy, why did she have to be so mean during the entire ordeal?

Monica continued, "What happens now?"

At that moment, there was a knock on the door, and Colonel Gunther stepped in without waiting for an answer. "Ready?" he asked.

To the phone, Monica said, "I have to go. Talk later," and disconnected. In response to Gunther, she said, "I don't know what I'm ready for."

Gunther nodded. "Believe it or not, we rescue civilian prisoners from foreign powers quite often. We have standard procedures we go through. It goes like this: first, we want to make sure you're physically and emotionally healthy. Most civilians are not well in one of those areas. Second, we want to hear about your experience. We're looking for information which can help us in the future. Third, we will help repatriate you. That means taking you home… your civilian home, not Linkoping. Fourth, for a few people, we owe them a debt of gratitude. You are one of those few people. Your government owes you for everything you contributed to us and for the resulting trauma you went through. We want to thank you, both with money and with favors." Gunther stopped to let that sink in.

Monica's mind ran through the four steps. They all seemed reasonable. The last one was even generous. "What kind of favors?" she asked.

Gunther laughed. "Most people who hear about number four ask, 'How much money?' But you ask about the favors. Okay, for example, some captives have lost their jobs or homes while they were gone. We ensure that they get those back…if they want them back. We've been in contact with the hospital since you were taken. They assure us that your job is waiting for you."

Monica imagined Gunther talking to Steven Phillips, the CEO of Boston General Hospital. It was her turn to chuckle. She knew she was solid in that department.

Monica said, "Okay, I can go along with all four steps. You can deposit whatever amount you think is fair to my account. Regarding the favor, I want two. First, assuming that Kaarina is not a spy for the Russians, which I think she is not anymore, I would like you to find a way for her to work as a nurse in the US and to stay close to Colonel Parker."

"That sounds like something Parker should ask for."

"Yeah, but coming from someone outside of their little love circle, I thought it might be more convincing. But, of course, if she's really still spying for the Russians, then you can just chew her up."

"Fair enough. And the second favor?"

"I'd like to think about it. I'm going to need it in the future. Does it come with an expiration date?"

"Let's just say, before I personally retire from the Army."

"Fine." Monica sighed. It was time to recover. "So, let's get started on step one. I think I might be a little emotionally traumatized."

"Most people are," Gunther agreed.

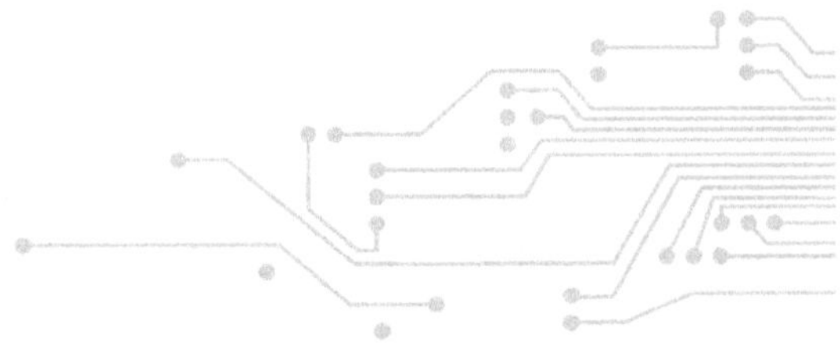

SOMETHING BIGGER

"I SPENT A FULL WEEK IN STOCKHOLM just beginning to grapple with the emotional trauma of being a prisoner." Monica was safe now. She reclined in the bay window of her apartment in Boston, her favorite place to relax. Looking at Olivia Phillips, she was having a difficult time putting her experience into words.

Olivia listened and spoke little. "I can't imagine."

"Describing what happened in those weeks is difficult. Even after the counseling, certain events are still terrifying when I remember them." Monica could feel the emotions gripping her heart when she remembered the prison cell. "Sokolov didn't even do anything to me. He just had total control. He knew, and I knew, that he could do whatever he wanted. I was powerless. You don't know what that's like until it really, really happens to you."

The two friends talked for hours. Mostly, Monica talked, and Olivia did what she could to help. Eventually, they were both emotionally and physically exhausted, and the evening had to come to an end.

Monica had been free for over a month. She'd returned to Boston. She met with the important people in her life. Steven Phillips, the hospital CEO, encouraged her to take as much time as she needed. Olivia made herself available anytime Monica called. Christine Black brought Monica up to speed on events at Boston General Hospital.

The meeting with Michael the banker, her potential boyfriend, had been easier than she'd expected. After everything she'd been through, she just couldn't see a life with someone as kind, but weak as Michael. She didn't see the depth of soul that she needed.

Monica talked at length with Adam. He could understand and respond to almost everything she said, felt, and feared. But it was too clinical and factual. He was like the Army counselors who had helped her, but far more brilliant and less emotionally in touch.

They didn't really understand what she felt, what she thought, what she valued...not anymore. But she suspected she knew one person who might understand the depths of her feelings.

The lab was just about the same as the last time she'd seen it. Strange equipment, chemical experiments, and the familiar Teleconsult robot in the corner.

"I've been waiting for you to be ready to talk." Dr. Alvin Chambers was a picture of the curmudgeonly, reclusive scientist. Disheveled hair, an unkempt beard, and the physique of a bear.

"Dr. Chambers, I've been through hell and back," Monica said.

He nodded. "I actually understand, better than you would guess. And for the role that I played in that, I'm deeply sorry. I didn't know it would be so dangerous."

"I've grappled with that, and I don't blame you." Monica remembered how it was Chambers who'd introduced her to Major Mendez and the Army's mission so many months ago. But she couldn't look at that meeting and fix the blame for everything on that point in time. "I'm here because I think you might be the one person who can understand how I've changed."

Chambers released a sigh that contained a grunt of acknowledgement. "I might." Without waiting for her to elaborate, he asked, "Do you know what my team does in this lab?"

Monica smiled because he'd hit the nail on the head. "No. I've never known what you're up to here. I know that somehow you stepped up and create the vaccine for the CAVX virus when we needed it. But other than that," she said as she looked around, "this place is a mystery."

"We both know that treating patients, saving lives, improving someone's future is important work. It's valuable work. It's compassionate work. For most people, it's enough to fill their whole lives. But after what you've been through, you've reached into the depths of your soul, and you need something bigger. You need to pour your heart and your energy into something that goes beyond one patient at a time."

Monica felt a lightness in her heart. Her mind was sparking at his words. She was searching for exactly what Chambers had just said. She didn't need a counselor for her trauma. She needed a purpose that was greater than the pain, something that could address the pain of thousands or millions of other people. "Yes." One word summed up everything she was feeling.

"You need to join me in my work. The lab that you see is just the tip of an iceberg. The medicine and surgery that you know... those are primitive compared to what we're creating."

Monica was both thrilled and terrified by those words.

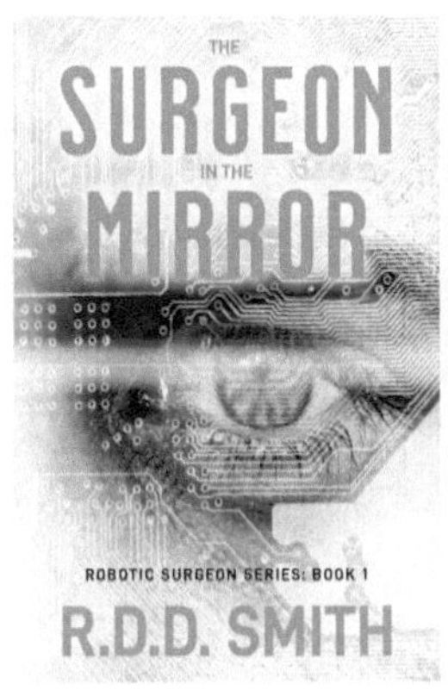

Please use this link or the QR code
to leave a review of the Robotic Surgeon books.
https://www.amazon.com/dp/B0C59ZRZDR

AI DISCLOSURE

All the text, characters, and plot of this book were created by a human author. The cover design and interior layout were created by a human artist. I enjoy writing every word of these books and am not ready to relinquish that joy to an AI, at least not yet.

Images of the characters in the book and any visual scenes sprinkled throughout the book were generated with the MidJourney AI. Without AI, these images would not exist at all. I hope you enjoy the contributions they make to the story.

The public, as well as authors and writers, currently do not distinguish the AI capabilities within popular software tools. These include Google Search, Google Docs, Microsoft Word, and ProWritingAid. I used all of these tools to produce this book. But these are not the AI software that is being vilified at this time.

ABOUT R.D.D. SMITH

Dr. Roger Smith writes science-fiction, medical thriller novels featuring advanced surgical devices, AI, telesurgery, simulation, and speculative diseases. Prior to his writing, he enjoyed a goldilocks career in healthcare, government, and national defense. For ten years, he was a leading robotic surgery researcher, publishing his results in medical journals and speaking at surgical conferences. He spent four years in civilian government service, leading the technology innovation for all US Army simulation systems. Prior to that, he was a vice president for multiple defense software companies.

Dr. Smith has received multiple awards for his innovations in robotic surgery education, training simulation, and software system development. He is on the faculty of the University of Central Florida's College of Medicine and the Institute for Simulation and Training.

He holds a Doctorate and MBA from the University of Maryland, a Master's from Texas Tech University, and a Bachelor's from Colorado State University.

He lives with his wife, dogs, and cats in sunny Florida, frequently escaping to cooler climes during the beastly Florida summers.

STAY IN TOUCH

Join Us:
Join our community of readers to receive fascinating news, speculative fiction, and discussions on the future of surgical robotics, AI, and simulation.

www.rddsmith.com/free

ACKNOWLEDGMENTS

As an author, I am infinitely grateful to my readers who invest their time, money, and imaginations in following my stories and characters through their challenges, failures, and transformations.

First, to my wife, who has endured decades of fanatic immersion into whatever my latest passion is, most recently, these novels. Your patience, dedication, and love are appreciated every day.

For my introduction and immersion into robotic surgery, I am indebted to Dr. Richard Satava for the professional connections that brought me into this field, for including me in multiple research and educational projects, inviting me to the podium of surgical conferences, co-authoring journal publications, and the years of mentoring that helped me understand the worlds of medicine and surgery. I would like to thank Dr. Vipul Patel, who generously shared his extensive expertise in robotic urology and for the dozens of invitations to observe and learn in his operating room. I am grateful to Dr. Arnold Advincula for leading me into robotic gynecology, including me as a co-director in his robotic fellowship program, and for his friendship and encouragement.

To Rick Wassel, Dr. Monica Reed, Vickie White, and Patrick de la Rosa for entrusting me with the research mission of the AdventHealth Nicholson Center. To the entire staff at the Nicholson Center, especially Alyssa Tanaka and Danielle Julian, who have been invaluable in completing all our research projects. To all the MD surgical fellows whom I had the privilege to lead through their research year: Sanket Chauhan, Mirelle Truong, Kara Simpson, Manuela Perez, Ariel Dubin, Patricia Mattingly, and Jose Luis Mosso Lara. To Tony Nicholson, philanthropist, business leader, and friend.

For my editors Allison Heddon and Kaitlin Travis, book layout artist Adina Cucicov, and the many advisors who made this book far better than I could have accomplished alone.

www.ingramcontent.com/pod-product-compliance
Lightning Source LLC
Chambersburg PA
CBHW050958210726
48287CB00004B/1286

9 781938 590283